INVISIBLE

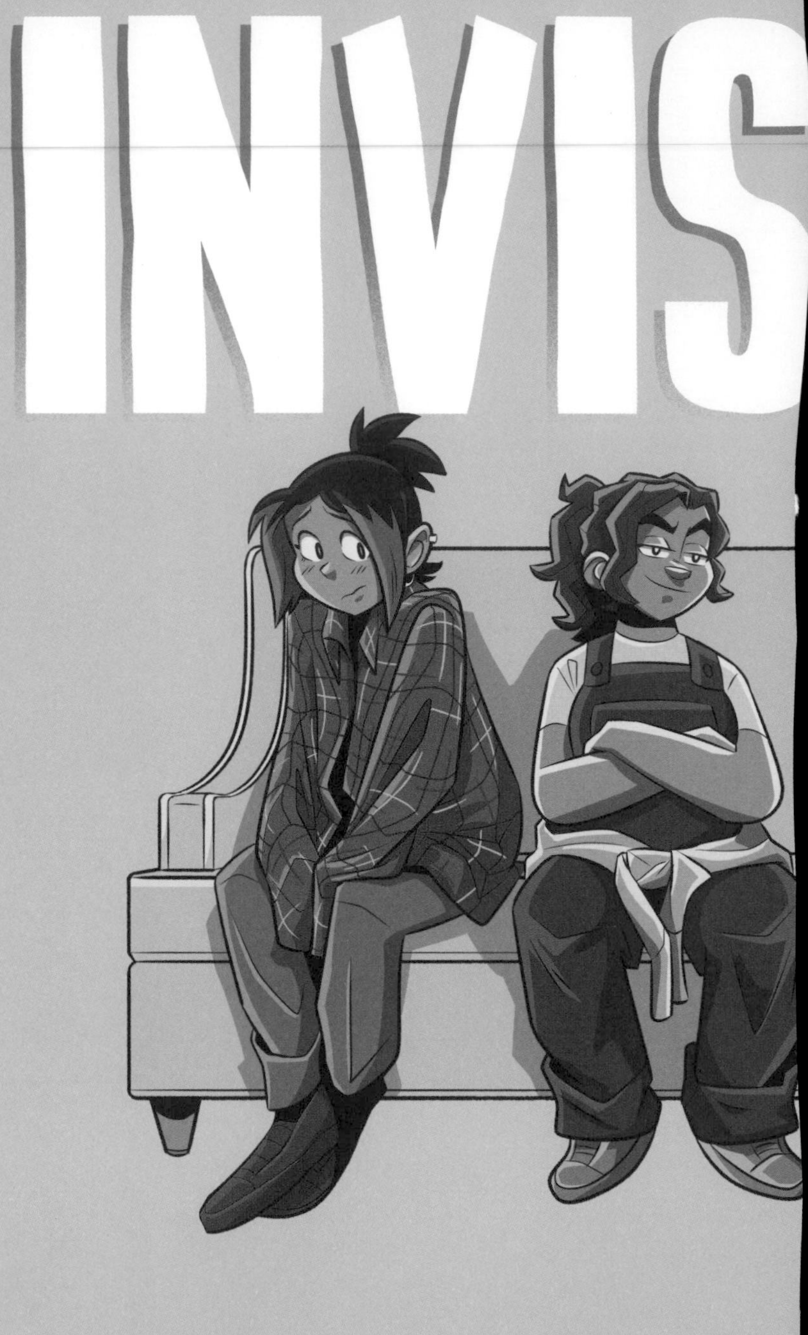
INVIS

IBLE

WRITTEN BY
CHRISTINA DIAZ GONZALEZ

ILLUSTRATED BY
GABRIELA EPSTEIN

WITH COLOR BY
LARK PIEN

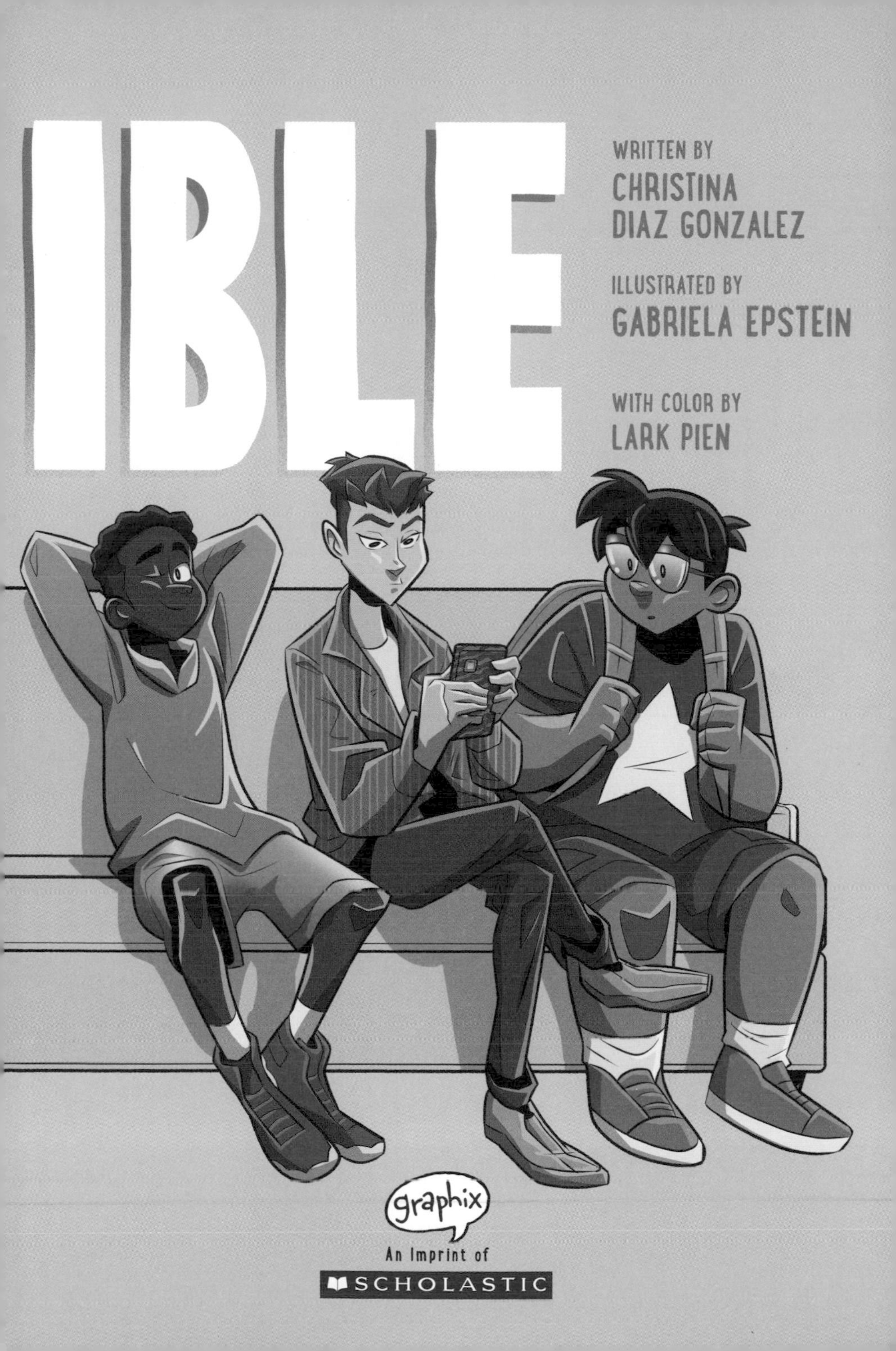

graphix
An Imprint of
SCHOLASTIC

Text copyright © 2022 by Christina Diaz Gonzalez
Art copyright © 2022 by Gabriela Epstein

Library of Congress Cataloging-in-Publication Data available

ISBN 978-1-338-19455-5 (hardcover)
ISBN 978-1-338-19454-8 (paperback)

10 9 8 7 6 5 4 3 2   22 23 24 25 26

Printed in China 62
First edition, August 2022

Color by Lark Pien
Edited by Emily Seife
Book design by Shivana Sookdeo
Creative Director: Phil Falco
Publisher: David Saylor

For the two Olivias

C.D.G.

Para mi familia en Chile — les amo mucho.
Gracias a la abuelita Sonia por su cariño,
a la tía Paulina por su apoyo y a la tía Chiti por sus
historias. Sobre todo, gracias a mi mamá por plantar
las semillas del arte y la poesía en nuestra vida.

G.E.

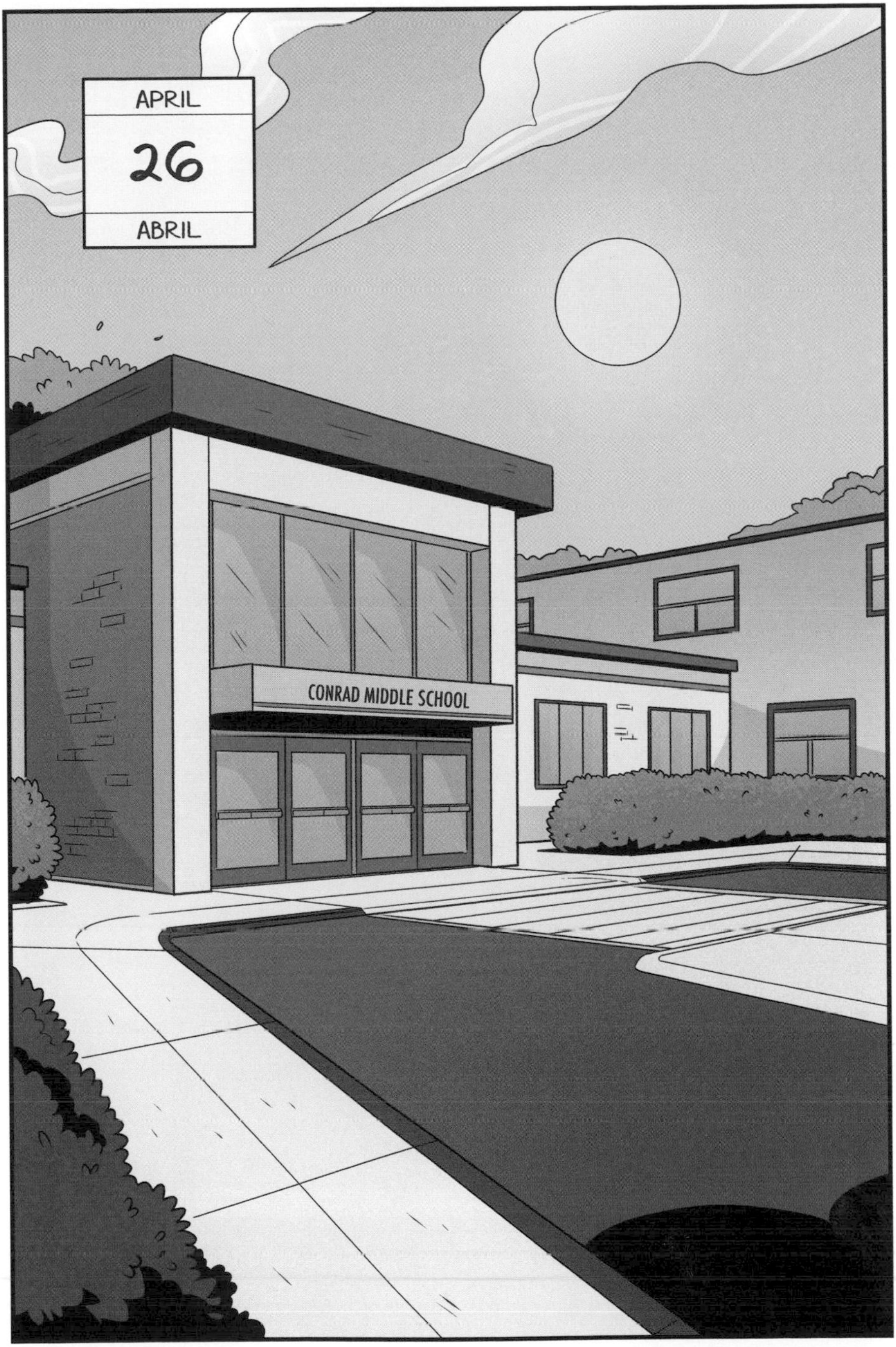
APRIL
26
ABRIL
CONRAD MIDDLE SCHOOL

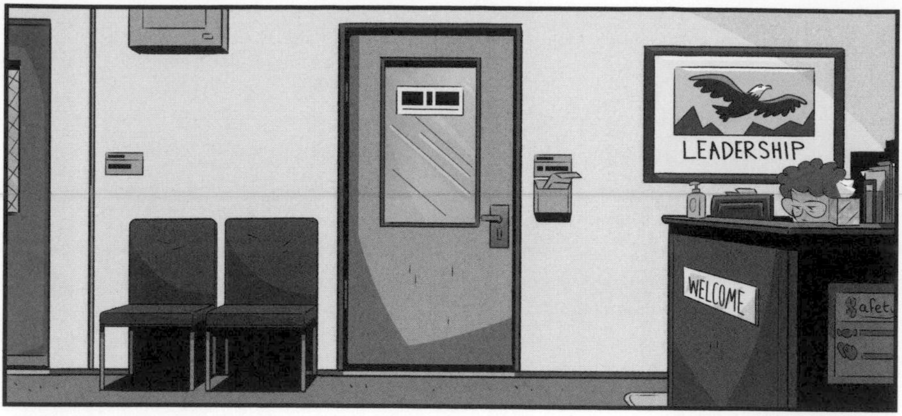
LEADERSHIP
WELCOME

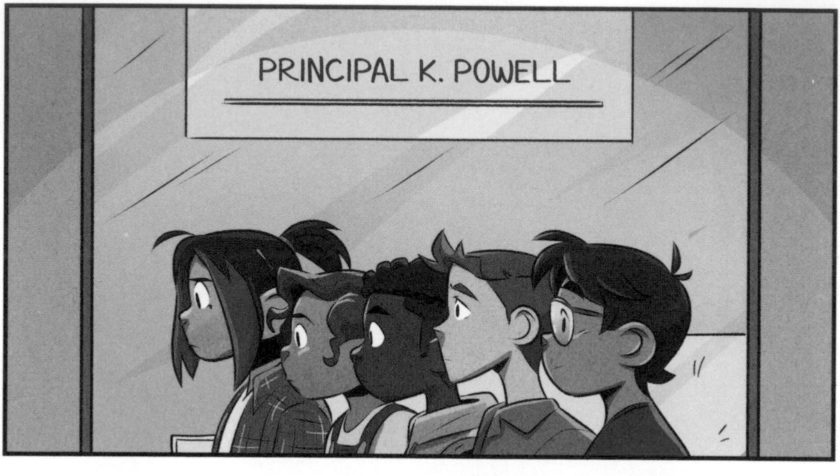
PRINCIPAL K. POWELL

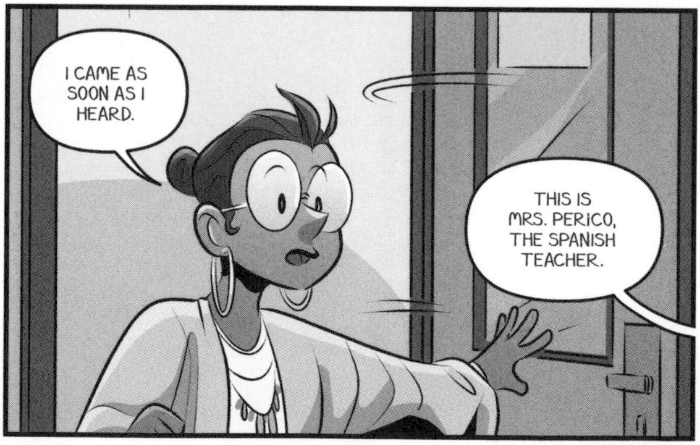
I CAME AS SOON AS I HEARD.
THIS IS MRS. PERICO, THE SPANISH TEACHER.

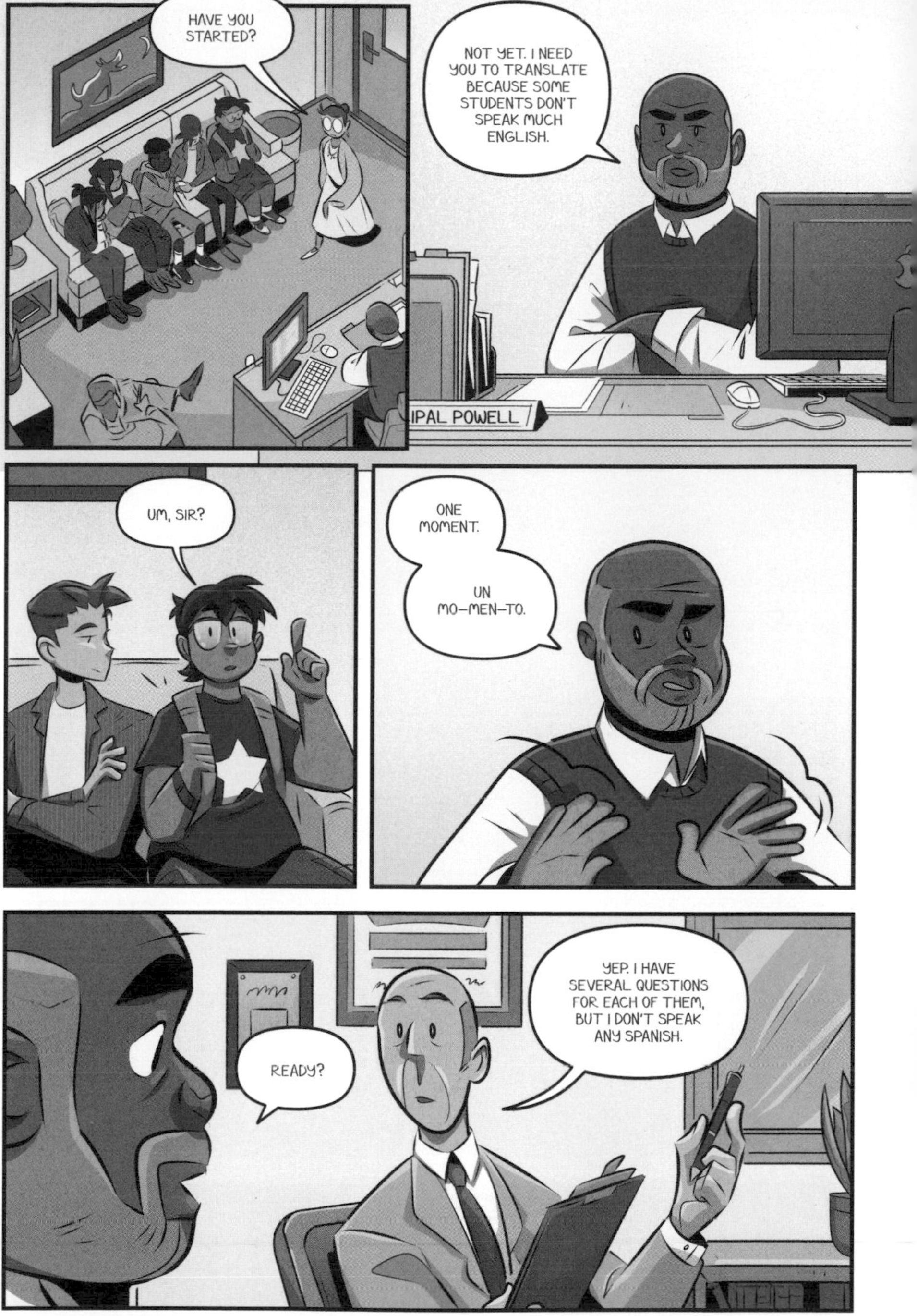
HAVE YOU STARTED?
NOT YET. I NEED YOU TO TRANSLATE BECAUSE SOME STUDENTS DON'T SPEAK MUCH ENGLISH.
IPAL POWELL
UM, SIR?
ONE MOMENT.
UN MO-MEN-TO.
READY?
YEP. I HAVE SEVERAL QUESTIONS FOR EACH OF THEM, BUT I DON'T SPEAK ANY SPANISH.

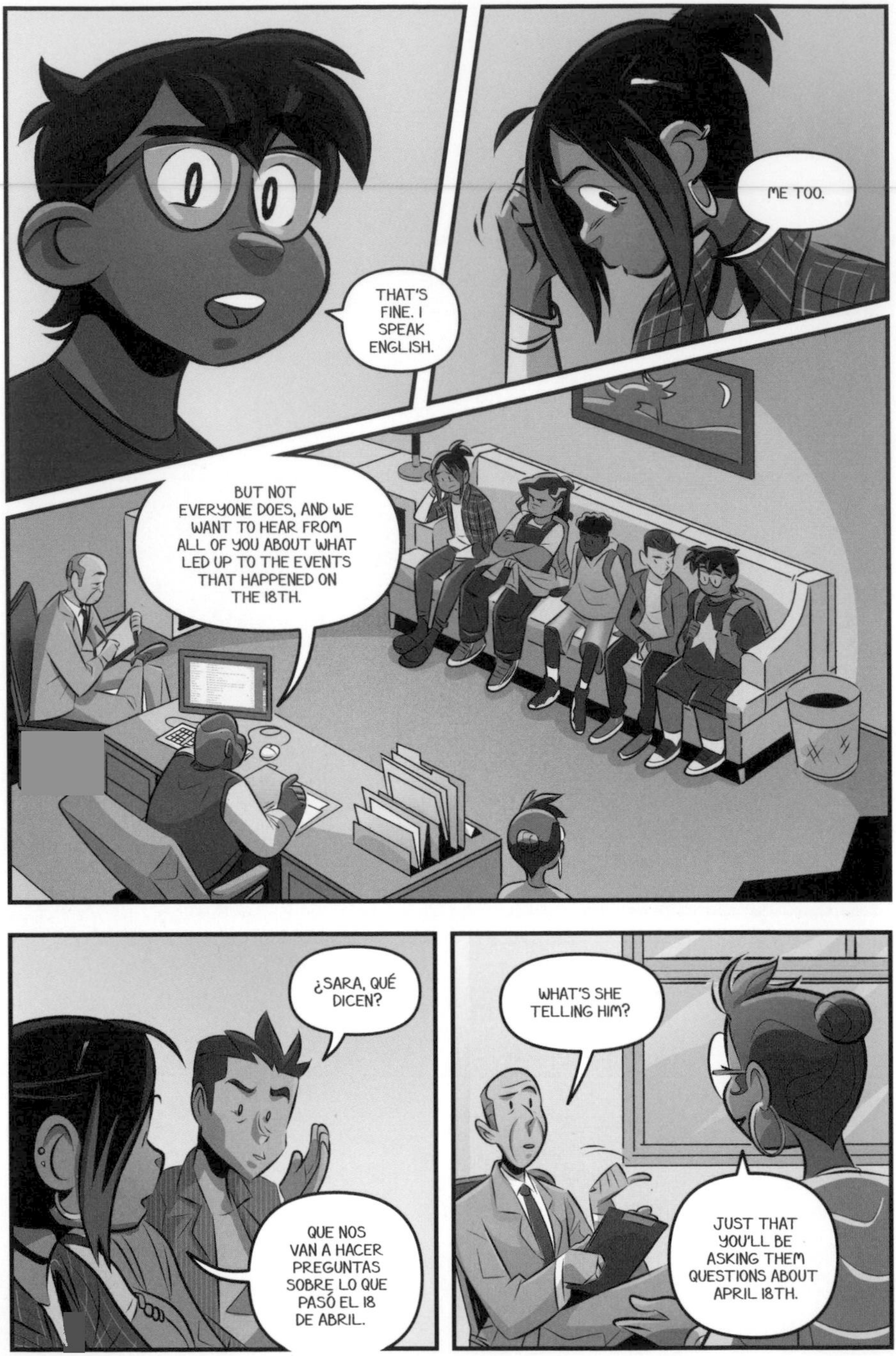
THAT'S FINE. I SPEAK ENGLISH.
ME TOO.
BUT NOT EVERYONE DOES, AND WE WANT TO HEAR FROM ALL OF YOU ABOUT WHAT LED UP TO THE EVENTS THAT HAPPENED ON THE 18TH.
¿SARA, QUÉ DICEN?
QUE NOS VAN A HACER PREGUNTAS SOBRE LO QUE PASÓ EL 18 DE ABRIL.
WHAT'S SHE TELLING HIM?
JUST THAT YOU'LL BE ASKING THEM QUESTIONS ABOUT APRIL 18TH.

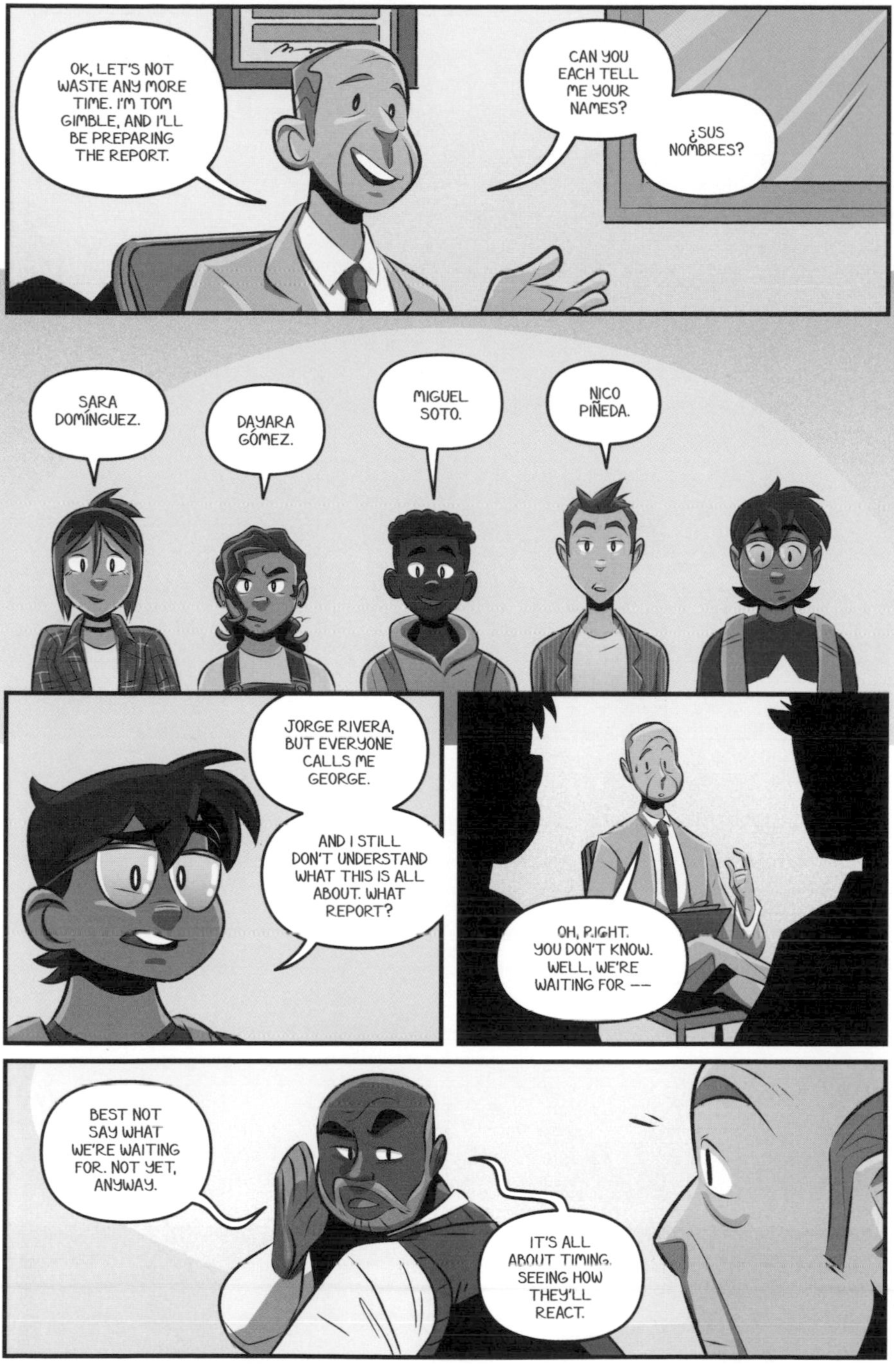
OK, LET'S NOT WASTE ANY MORE TIME. I'M TOM GIMBLE, AND I'LL BE PREPARING THE REPORT.
CAN YOU EACH TELL ME YOUR NAMES?
¿SUS NOMBRES?
SARA DOMÍNGUEZ.
DAYARA GÓMEZ.
MIGUEL SOTO.
NICO PIÑEDA.
JORGE RIVERA, BUT EVERYONE CALLS ME GEORGE.
AND I STILL DON'T UNDERSTAND WHAT THIS IS ALL ABOUT. WHAT REPORT?
OH, RIGHT. YOU DON'T KNOW. WELL, WE'RE WAITING FOR ––
BEST NOT SAY WHAT WE'RE WAITING FOR. NOT YET, ANYWAY.
IT'S ALL ABOUT TIMING. SEEING HOW THEY'LL REACT.

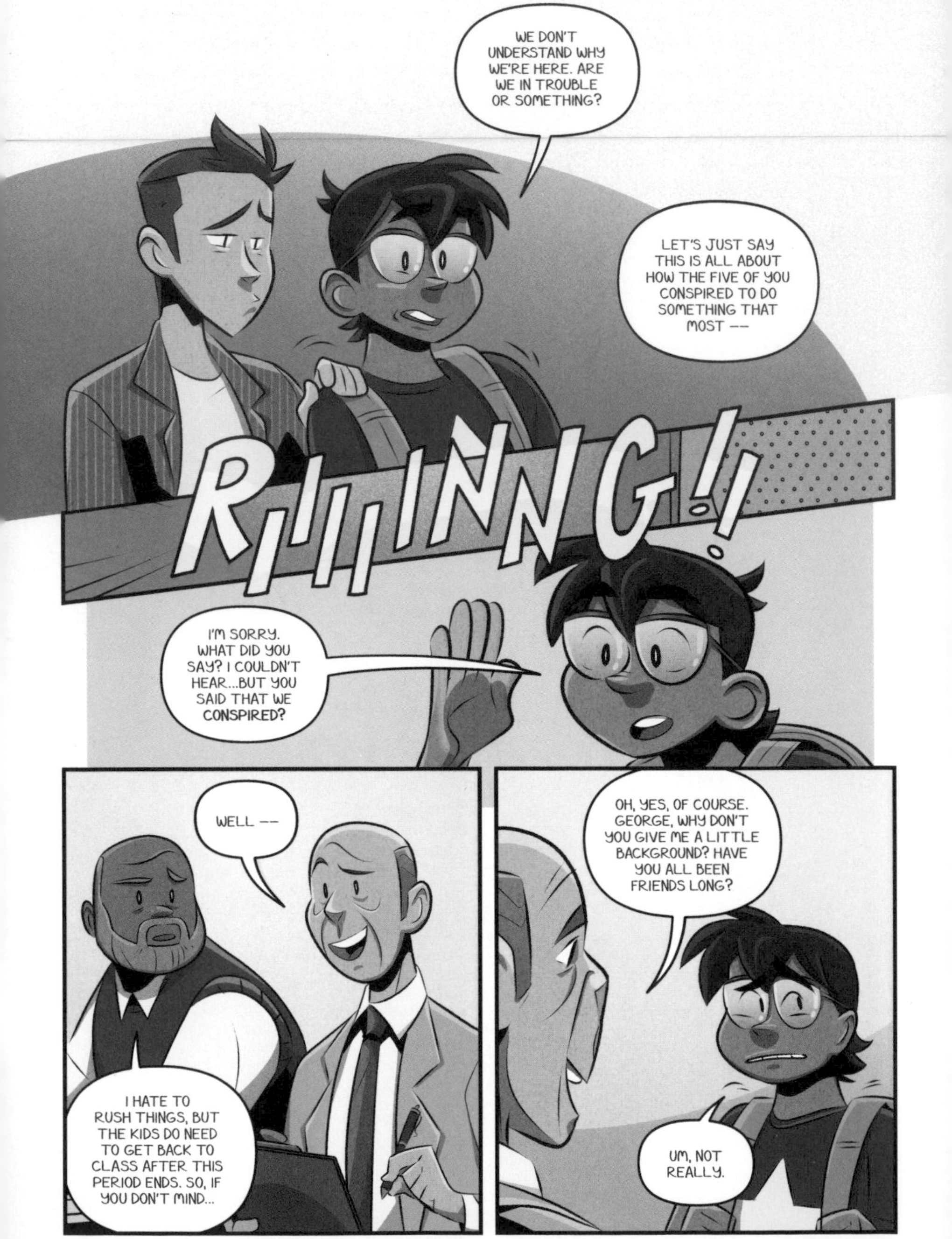
WE DON'T UNDERSTAND WHY WE'RE HERE. ARE WE IN TROUBLE OR SOMETHING?
LET'S JUST SAY THIS IS ALL ABOUT HOW THE FIVE OF YOU CONSPIRED TO DO SOMETHING THAT MOST --
RIIIINNG!!
I'M SORRY. WHAT DID YOU SAY? I COULDN'T HEAR...BUT YOU SAID THAT WE CONSPIRED?
WELL --
I HATE TO RUSH THINGS, BUT THE KIDS DO NEED TO GET BACK TO CLASS AFTER THIS PERIOD ENDS. SO, IF YOU DON'T MIND...
OH, YES, OF COURSE. GEORGE, WHY DON'T YOU GIVE ME A LITTLE BACKGROUND? HAVE YOU ALL BEEN FRIENDS LONG?
UM, NOT REALLY.

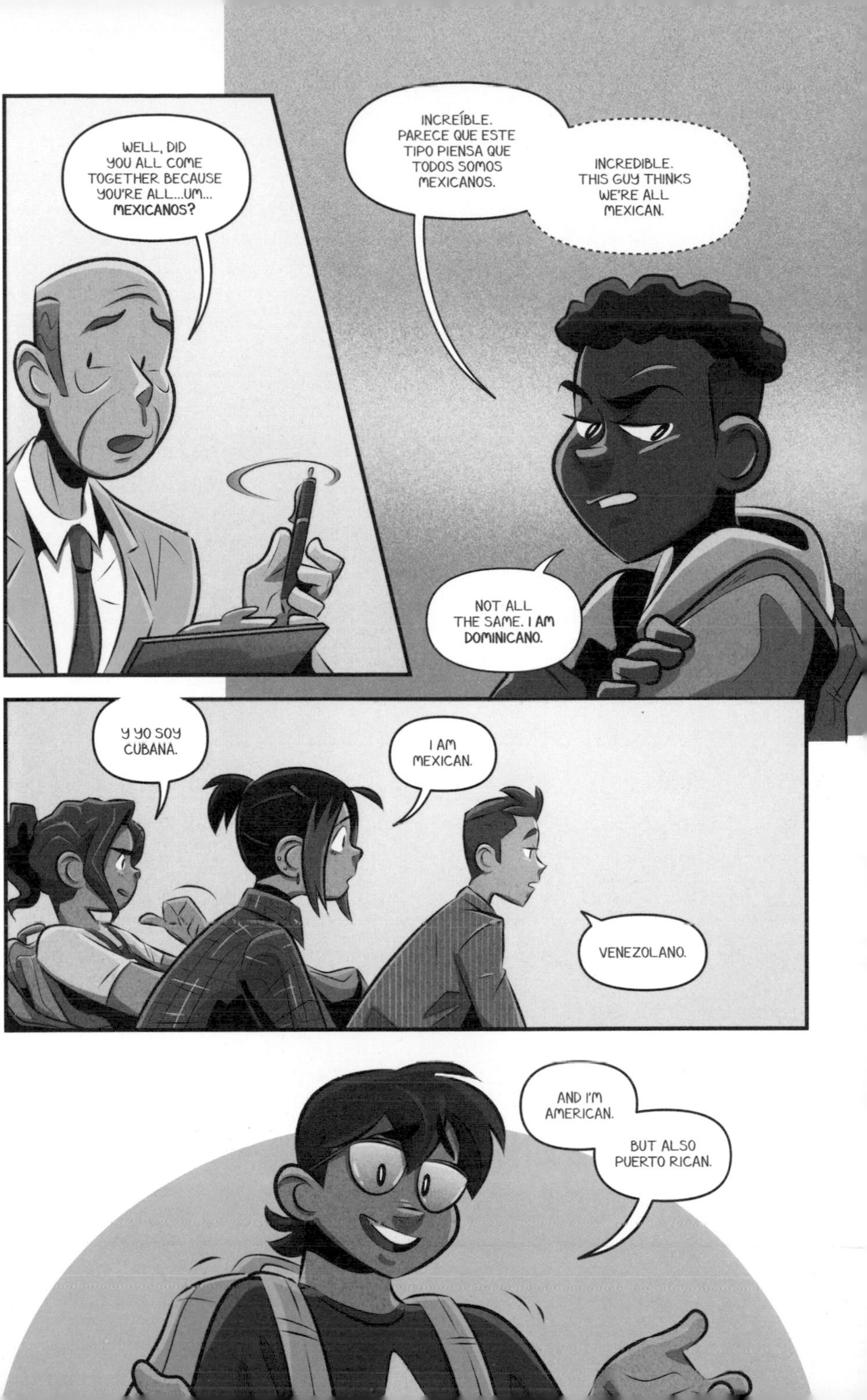
WELL, DID YOU ALL COME TOGETHER BECAUSE YOU'RE ALL...UM... MEXICANOS?
INCREÍBLE. PARECE QUE ESTE TIPO PIENSA QUE TODOS SOMOS MEXICANOS.
INCREDIBLE. THIS GUY THINKS WE'RE ALL MEXICAN.
NOT ALL THE SAME. I AM DOMINICANO.
Y YO SOY CUBANA.
I AM MEXICAN.
VENEZOLANO.
AND I'M AMERICAN.
BUT ALSO PUERTO RICAN.

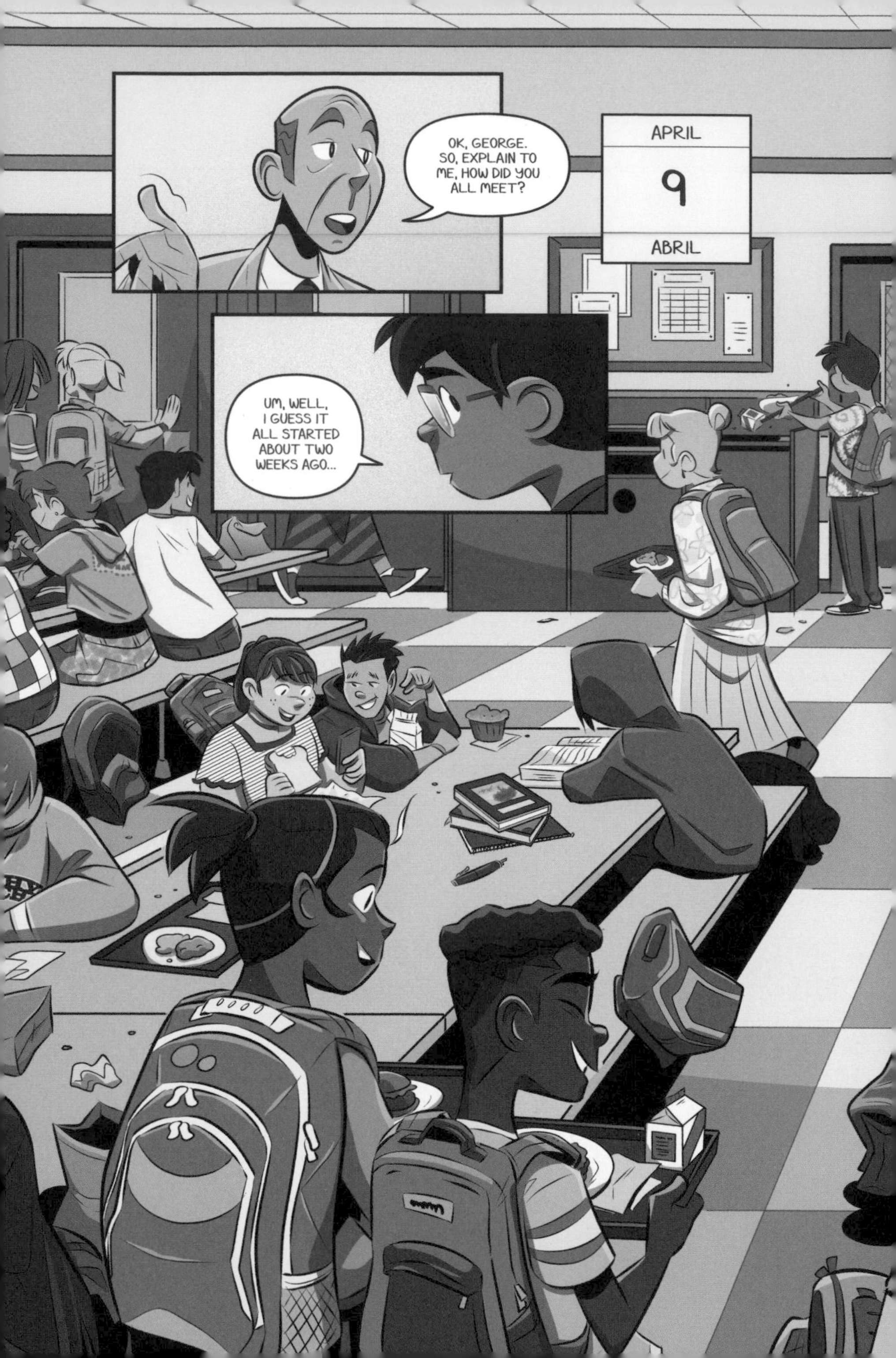
OK, GEORGE. SO, EXPLAIN TO ME, HOW DID YOU ALL MEET?
APRIL
9
ABRIL
UM, WELL, I GUESS IT ALL STARTED ABOUT TWO WEEKS AGO...

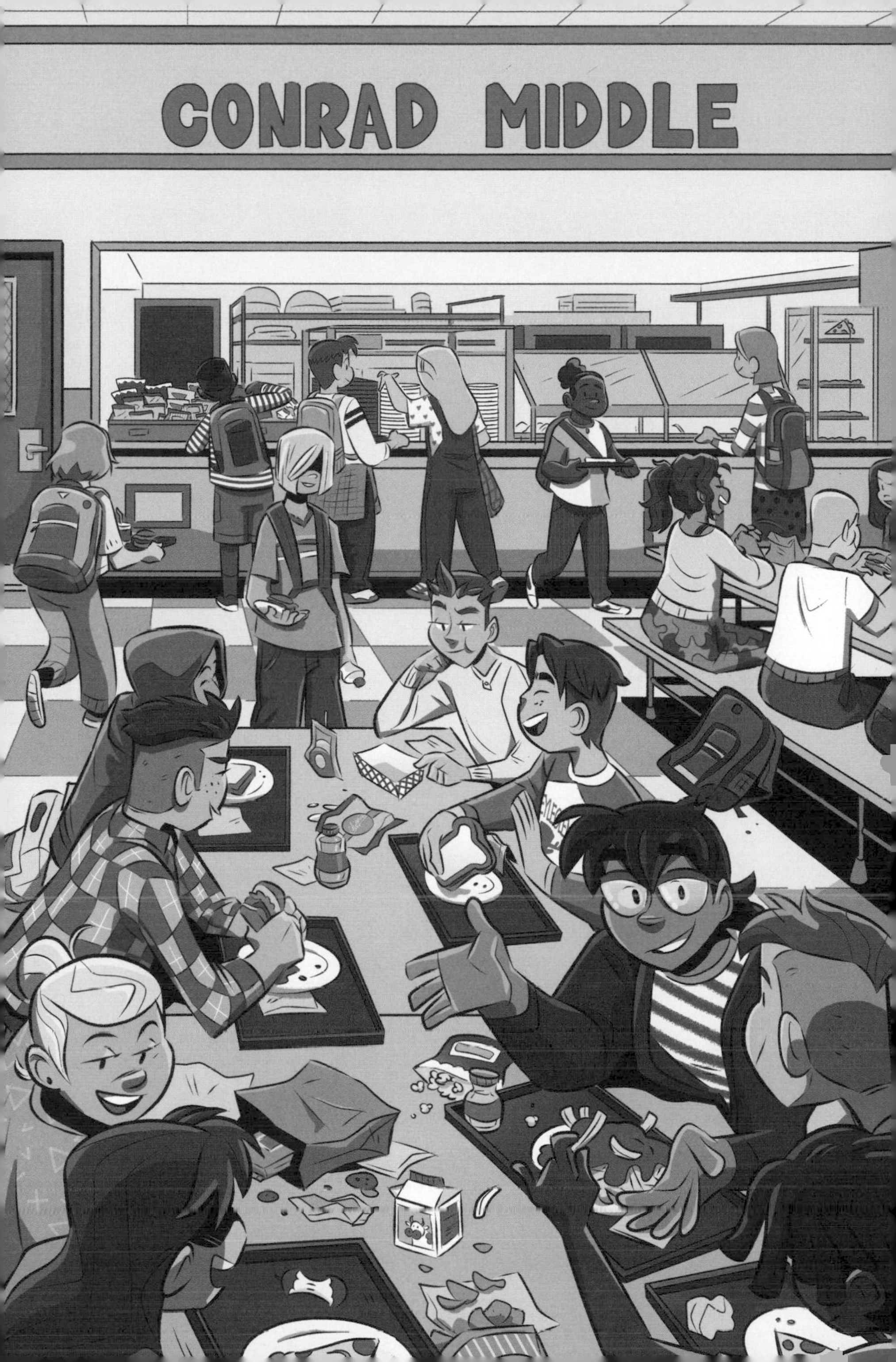
CONRAD MIDDLE

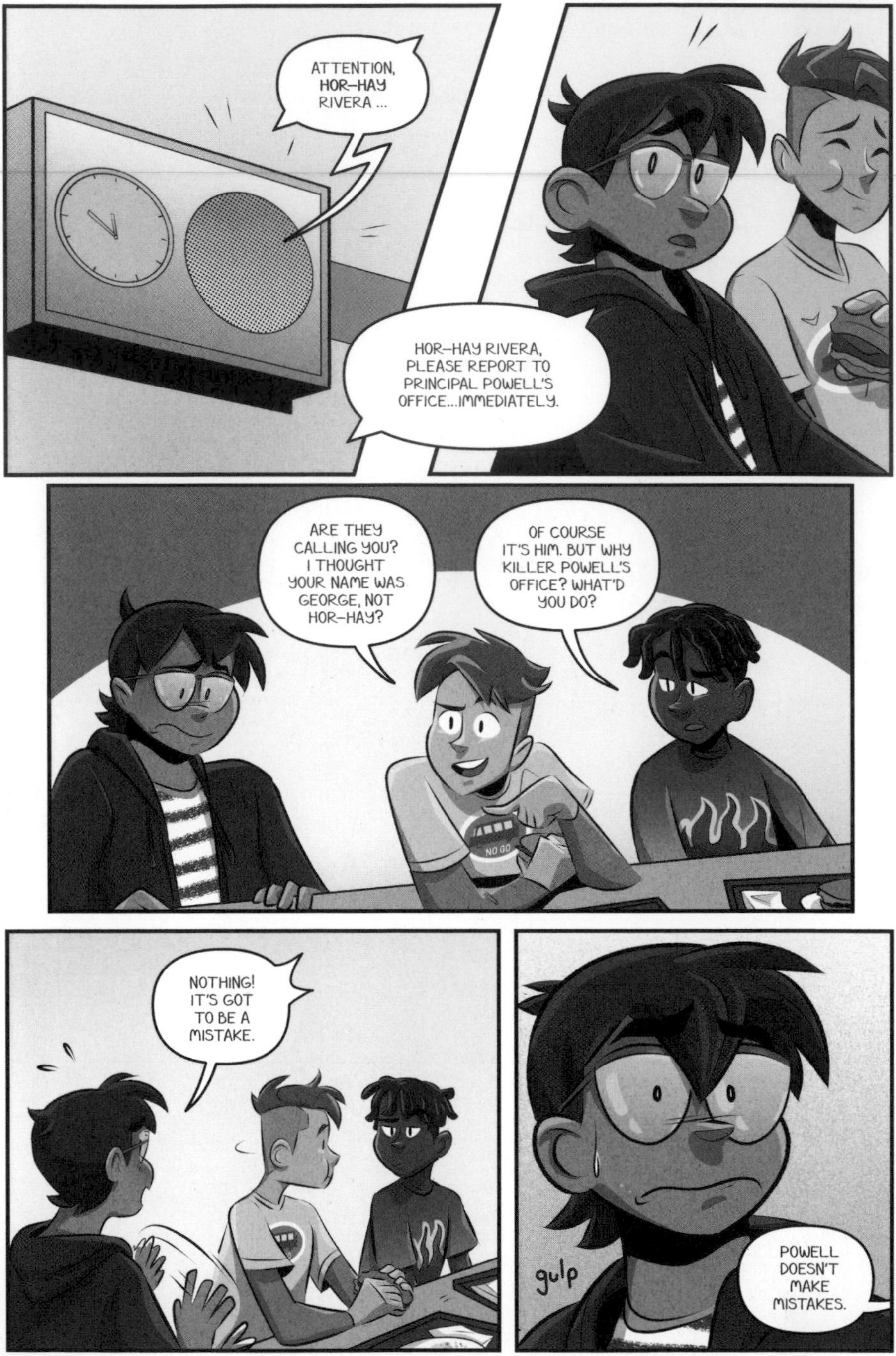
ATTENTION, HOR–HAY RIVERA ...
HOR–HAY RIVERA, PLEASE REPORT TO PRINCIPAL POWELL'S OFFICE...IMMEDIATELY.
ARE THEY CALLING YOU? I THOUGHT YOUR NAME WAS GEORGE, NOT HOR–HAY?
OF COURSE IT'S HIM. BUT WHY KILLER POWELL'S OFFICE? WHAT'D YOU DO?
NO GO
NOTHING! IT'S GOT TO BE A MISTAKE.
gulp
POWELL DOESN'T MAKE MISTAKES.

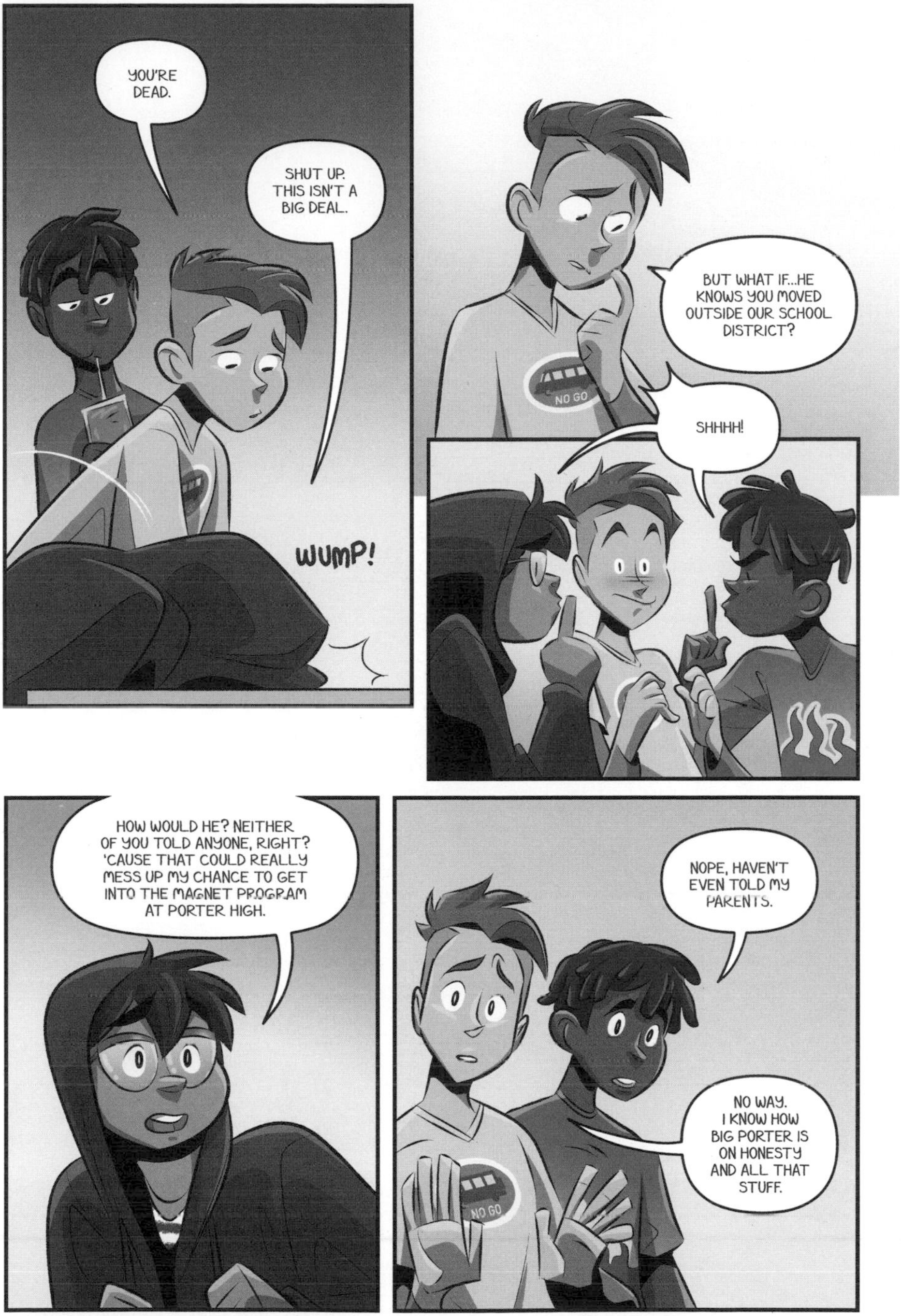
YOU'RE DEAD.
SHUT UP. THIS ISN'T A BIG DEAL.
WUMP!
BUT WHAT IF...HE KNOWS YOU MOVED OUTSIDE OUR SCHOOL DISTRICT?
SHHHH!
NO GO
HOW WOULD HE? NEITHER OF YOU TOLD ANYONE, RIGHT? 'CAUSE THAT COULD REALLY MESS UP MY CHANCE TO GET INTO THE MAGNET PROGRAM AT PORTER HIGH.
NOPE, HAVEN'T EVEN TOLD MY PARENTS.
NO WAY. I KNOW HOW BIG PORTER IS ON HONESTY AND ALL THAT STUFF.
NO GO

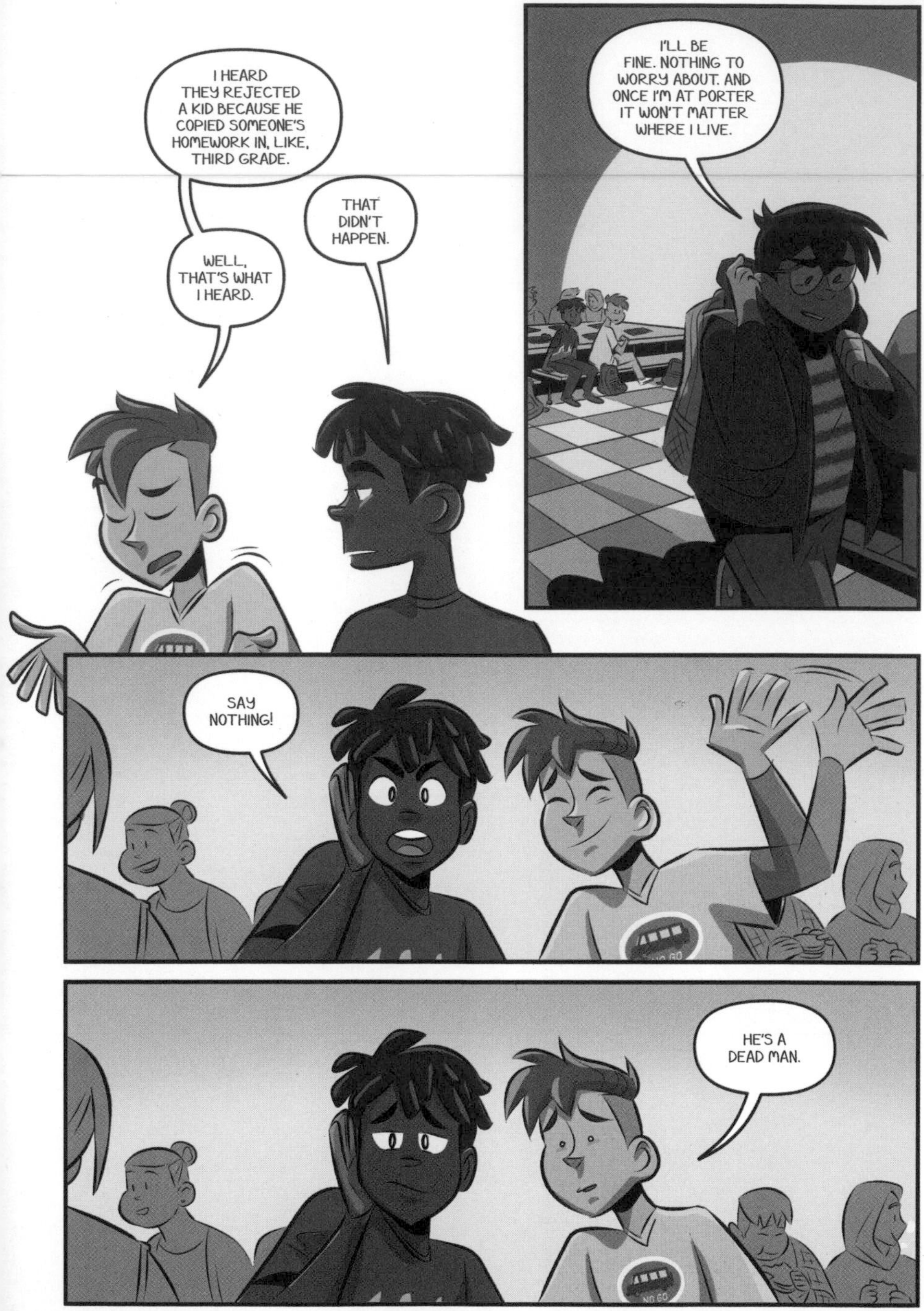
I HEARD THEY REJECTED A KID BECAUSE HE COPIED SOMEONE'S HOMEWORK IN, LIKE, THIRD GRADE.
WELL, THAT'S WHAT I HEARD.
THAT DIDN'T HAPPEN.
I'LL BE FINE. NOTHING TO WORRY ABOUT. AND ONCE I'M AT PORTER IT WON'T MATTER WHERE I LIVE.
SAY NOTHING!
HE'S A DEAD MAN.

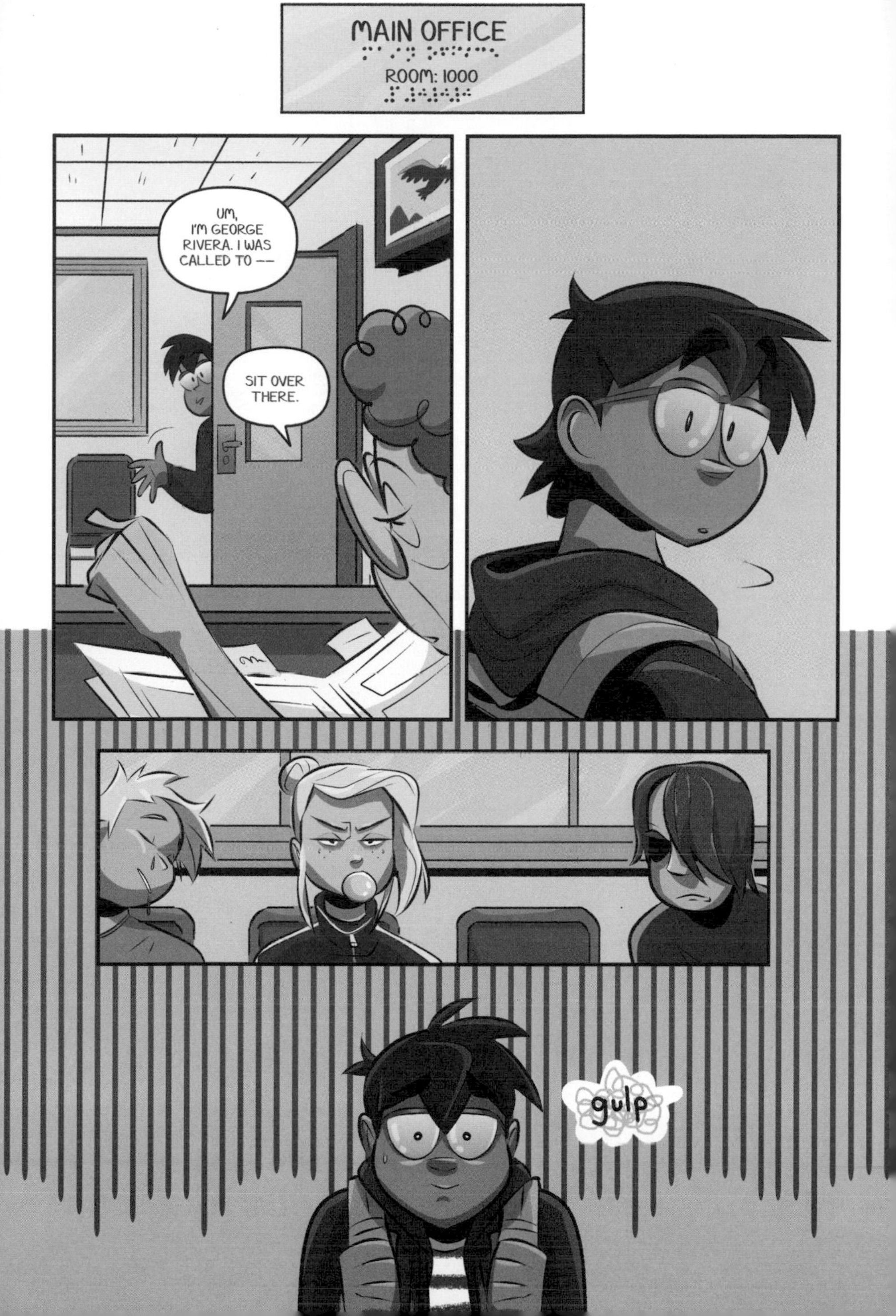
MAIN OFFICE
ROOM: 1000
UM, I'M GEORGE RIVERA. I WAS CALLED TO --
SIT OVER THERE.
gulp

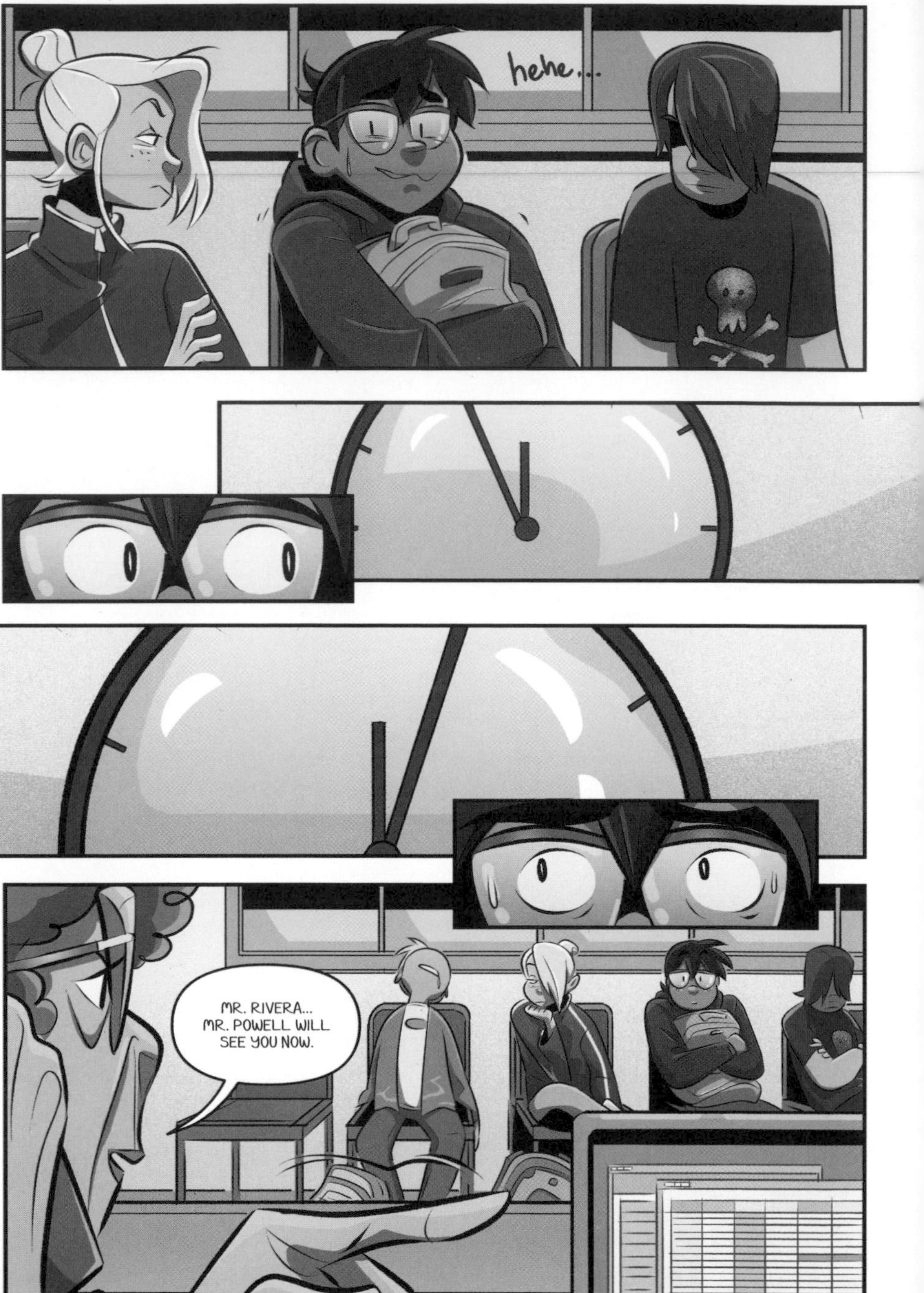
hehe...
MR. RIVERA...
MR. POWELL WILL
SEE YOU NOW.

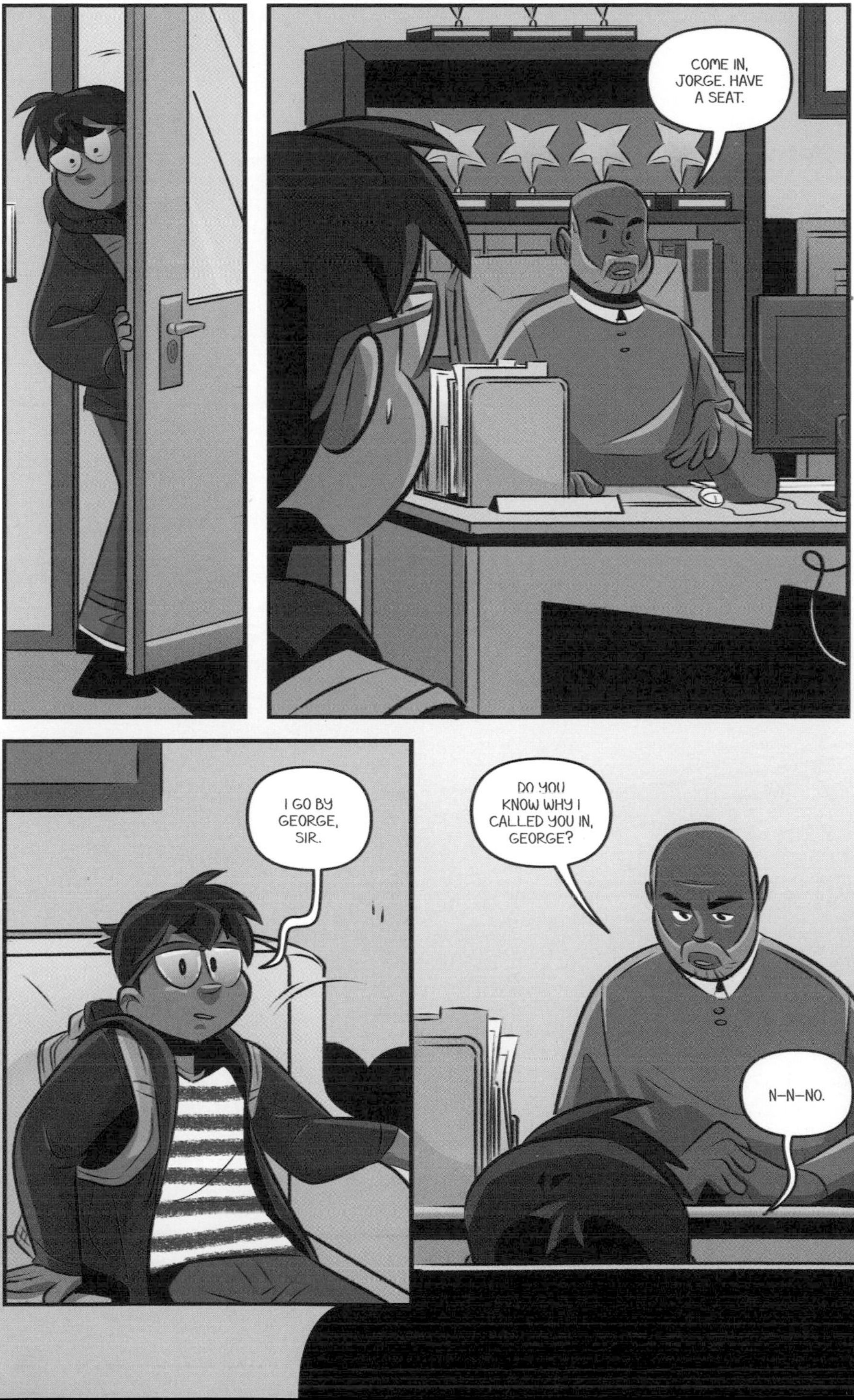
COME IN, JORGE. HAVE A SEAT.
I GO BY GEORGE, SIR.
DO YOU KNOW WHY I CALLED YOU IN, GEORGE?
N-N-NO.

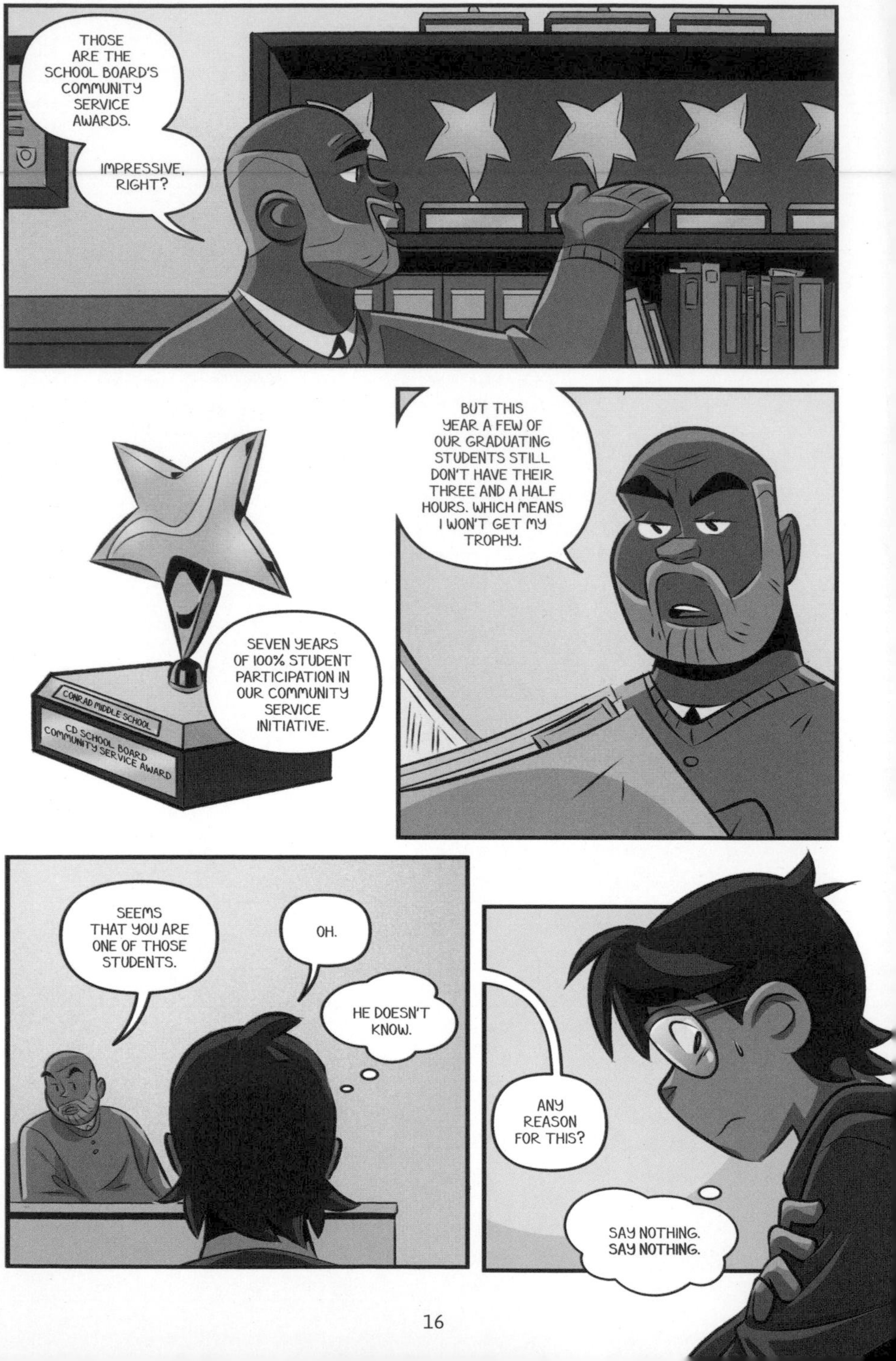
THOSE ARE THE SCHOOL BOARD'S COMMUNITY SERVICE AWARDS.
IMPRESSIVE, RIGHT?
CONRAD MIDDLE SCHOOL
CD SCHOOL BOARD COMMUNITY SERVICE AWARD
SEVEN YEARS OF 100% STUDENT PARTICIPATION IN OUR COMMUNITY SERVICE INITIATIVE.
BUT THIS YEAR A FEW OF OUR GRADUATING STUDENTS STILL DON'T HAVE THEIR THREE AND A HALF HOURS. WHICH MEANS I WON'T GET MY TROPHY.
SEEMS THAT YOU ARE ONE OF THOSE STUDENTS.
OH.
HE DOESN'T KNOW.
ANY REASON FOR THIS?
SAY NOTHING. **SAY NOTHING.**

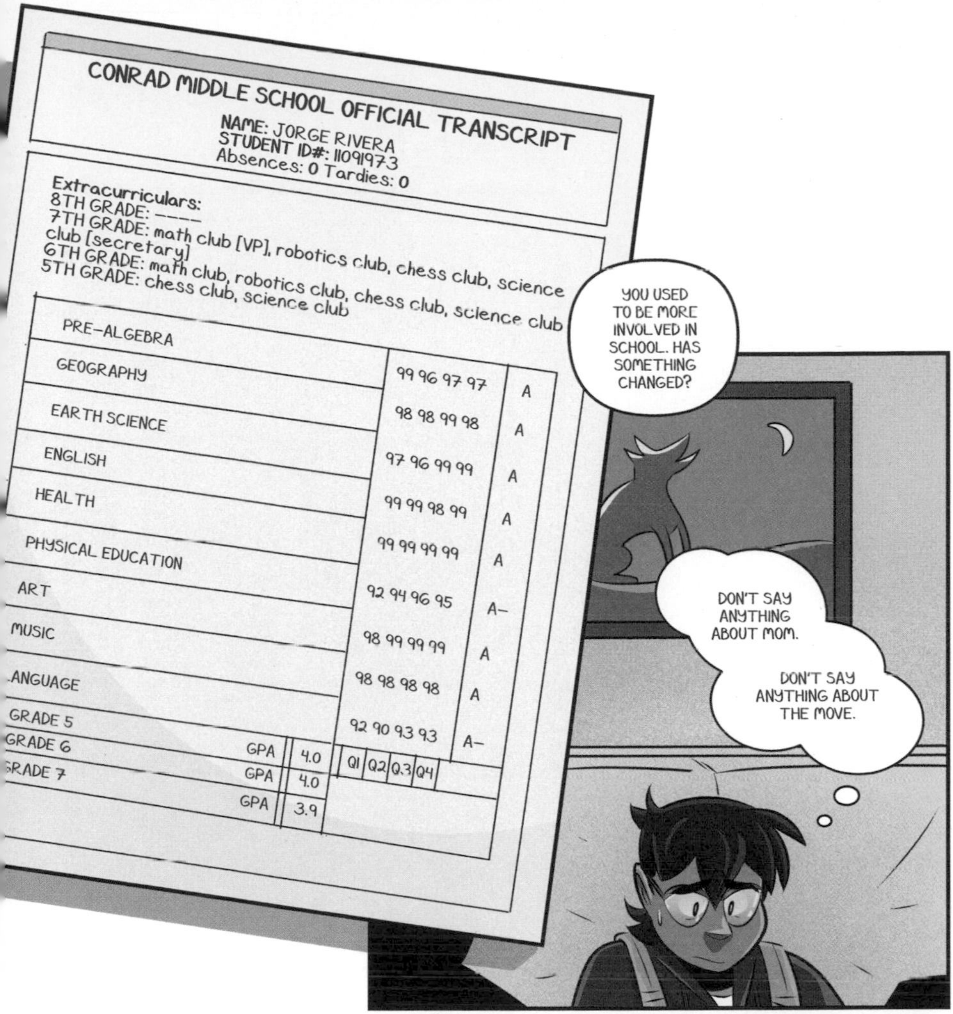
CONRAD MIDDLE SCHOOL OFFICIAL TRANSCRIPT
NAME: JORGE RIVERA
STUDENT ID#: 11091973
Absences: 0 Tardies: 0
Extracurriculars:
8TH GRADE: ----
7TH GRADE: math club [VP], robotics club, chess club, science club [secretary]
6TH GRADE: math club, robotics club, chess club, science club
5TH GRADE: chess club, science club
PRE-ALGEBRA
GEOGRAPHY
EARTH SCIENCE
ENGLISH
HEALTH
PHYSICAL EDUCATION
ART
MUSIC
LANGUAGE
99 96 97 97 A
98 98 99 98 A
97 96 99 99 A
99 99 98 99 A
99 99 99 99 A
92 94 96 95 A-
98 99 99 99 A
98 98 98 98 A
92 90 93 93 A-
Q1 Q2 Q3 Q4
GRADE 5 GPA 4.0
GRADE 6 GPA 4.0
GRADE 7 GPA 3.9
YOU USED TO BE MORE INVOLVED IN SCHOOL. HAS SOMETHING CHANGED?
DON'T SAY ANYTHING ABOUT MOM.
DON'T SAY ANYTHING ABOUT THE MOVE.

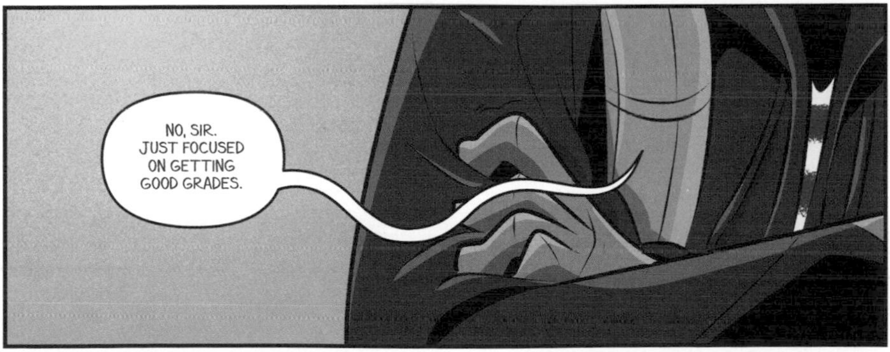
NO, SIR. JUST FOCUSED ON GETTING GOOD GRADES.

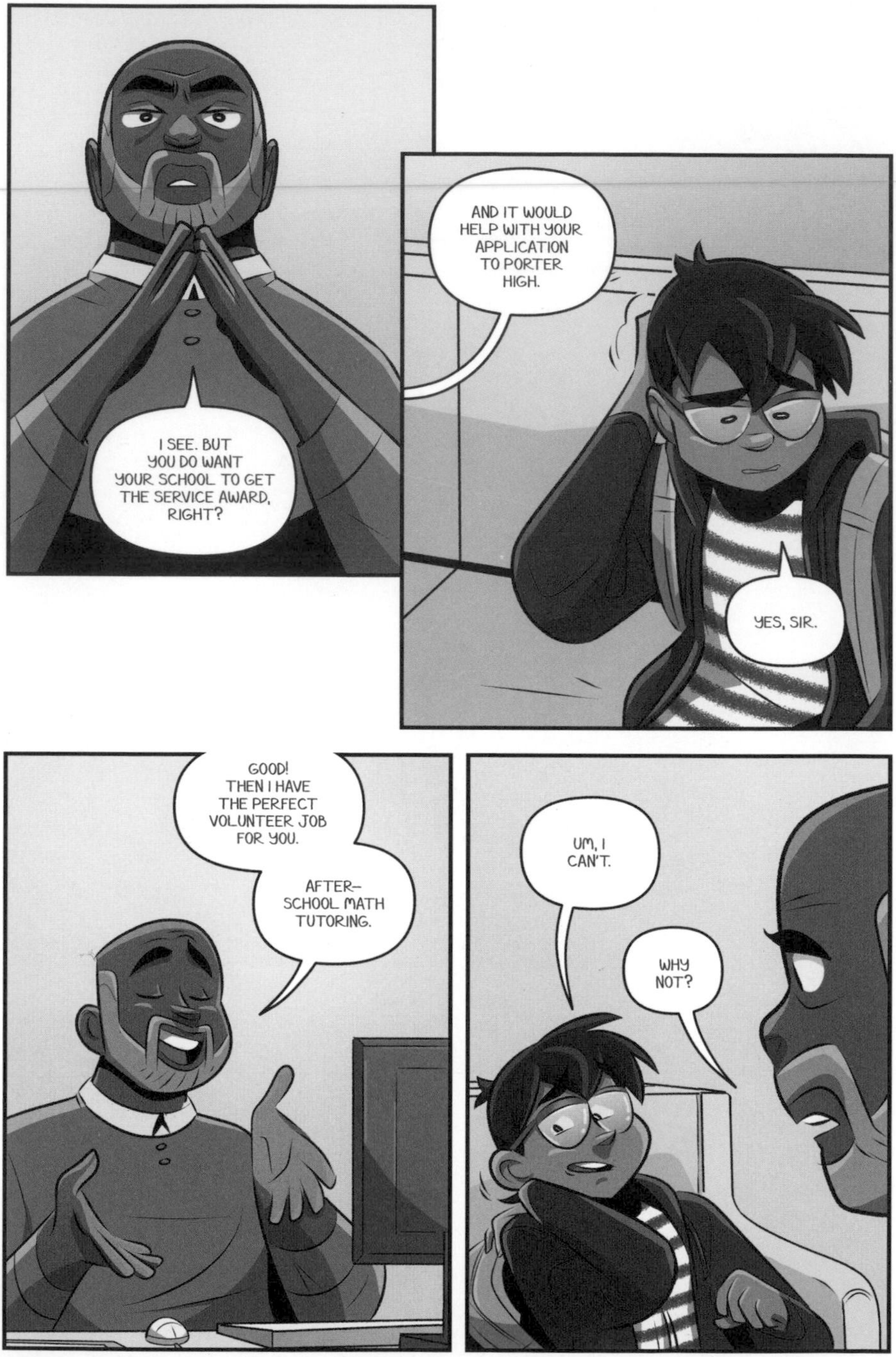

I SEE. BUT YOU DO WANT YOUR SCHOOL TO GET THE SERVICE AWARD, RIGHT?
AND IT WOULD HELP WITH YOUR APPLICATION TO PORTER HIGH.
YES, SIR.
GOOD! THEN I HAVE THE PERFECT VOLUNTEER JOB FOR YOU.
AFTER-SCHOOL MATH TUTORING.
UM, I CAN'T.
WHY NOT?

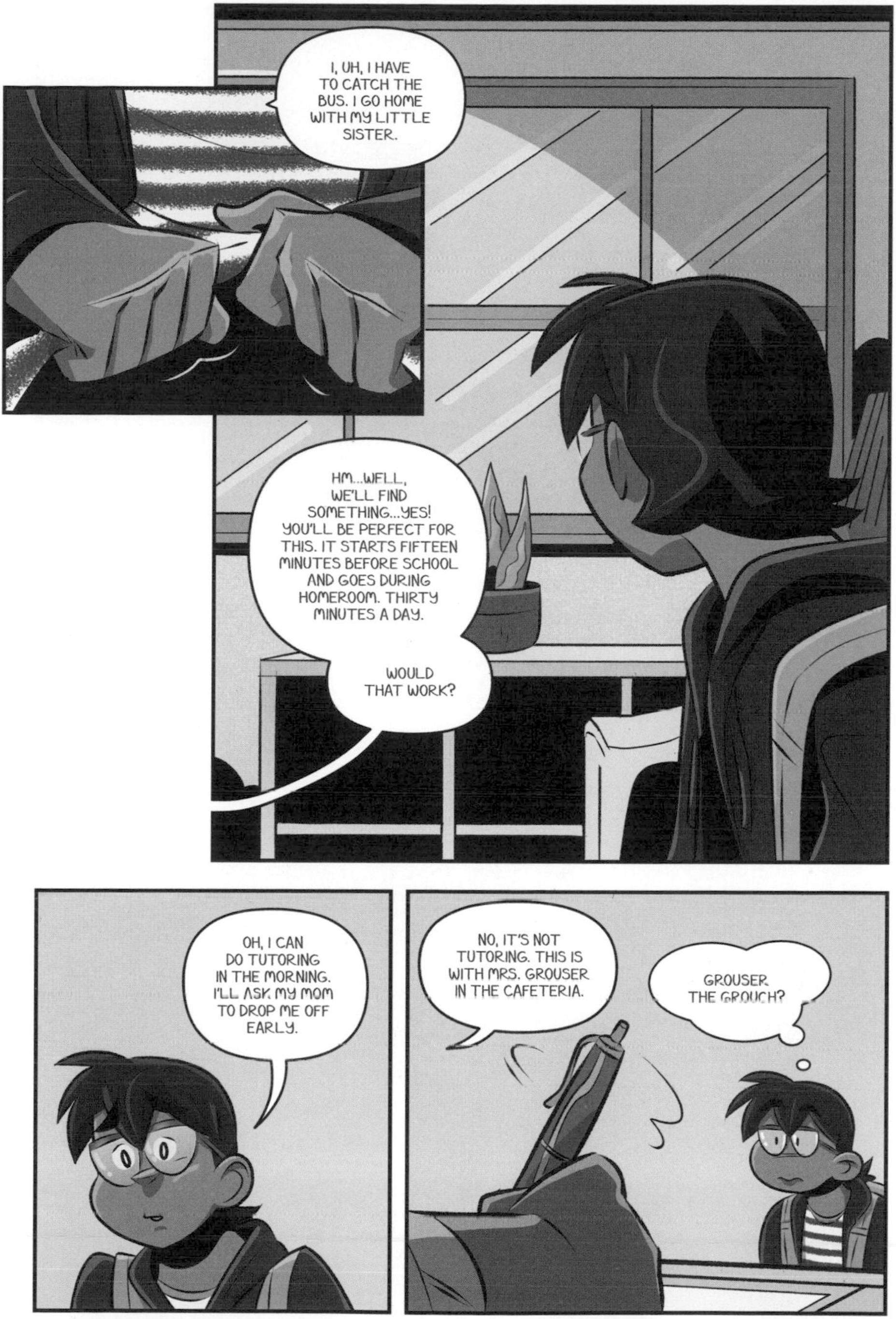
I, UH, I HAVE TO CATCH THE BUS. I GO HOME WITH MY LITTLE SISTER.
HM...WELL, WE'LL FIND SOMETHING...YES! YOU'LL BE PERFECT FOR THIS. IT STARTS FIFTEEN MINUTES BEFORE SCHOOL AND GOES DURING HOMEROOM. THIRTY MINUTES A DAY.
WOULD THAT WORK?
OH, I CAN DO TUTORING IN THE MORNING. I'LL ASK MY MOM TO DROP ME OFF EARLY.
NO, IT'S NOT TUTORING. THIS IS WITH MRS. GROUSER IN THE CAFETERIA.
GROUSER THE GROUCH?

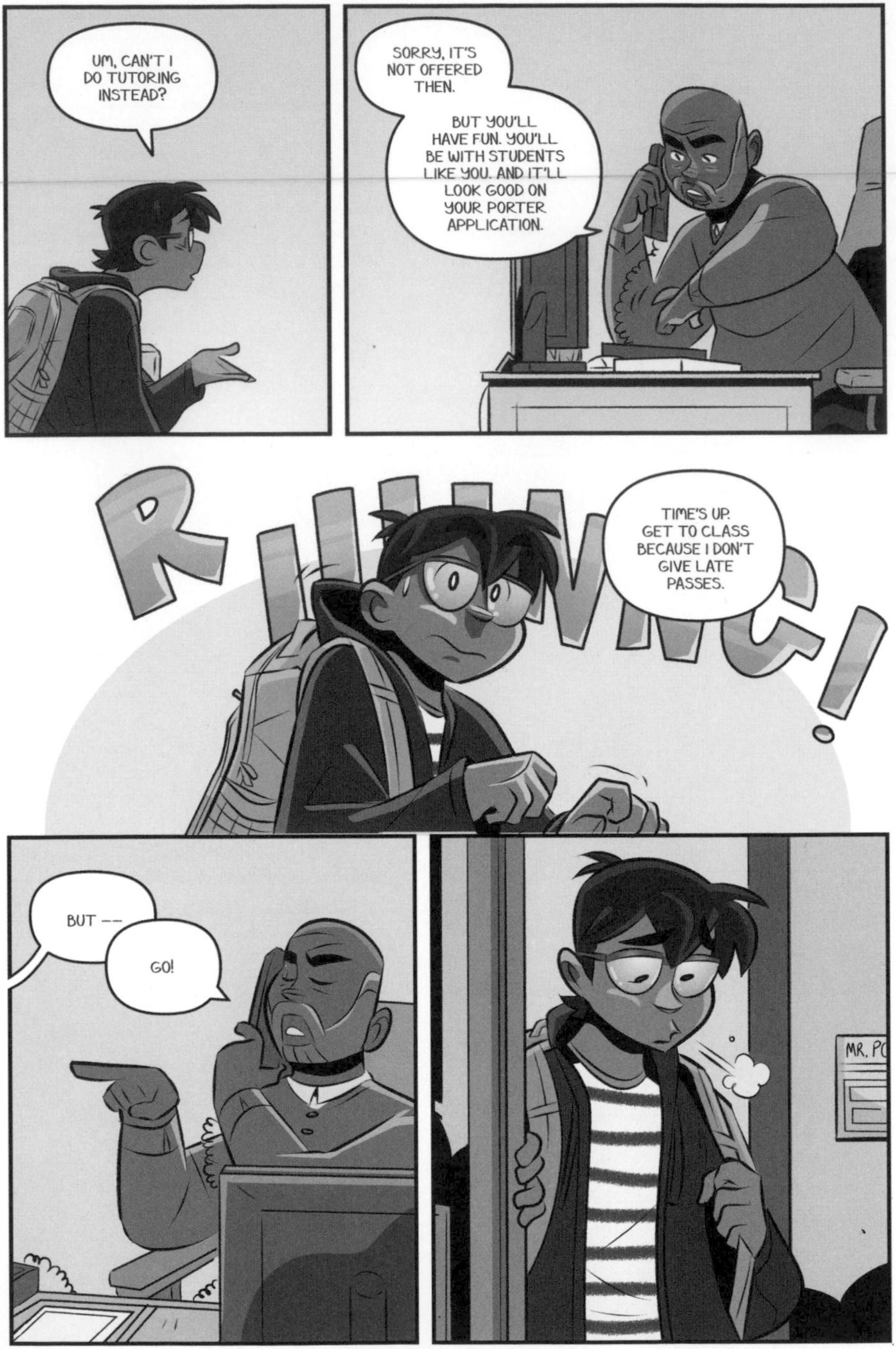
UM, CAN'T I DO TUTORING INSTEAD?
SORRY, IT'S NOT OFFERED THEN.
BUT YOU'LL HAVE FUN. YOU'LL BE WITH STUDENTS LIKE YOU. AND IT'LL LOOK GOOD ON YOUR PORTER APPLICATION.
RIIIING!
TIME'S UP. GET TO CLASS BECAUSE I DON'T GIVE LATE PASSES.
BUT --
GO!
MR. P

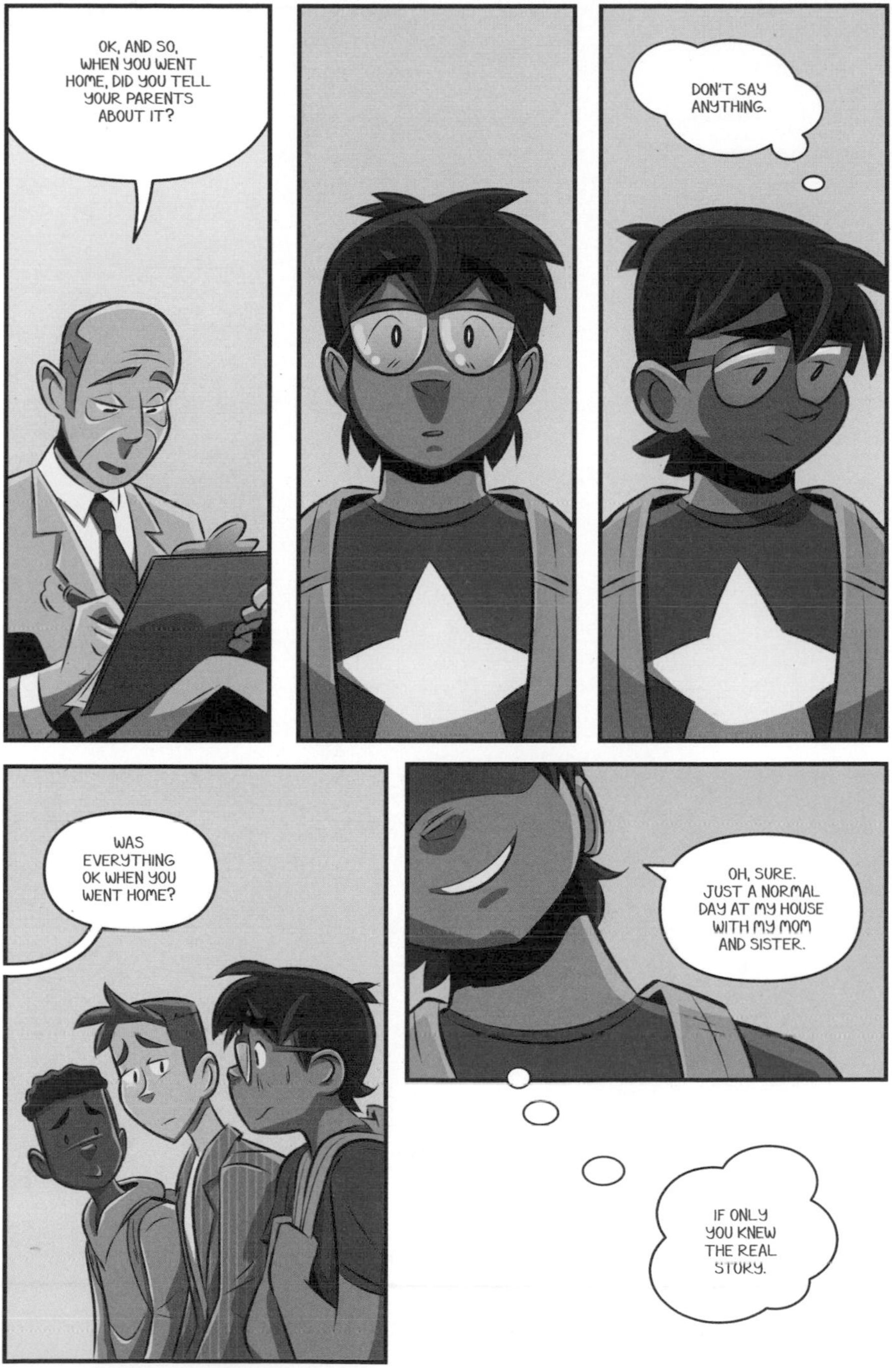
OK, AND SO, WHEN YOU WENT HOME, DID YOU TELL YOUR PARENTS ABOUT IT?
DON'T SAY ANYTHING.
WAS EVERYTHING OK WHEN YOU WENT HOME?
OH, SURE. JUST A NORMAL DAY AT MY HOUSE WITH MY MOM AND SISTER.
IF ONLY YOU KNEW THE REAL STORY.

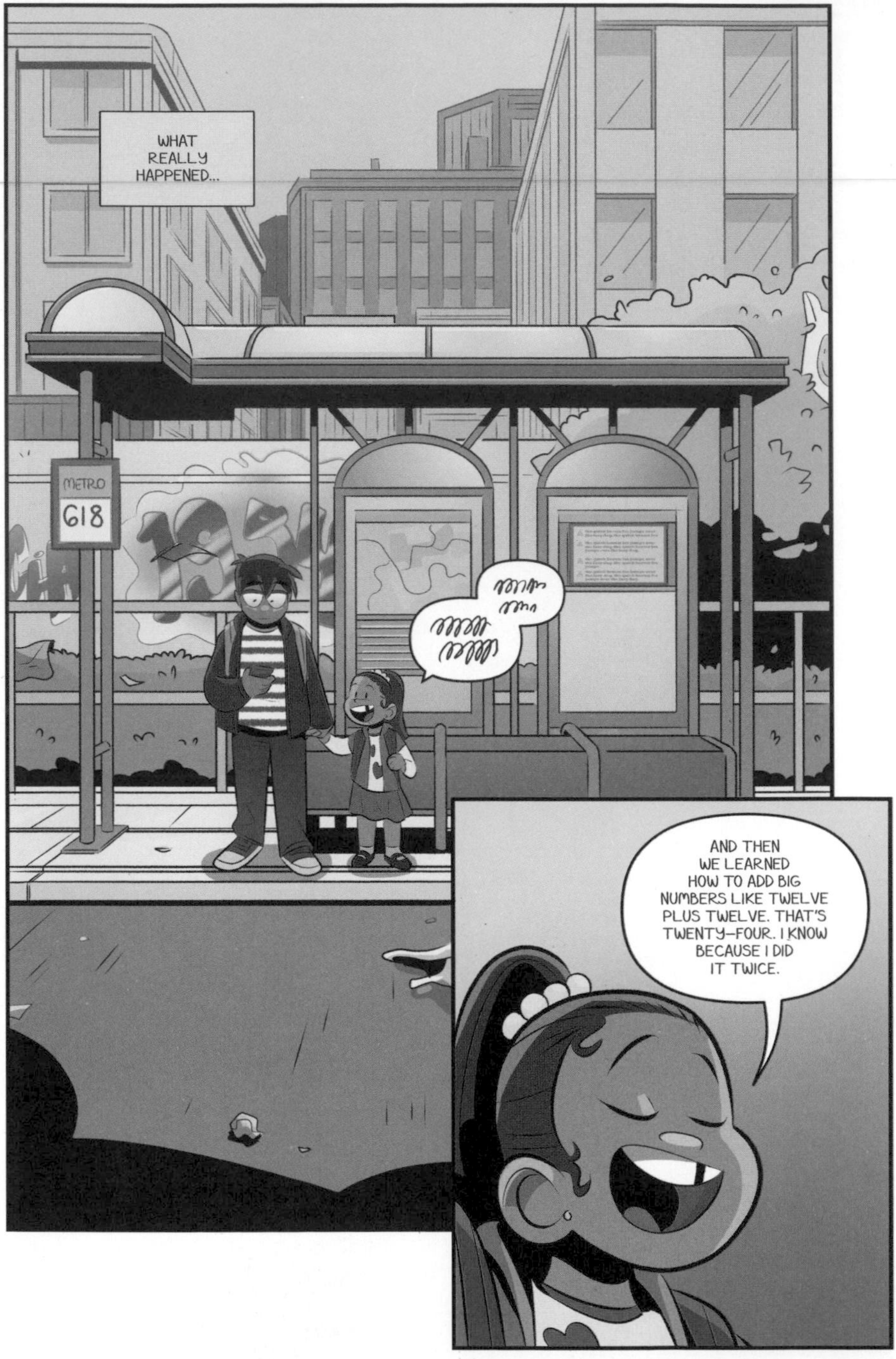

WHAT REALLY HAPPENED...
METRO
618
AND THEN WE LEARNED HOW TO ADD BIG NUMBERS LIKE TWELVE PLUS TWELVE. THAT'S TWENTY-FOUR. I KNOW BECAUSE I DID IT TWICE.

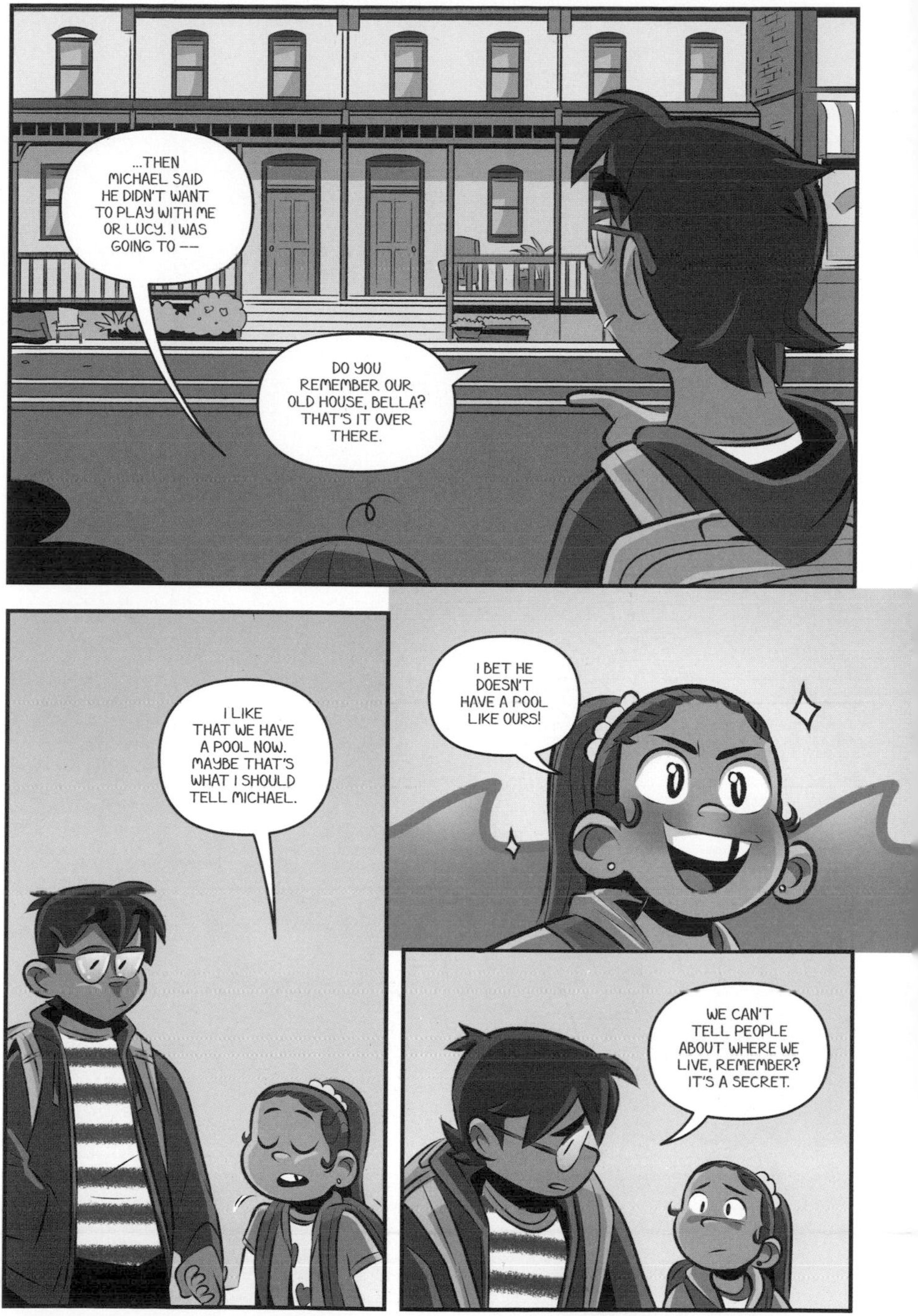
...THEN MICHAEL SAID HE DIDN'T WANT TO PLAY WITH ME OR LUCY. I WAS GOING TO --
DO YOU REMEMBER OUR OLD HOUSE, BELLA? THAT'S IT OVER THERE.
I LIKE THAT WE HAVE A POOL NOW. MAYBE THAT'S WHAT I SHOULD TELL MICHAEL.
I BET HE DOESN'T HAVE A POOL LIKE OURS!
WE CAN'T TELL PEOPLE ABOUT WHERE WE LIVE, REMEMBER? IT'S A SECRET.

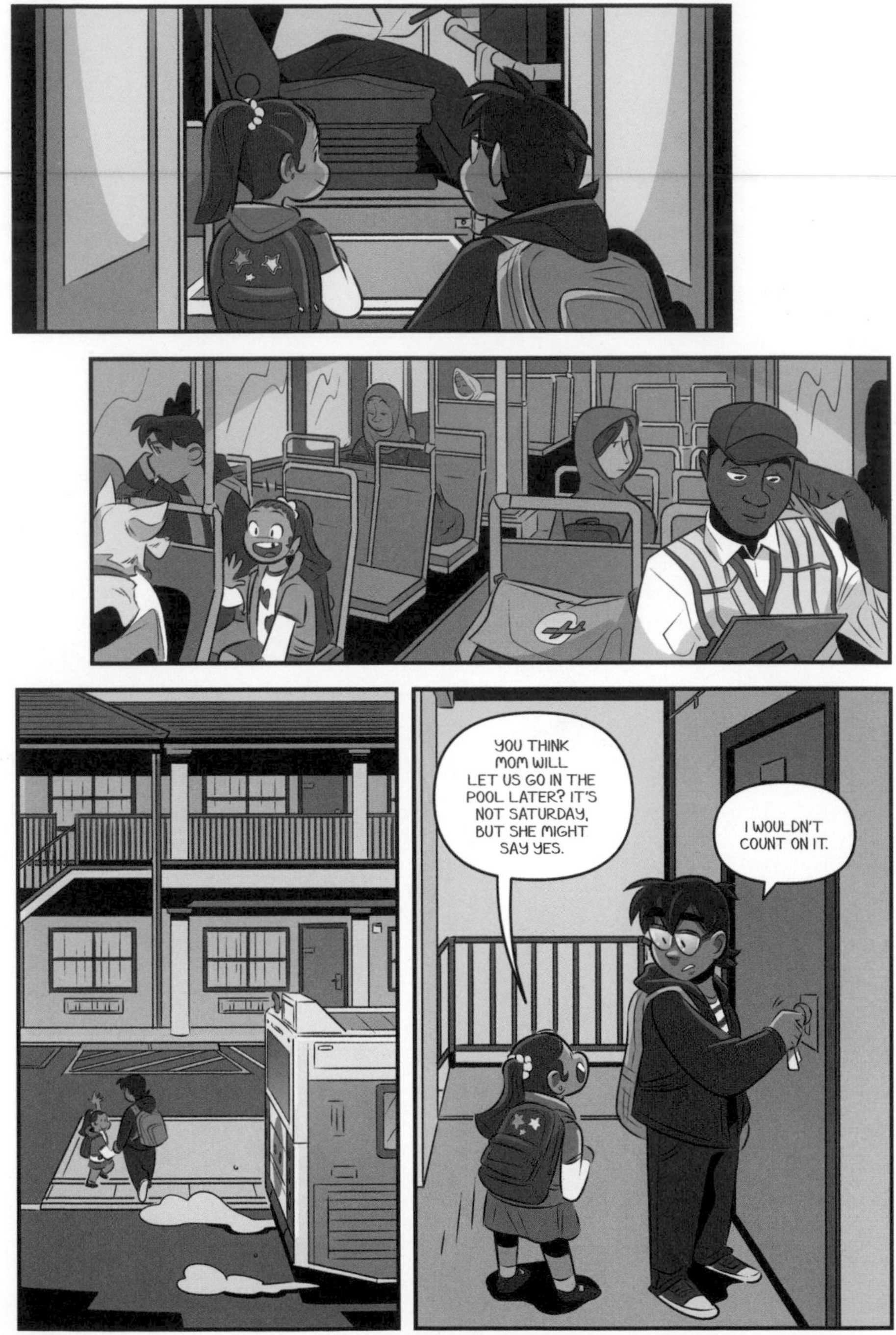
YOU THINK MOM WILL LET US GO IN THE POOL LATER? IT'S NOT SATURDAY, BUT SHE MIGHT SAY YES.
I WOULDN'T COUNT ON IT.

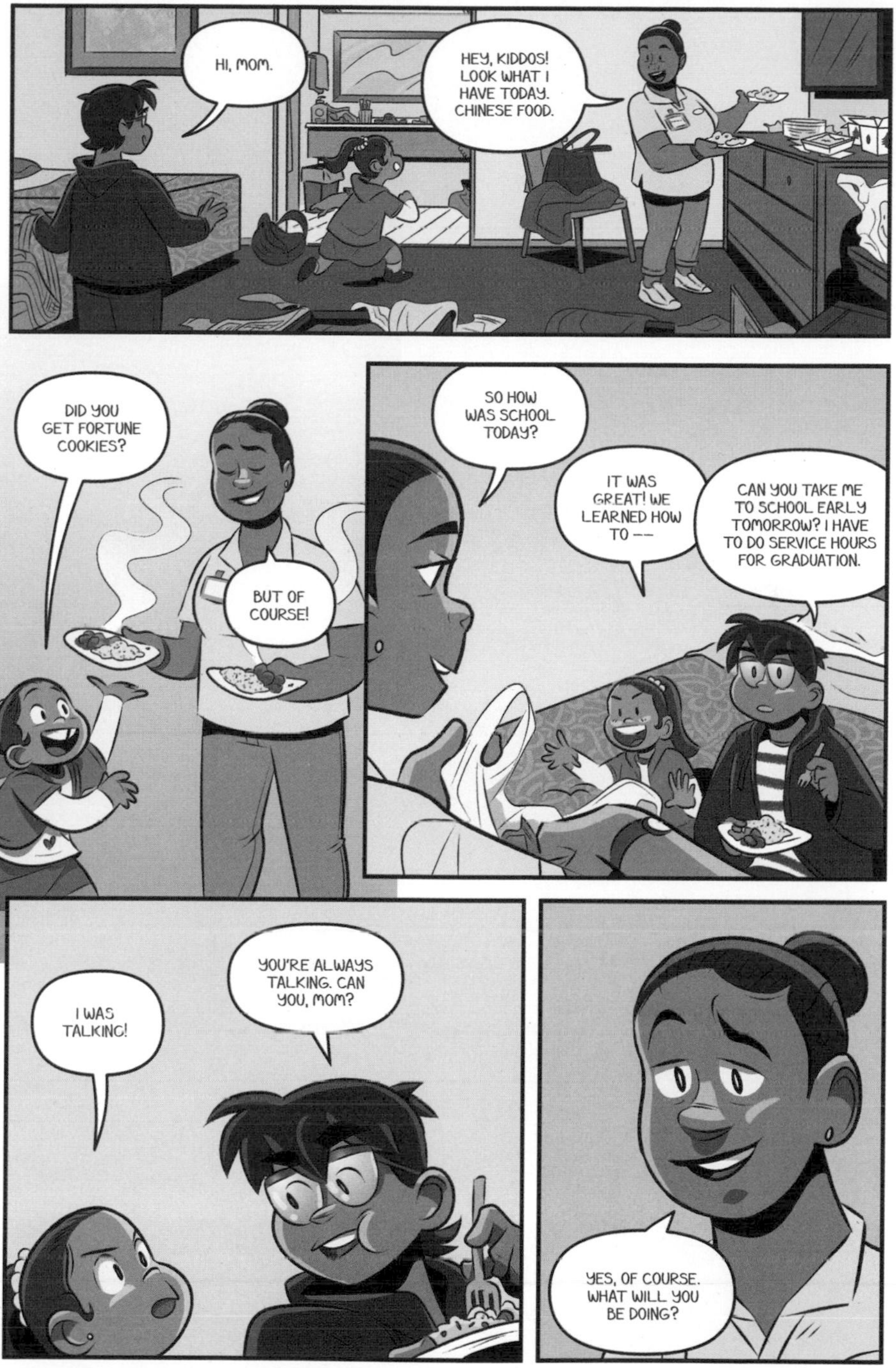
HI, MOM.
HEY, KIDDOS! LOOK WHAT I HAVE TODAY. CHINESE FOOD.
DID YOU GET FORTUNE COOKIES?
BUT OF COURSE!
SO HOW WAS SCHOOL TODAY?
IT WAS GREAT! WE LEARNED HOW TO --
CAN YOU TAKE ME TO SCHOOL EARLY TOMORROW? I HAVE TO DO SERVICE HOURS FOR GRADUATION.
I WAS TALKING!
YOU'RE ALWAYS TALKING. CAN YOU, MOM?
YES, OF COURSE. WHAT WILL YOU BE DOING?

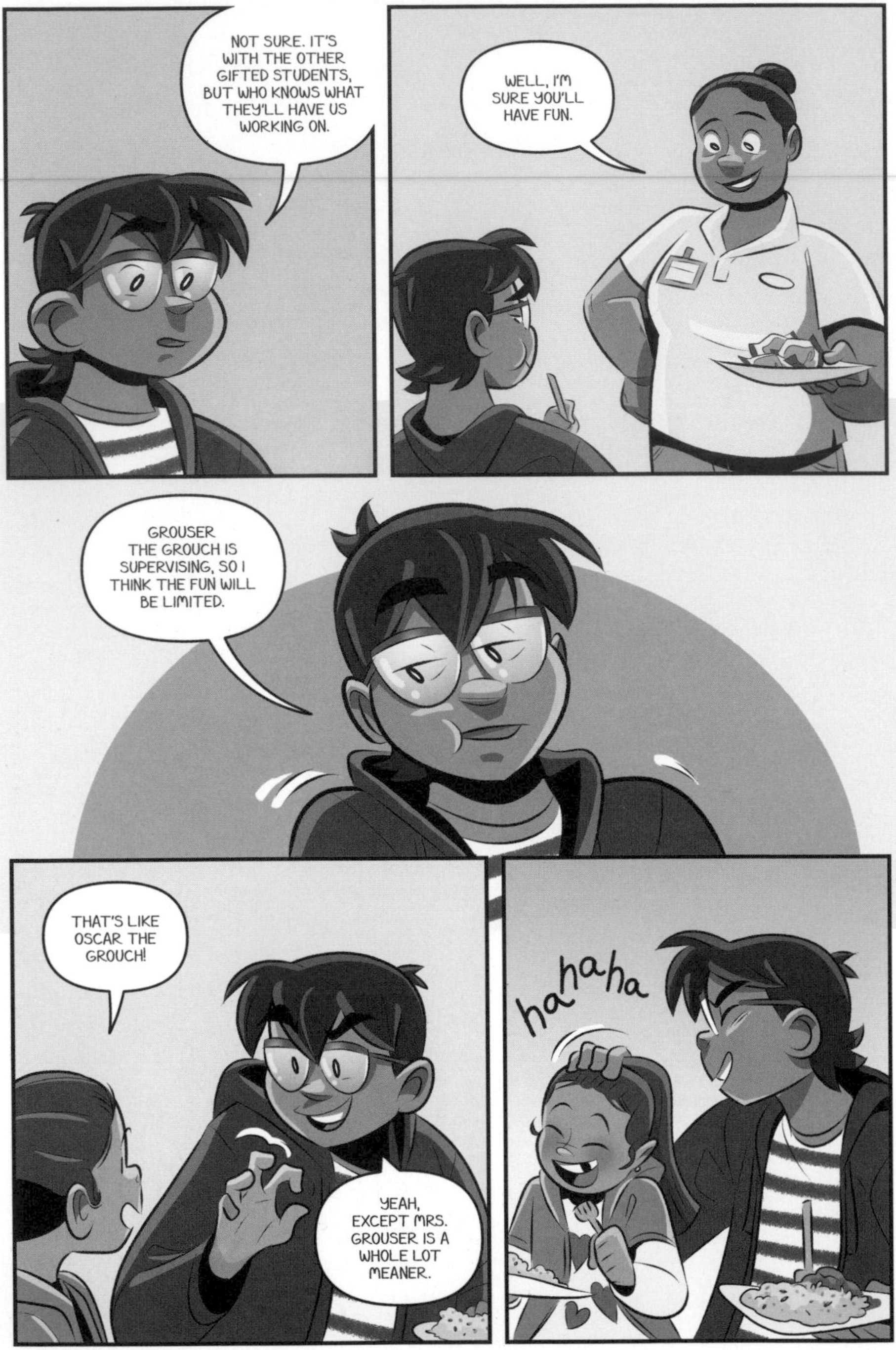
NOT SURE. IT'S WITH THE OTHER GIFTED STUDENTS, BUT WHO KNOWS WHAT THEY'LL HAVE US WORKING ON.
WELL, I'M SURE YOU'LL HAVE FUN.
GROUSER THE GROUCH IS SUPERVISING, SO I THINK THE FUN WILL BE LIMITED.
THAT'S LIKE OSCAR THE GROUCH!
YEAH, EXCEPT MRS. GROUSER IS A WHOLE LOT MEANER.
hahahaha

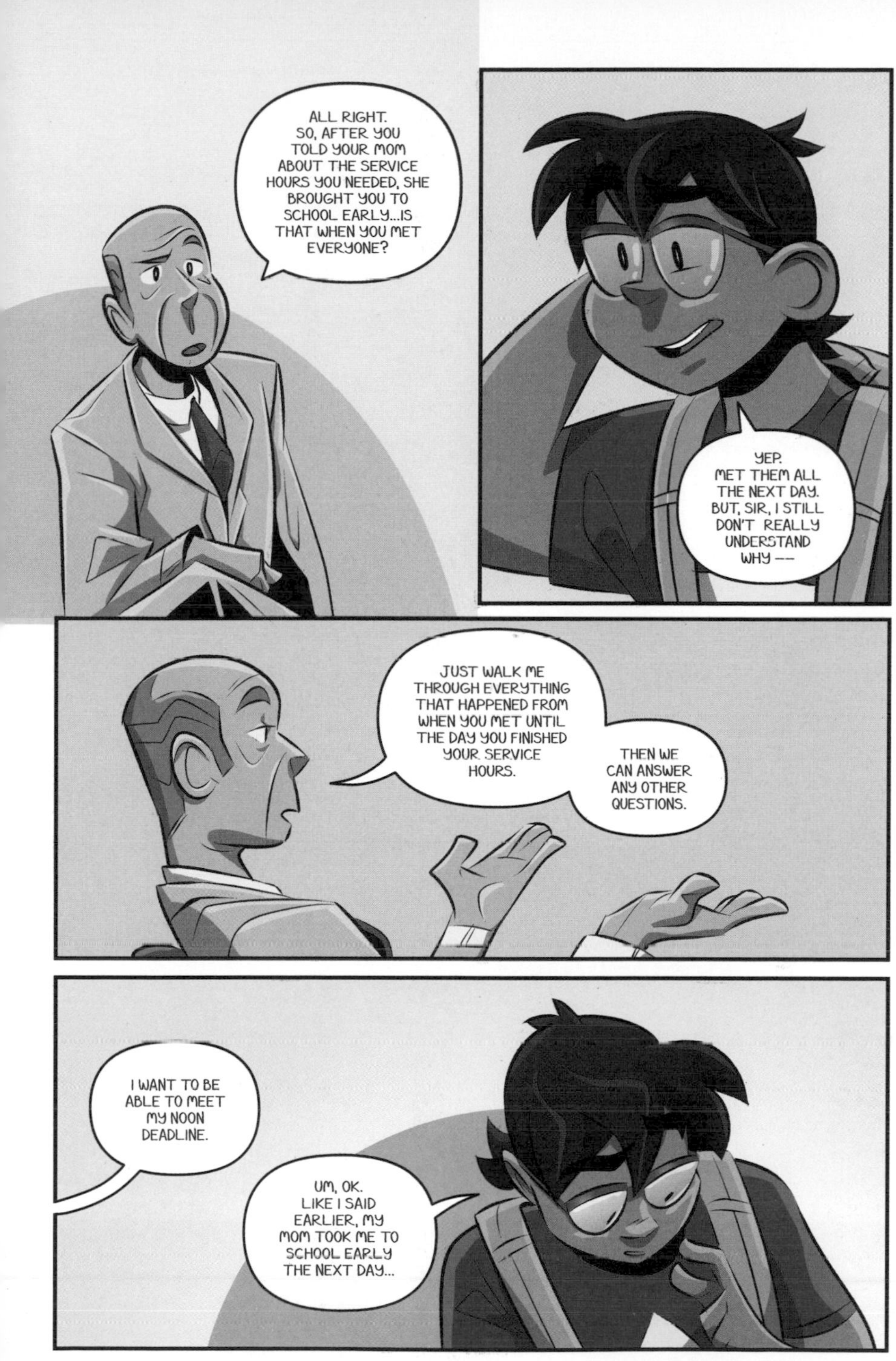
ALL RIGHT. SO, AFTER YOU TOLD YOUR MOM ABOUT THE SERVICE HOURS YOU NEEDED, SHE BROUGHT YOU TO SCHOOL EARLY...IS THAT WHEN YOU MET EVERYONE?
YEP. MET THEM ALL THE NEXT DAY. BUT, SIR, I STILL DON'T REALLY UNDERSTAND WHY --
JUST WALK ME THROUGH EVERYTHING THAT HAPPENED FROM WHEN YOU MET UNTIL THE DAY YOU FINISHED YOUR SERVICE HOURS.
THEN WE CAN ANSWER ANY OTHER QUESTIONS.
I WANT TO BE ABLE TO MEET MY NOON DEADLINE.
UM, OK. LIKE I SAID EARLIER, MY MOM TOOK ME TO SCHOOL EARLY THE NEXT DAY...

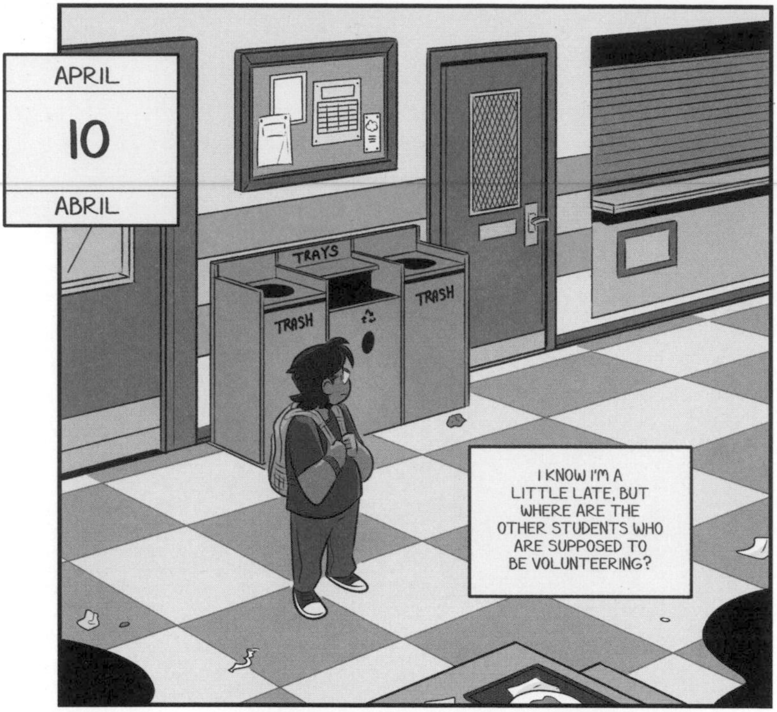
APRIL
10
ABRIL
TRAYS
TRASH
TRASH
I KNOW I'M A LITTLE LATE, BUT WHERE ARE THE OTHER STUDENTS WHO ARE SUPPOSED TO BE VOLUNTEERING?

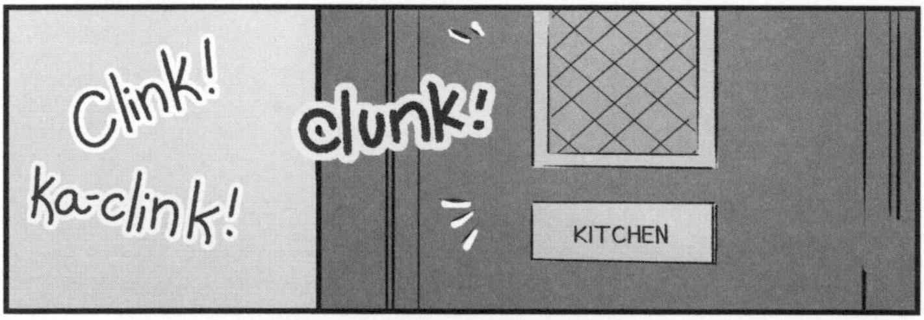
Clink!
ka-clink!
clunk!
KITCHEN

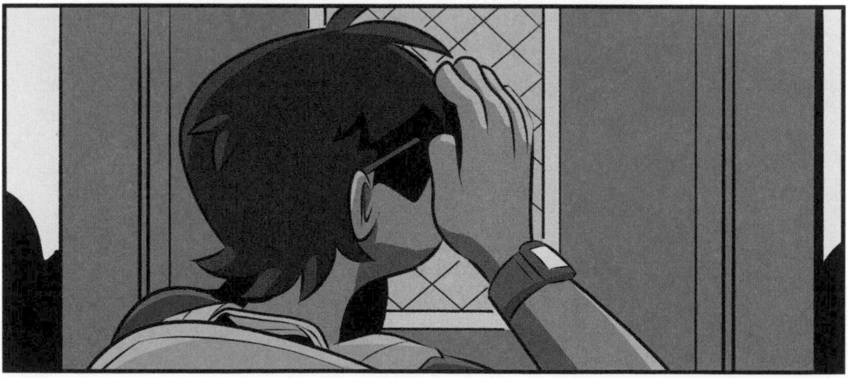

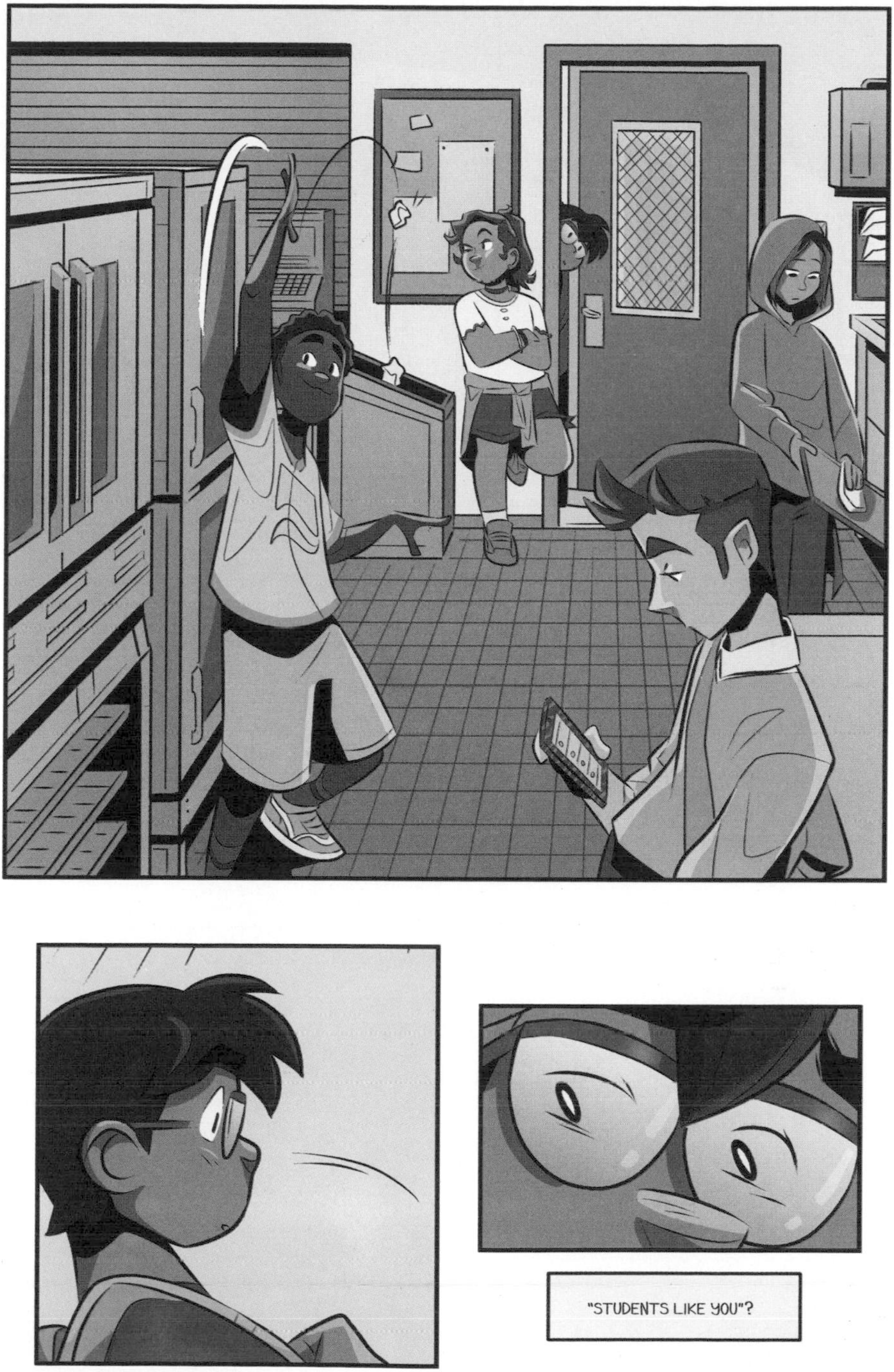
"STUDENTS LIKE YOU"?

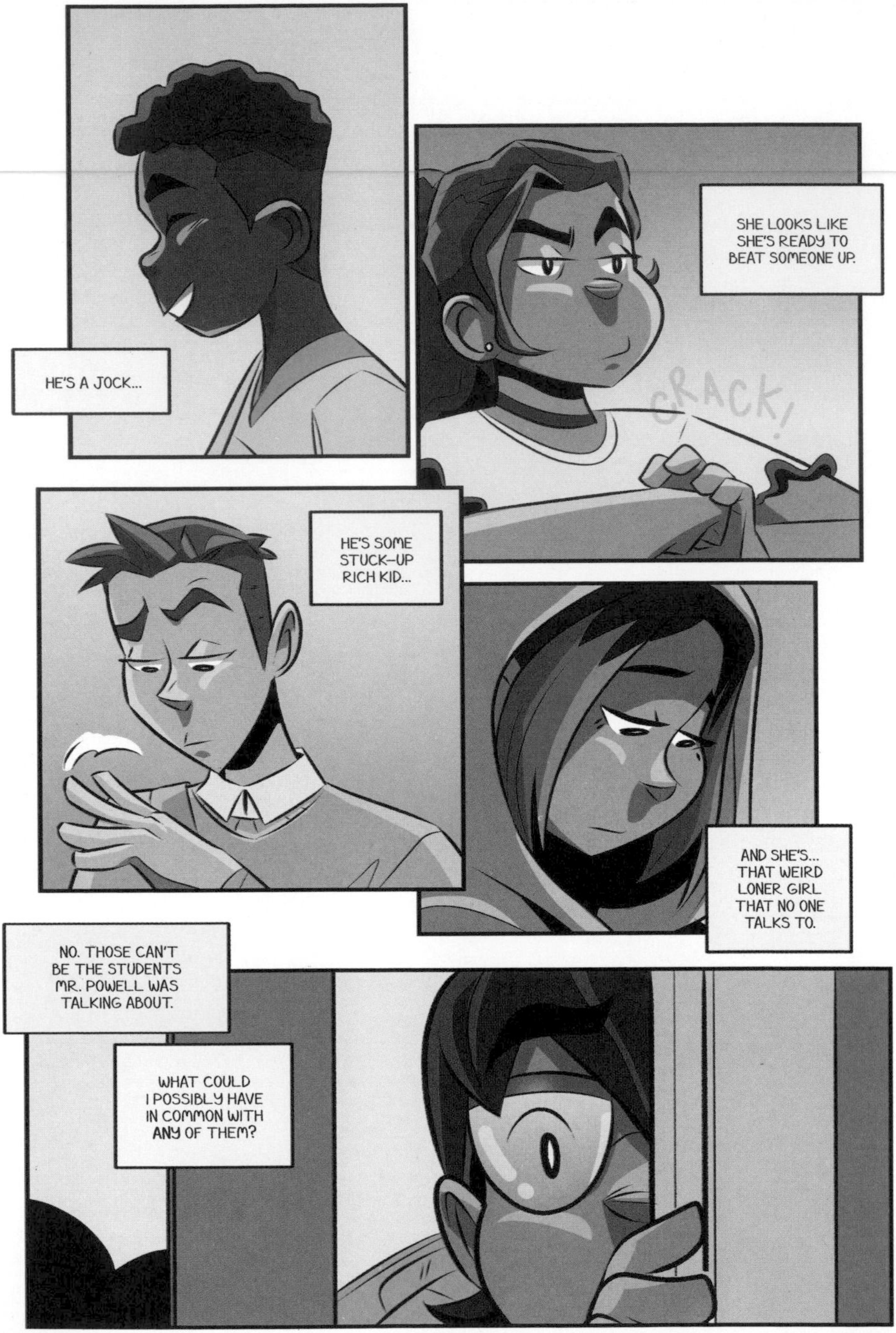
HE'S A JOCK...
SHE LOOKS LIKE SHE'S READY TO BEAT SOMEONE UP.
CRACK!
HE'S SOME STUCK-UP RICH KID...
AND SHE'S... THAT WEIRD LONER GIRL THAT NO ONE TALKS TO.
NO. THOSE CAN'T BE THE STUDENTS MR. POWELL WAS TALKING ABOUT.
WHAT COULD I POSSIBLY HAVE IN COMMON WITH ANY OF THEM?

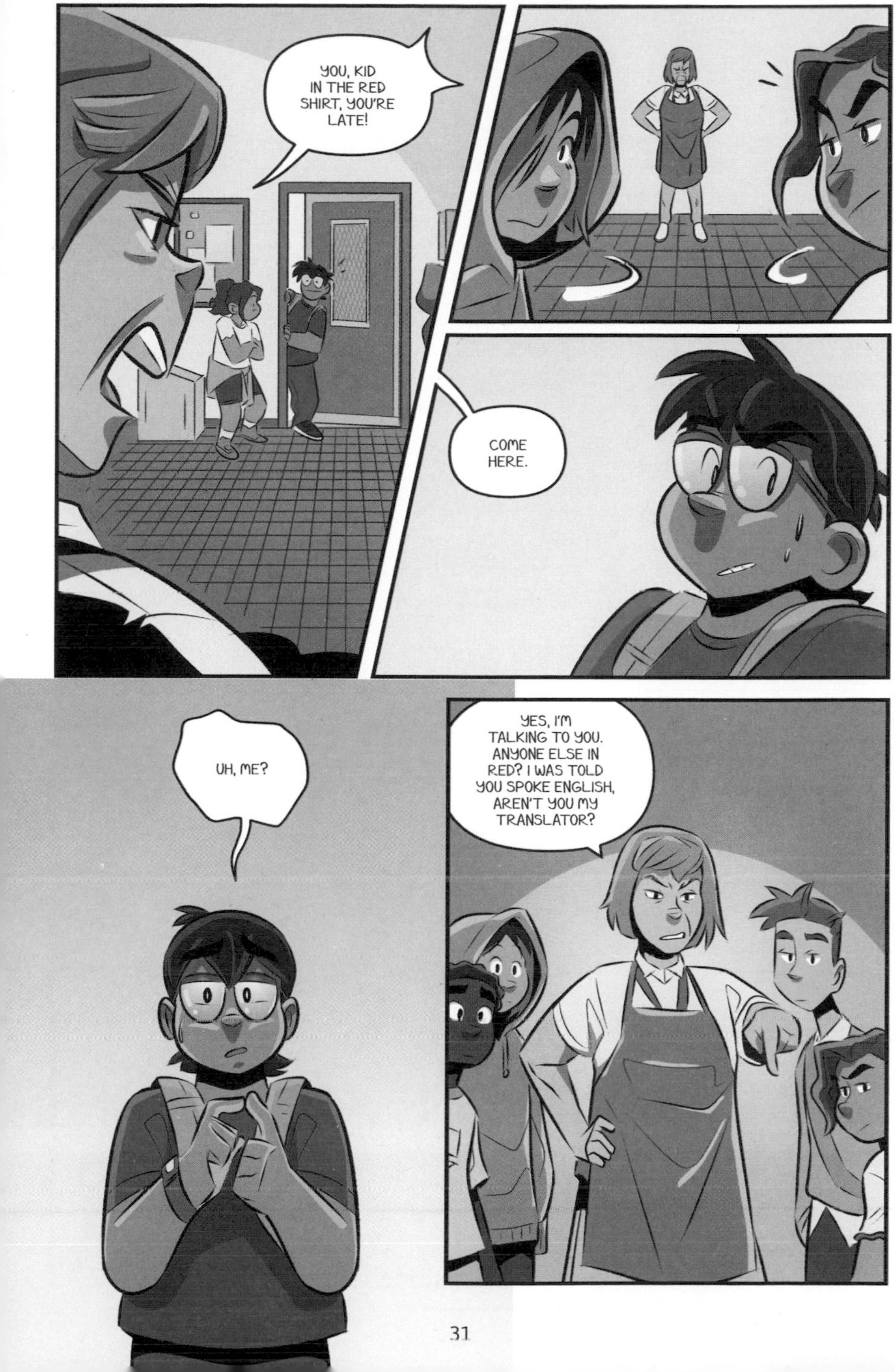
YOU, KID IN THE RED SHIRT, YOU'RE LATE!
COME HERE.
UH, ME?
YES, I'M TALKING TO YOU. ANYONE ELSE IN RED? I WAS TOLD YOU SPOKE ENGLISH, AREN'T YOU MY TRANSLATOR?

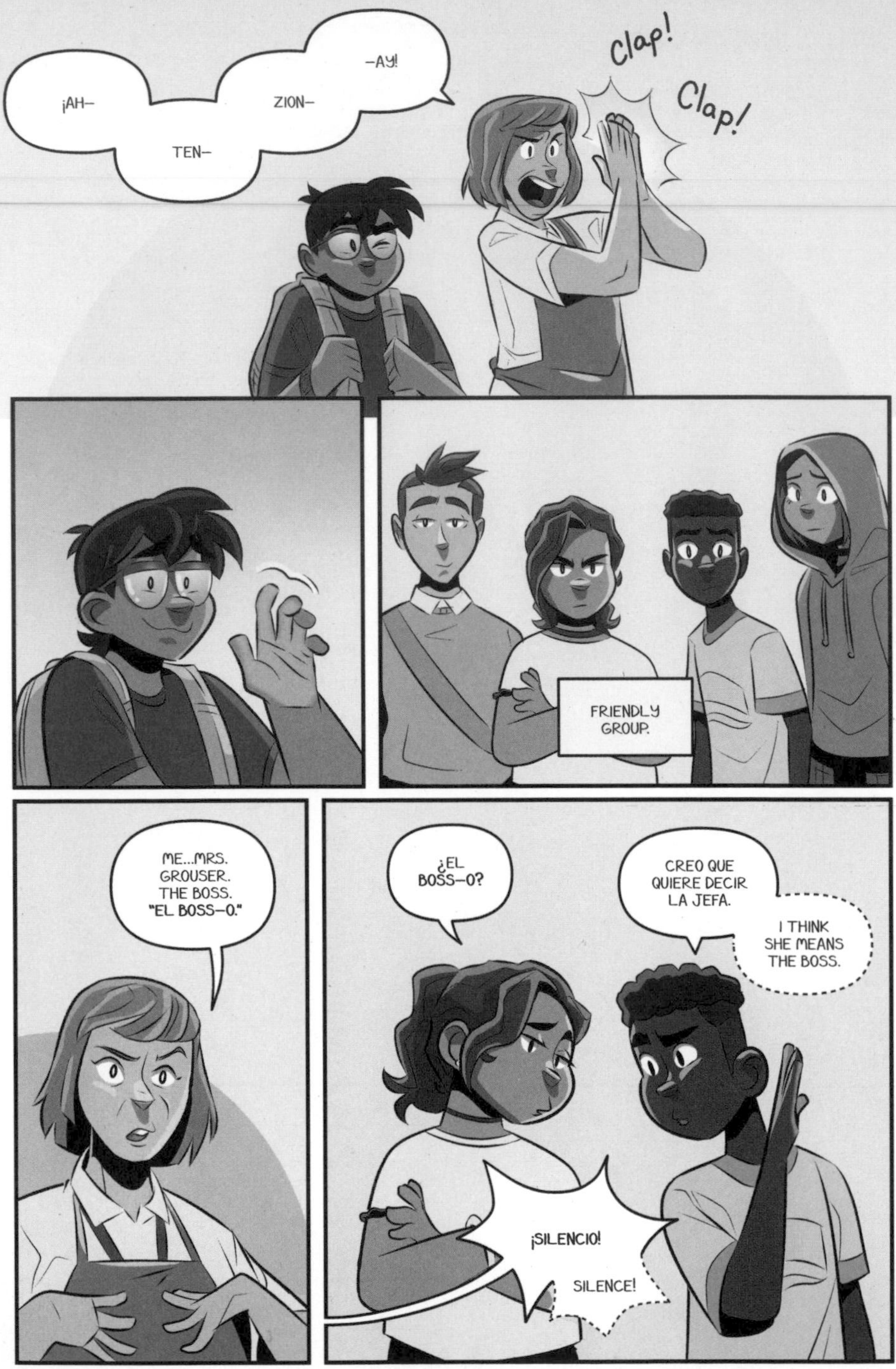
¡AH—
TEN—
ZION—
—AY!
Clap!
Clap!
FRIENDLY GROUP.
ME...MRS. GROUSER. THE BOSS. "EL BOSS—O."
¿EL BOSS—O?
CREO QUE QUIERE DECIR LA JEFA.
I THINK SHE MEANS THE BOSS.
¡SILENCIO!
SILENCE!

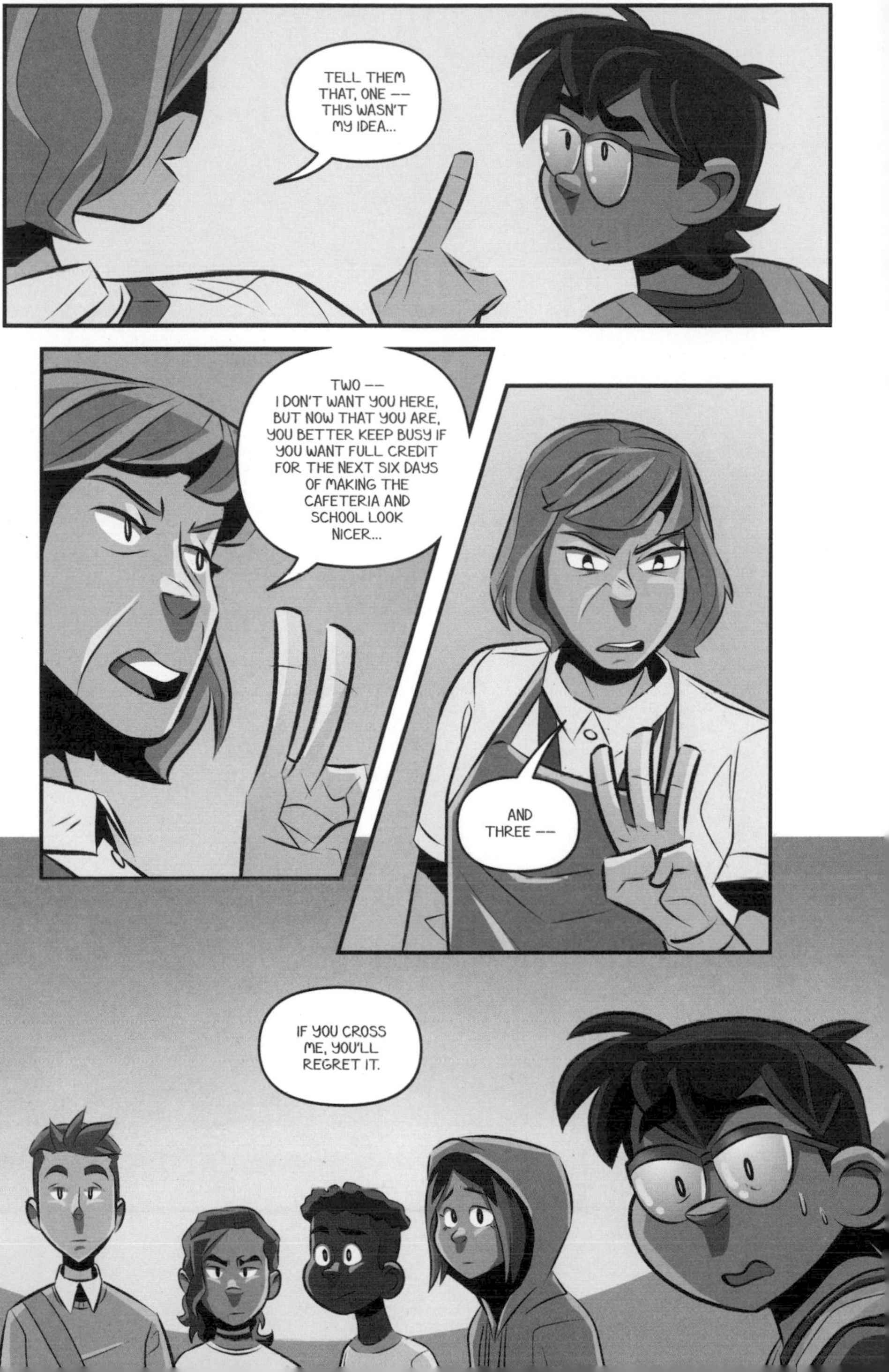
TELL THEM THAT, ONE -- THIS WASN'T MY IDEA...
TWO -- I DON'T WANT YOU HERE, BUT NOW THAT YOU ARE, YOU BETTER KEEP BUSY IF YOU WANT FULL CREDIT FOR THE NEXT SIX DAYS OF MAKING THE CAFETERIA AND SCHOOL LOOK NICER...
AND THREE --
IF YOU CROSS ME, YOU'LL REGRET IT.

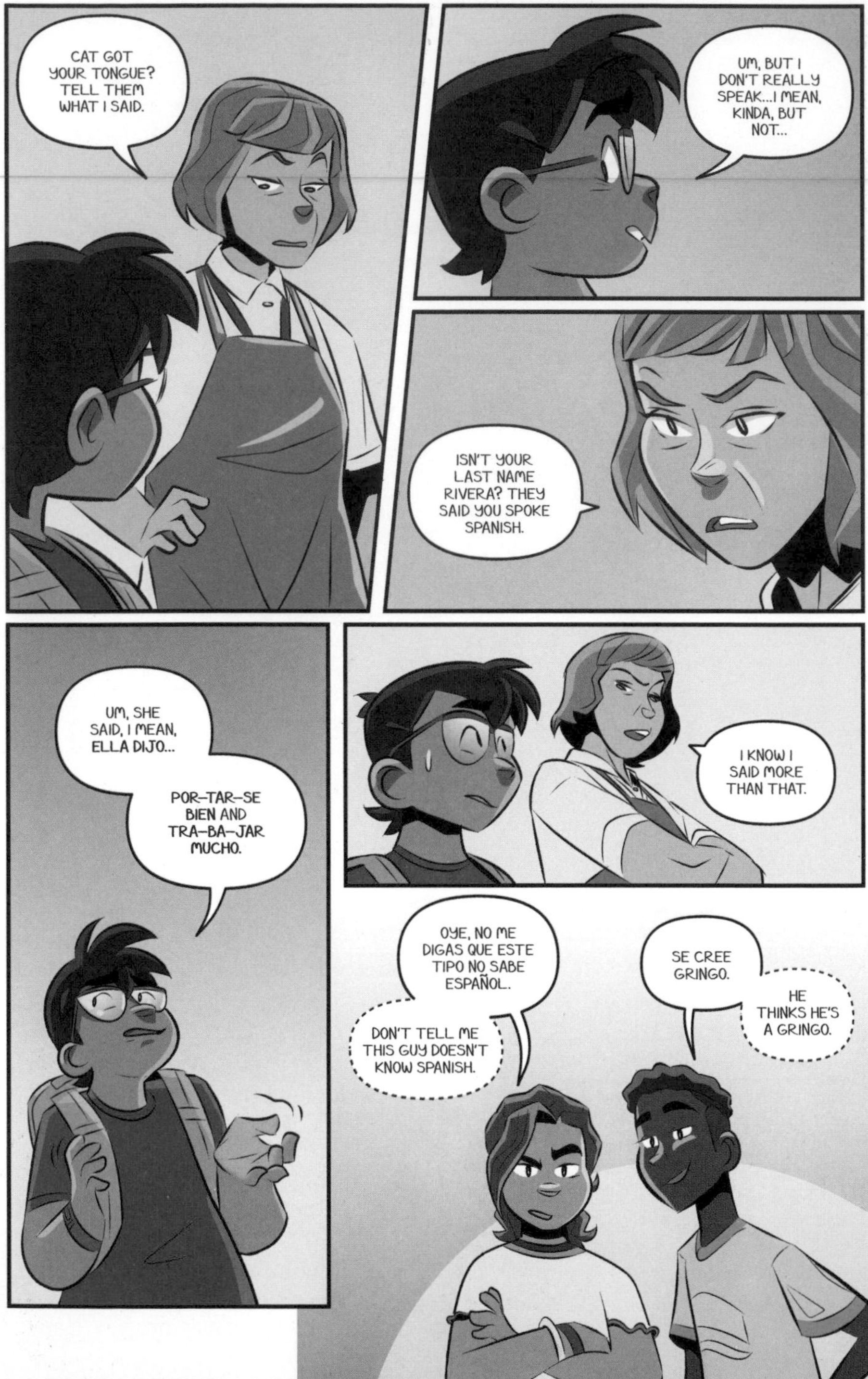
CAT GOT YOUR TONGUE? TELL THEM WHAT I SAID.
UM, BUT I DON'T REALLY SPEAK...I MEAN, KINDA, BUT NOT...
ISN'T YOUR LAST NAME RIVERA? THEY SAID YOU SPOKE SPANISH.
UM, SHE SAID, I MEAN, ELLA DIJO...
POR-TAR-SE BIEN AND TRA-BA-JAR MUCHO.
I KNOW I SAID MORE THAN THAT.
OYE, NO ME DIGAS QUE ESTE TIPO NO SABE ESPAÑOL.
DON'T TELL ME THIS GUY DOESN'T KNOW SPANISH.
SE CREE GRINGO.
HE THINKS HE'S A GRINGO.

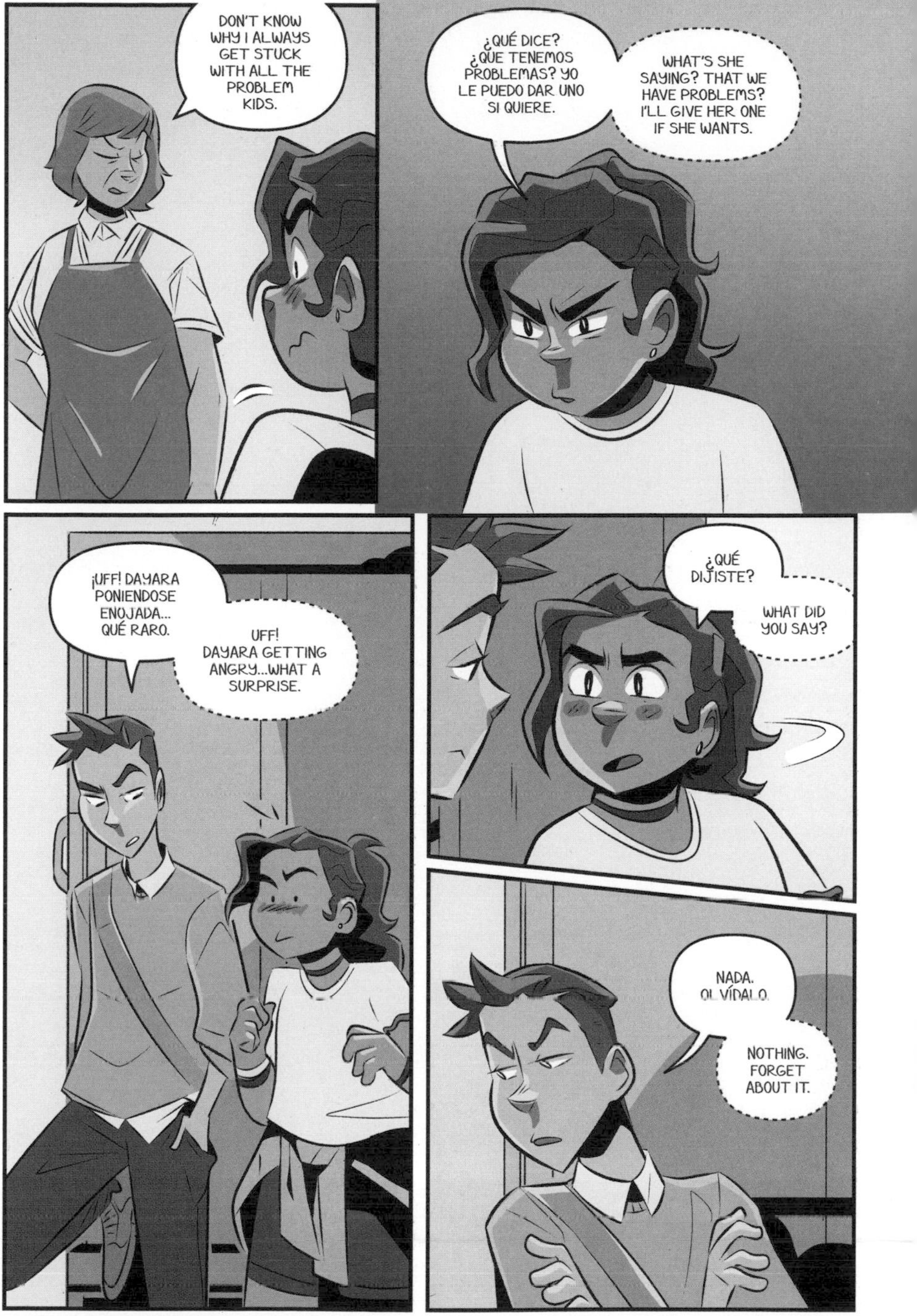
DON'T KNOW WHY I ALWAYS GET STUCK WITH ALL THE PROBLEM KIDS.
¿QUÉ DICE? ¿QUE TENEMOS PROBLEMAS? YO LE PUEDO DAR UNO SI QUIERE.
WHAT'S SHE SAYING? THAT WE HAVE PROBLEMS? I'LL GIVE HER ONE IF SHE WANTS.
¡UFF! DAYARA PONIENDOSE ENOJADA... QUÉ RARO.
UFF! DAYARA GETTING ANGRY...WHAT A SURPRISE.
¿QUÉ DIJISTE?
WHAT DID YOU SAY?
NADA. OLVÍDALO.
NOTHING. FORGET ABOUT IT.

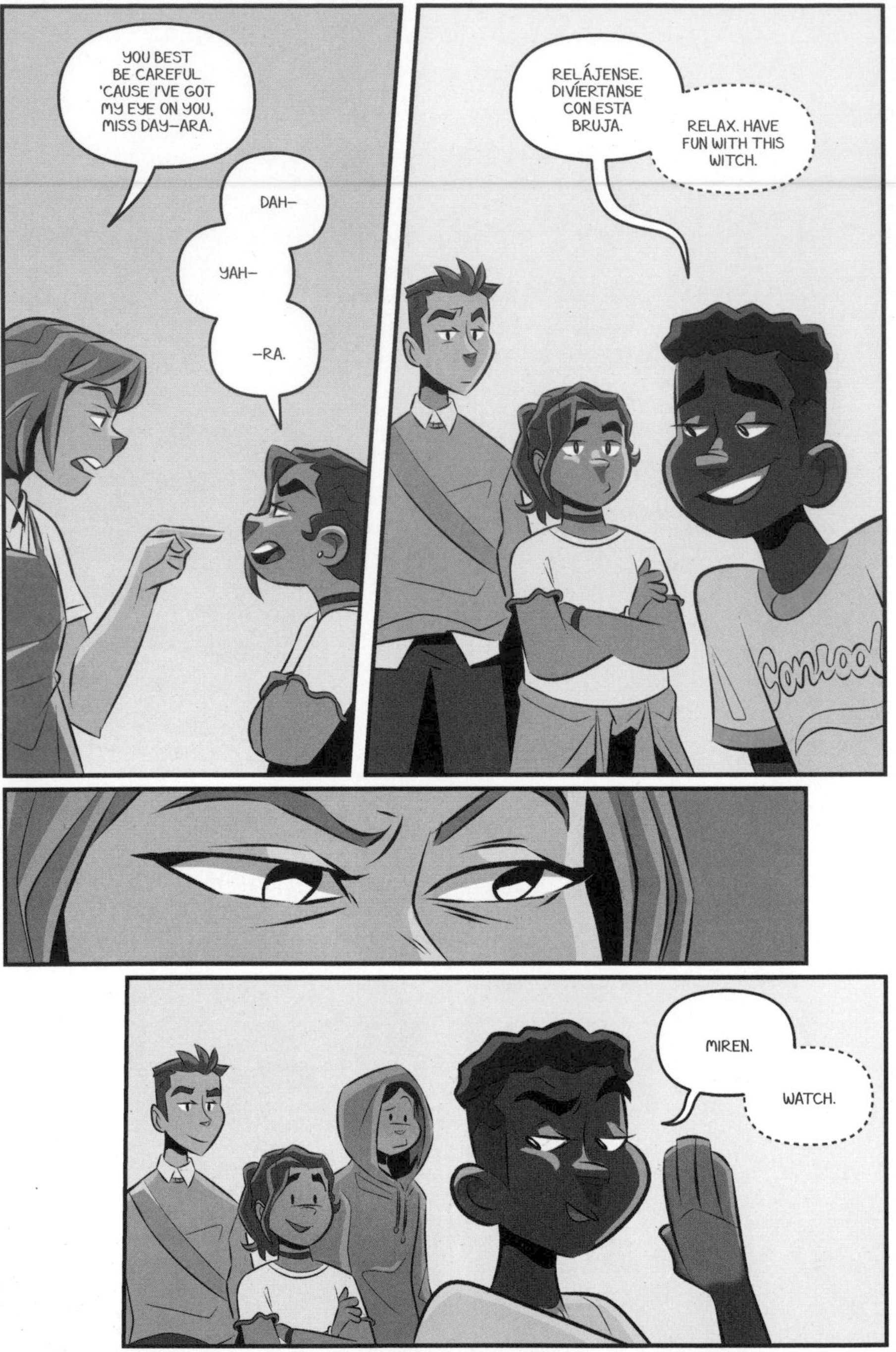

YOU BEST BE CAREFUL 'CAUSE I'VE GOT MY EYE ON YOU, MISS DAY—ARA.
DAH—
YAH—
—RA.
RELÁJENSE. DIVÍERTANSE CON ESTA BRUJA.
RELAX. HAVE FUN WITH THIS WITCH.
MIREN.
WATCH.

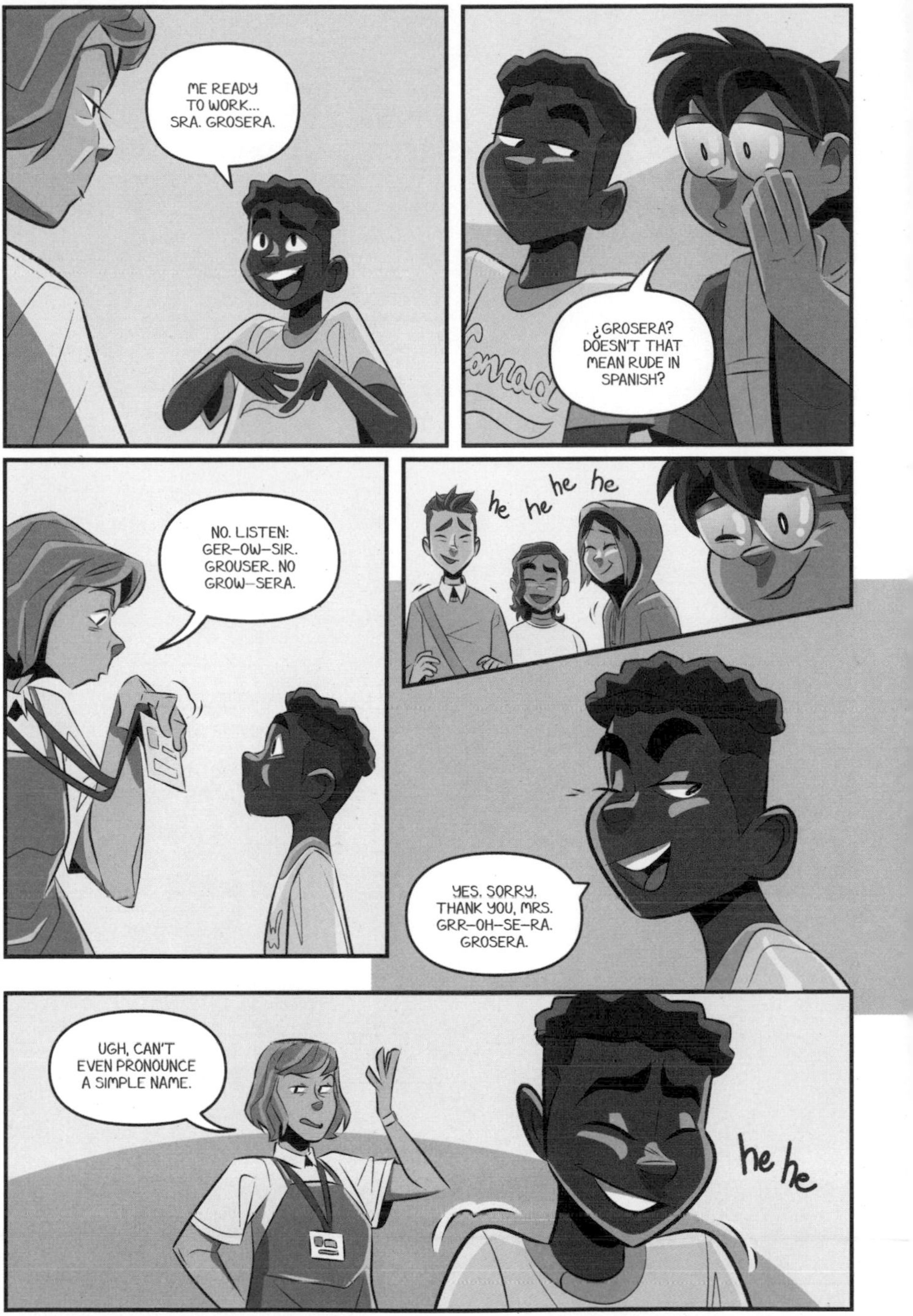
ME READY TO WORK... SRA. GROSERA.
¿GROSERA? DOESN'T THAT MEAN RUDE IN SPANISH?
NO. LISTEN: GER–OW–SIR. GROUSER. NO GROW–SERA.
he he he he
YES. SORRY. THANK YOU, MRS. GRR–OH–SE–RA. GROSERA.
UGH, CAN'T EVEN PRONOUNCE A SIMPLE NAME.
he he

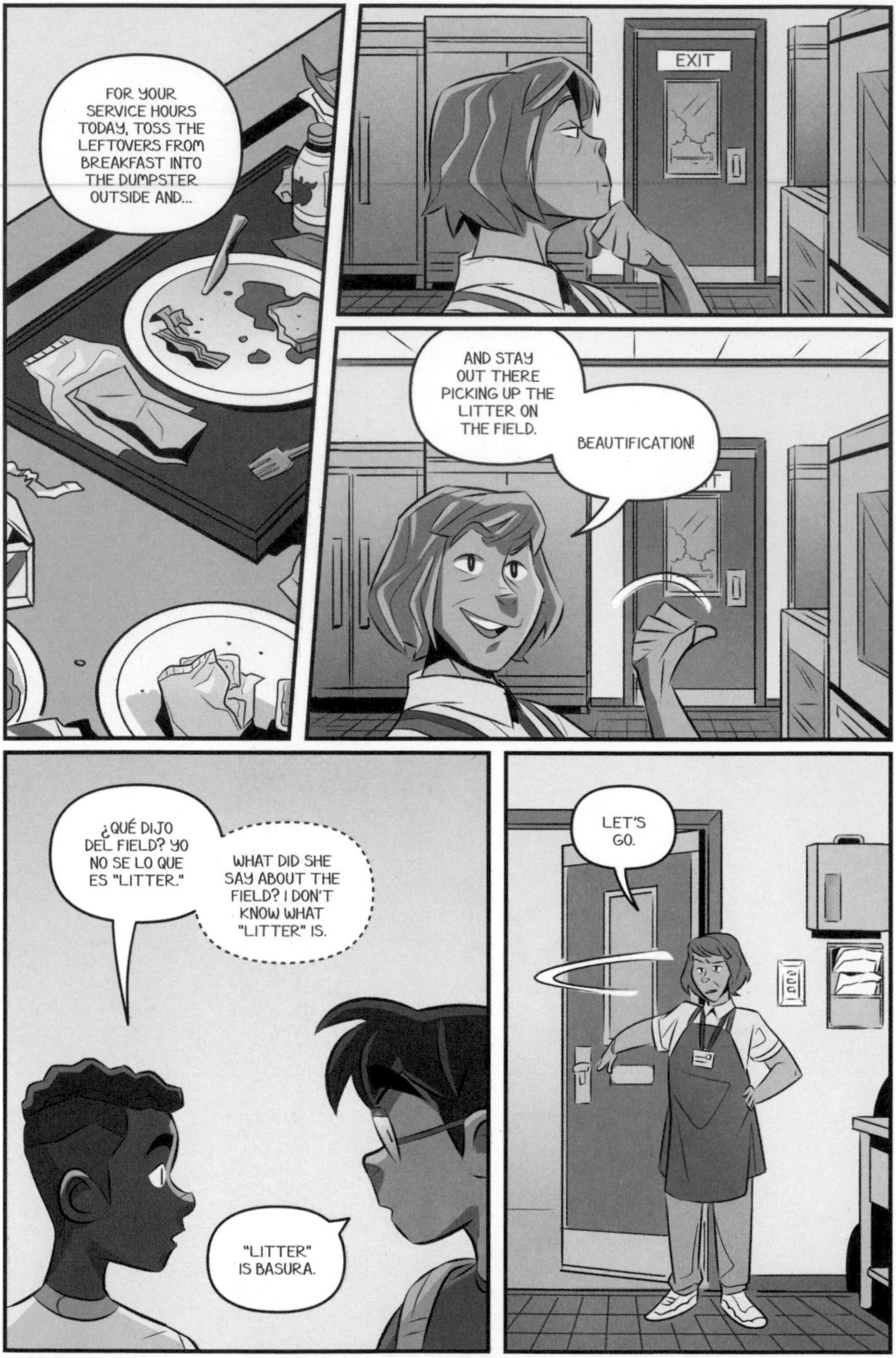
FOR YOUR SERVICE HOURS TODAY, TOSS THE LEFTOVERS FROM BREAKFAST INTO THE DUMPSTER OUTSIDE AND...
EXIT
AND STAY OUT THERE PICKING UP THE LITTER ON THE FIELD.
BEAUTIFICATION!
¿QUÉ DIJO DEL FIELD? YO NO SE LO QUE ES "LITTER."
WHAT DID SHE SAY ABOUT THE FIELD? I DON'T KNOW WHAT "LITTER" IS.
"LITTER" IS BASURA.
LET'S GO.

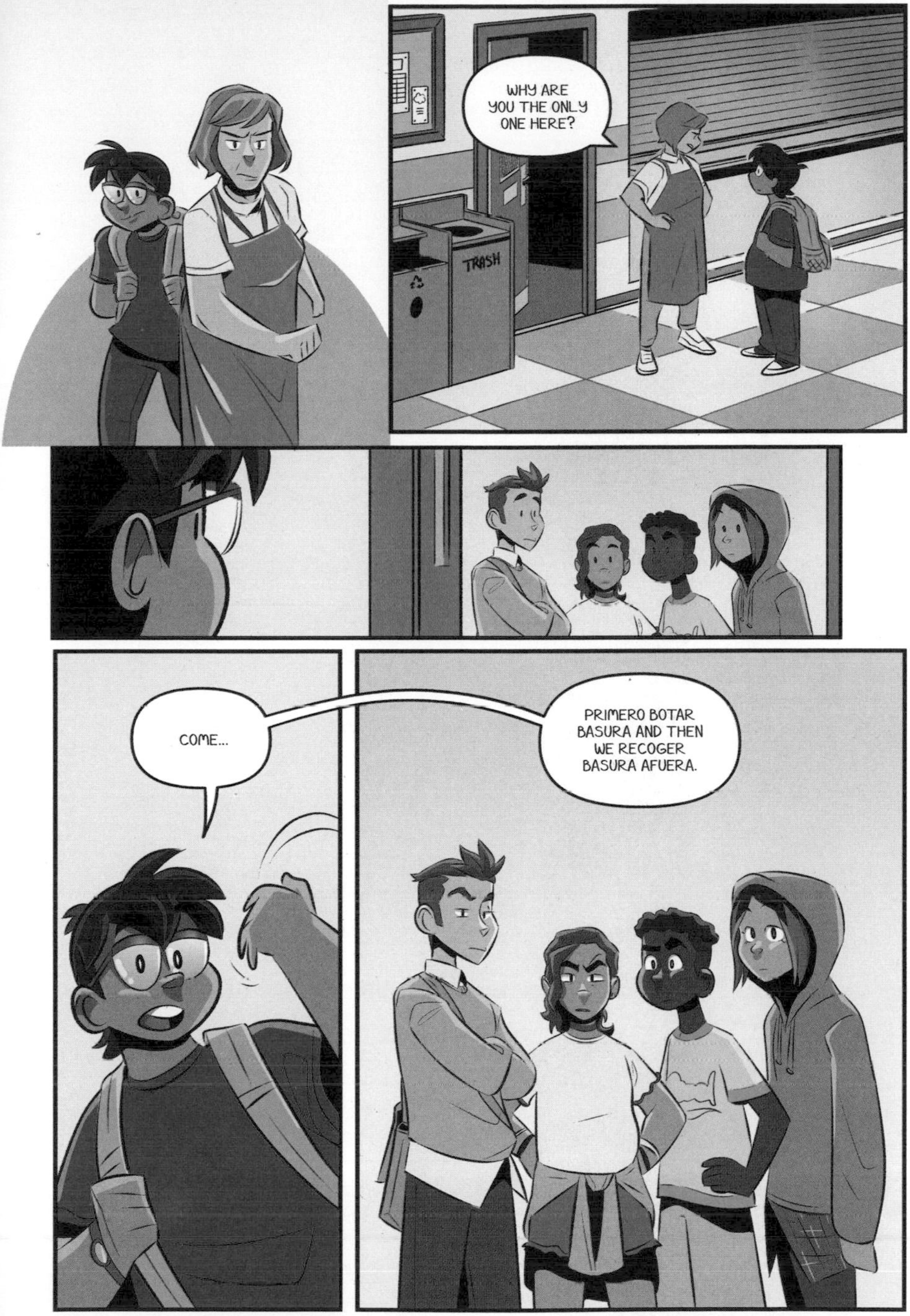
WHY ARE YOU THE ONLY ONE HERE?
TRASH
COME...
PRIMERO BOTAR BASURA AND THEN WE RECOGER BASURA AFUERA.

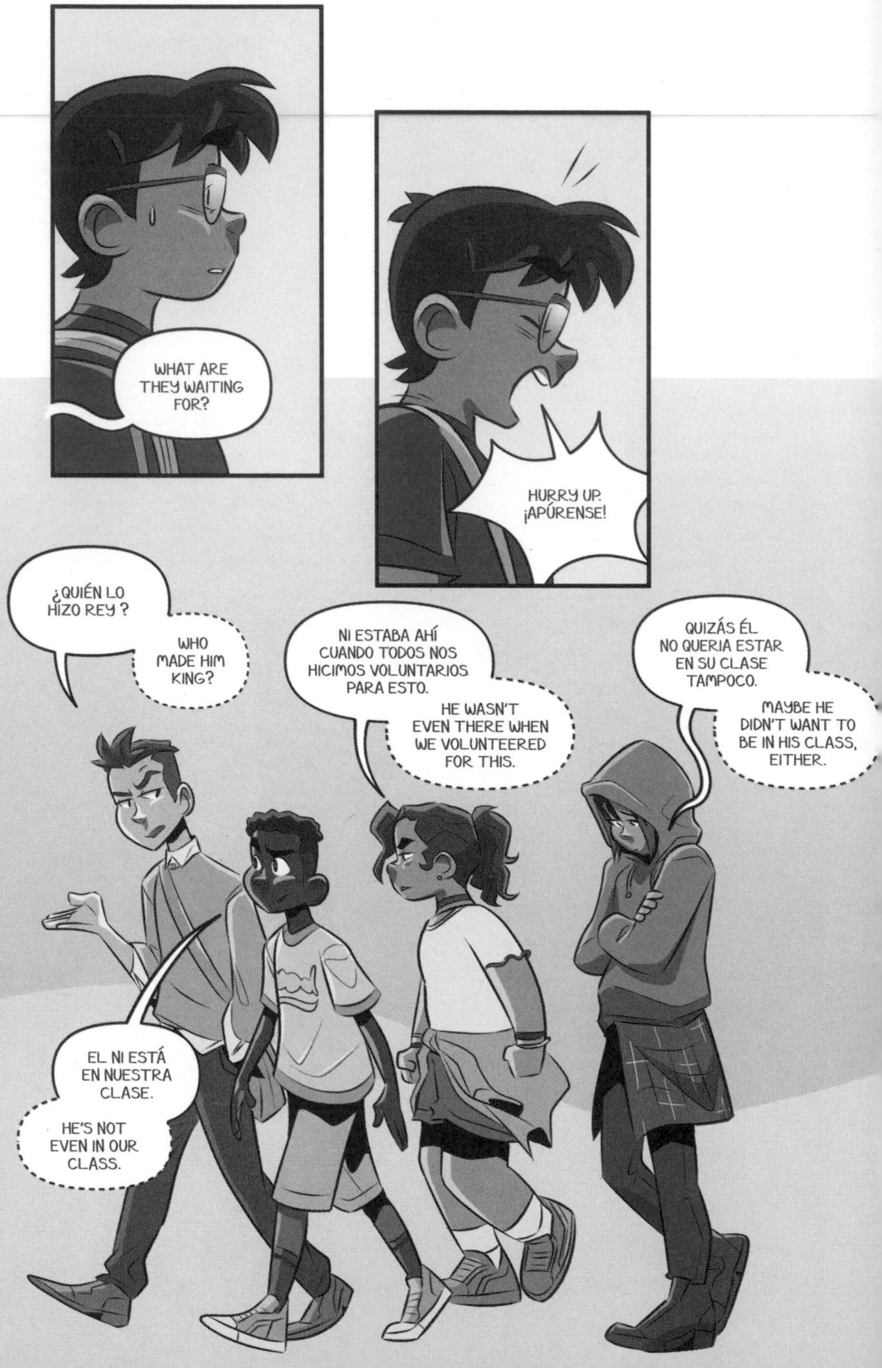
WHAT ARE THEY WAITING FOR?
HURRY UP. ¡APÚRENSE!
¿QUIÉN LO HIZO REY ?
WHO MADE HIM KING?
NI ESTABA AHÍ CUANDO TODOS NOS HICIMOS VOLUNTARIOS PARA ESTO.
HE WASN'T EVEN THERE WHEN WE VOLUNTEERED FOR THIS.
QUIZÁS ÉL NO QUERIA ESTAR EN SU CLASE TAMPOCO.
MAYBE HE DIDN'T WANT TO BE IN HIS CLASS, EITHER.
EL NI ESTÁ EN NUESTRA CLASE.
HE'S NOT EVEN IN OUR CLASS.

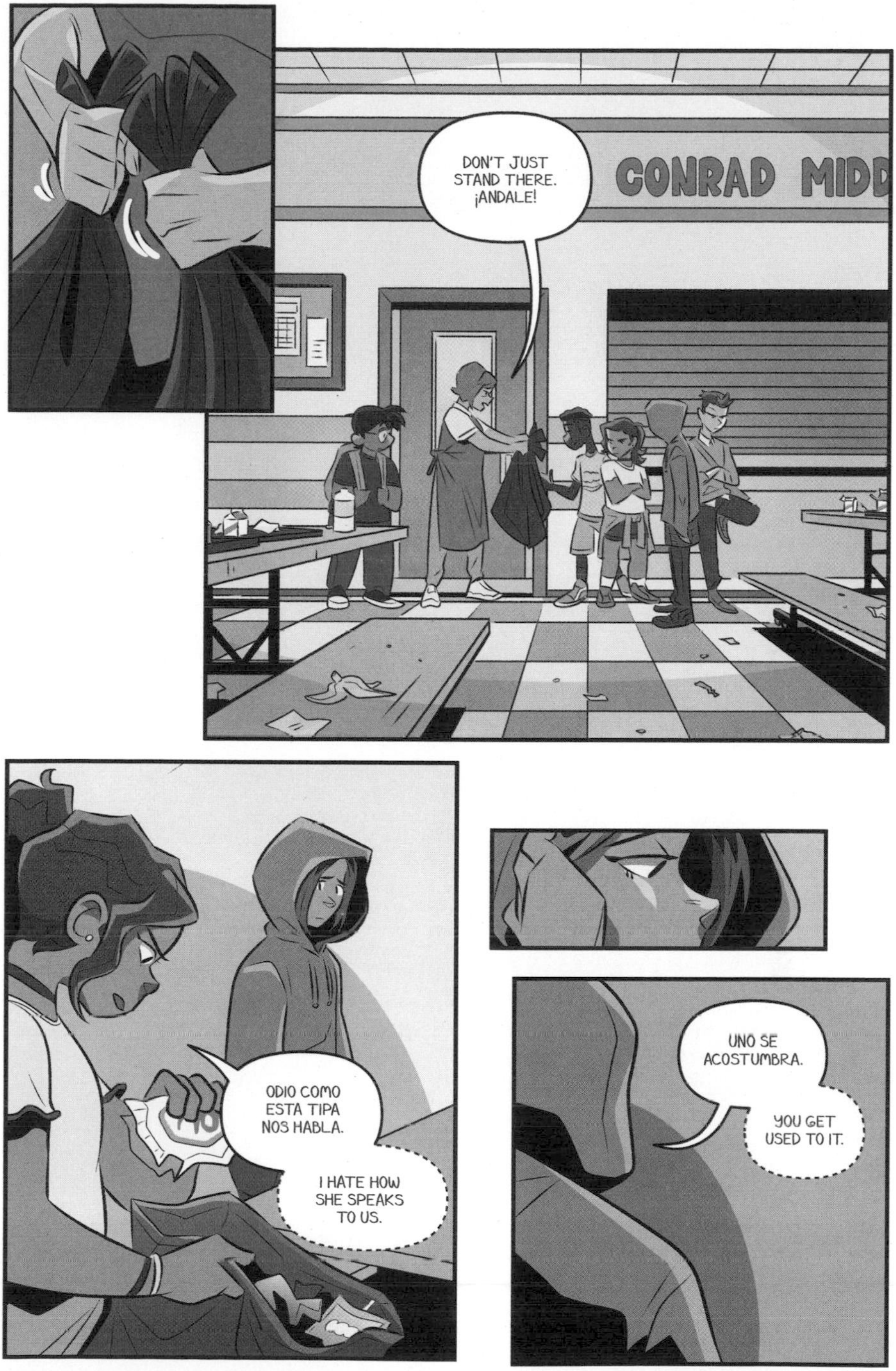
DON'T JUST STAND THERE. ¡ANDALE!
CONRAD MIDD
ODIO COMO ESTA TIPA NOS HABLA.
I HATE HOW SHE SPEAKS TO US.
UNO SE ACOSTUMBRA.
YOU GET USED TO IT.

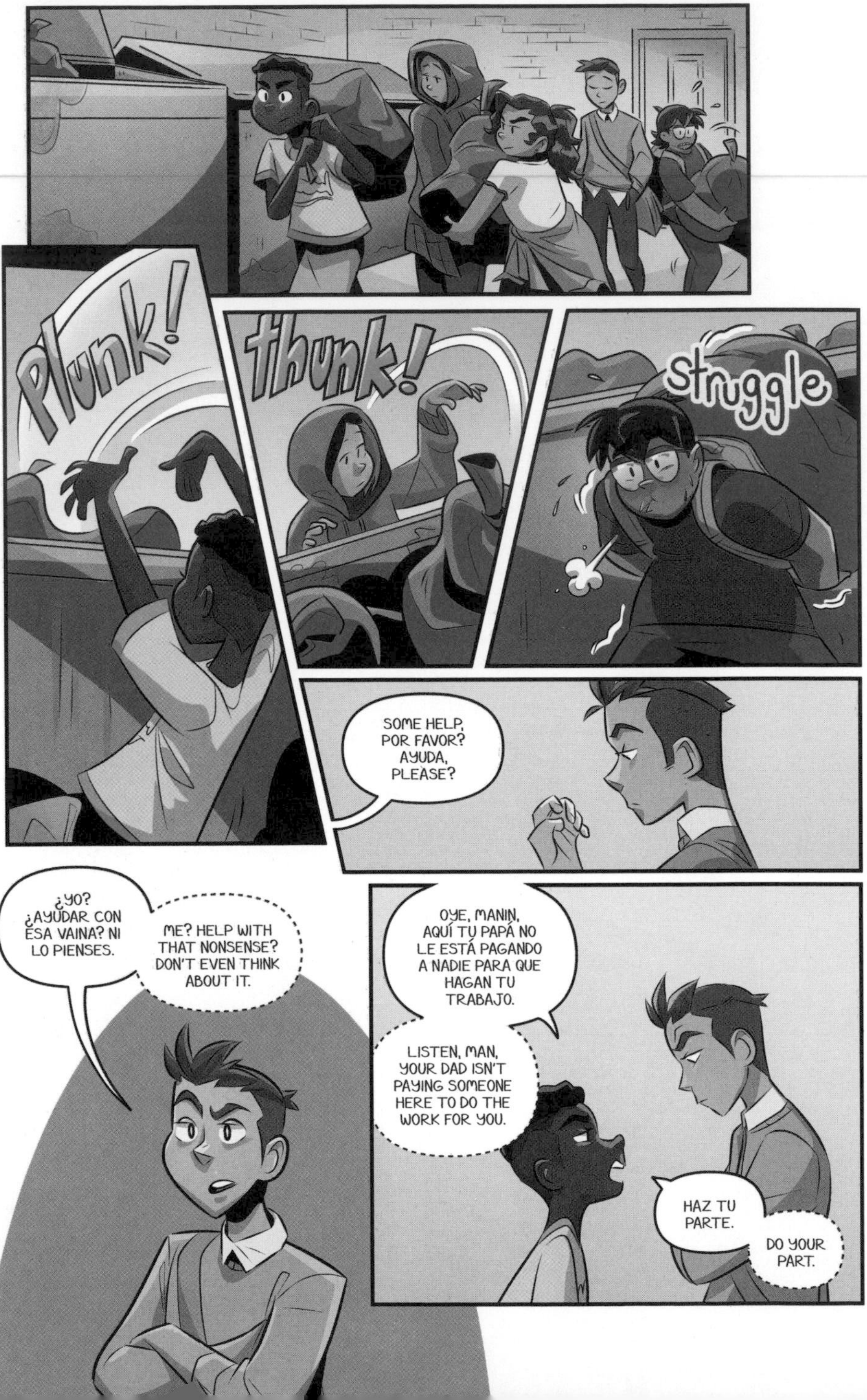
Plunk!
thunk!
struggle
SOME HELP, POR FAVOR? AYUDA, PLEASE?
¿YO? ¿AYUDAR CON ESA VAINA? NI LO PIENSES.
ME? HELP WITH THAT NONSENSE? DON'T EVEN THINK ABOUT IT.
OYE, MANIN, AQUÍ TU PAPÁ NO LE ESTÁ PAGANDO A NADIE PARA QUE HAGAN TU TRABAJO.
LISTEN, MAN, YOUR DAD ISN'T PAYING SOMEONE HERE TO DO THE WORK FOR YOU.
HAZ TU PARTE.
DO YOUR PART.

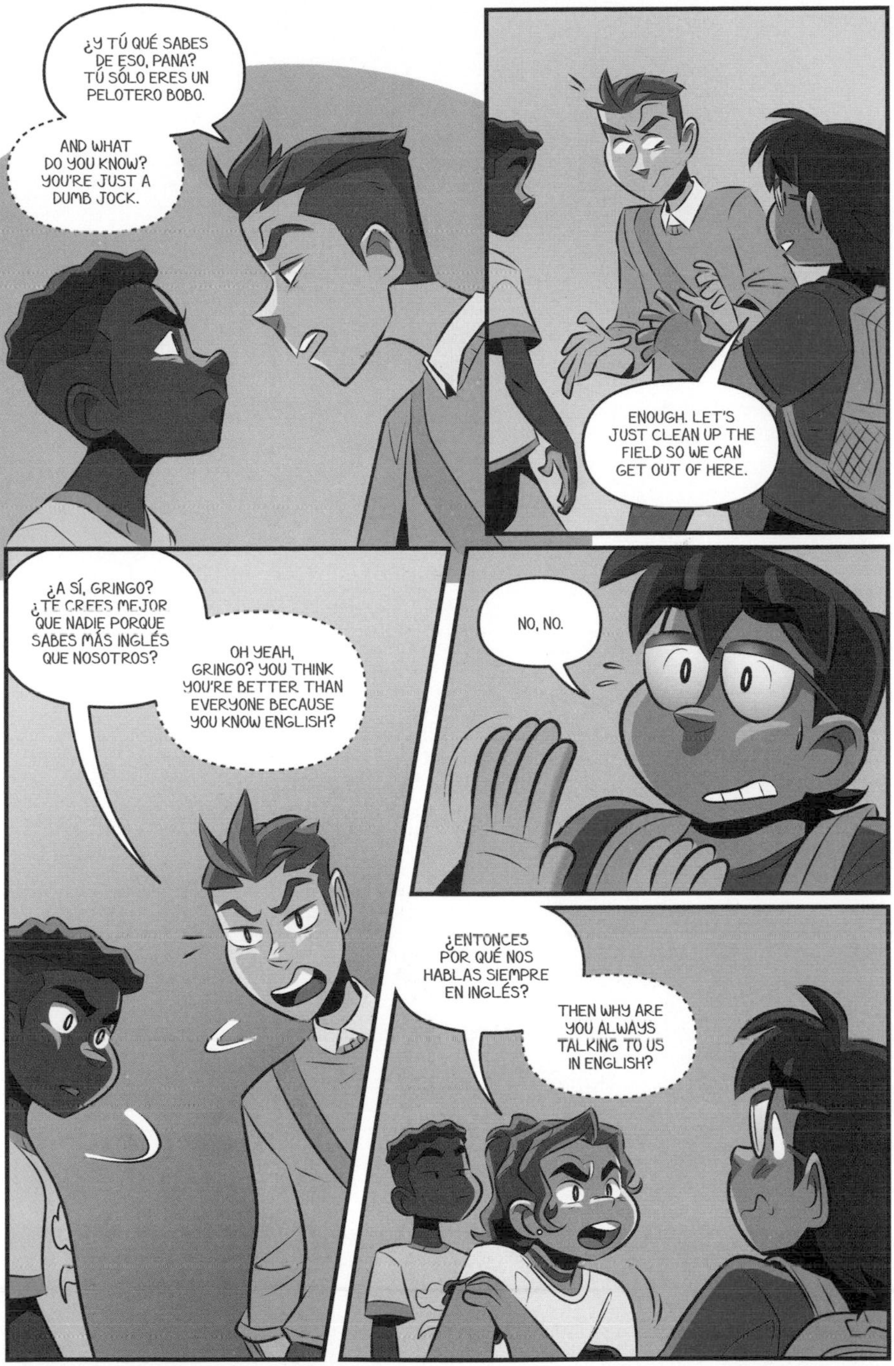
¿Y TÚ QUÉ SABES DE ESO, PANA? TÚ SÓLO ERES UN PELOTERO BOBO.
AND WHAT DO YOU KNOW? YOU'RE JUST A DUMB JOCK.
ENOUGH. LET'S JUST CLEAN UP THE FIELD SO WE CAN GET OUT OF HERE.
¿A SÍ, GRINGO? ¿TE CREES MEJOR QUE NADIE PORQUE SABES MÁS INGLÉS QUE NOSOTROS?
OH YEAH, GRINGO? YOU THINK YOU'RE BETTER THAN EVERYONE BECAUSE YOU KNOW ENGLISH?
NO, NO.
¿ENTONCES POR QUÉ NOS HABLAS SIEMPRE EN INGLÉS?
THEN WHY ARE YOU ALWAYS TALKING TO US IN ENGLISH?

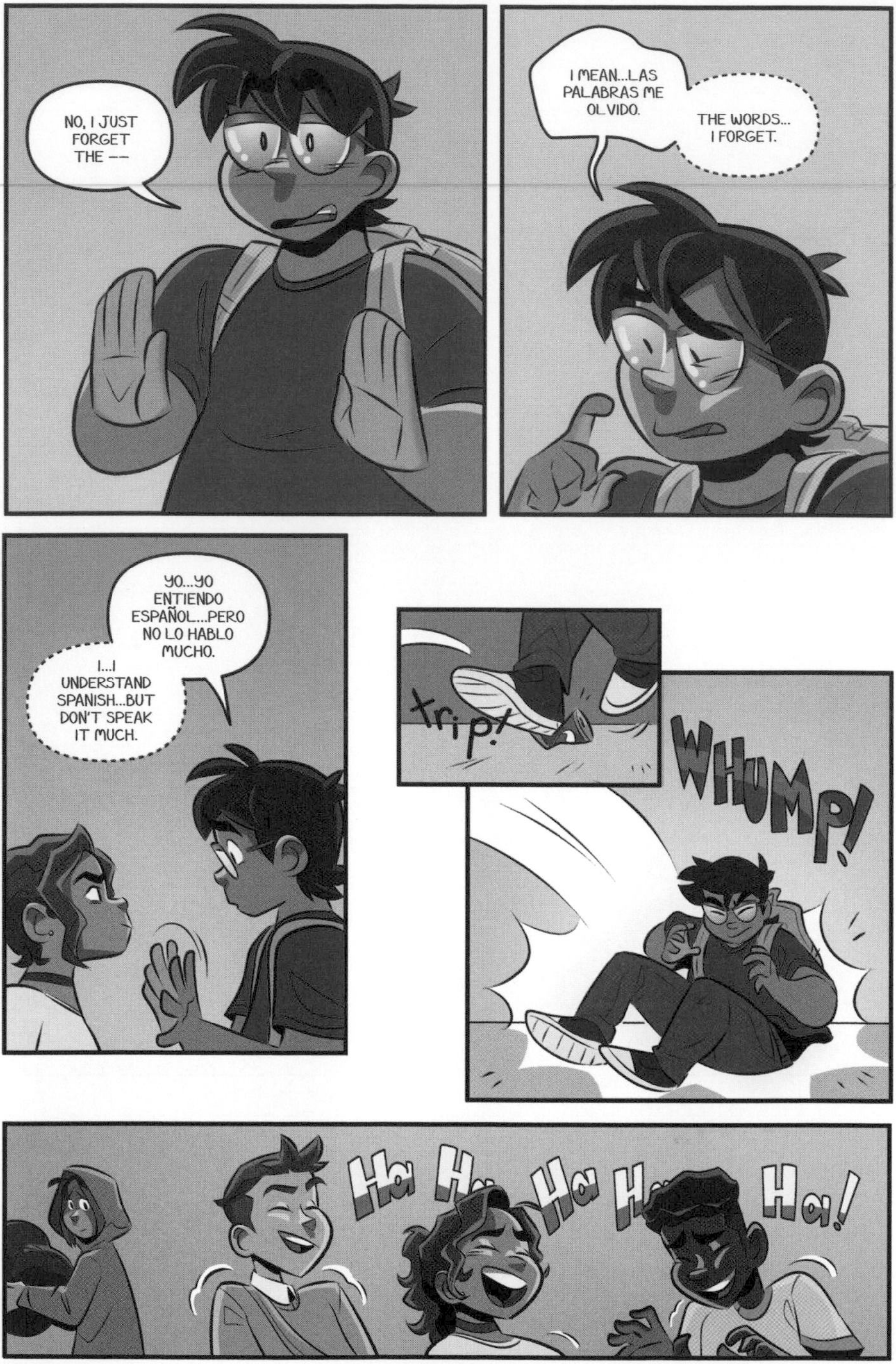
NO, I JUST FORGET THE --
I MEAN...LAS PALABRAS ME OLVIDO.
THE WORDS... I FORGET.
YO...YO ENTIENDO ESPAÑOL...PERO NO LO HABLO MUCHO.
I...I UNDERSTAND SPANISH...BUT DON'T SPEAK IT MUCH.
trip!
WHUMP!
Ha Ha Ha Ha Ha!

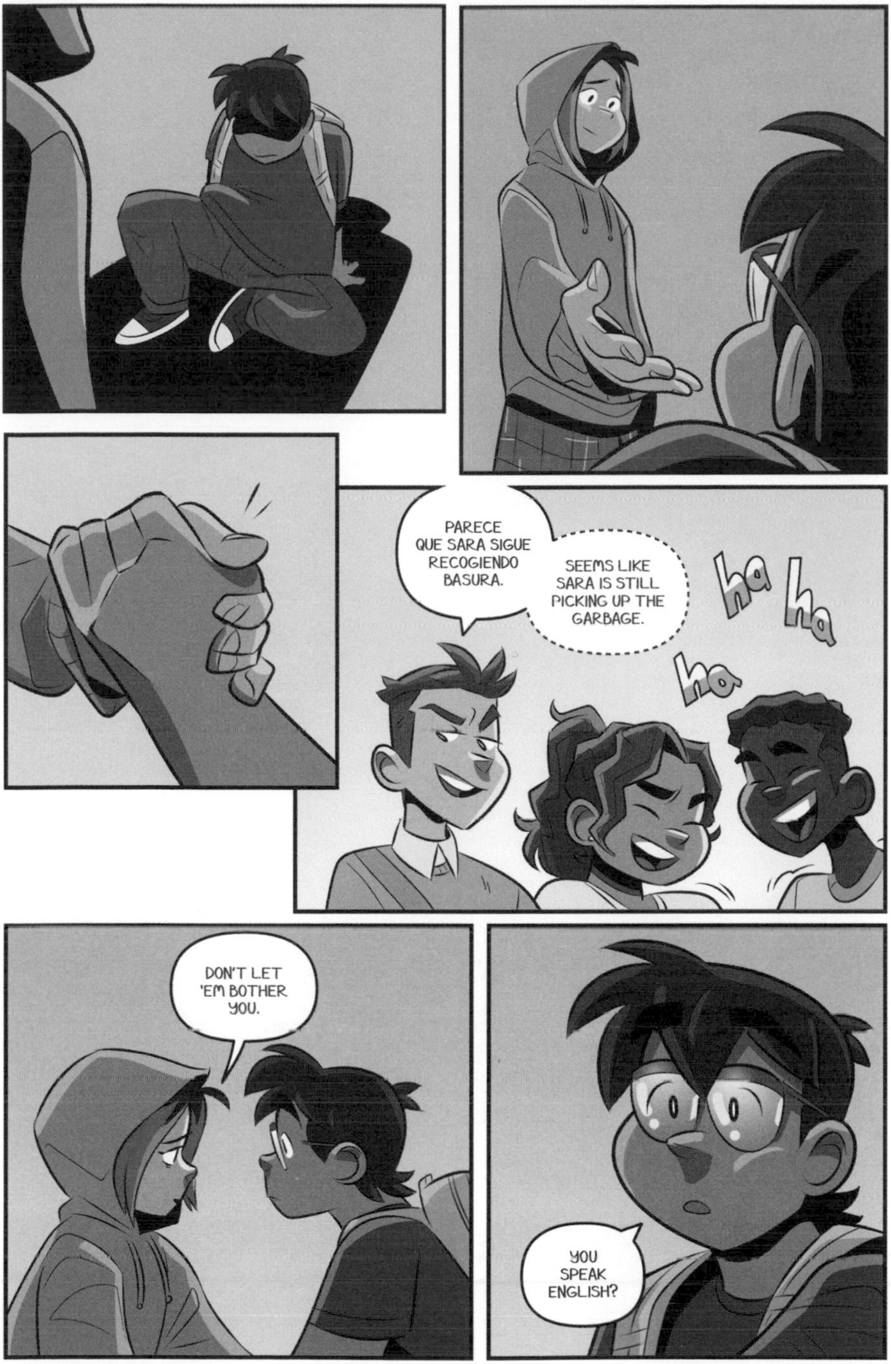
PARECE QUE SARA SIGUE RECOGIENDO BASURA.
SEEMS LIKE SARA IS STILL PICKING UP THE GARBAGE.
ha ha ha
DON'T LET 'EM BOTHER YOU.
YOU SPEAK ENGLISH?

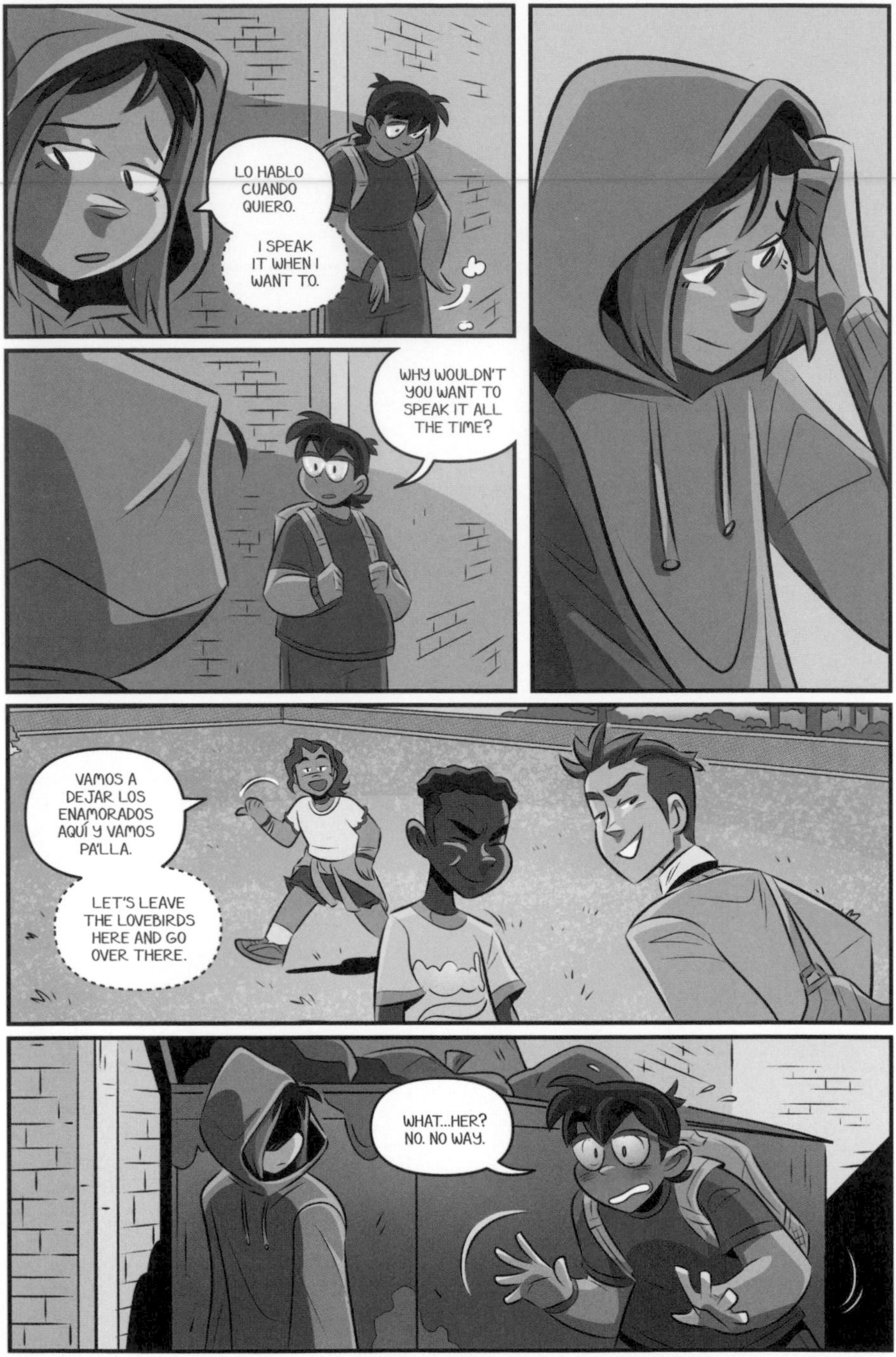
LO HABLO CUANDO QUIERO.
I SPEAK IT WHEN I WANT TO.
WHY WOULDN'T YOU WANT TO SPEAK IT ALL THE TIME?
VAMOS A DEJAR LOS ENAMORADOS AQUÍ Y VAMOS PA'LLA.
LET'S LEAVE THE LOVEBIRDS HERE AND GO OVER THERE.
WHAT...HER? NO. NO WAY.

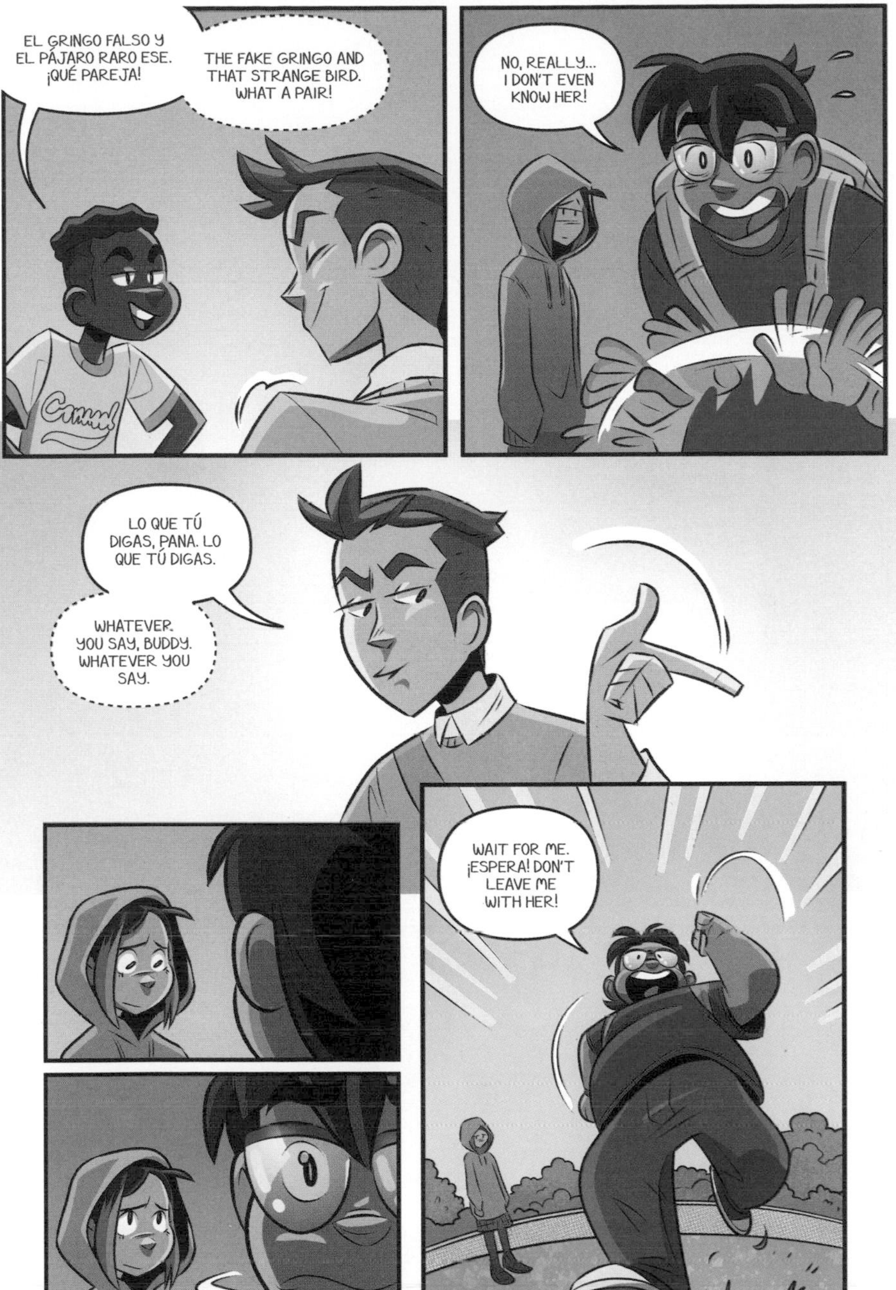
EL GRINGO FALSO Y EL PÁJARO RARO ESE. ¡QUÉ PAREJA!
THE FAKE GRINGO AND THAT STRANGE BIRD. WHAT A PAIR!
NO, REALLY... I DON'T EVEN KNOW HER!
LO QUE TÚ DIGAS, PANA. LO QUE TÚ DIGAS.
WHATEVER. YOU SAY, BUDDY. WHATEVER YOU SAY.
WAIT FOR ME. ¡ESPERA! DON'T LEAVE ME WITH HER!

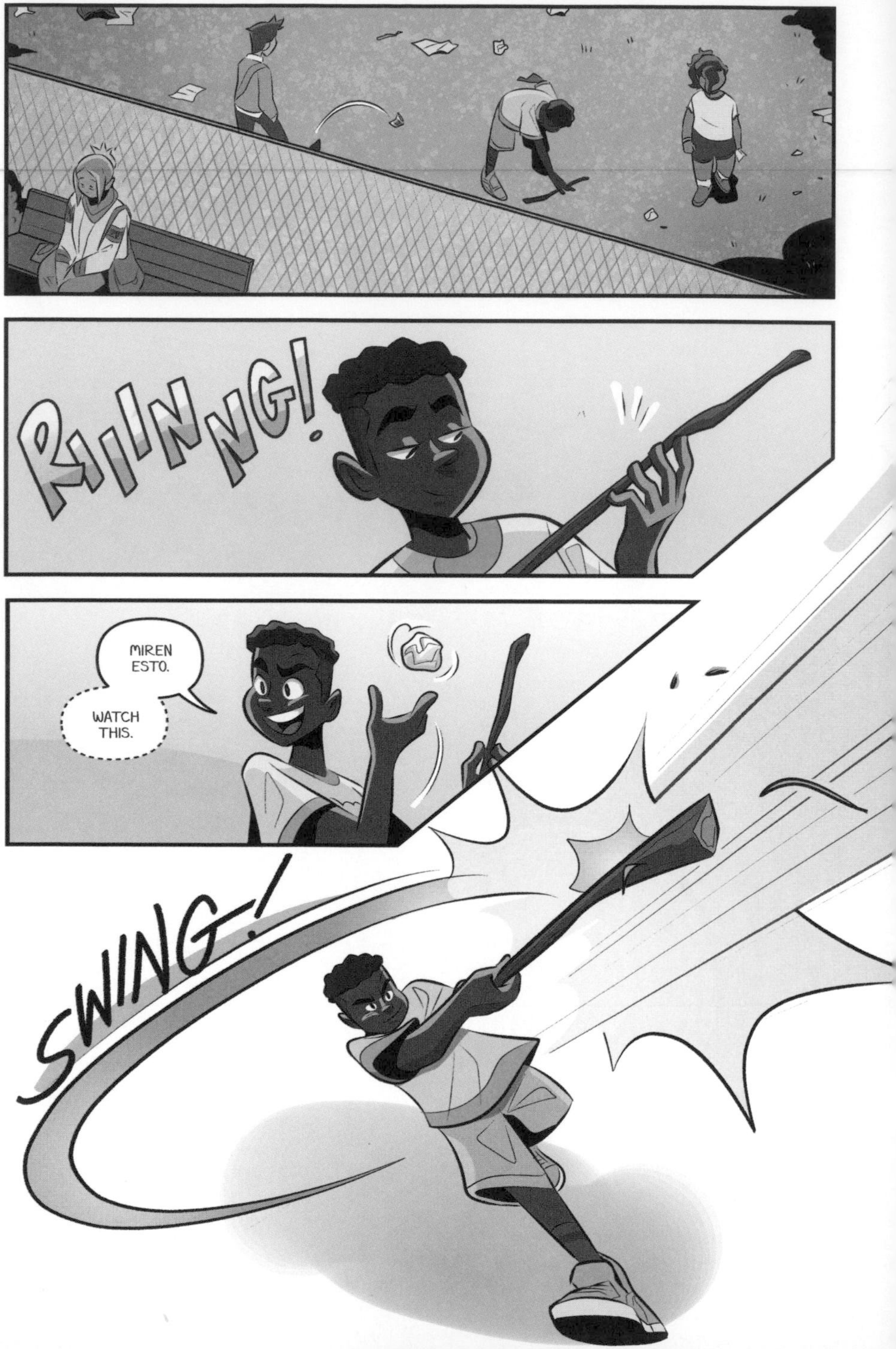
RIIINNG!
MIREN ESTO.
WATCH THIS.
SWING!

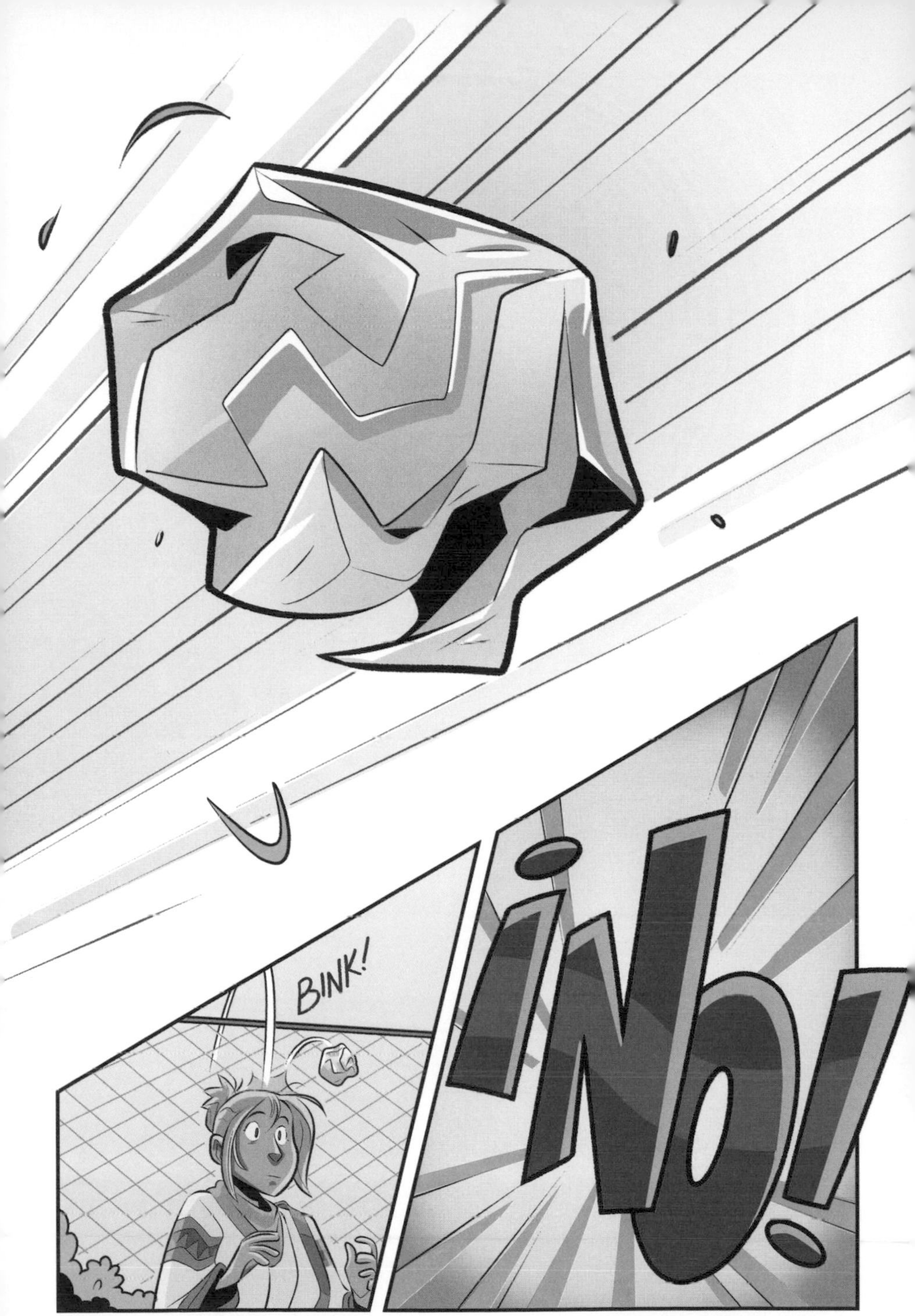
BINK!
¡NO!

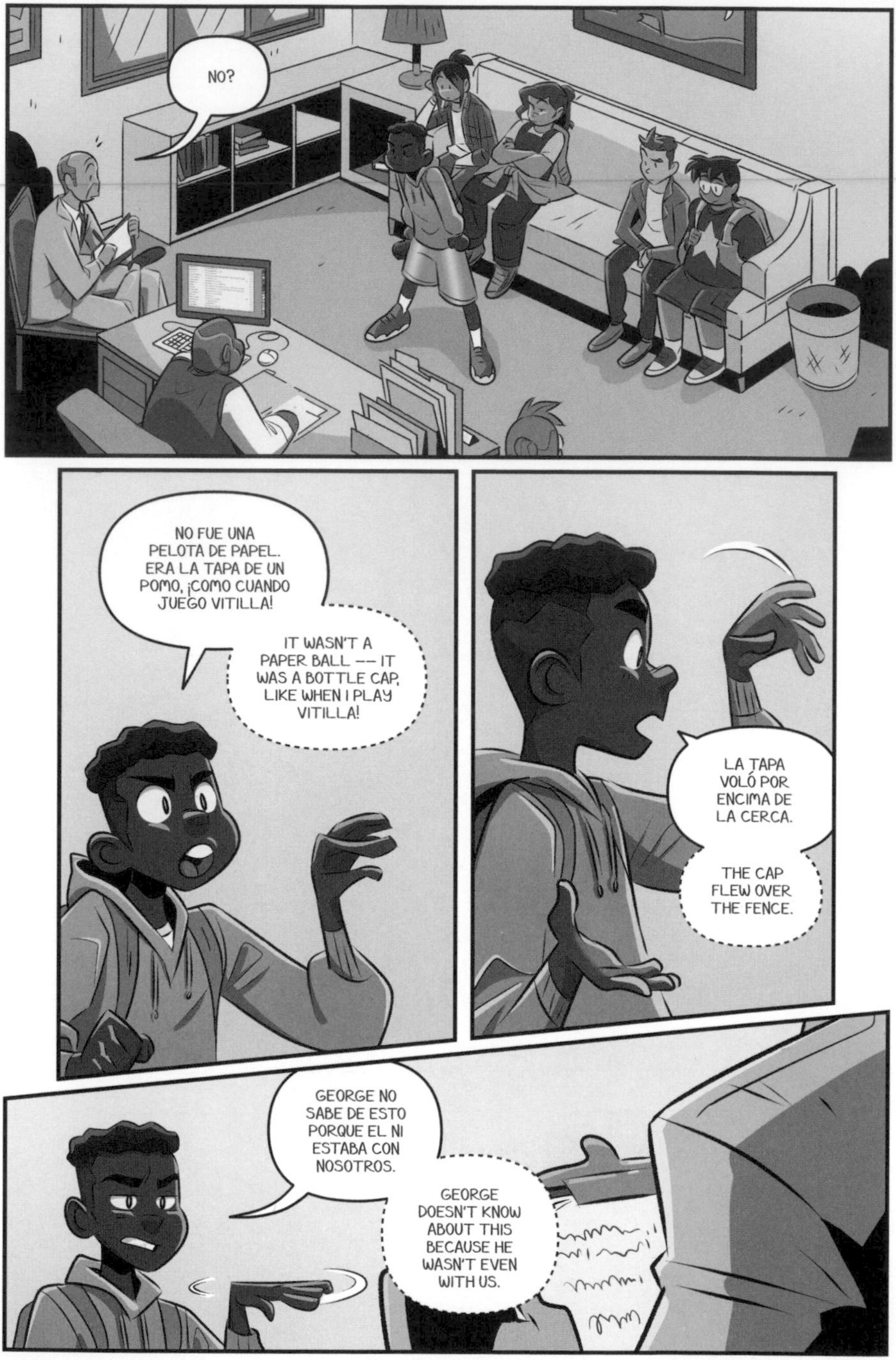
NO?
NO FUE UNA PELOTA DE PAPEL. ERA LA TAPA DE UN POMO, ¡COMO CUANDO JUEGO VITILLA!
IT WASN'T A PAPER BALL -- IT WAS A BOTTLE CAP, LIKE WHEN I PLAY VITILLA!
LA TAPA VOLÓ POR ENCIMA DE LA CERCA.
THE CAP FLEW OVER THE FENCE.
GEORGE NO SABE DE ESTO PORQUE EL NI ESTABA CON NOSOTROS.
GEORGE DOESN'T KNOW ABOUT THIS BECAUSE HE WASN'T EVEN WITH US.

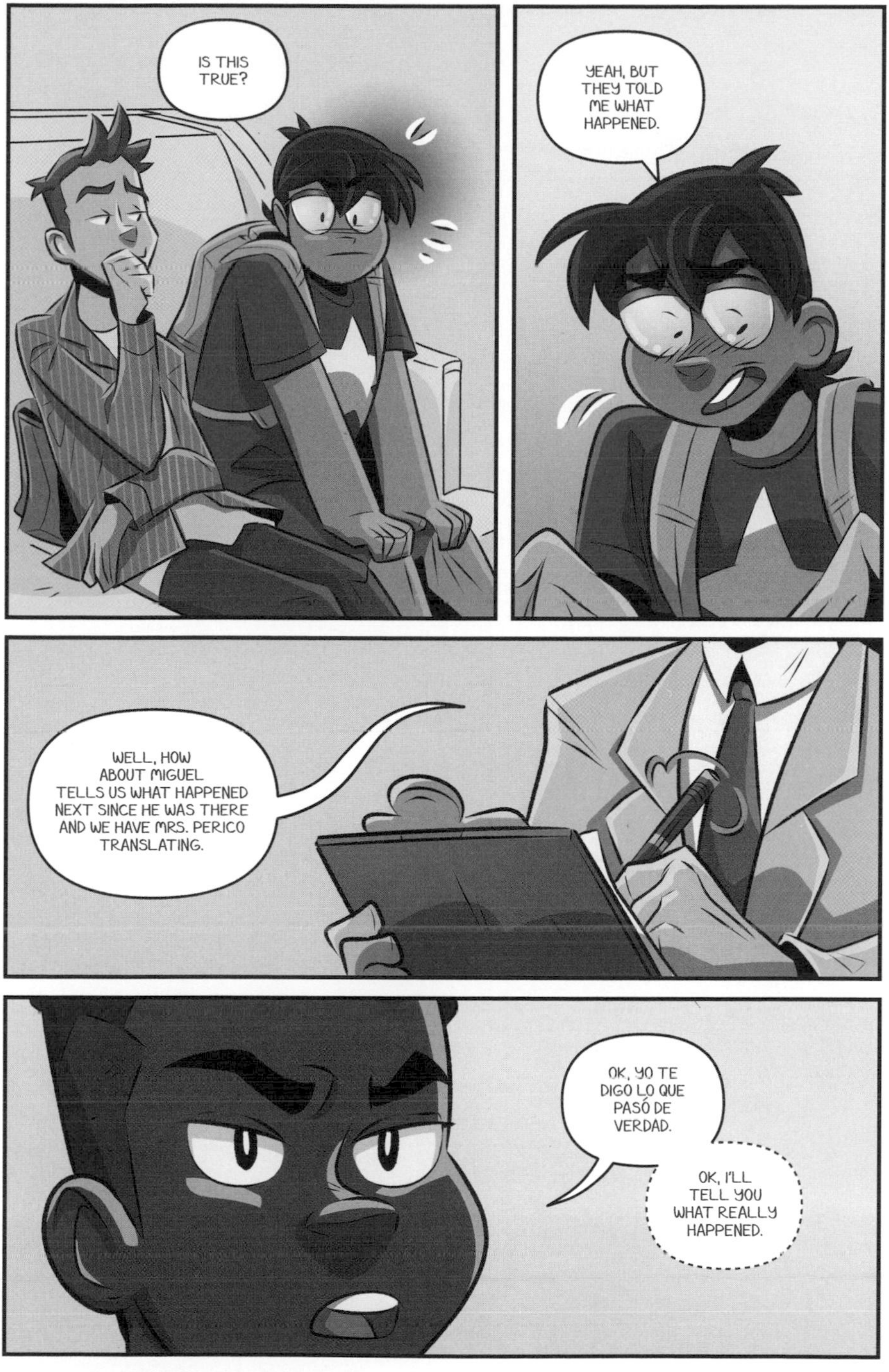
IS THIS TRUE?
YEAH, BUT THEY TOLD ME WHAT HAPPENED.
WELL, HOW ABOUT MIGUEL TELLS US WHAT HAPPENED NEXT SINCE HE WAS THERE AND WE HAVE MRS. PERICO TRANSLATING.
OK, YO TE DIGO LO QUE PASÓ DE VERDAD.
OK, I'LL TELL YOU WHAT REALLY HAPPENED.

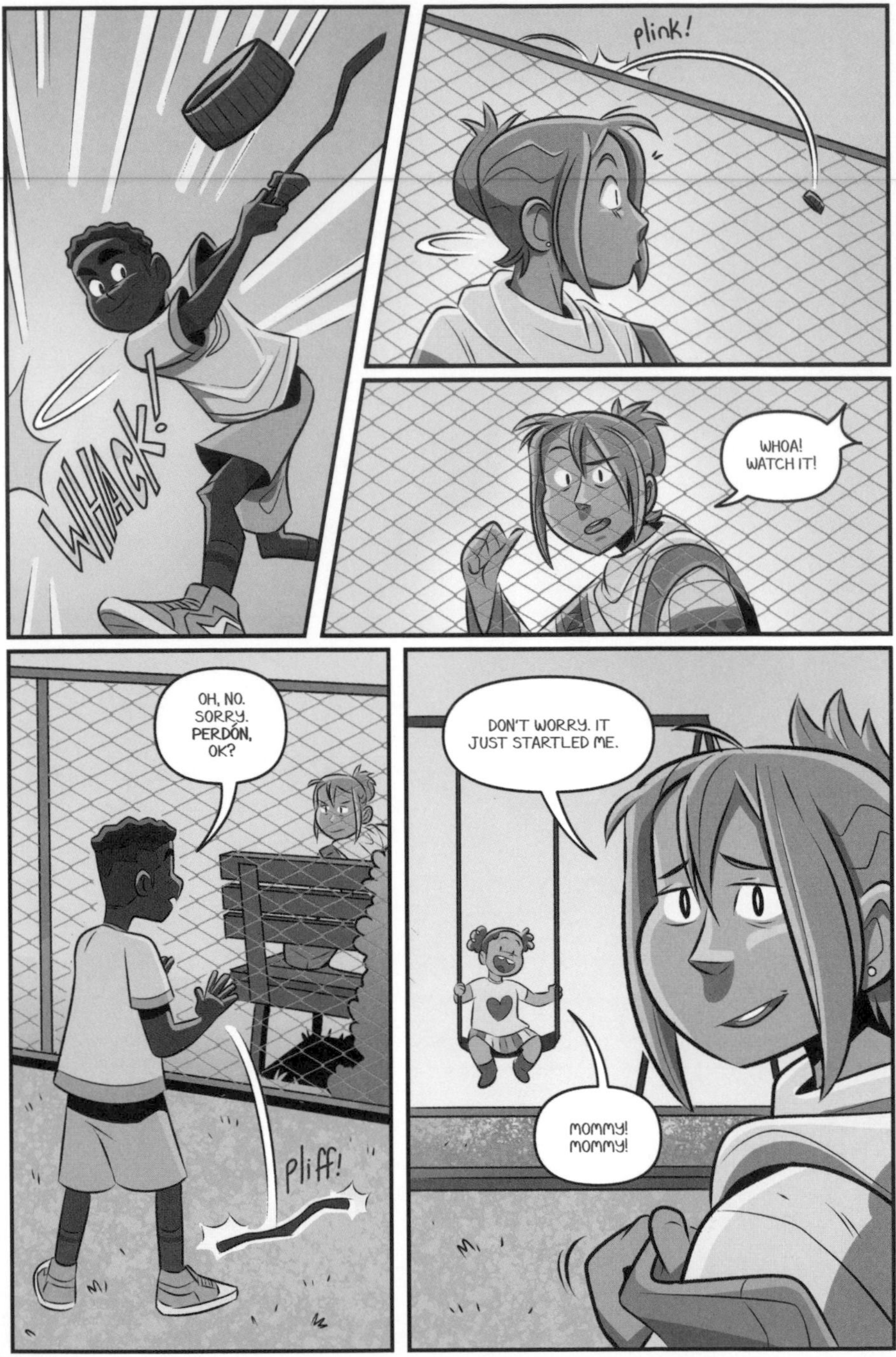
WHACK!
plink!
WHOA! WATCH IT!
OH, NO. SORRY. PERDÓN, OK?
pliff!
DON'T WORRY. IT JUST STARTLED ME.
MOMMY! MOMMY!

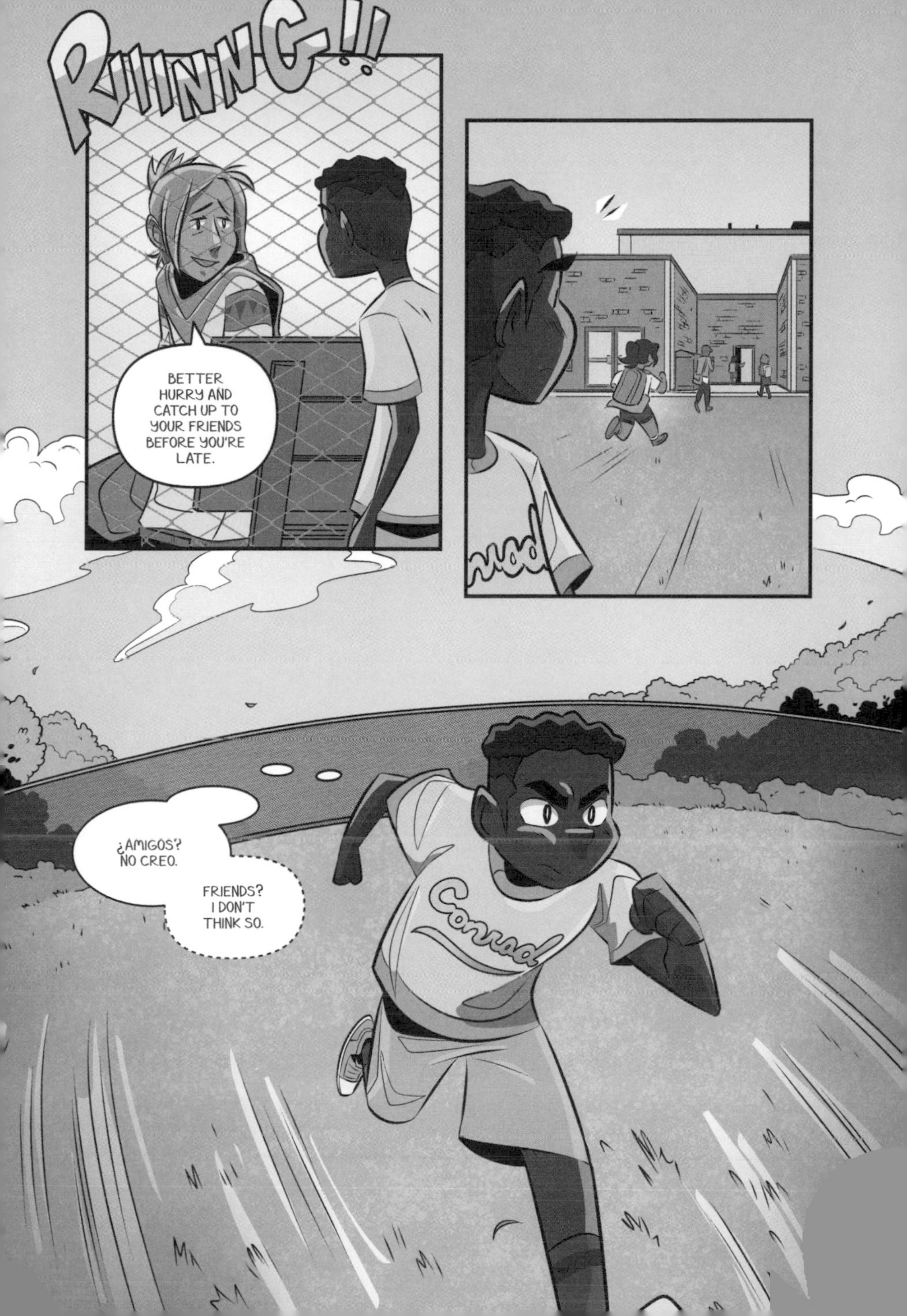
RIIINNG!!!
BETTER HURRY AND CATCH UP TO YOUR FRIENDS BEFORE YOU'RE LATE.
¿AMIGOS? NO CREO.
FRIENDS? I DON'T THINK SO.
Conrad

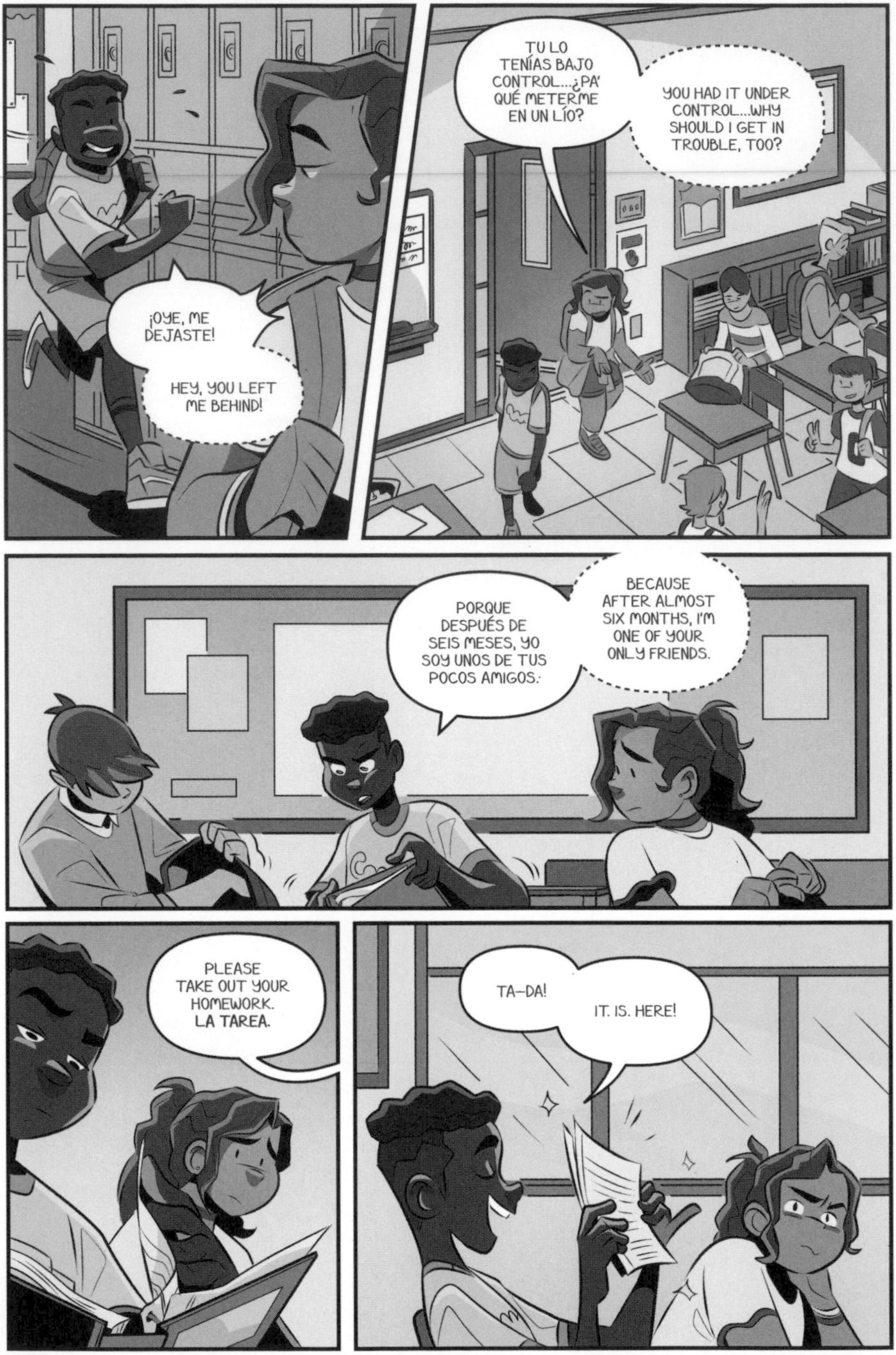
¡OYE, ME DEJASTE!
HEY, YOU LEFT ME BEHIND!
TU LO TENÍAS BAJO CONTROL...¿PA' QUÉ METERME EN UN LÍO?
YOU HAD IT UNDER CONTROL...WHY SHOULD I GET IN TROUBLE, TOO?
PORQUE DESPUÉS DE SEIS MESES, YO SOY UNOS DE TUS POCOS AMIGOS.
BECAUSE AFTER ALMOST SIX MONTHS, I'M ONE OF YOUR ONLY FRIENDS.
PLEASE TAKE OUT YOUR HOMEWORK. **LA TAREA.**
TA-DA!
IT. IS. HERE!

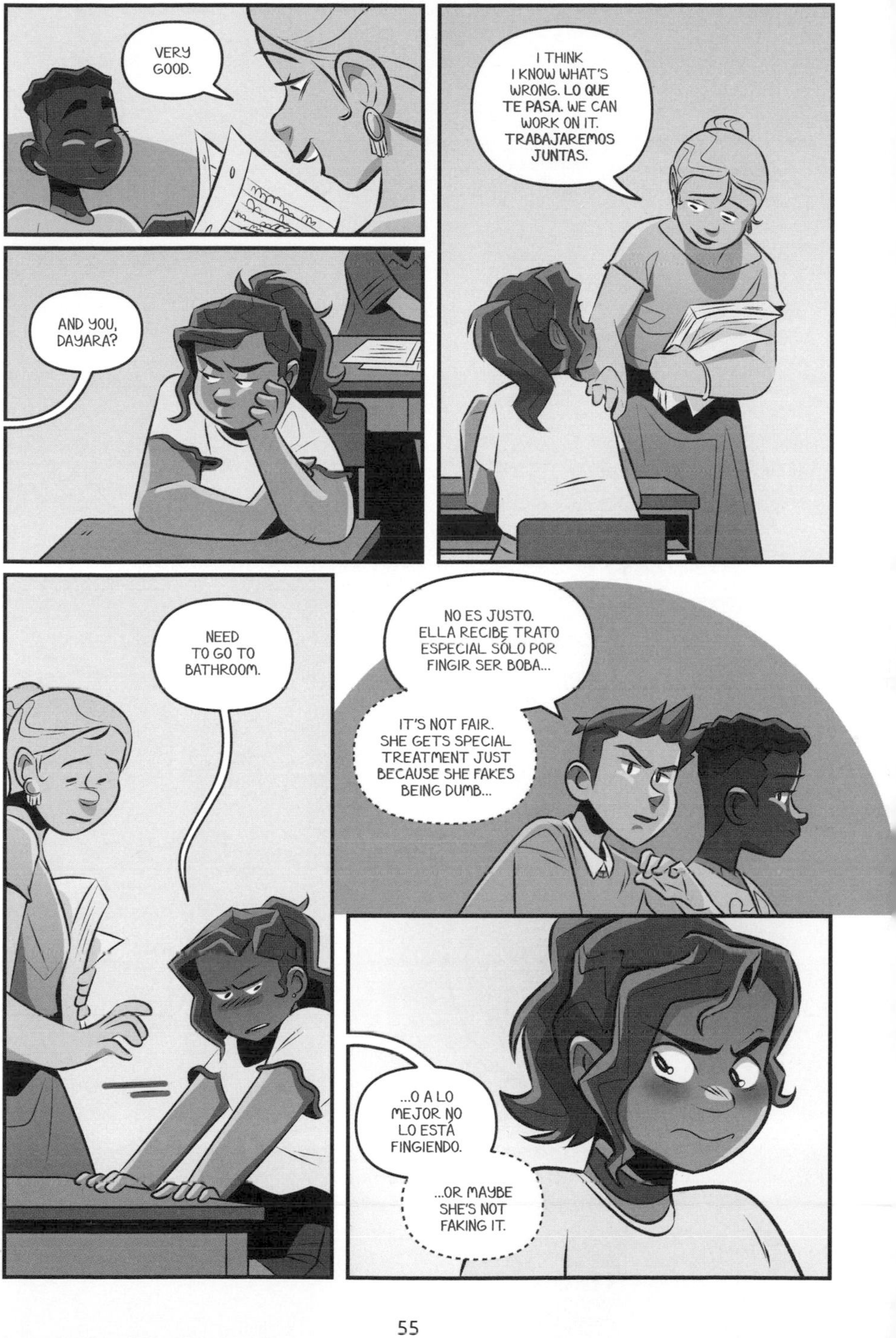
VERY GOOD.
I THINK I KNOW WHAT'S WRONG. LO QUE TE PASA. WE CAN WORK ON IT. TRABAJAREMOS JUNTAS.
AND YOU, DAYARA?
NEED TO GO TO BATHROOM.
NO ES JUSTO. ELLA RECIBE TRATO ESPECIAL SÓLO POR FINGIR SER BOBA...
IT'S NOT FAIR. SHE GETS SPECIAL TREATMENT JUST BECAUSE SHE FAKES BEING DUMB...
...O A LO MEJOR NO LO ESTÁ FINGIENDO.
...OR MAYBE SHE'S NOT FAKING IT.

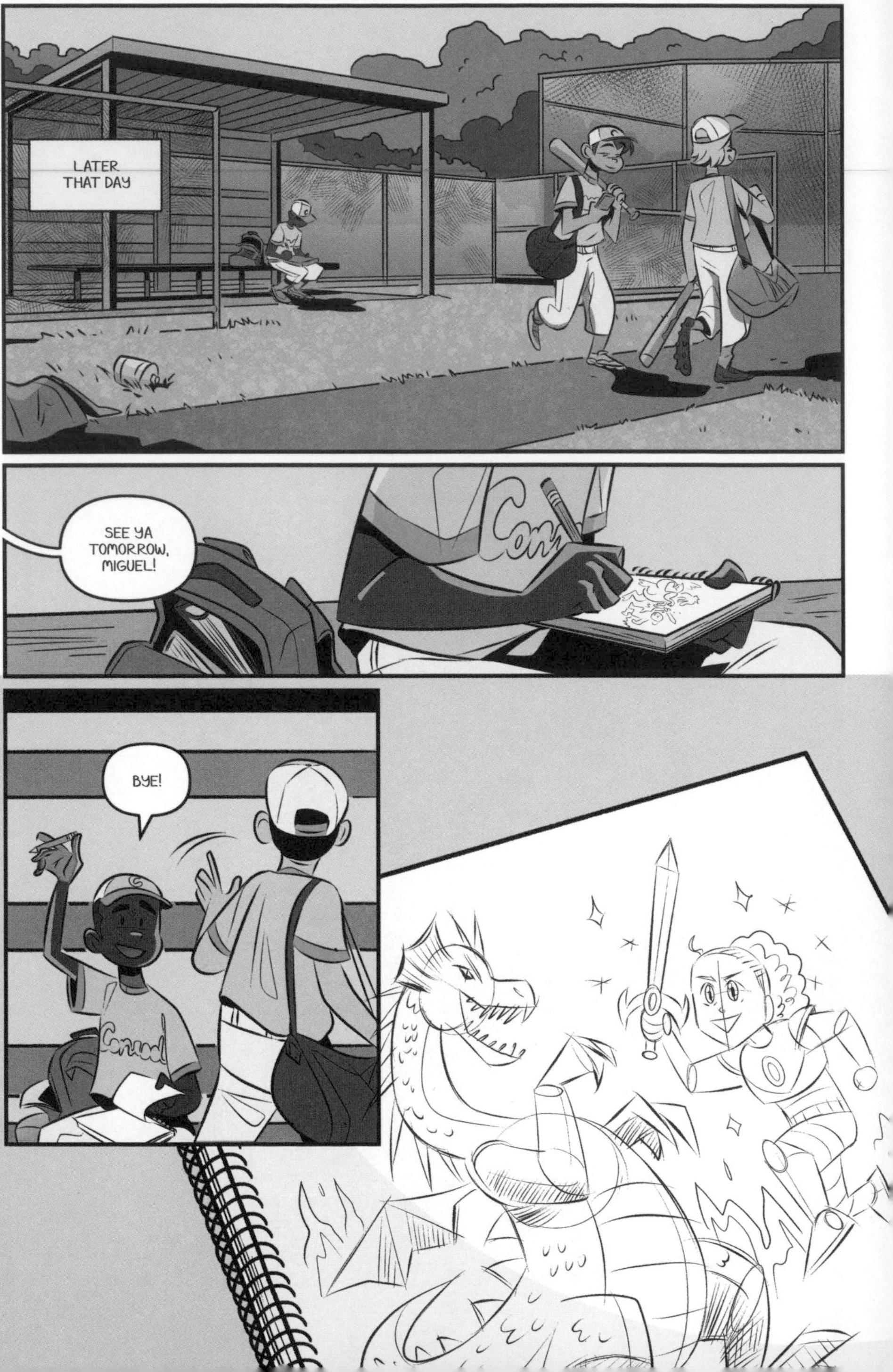
LATER THAT DAY
SEE YA TOMORROW, MIGUEL!
BYE!

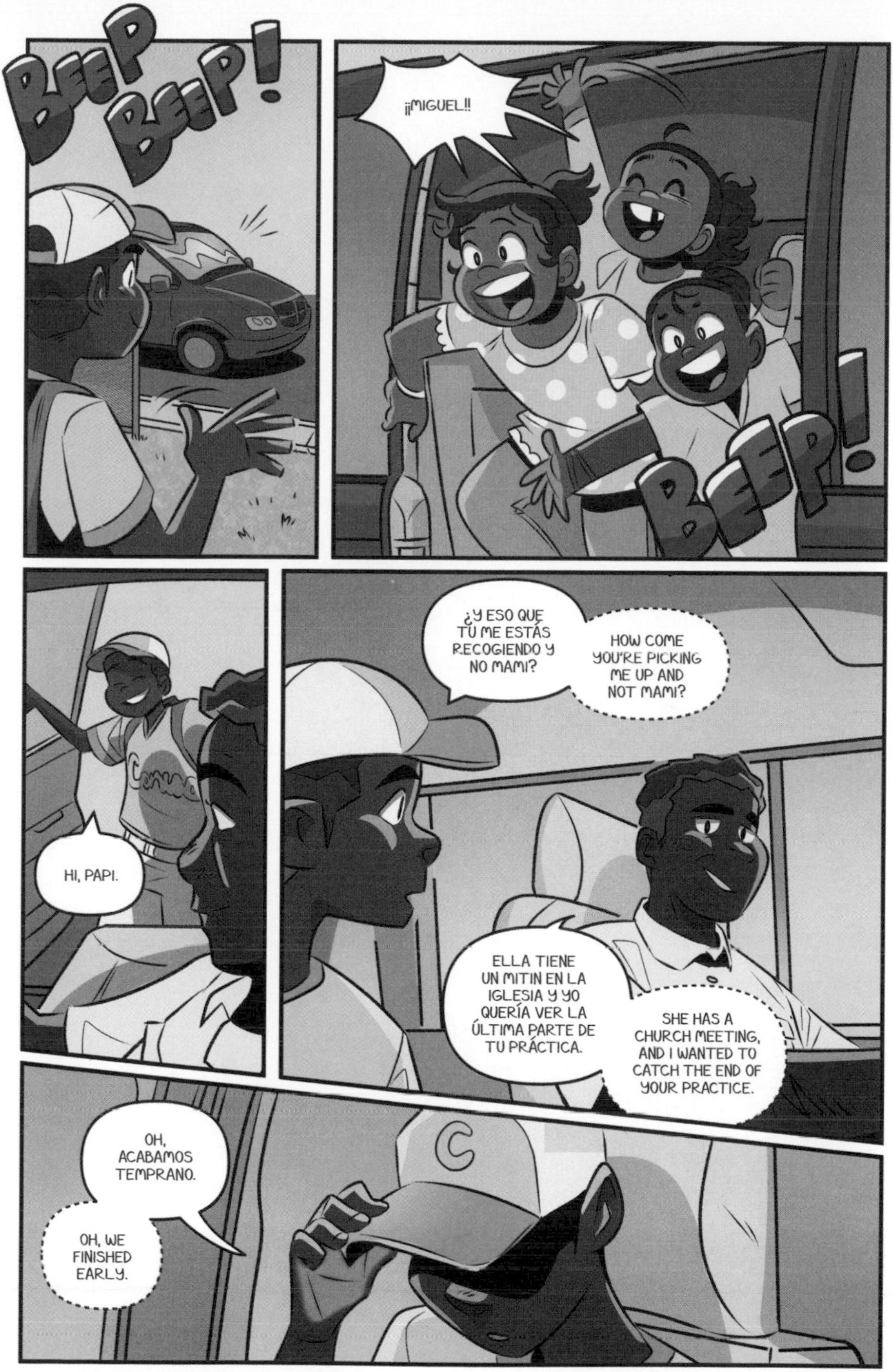
BEEP BEEP!
¡¡MIGUEL!!
BEEP!
HI, PAPI.
¿Y ESO QUE TÚ ME ESTÁS RECOGIENDO Y NO MAMI?
HOW COME YOU'RE PICKING ME UP AND NOT MAMI?
ELLA TIENE UN MITIN EN LA IGLESIA Y YO QUERÍA VER LA ÚLTIMA PARTE DE TU PRÁCTICA.
SHE HAS A CHURCH MEETING, AND I WANTED TO CATCH THE END OF YOUR PRACTICE.
OH, ACABAMOS TEMPRANO.
OH, WE FINISHED EARLY.

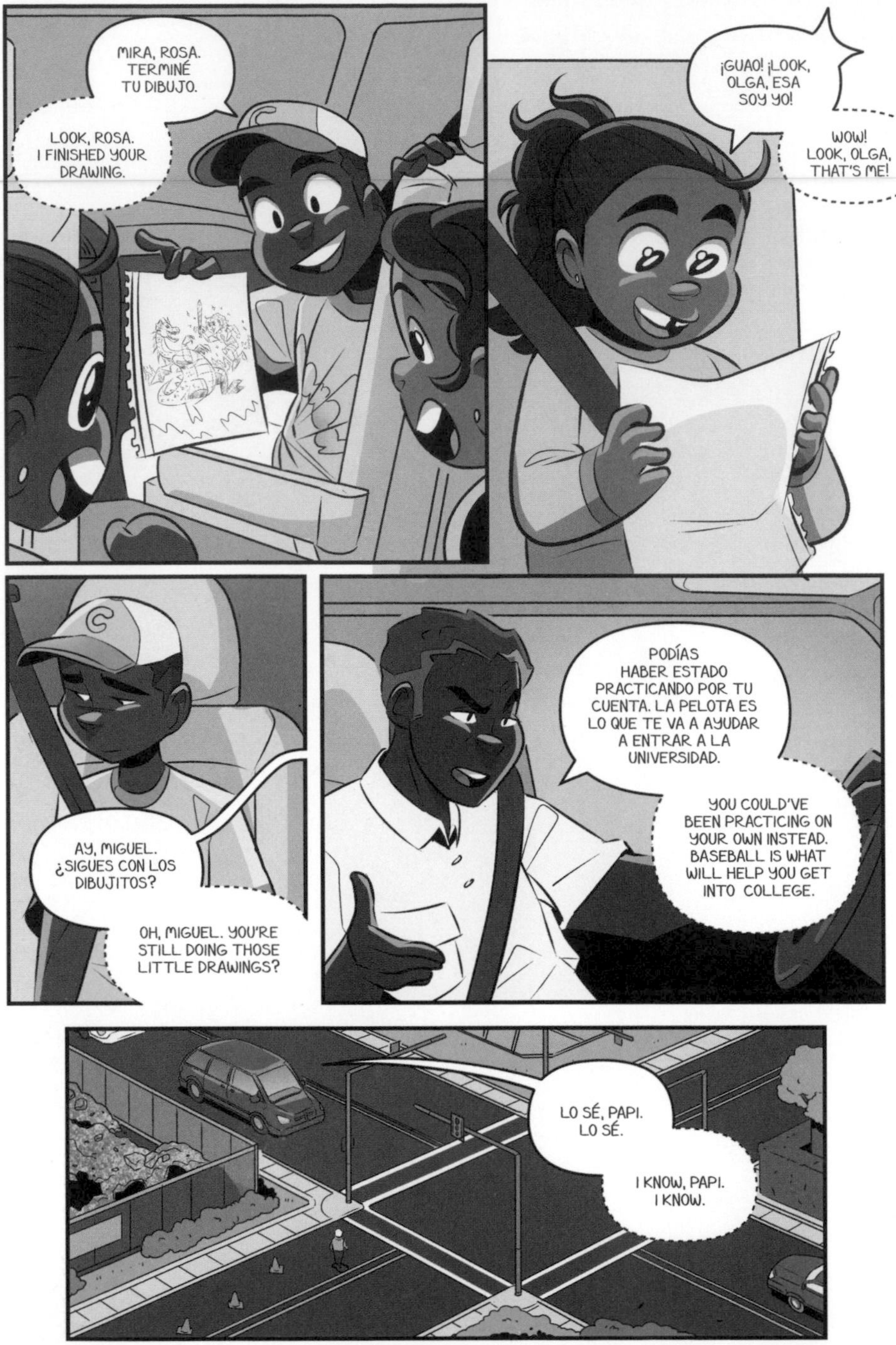
MIRA, ROSA. TERMINÉ TU DIBUJO.
LOOK, ROSA. I FINISHED YOUR DRAWING.
¡GUAO! ¡LOOK, OLGA, ESA SOY YO!
WOW! LOOK, OLGA, THAT'S ME!
AY, MIGUEL. ¿SIGUES CON LOS DIBUJITOS?
OH, MIGUEL. YOU'RE STILL DOING THOSE LITTLE DRAWINGS?
PODÍAS HABER ESTADO PRACTICANDO POR TU CUENTA. LA PELOTA ES LO QUE TE VA A AYUDAR A ENTRAR A LA UNIVERSIDAD.
YOU COULD'VE BEEN PRACTICING ON YOUR OWN INSTEAD. BASEBALL IS WHAT WILL HELP YOU GET INTO COLLEGE.
LO SÉ, PAPI. LO SÉ.
I KNOW, PAPI. I KNOW.

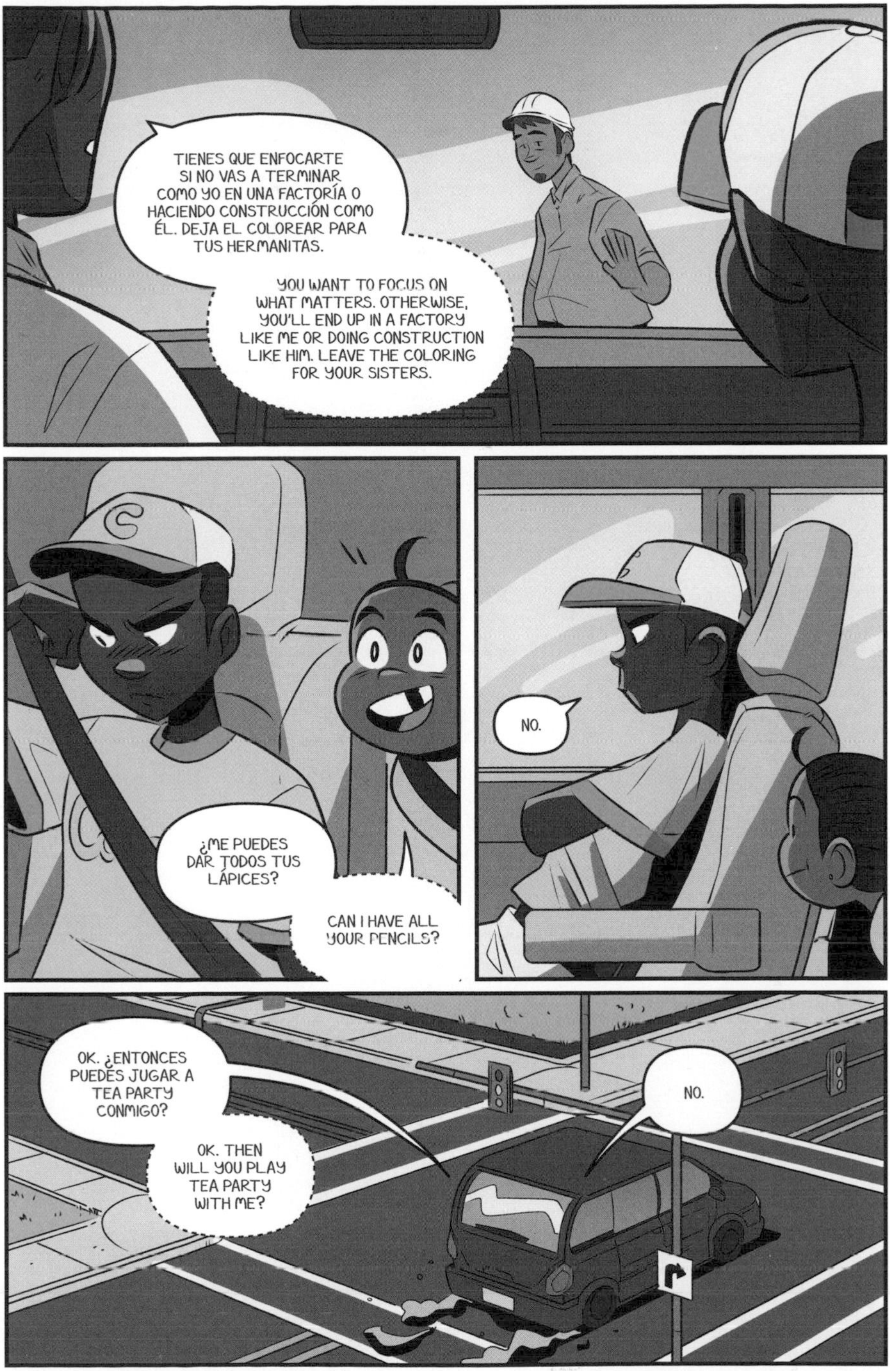
TIENES QUE ENFOCARTE SI NO VAS A TERMINAR COMO YO EN UNA FACTORÍA O HACIENDO CONSTRUCCIÓN COMO ÉL. DEJA EL COLOREAR PARA TUS HERMANITAS.
YOU WANT TO FOCUS ON WHAT MATTERS. OTHERWISE, YOU'LL END UP IN A FACTORY LIKE ME OR DOING CONSTRUCTION LIKE HIM. LEAVE THE COLORING FOR YOUR SISTERS.
¿ME PUEDES DAR TODOS TUS LÁPICES?
CAN I HAVE ALL YOUR PENCILS?
NO.
OK. ¿ENTONCES PUEDES JUGAR A TEA PARTY CONMIGO?
OK. THEN WILL YOU PLAY TEA PARTY WITH ME?
NO.

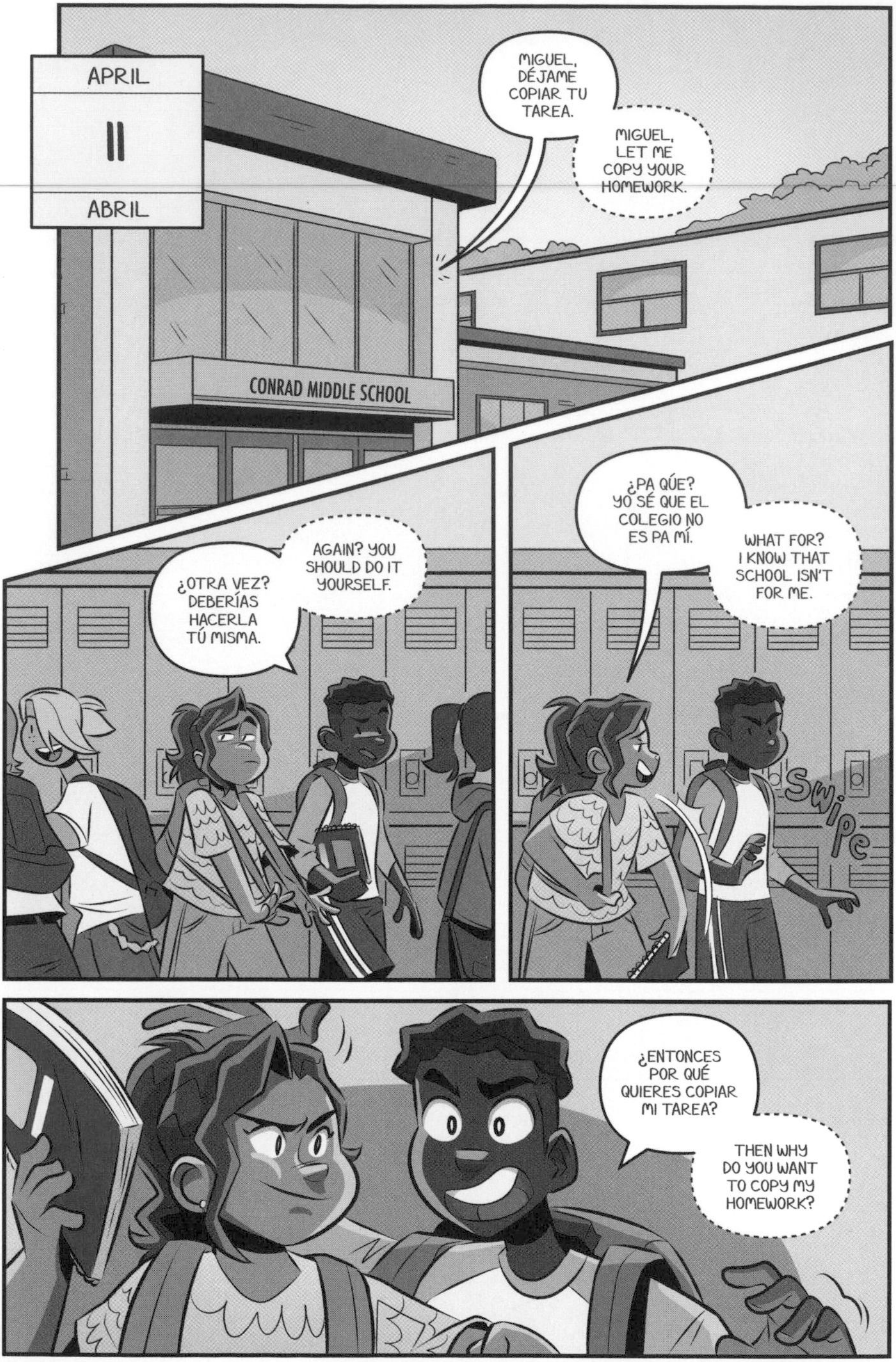
APRIL
11
ABRIL
MIGUEL, DÉJAME COPIAR TU TAREA.
MIGUEL, LET ME COPY YOUR HOMEWORK.
CONRAD MIDDLE SCHOOL
¿OTRA VEZ? DEBERÍAS HACERLA TÚ MISMA.
AGAIN? YOU SHOULD DO IT YOURSELF.
¿PA QÚE? YO SÉ QUE EL COLEGIO NO ES PA MÍ.
WHAT FOR? I KNOW THAT SCHOOL ISN'T FOR ME.
SWIPE
¿ENTONCES POR QUÉ QUIERES COPIAR MI TAREA?
THEN WHY DO YOU WANT TO COPY MY HOMEWORK?

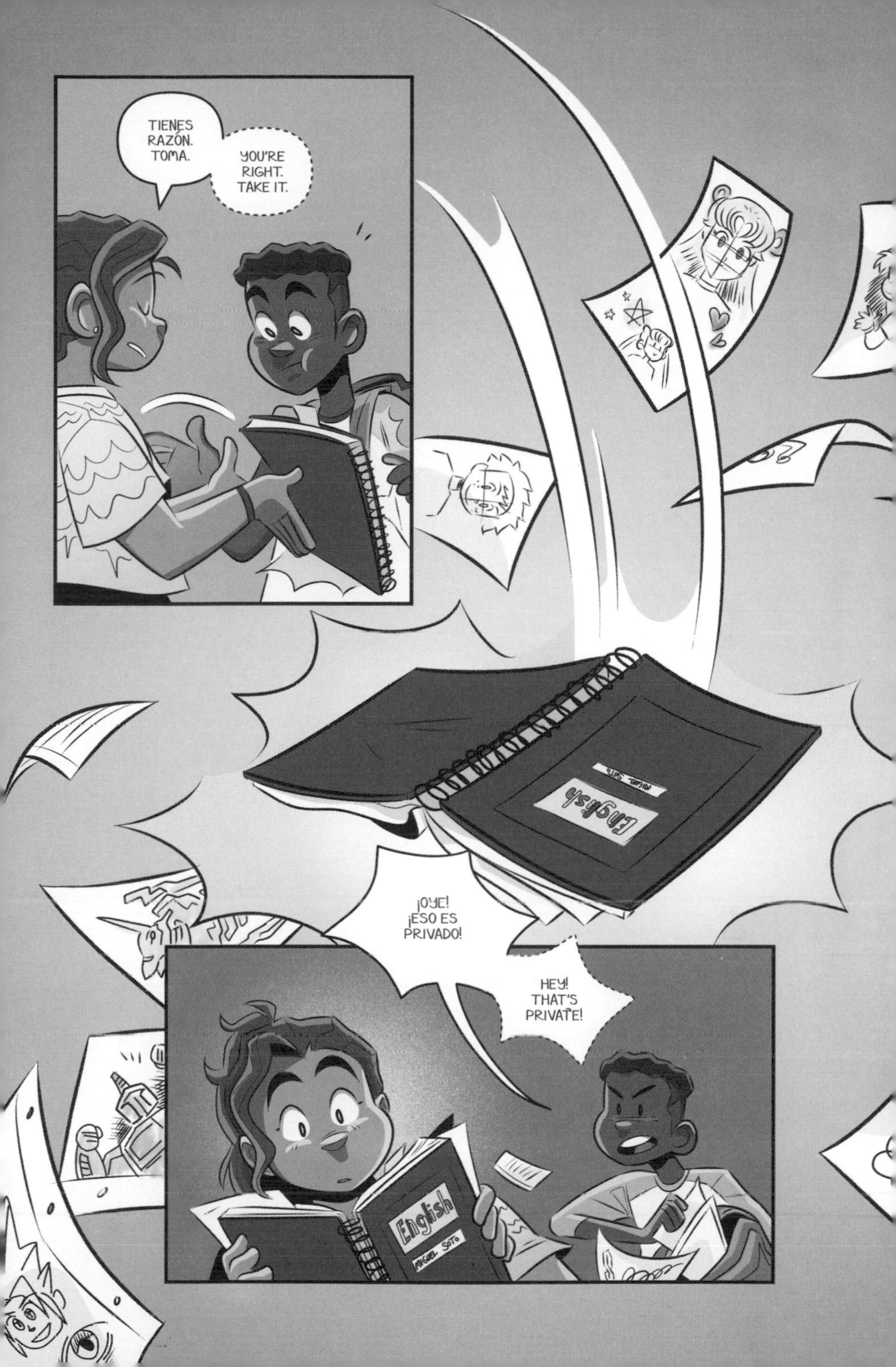
TIENES RAZÓN. TOMA.
YOU'RE RIGHT. TAKE IT.
English
MIGUEL SOTO
¡OYE! ¡ESO ES PRIVADO!
HEY! THAT'S PRIVATE!
English
MIGUEL SOTO

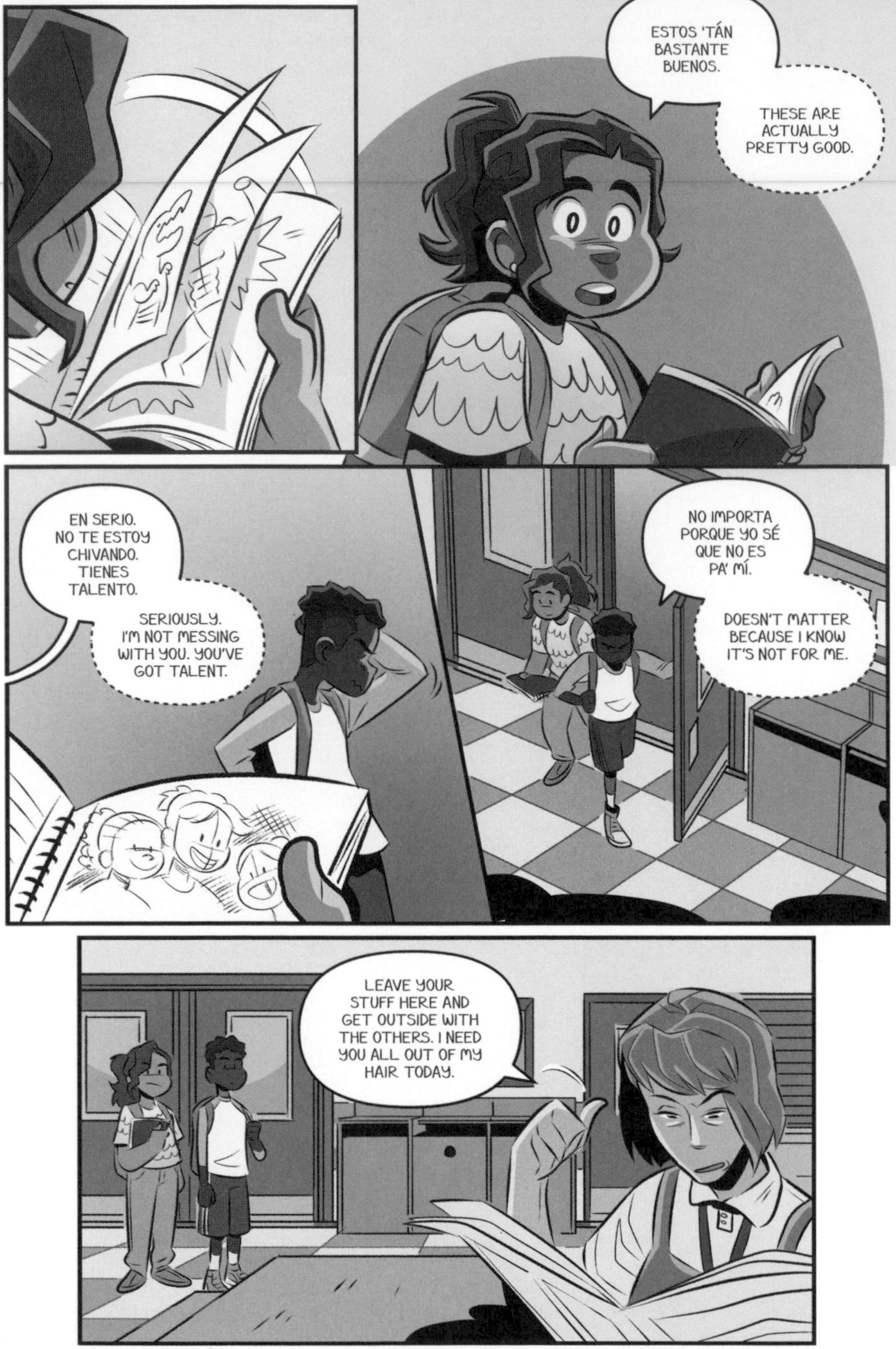
ESTOS 'TÁN BASTANTE BUENOS.
THESE ARE ACTUALLY PRETTY GOOD.
EN SERIO. NO TE ESTOY CHIVANDO. TIENES TALENTO.
SERIOUSLY. I'M NOT MESSING WITH YOU. YOU'VE GOT TALENT.
NO IMPORTA PORQUE YO SÉ QUE NO ES PA' MÍ.
DOESN'T MATTER BECAUSE I KNOW IT'S NOT FOR ME.
LEAVE YOUR STUFF HERE AND GET OUTSIDE WITH THE OTHERS. I NEED YOU ALL OUT OF MY HAIR TODAY.

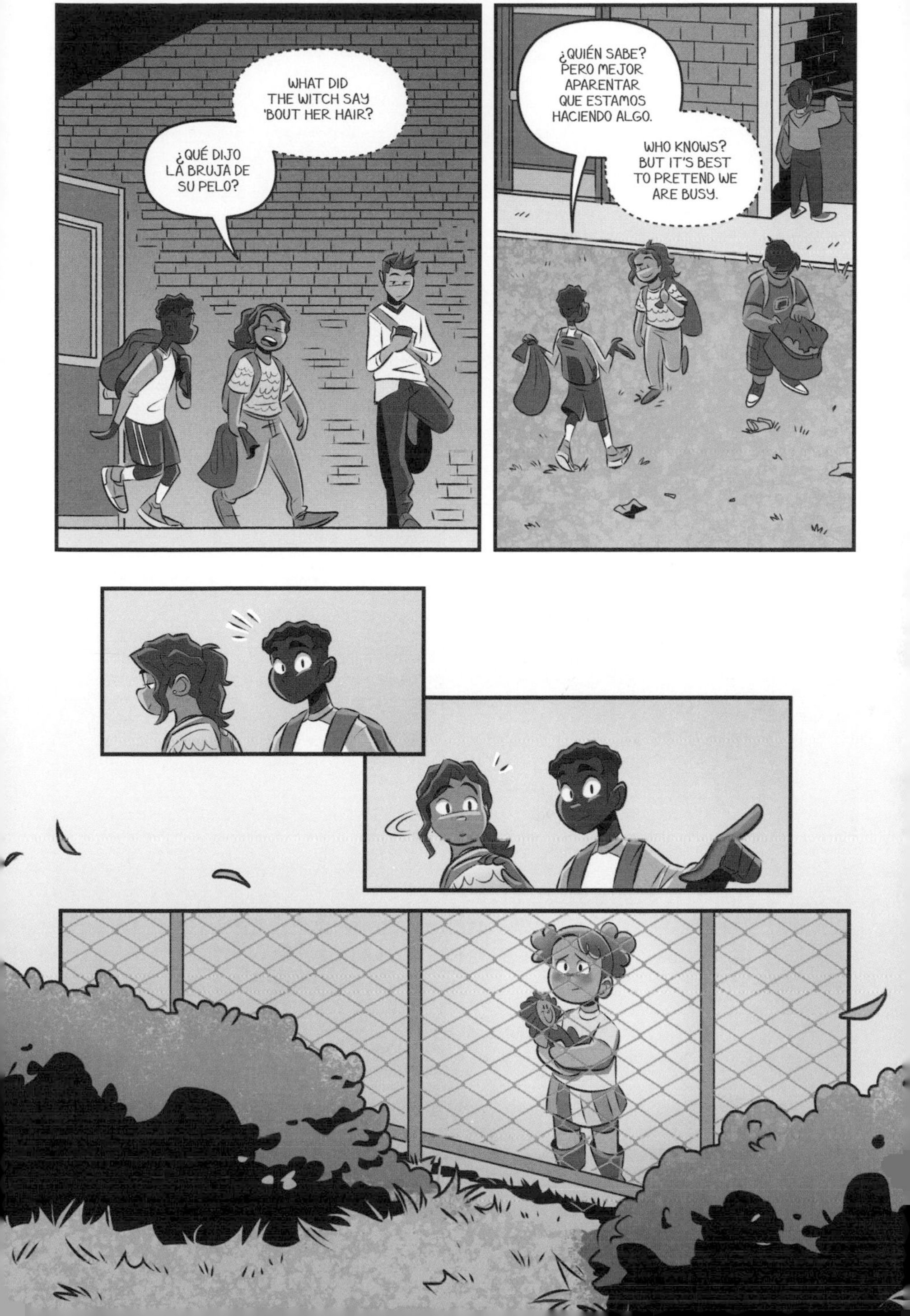
WHAT DID THE WITCH SAY 'BOUT HER HAIR?
¿QUÉ DIJO LA BRUJA DE SU PELO?
¿QUIÉN SABE? PERO MEJOR APARENTAR QUE ESTAMOS HACIENDO ALGO.
WHO KNOWS? BUT IT'S BEST TO PRETEND WE ARE BUSY.

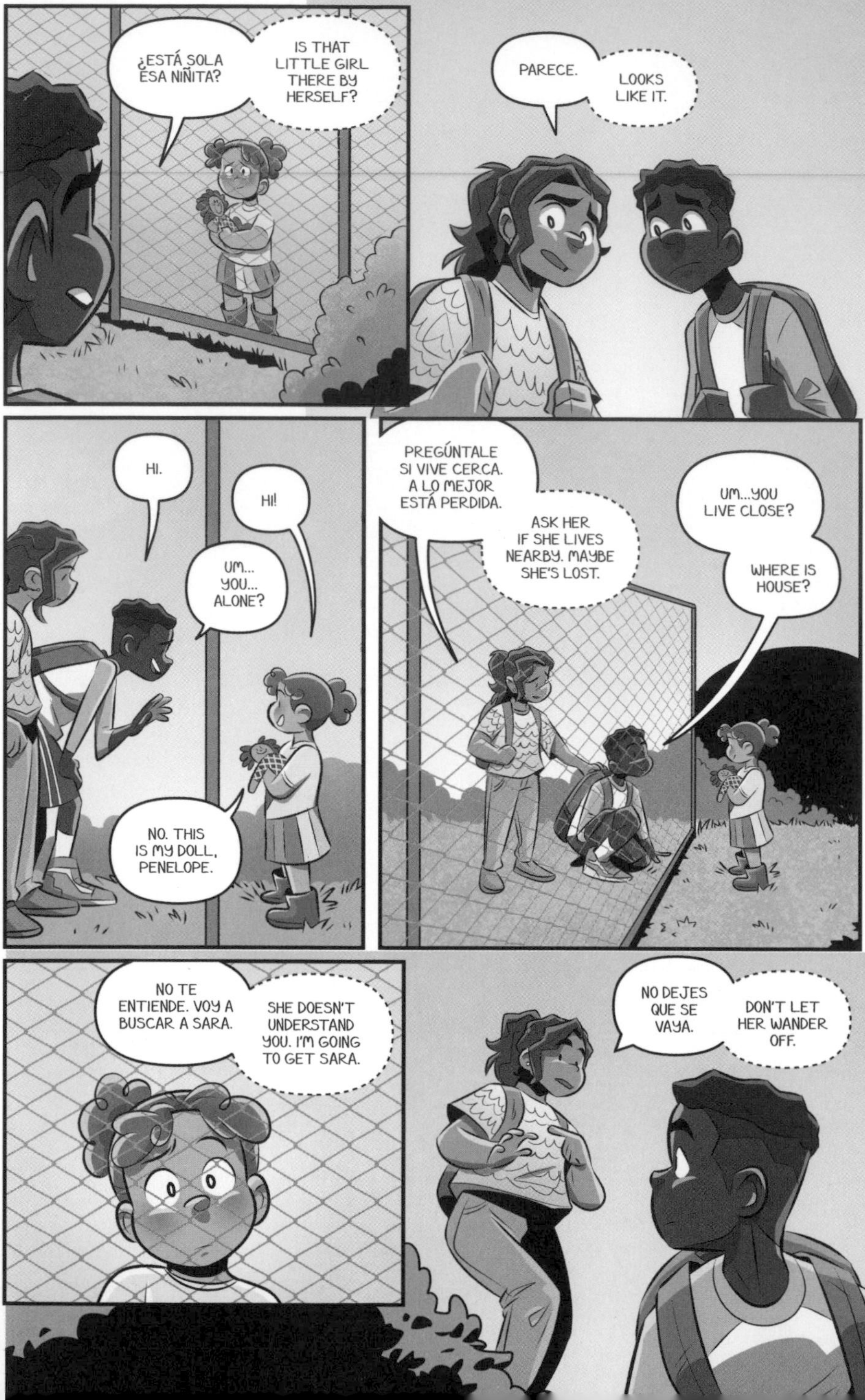
¿ESTÁ SOLA ESA NIÑITA?
IS THAT LITTLE GIRL THERE BY HERSELF?
PARECE.
LOOKS LIKE IT.
HI.
HI!
UM... YOU... ALONE?
NO. THIS IS MY DOLL, PENELOPE.
PREGÚNTALE SI VIVE CERCA. A LO MEJOR ESTÁ PERDIDA.
ASK HER IF SHE LIVES NEARBY. MAYBE SHE'S LOST.
UM...YOU LIVE CLOSE?
WHERE IS HOUSE?
NO TE ENTIENDE. VOY A BUSCAR A SARA.
SHE DOESN'T UNDERSTAND YOU. I'M GOING TO GET SARA.
NO DEJES QUE SE VAYA.
DON'T LET HER WANDER OFF.

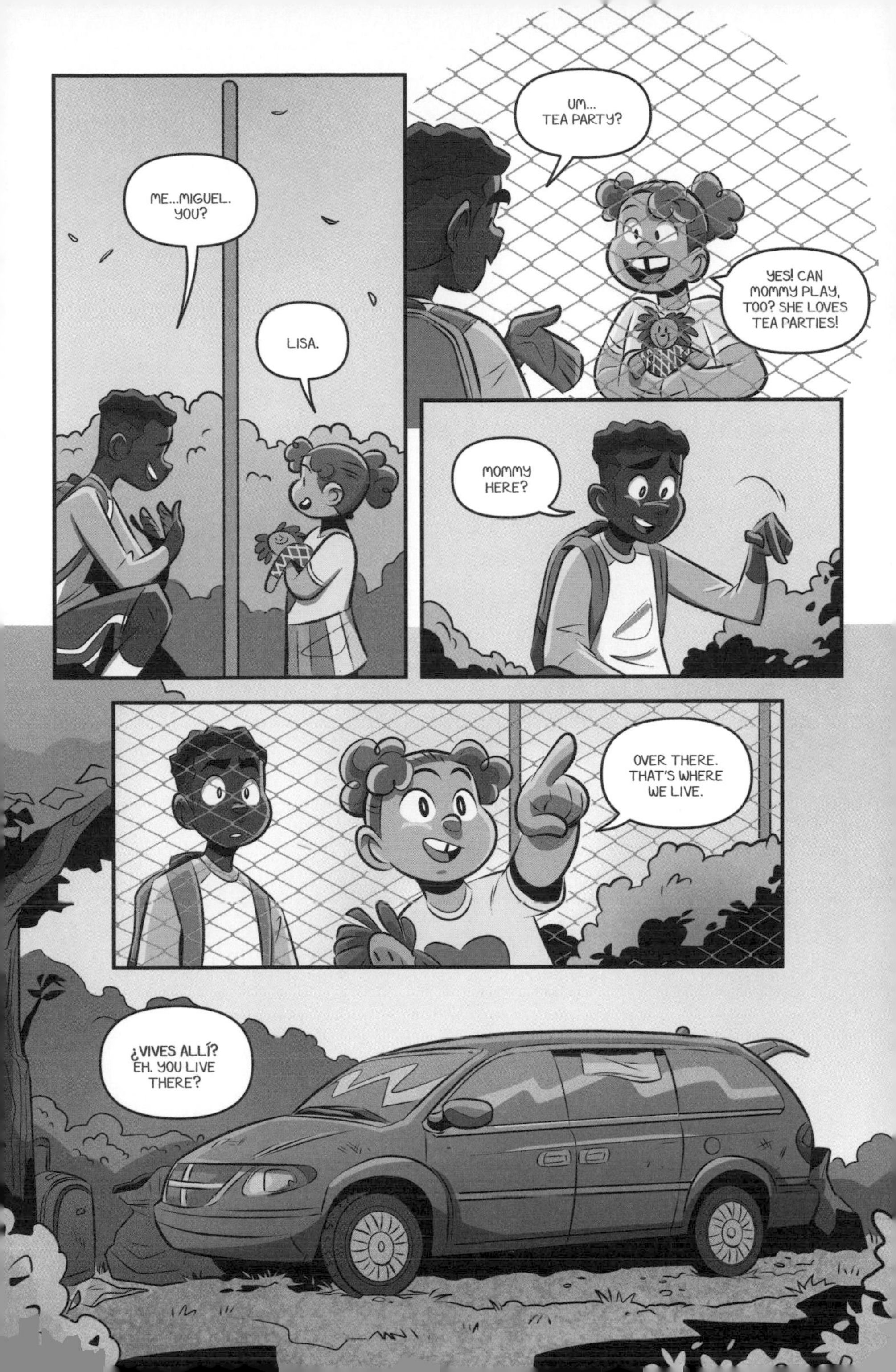

ME...MIGUEL. YOU?
LISA.
UM... TEA PARTY?
YES! CAN MOMMY PLAY, TOO? SHE LOVES TEA PARTIES!
MOMMY HERE?
OVER THERE. THAT'S WHERE WE LIVE.
¿VIVES ALLÍ? EH. YOU LIVE THERE?

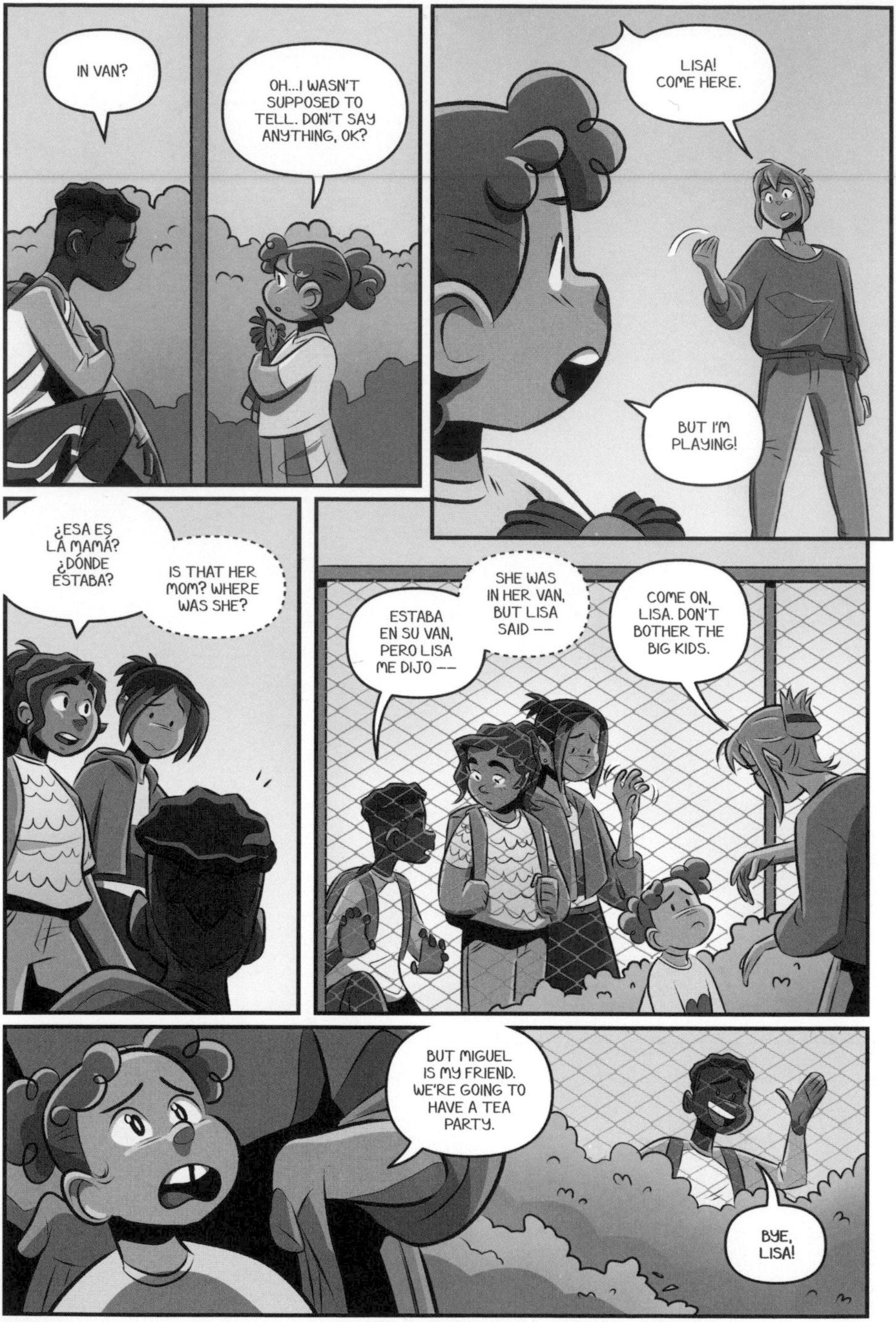
IN VAN?
OH...I WASN'T SUPPOSED TO TELL. DON'T SAY ANYTHING, OK?
LISA! COME HERE.
BUT I'M PLAYING!
¿ESA ES LA MAMÁ? ¿DÓNDE ESTABA?
IS THAT HER MOM? WHERE WAS SHE?
ESTABA EN SU VAN, PERO LISA ME DIJO --
SHE WAS IN HER VAN, BUT LISA SAID --
COME ON, LISA. DON'T BOTHER THE BIG KIDS.
BUT MIGUEL IS MY FRIEND. WE'RE GOING TO HAVE A TEA PARTY.
BYE, LISA!

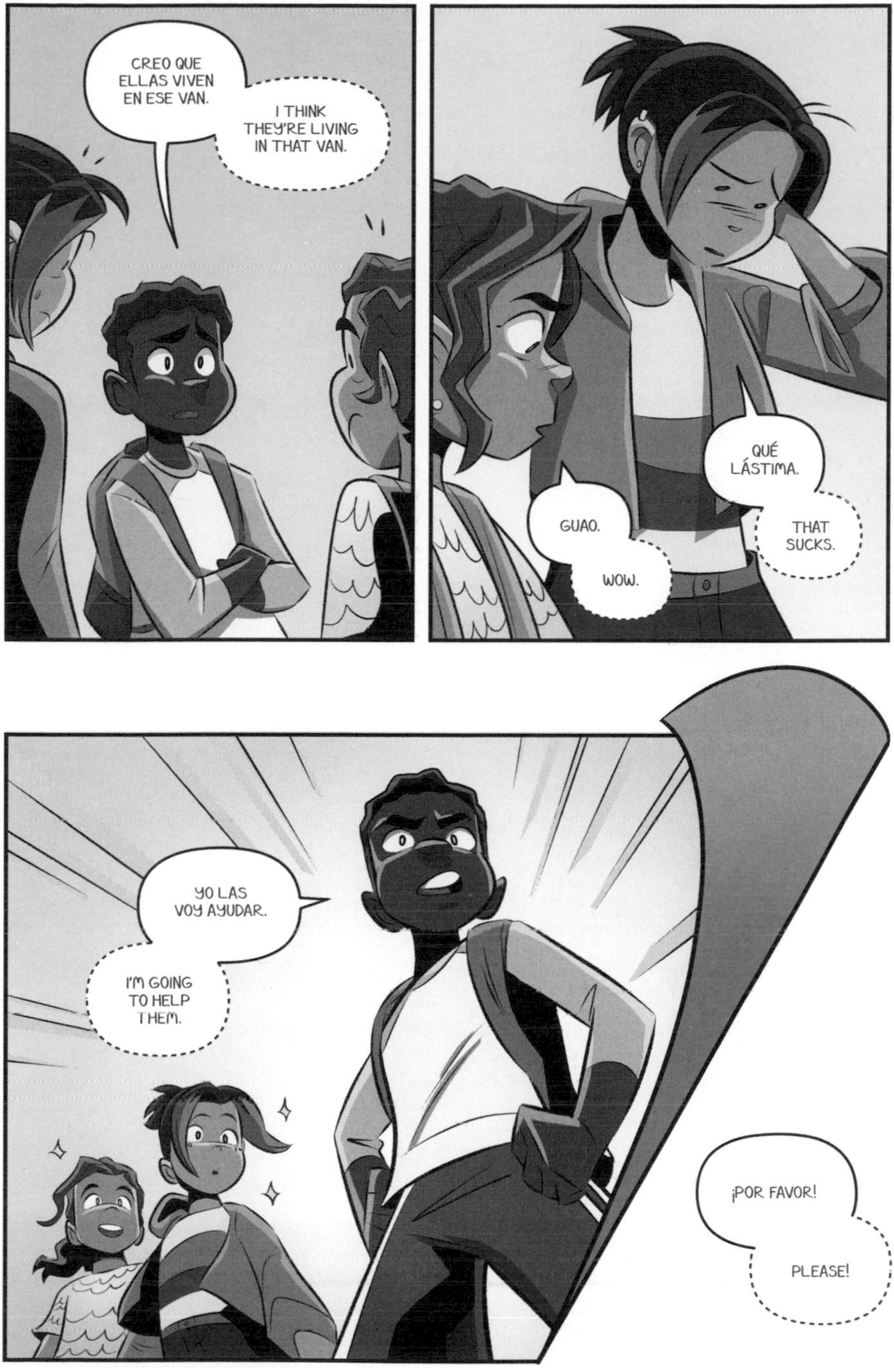
CREO QUE ELLAS VIVEN EN ESE VAN.
I THINK THEY'RE LIVING IN THAT VAN.
QUÉ LÁSTIMA.
THAT SUCKS.
GUAO.
WOW.
YO LAS VOY AYUDAR.
I'M GOING TO HELP THEM.
¡POR FAVOR!
PLEASE!

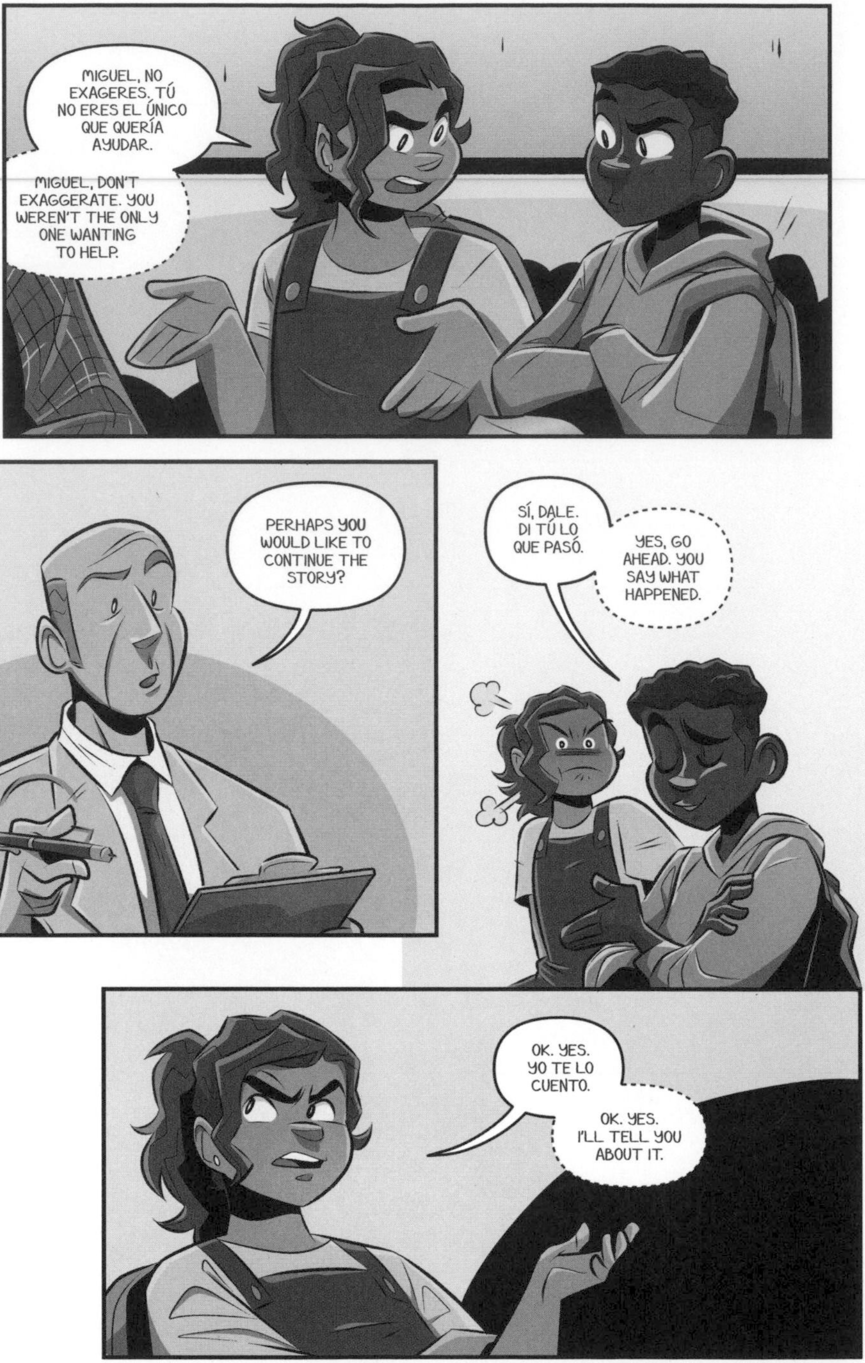
MIGUEL, NO EXAGERES. TÚ NO ERES EL ÚNICO QUE QUERÍA AYUDAR.
MIGUEL, DON'T EXAGGERATE. YOU WEREN'T THE ONLY ONE WANTING TO HELP.
PERHAPS YOU WOULD LIKE TO CONTINUE THE STORY?
SÍ, DALE. DI TÚ LO QUE PASÓ.
YES, GO AHEAD. YOU SAY WHAT HAPPENED.
OK. YES. YO TE LO CUENTO.
OK. YES. I'LL TELL YOU ABOUT IT.

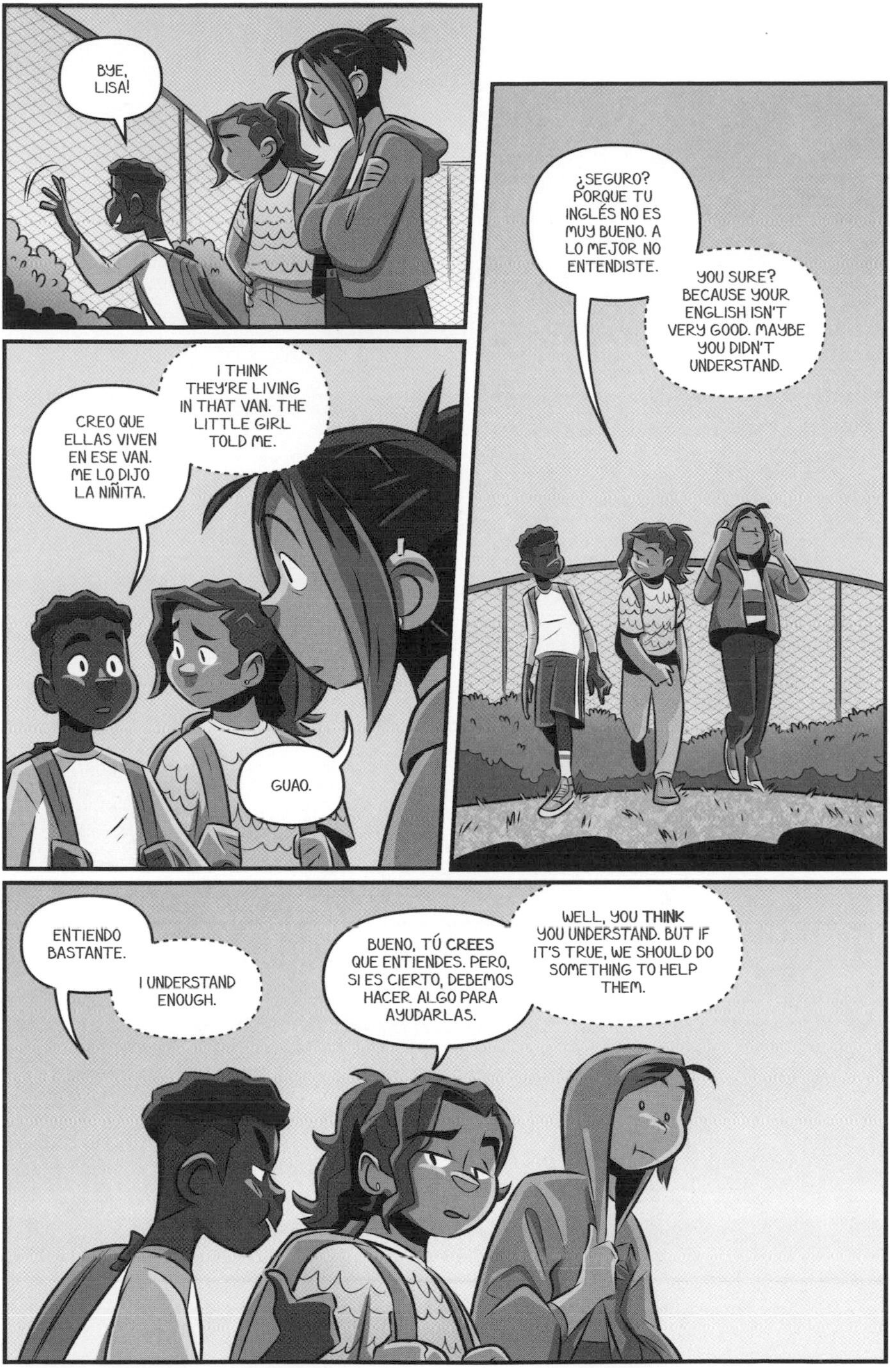

BYE, LISA!
CREO QUE ELLAS VIVEN EN ESE VAN. ME LO DIJO LA NIÑITA.
I THINK THEY'RE LIVING IN THAT VAN. THE LITTLE GIRL TOLD ME.
GUAO.
¿SEGURO? PORQUE TU INGLÉS NO ES MUY BUENO. A LO MEJOR NO ENTENDISTE.
YOU SURE? BECAUSE YOUR ENGLISH ISN'T VERY GOOD. MAYBE YOU DIDN'T UNDERSTAND.
ENTIENDO BASTANTE.
I UNDERSTAND ENOUGH.
BUENO, TÚ **CREES** QUE ENTIENDES. PERO, SI ES CIERTO, DEBEMOS HACER ALGO PARA AYUDARLAS.
WELL, YOU **THINK** YOU UNDERSTAND. BUT IF IT'S TRUE, WE SHOULD DO SOMETHING TO HELP THEM.

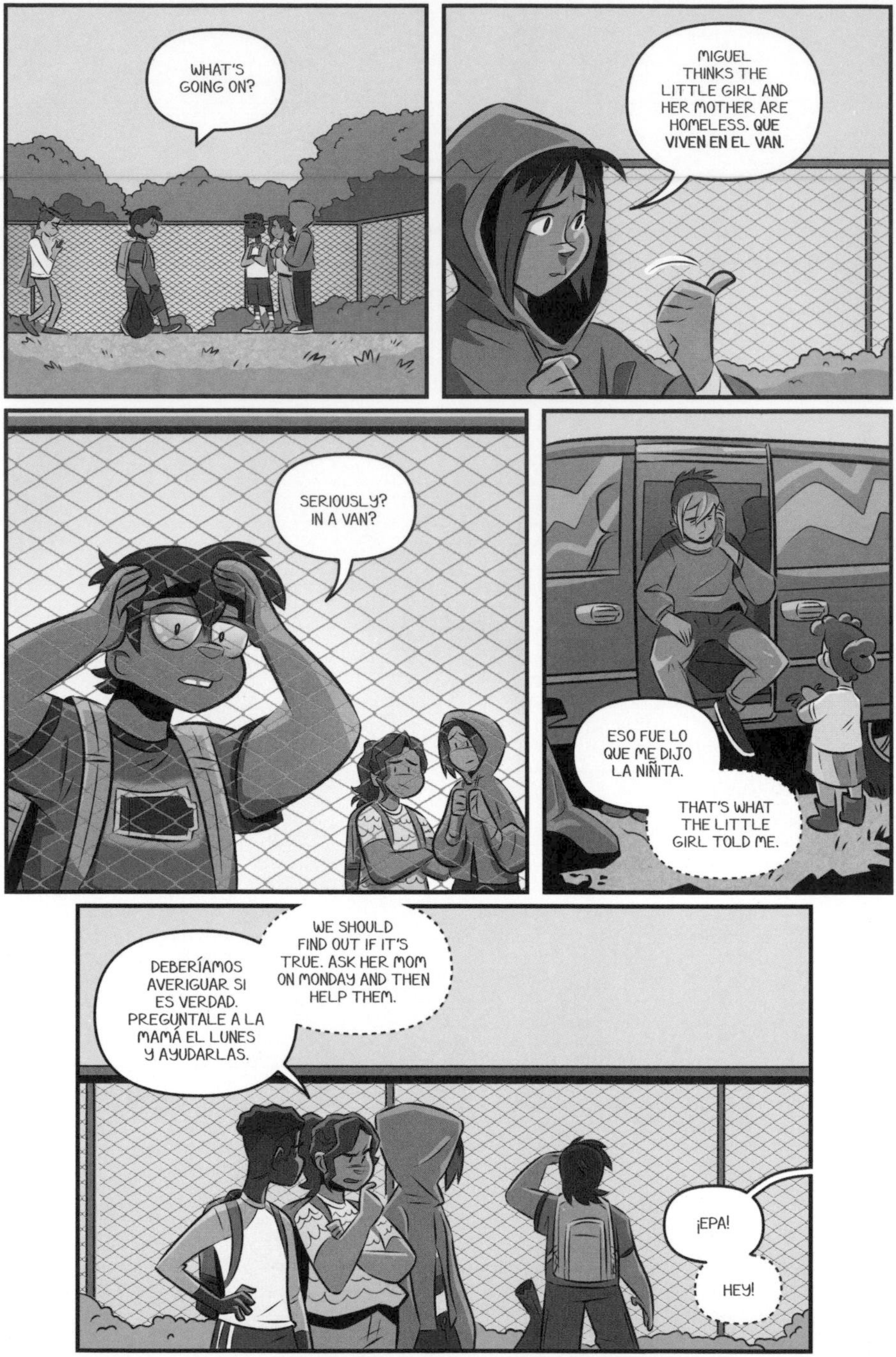
WHAT'S GOING ON?
MIGUEL THINKS THE LITTLE GIRL AND HER MOTHER ARE HOMELESS. QUE VIVEN EN EL VAN.
SERIOUSLY? IN A VAN?
ESO FUE LO QUE ME DIJO LA NIÑITA.
THAT'S WHAT THE LITTLE GIRL TOLD ME.
DEBERÍAMOS AVERIGUAR SI ES VERDAD. PREGUNTALE A LA MAMÁ EL LUNES Y AYUDARLAS.
WE SHOULD FIND OUT IF IT'S TRUE. ASK HER MOM ON MONDAY AND THEN HELP THEM.
¡EPA!
HEY!

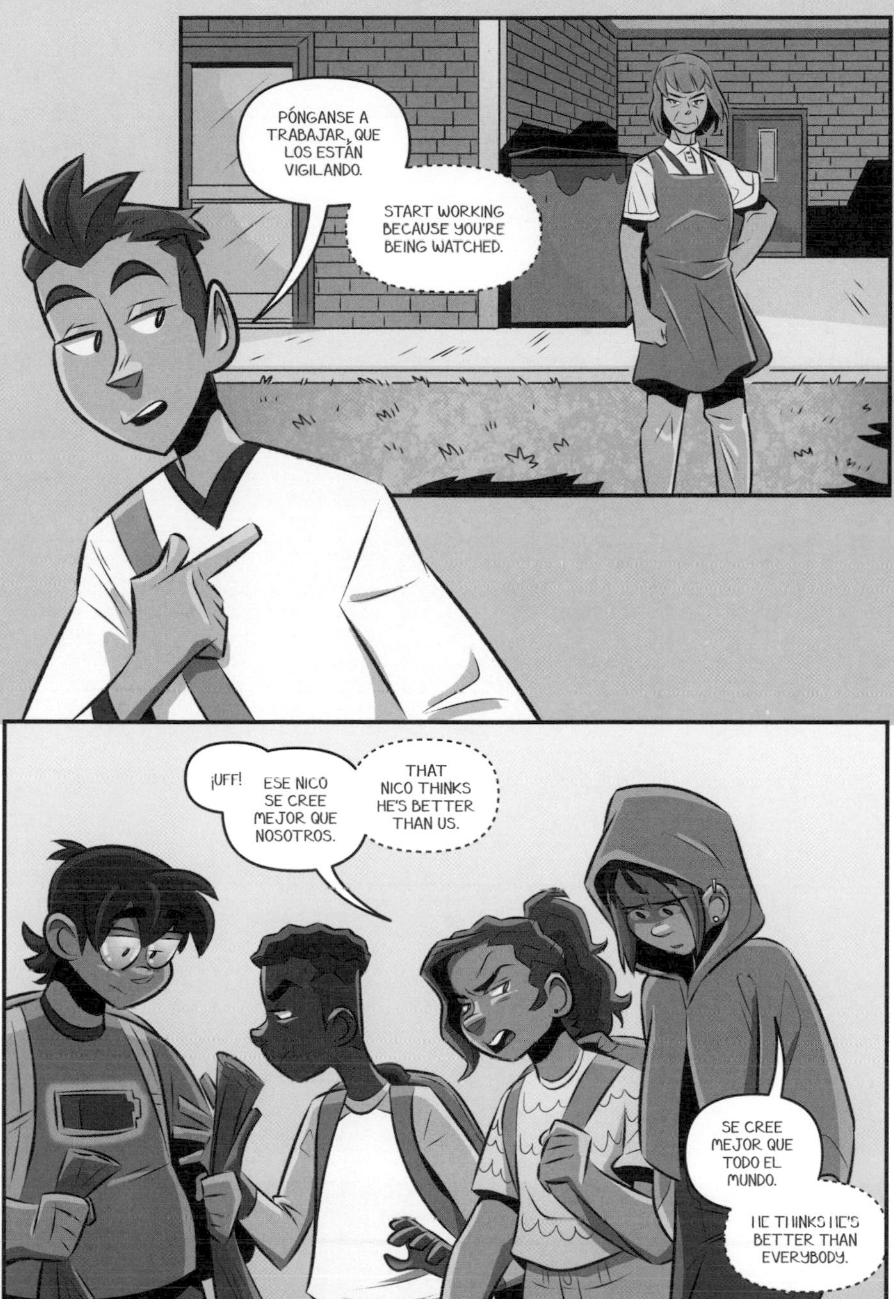
PÓNGANSE A TRABAJAR, QUE LOS ESTÁN VIGILANDO.
START WORKING BECAUSE YOU'RE BEING WATCHED.
¡UFF!
ESE NICO SE CREE MEJOR QUE NOSOTROS.
THAT NICO THINKS HE'S BETTER THAN US.
SE CREE MEJOR QUE TODO EL MUNDO.
HE THINKS HE'S BETTER THAN EVERYBODY.

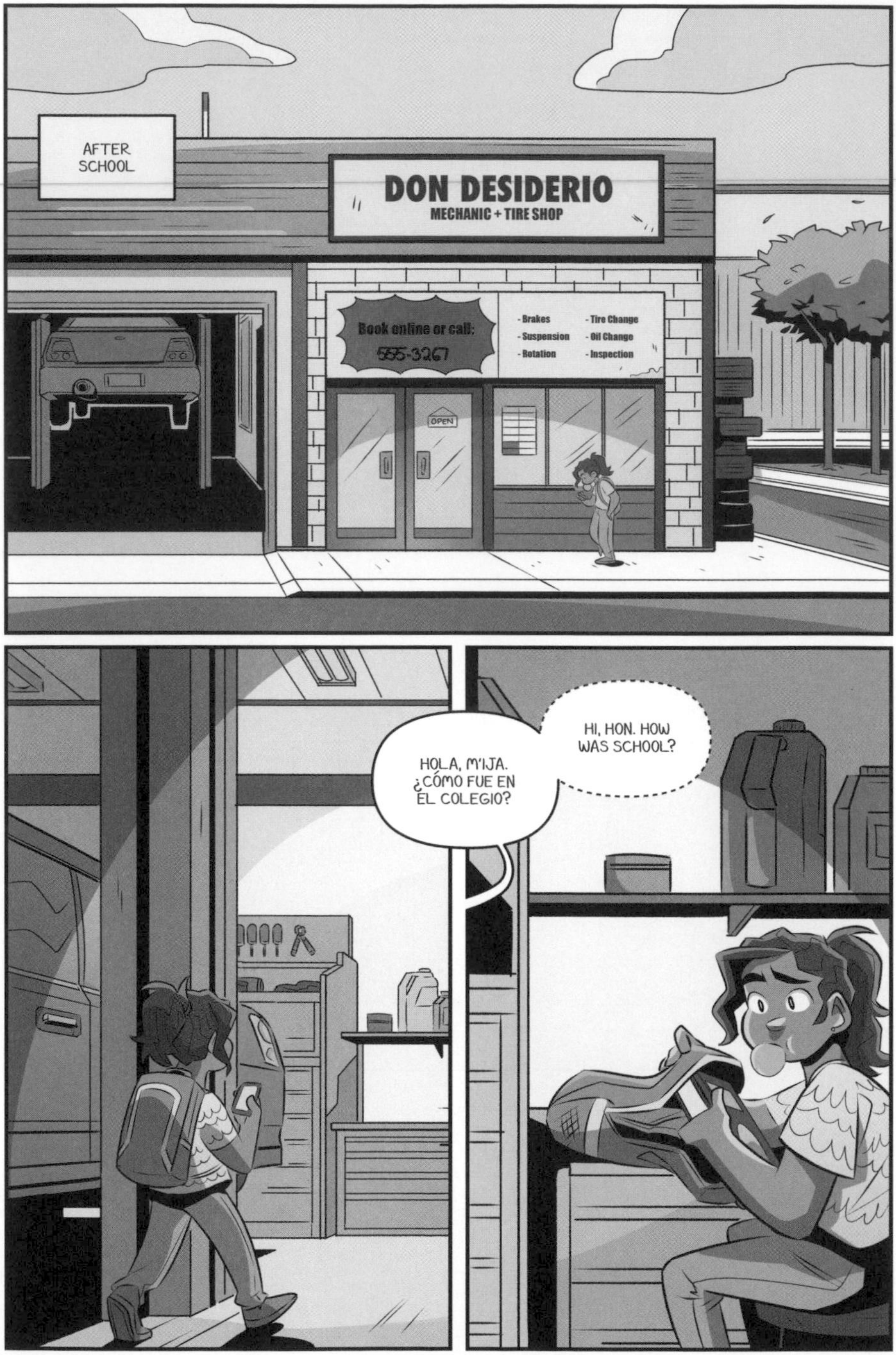
AFTER SCHOOL
DON DESIDERIO
MECHANIC + TIRE SHOP
Book online or call:
555-3267
- Brakes
- Suspension
- Rotation
- Tire Change
- Oil Change
- Inspection
OPEN
HOLA, M'IJA. ¿CÓMO FUE EN EL COLEGIO?
HI, HON. HOW WAS SCHOOL?

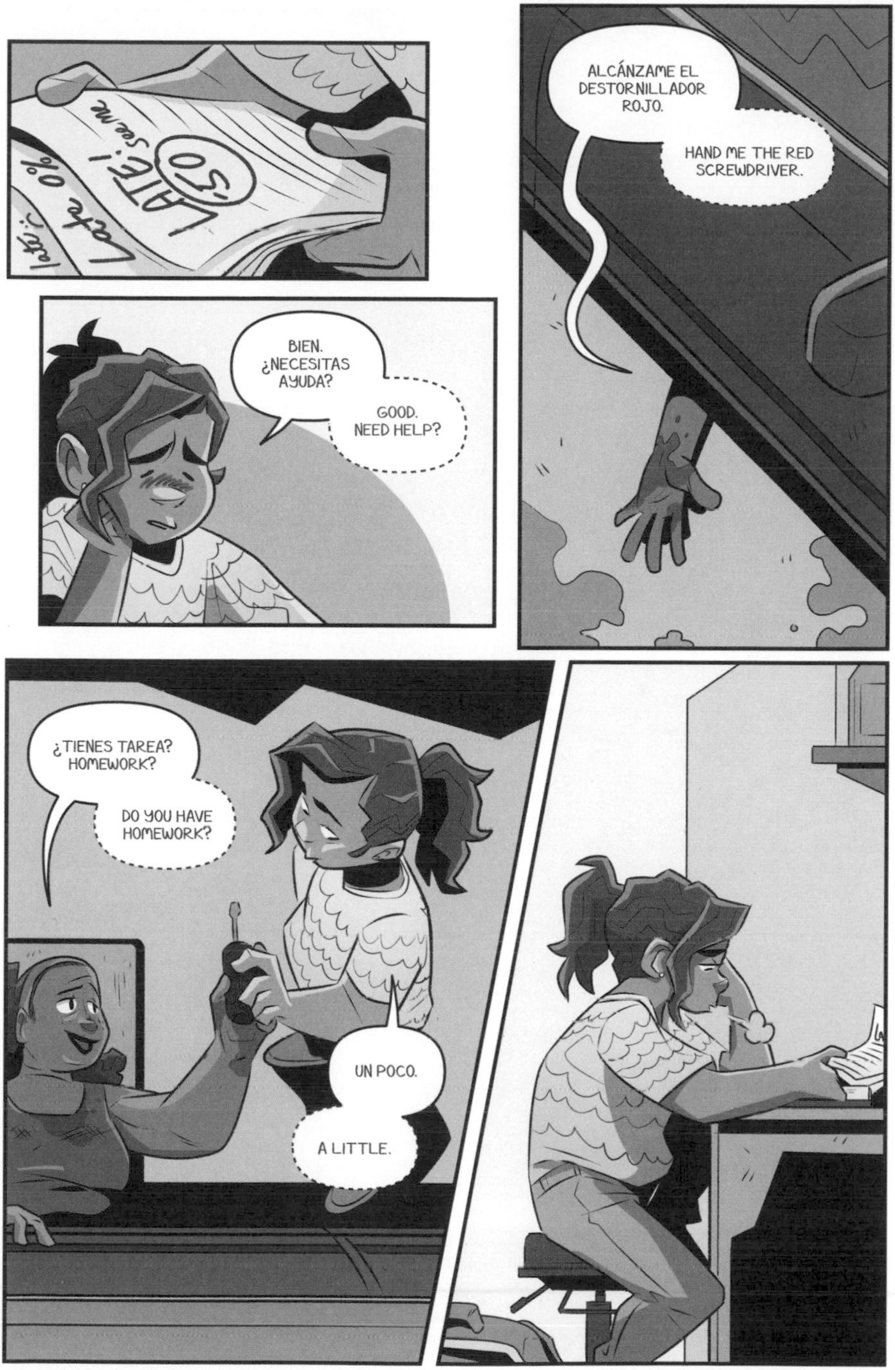
LATE!
50
see me
Late 0%
BIEN. ¿NECESITAS AYUDA?
GOOD. NEED HELP?
ALCÁNZAME EL DESTORNILLADOR ROJO.
HAND ME THE RED SCREWDRIVER.
¿TIENES TAREA? HOMEWORK?
DO YOU HAVE HOMEWORK?
UN POCO.
A LITTLE.

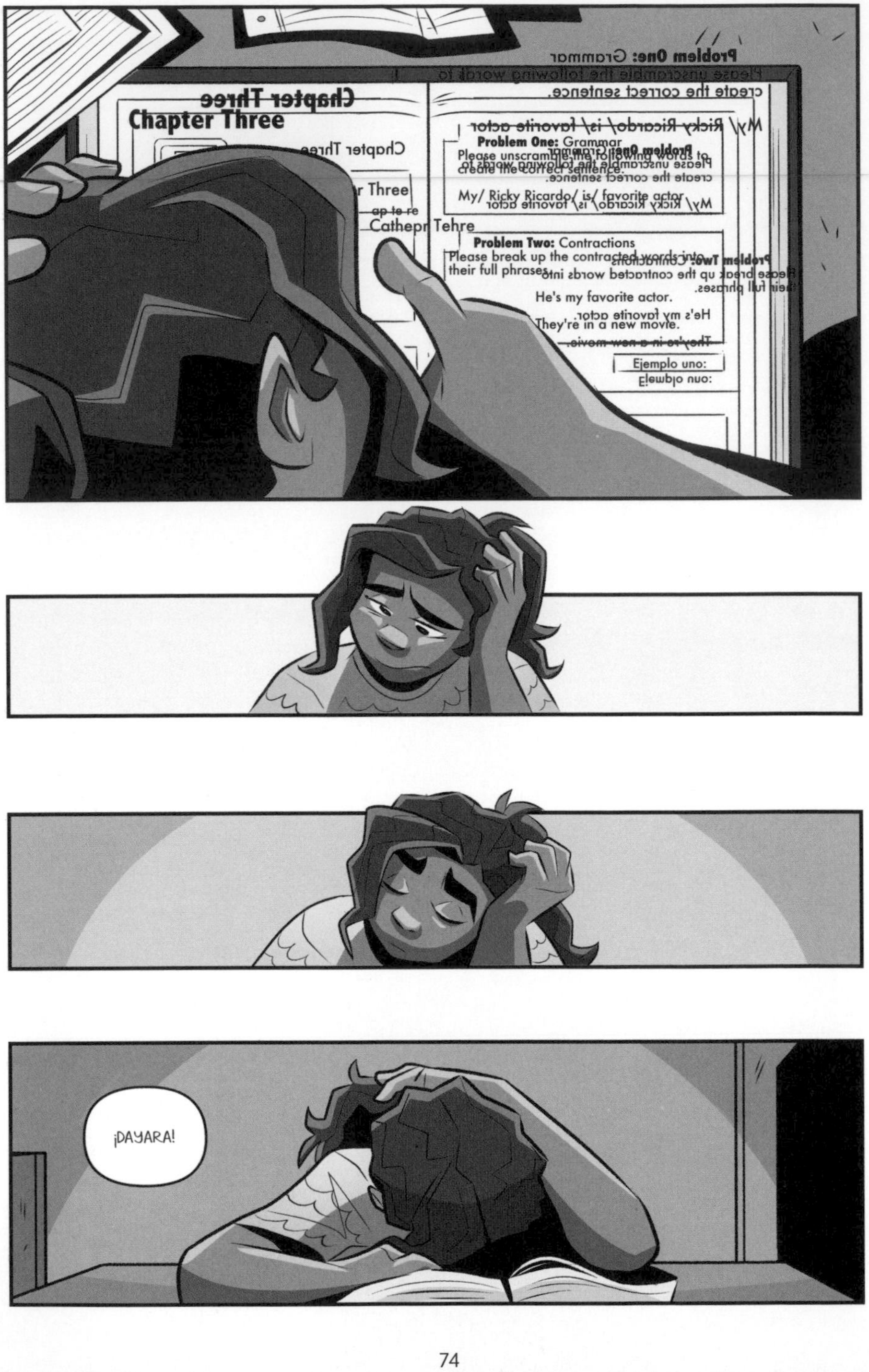
Chapter Three
Chapter Three
r Three
Cathepr Tehre
Problem One: Grammar
Please unscramble the following words to create the correct sentence.
My/ Ricky Ricardo/ is/ favorite actor
Problem Two: Contractions
Please break up the contracted words into their full phrases.
He's my favorite actor.
They're in a new movie.
Ejemplo uno:
¡DAYARA!

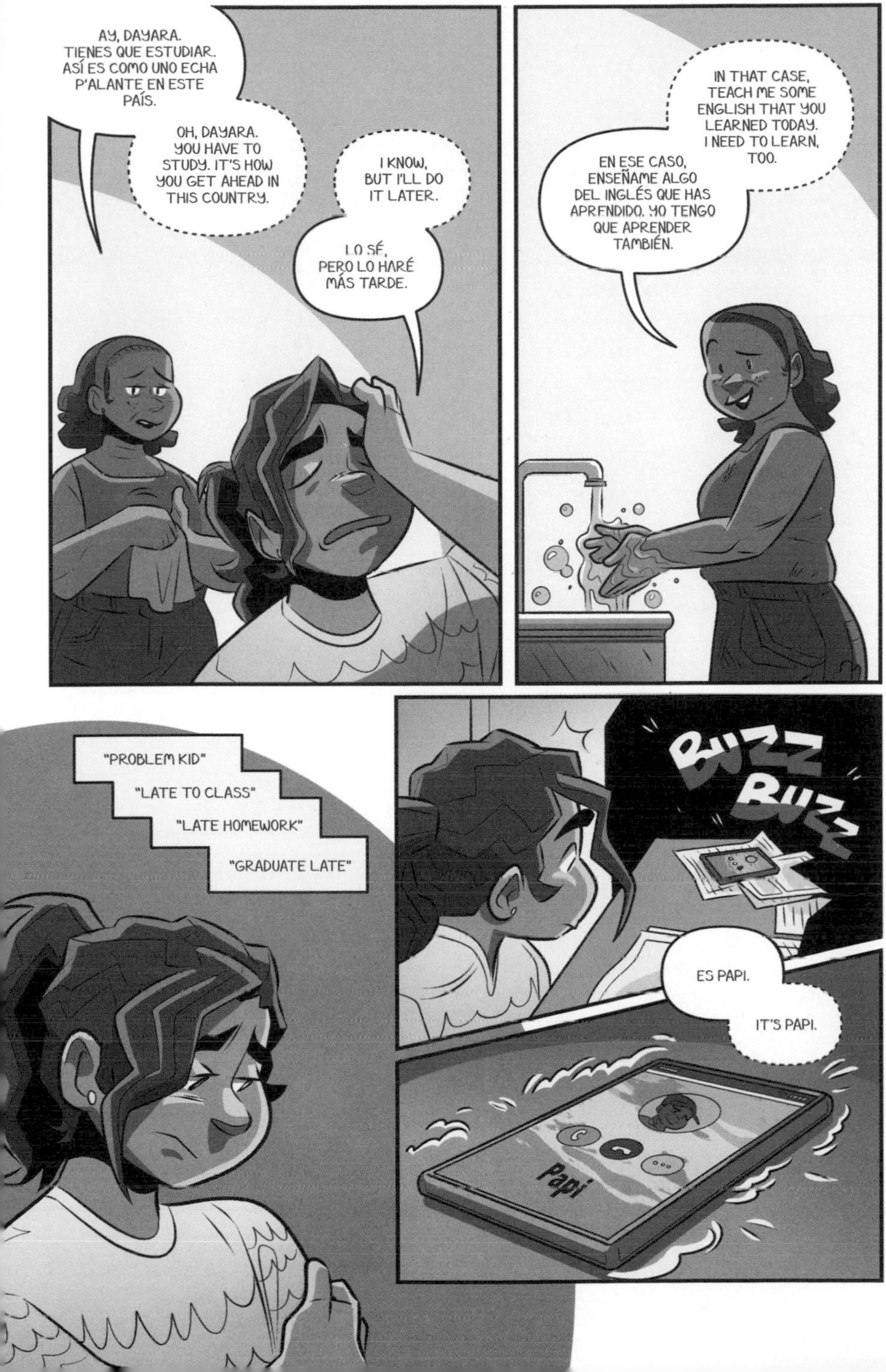
AY, DAYARA.
TIENES QUE ESTUDIAR.
ASÍ ES COMO UNO ECHA
P'ALANTE EN ESTE
PAÍS.
OH, DAYARA. YOU HAVE TO STUDY. IT'S HOW YOU GET AHEAD IN THIS COUNTRY.
I KNOW, BUT I'LL DO IT LATER.
LO SÉ, PERO LO HARÉ MÁS TARDE.
IN THAT CASE, TEACH ME SOME ENGLISH THAT YOU LEARNED TODAY. I NEED TO LEARN, TOO.
EN ESE CASO, ENSEÑAME ALGO DEL INGLÉS QUE HAS APRENDIDO. YO TENGO QUE APRENDER TAMBIÉN.
"PROBLEM KID"
"LATE TO CLASS"
"LATE HOMEWORK"
"GRADUATE LATE"
BUZZ
BUZZ
ES PAPI.
IT'S PAPI.
Papi

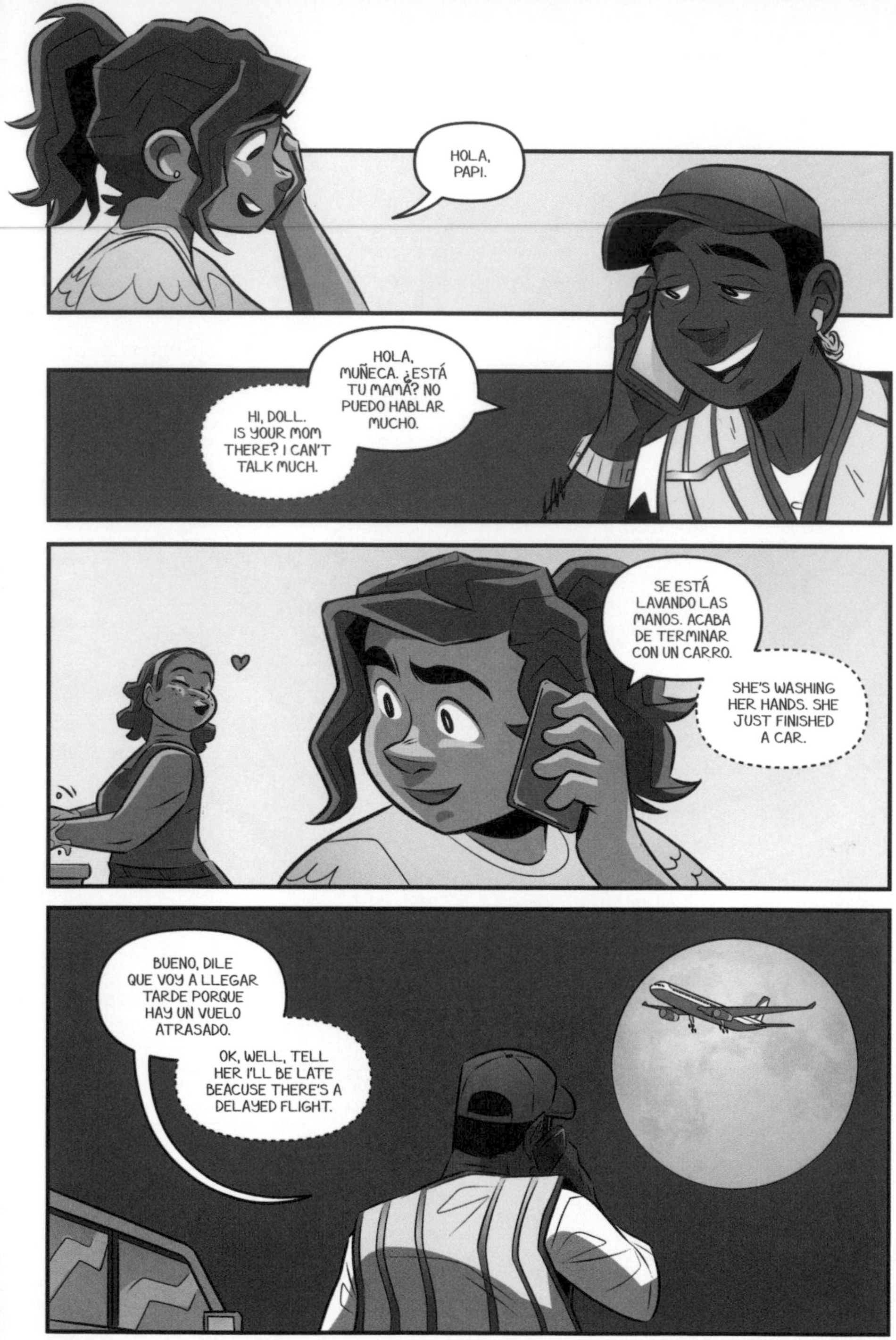

HOLA, PAPI.
HOLA, MUÑECA. ¿ESTÁ TU MAMÁ? NO PUEDO HABLAR MUCHO.
HI, DOLL. IS YOUR MOM THERE? I CAN'T TALK MUCH.
SE ESTÁ LAVANDO LAS MANOS. ACABA DE TERMINAR CON UN CARRO.
SHE'S WASHING HER HANDS. SHE JUST FINISHED A CAR.
BUENO, DILE QUE VOY A LLEGAR TARDE PORQUE HAY UN VUELO ATRASADO.
OK, WELL, TELL HER I'LL BE LATE BEACUSE THERE'S A DELAYED FLIGHT.

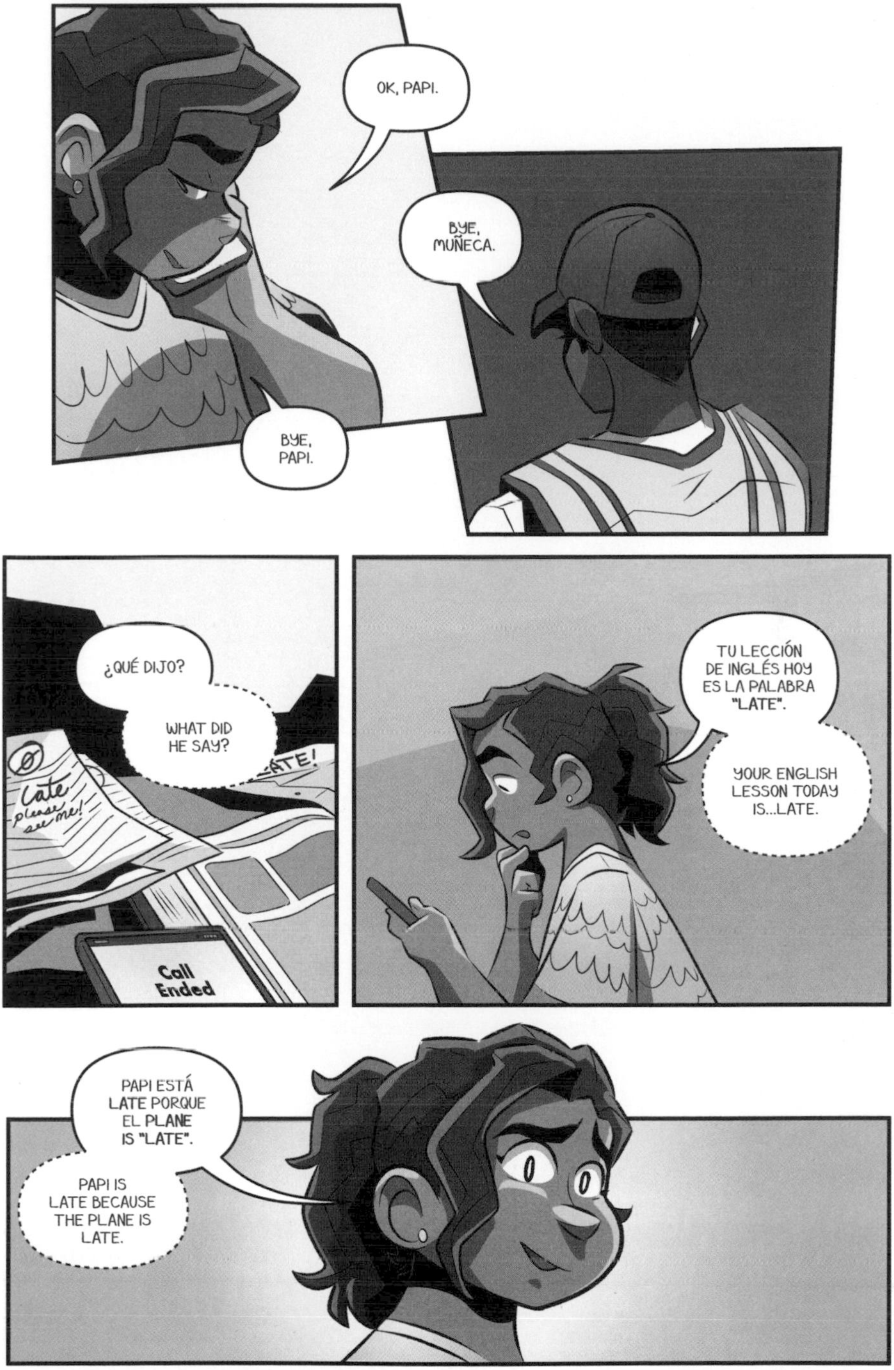
OK, PAPI.
BYE, MUÑECA.
BYE, PAPI.
¿QUÉ DIJO?
WHAT DID HE SAY?
LATE please see me!
LATE!
Call Ended
TU LECCIÓN DE INGLÉS HOY ES LA PALABRA "LATE".
YOUR ENGLISH LESSON TODAY IS...LATE.
PAPI ESTÁ LATE PORQUE EL PLANE IS "LATE".
PAPI IS LATE BECAUSE THE PLANE IS LATE.

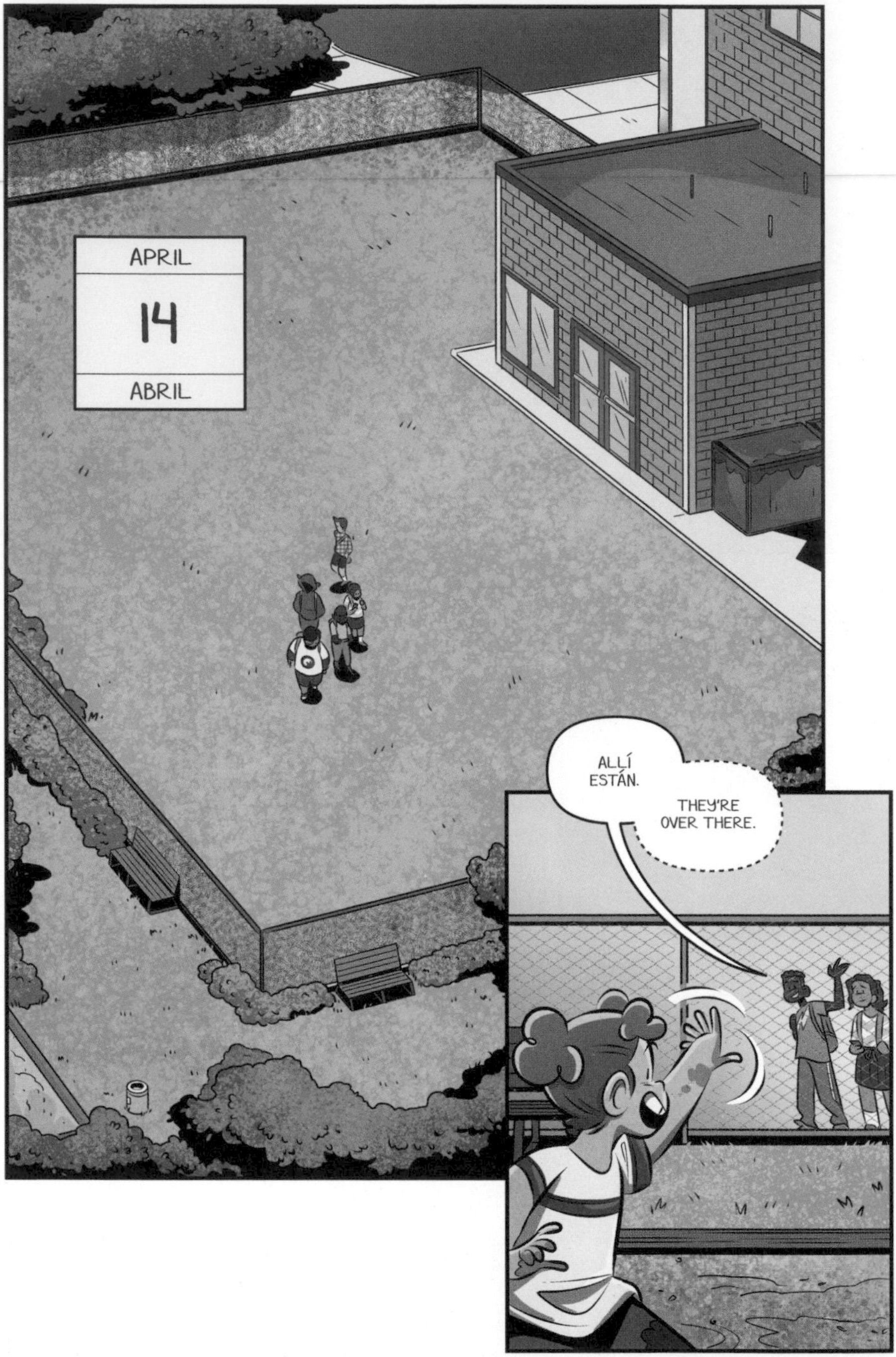
APRIL
14
ABRIL
ALLÍ ESTÁN.
THEY'RE OVER THERE.

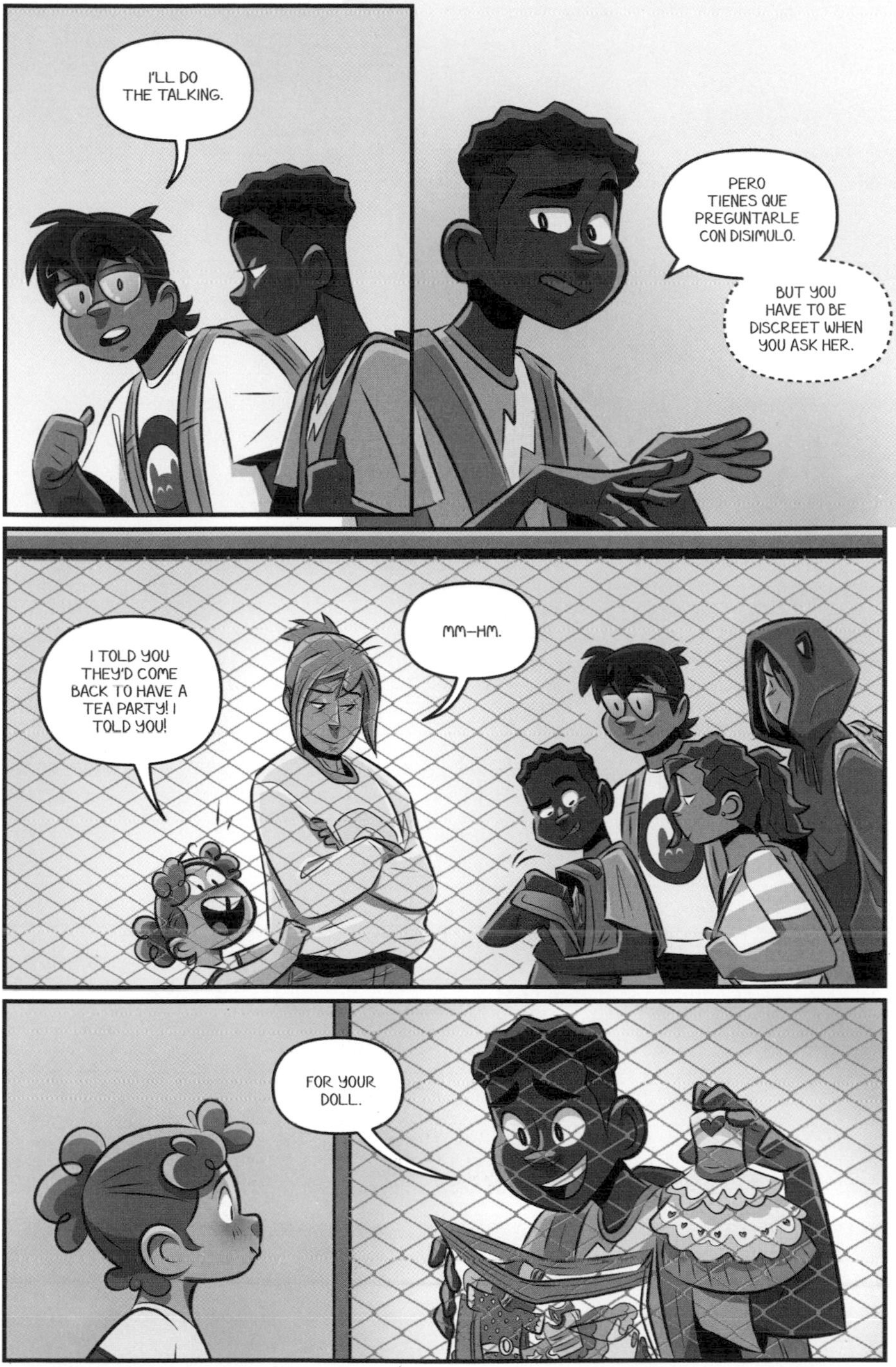
I'LL DO THE TALKING.
PERO TIENES QUE PREGUNTARLE CON DISIMULO.
BUT YOU HAVE TO BE DISCREET WHEN YOU ASK HER.
I TOLD YOU THEY'D COME BACK TO HAVE A TEA PARTY! I TOLD YOU!
MM-HM.
FOR YOUR DOLL.

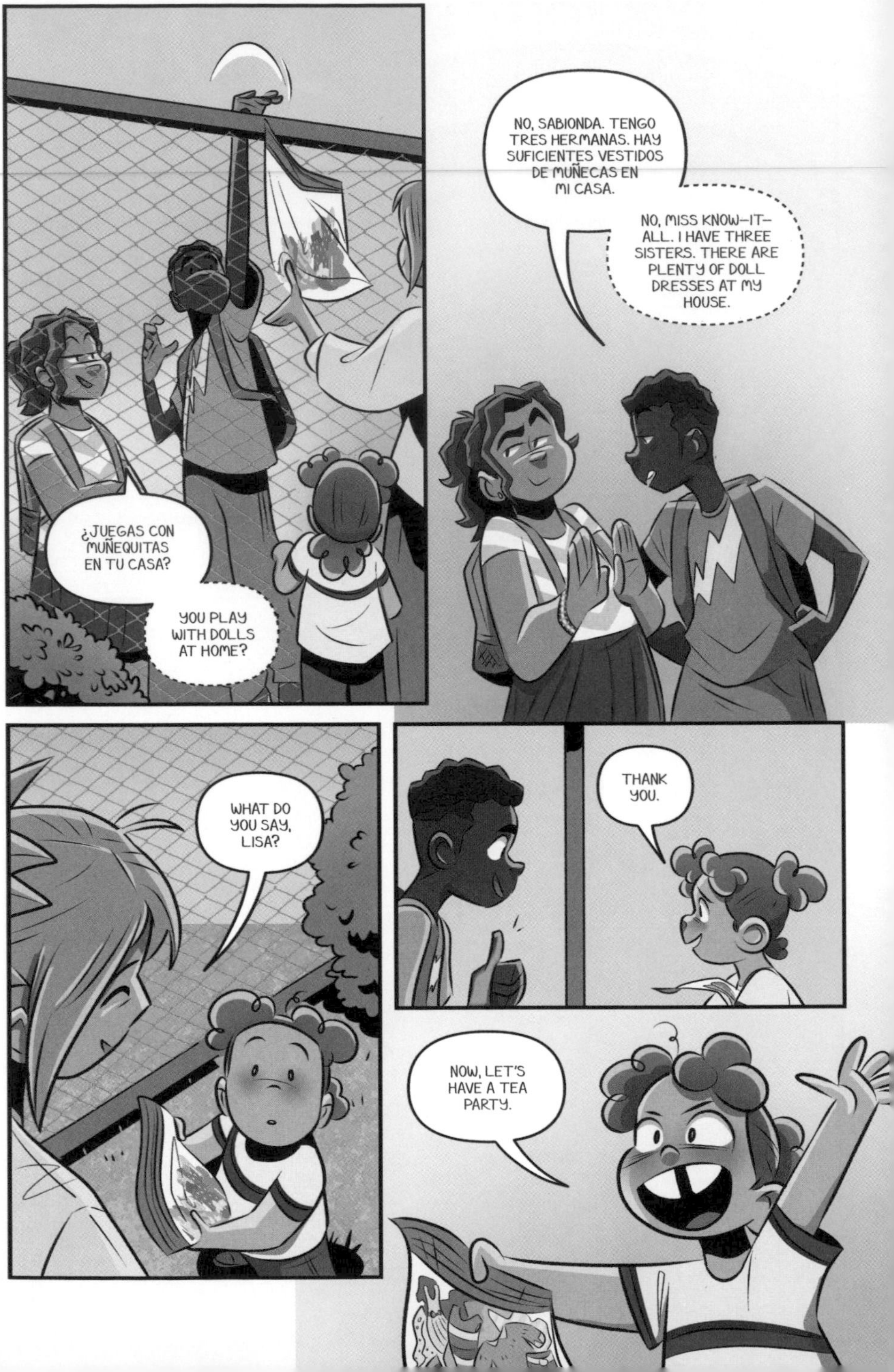
¿JUEGAS CON MUÑEQUITAS EN TU CASA?
YOU PLAY WITH DOLLS AT HOME?
NO, SABIONDA. TENGO TRES HERMANAS. HAY SUFICIENTES VESTIDOS DE MUÑECAS EN MI CASA.
NO, MISS KNOW-IT-ALL. I HAVE THREE SISTERS. THERE ARE PLENTY OF DOLL DRESSES AT MY HOUSE.
WHAT DO YOU SAY, LISA?
THANK YOU.
NOW, LET'S HAVE A TEA PARTY.

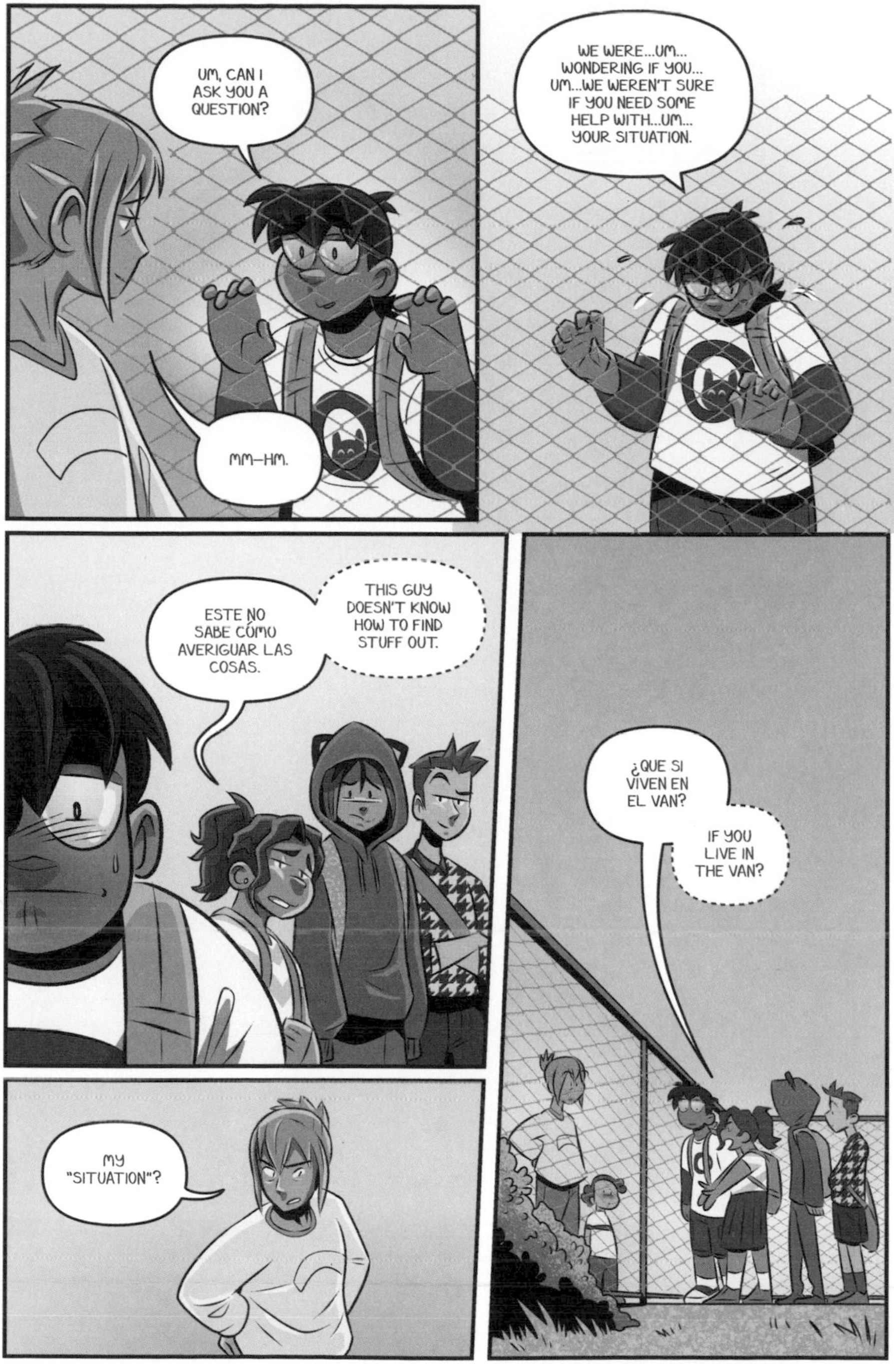
UM, CAN I ASK YOU A QUESTION?
MM-HM.
WE WERE...UM... WONDERING IF YOU... UM...WE WEREN'T SURE IF YOU NEED SOME HELP WITH...UM... YOUR SITUATION.
ESTE NO SABE CÓMO AVERIGUAR LAS COSAS.
THIS GUY DOESN'T KNOW HOW TO FIND STUFF OUT.
MY "SITUATION"?
¿QUE SI VIVEN EN EL VAN?
IF YOU LIVE IN THE VAN?

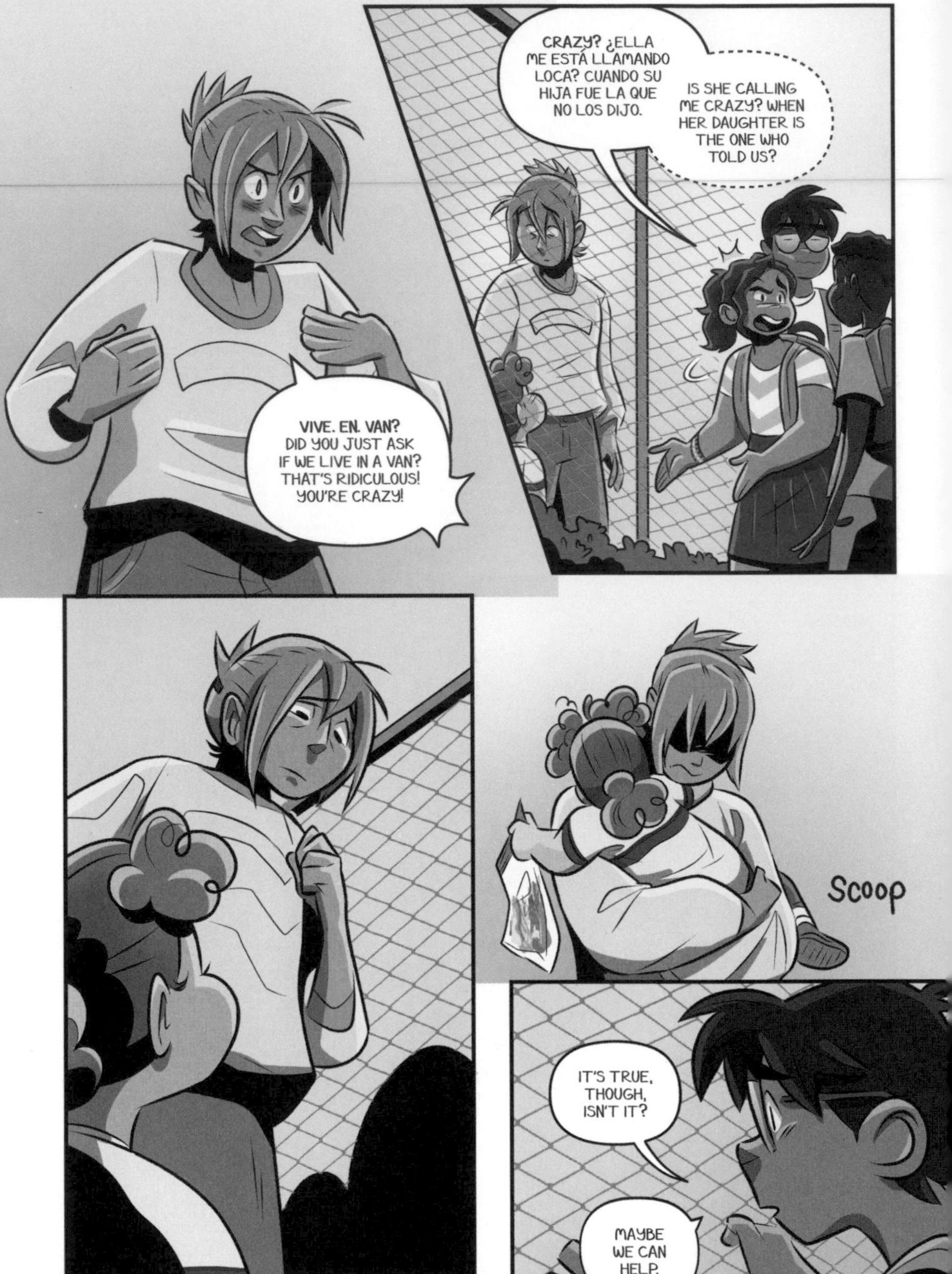
CRAZY? ¿ELLA ME ESTÁ LLAMANDO LOCA? CUANDO SU HIJA FUE LA QUE NO LOS DIJO.
IS SHE CALLING ME CRAZY? WHEN HER DAUGHTER IS THE ONE WHO TOLD US?
VIVE. EN. VAN? DID YOU JUST ASK IF WE LIVE IN A VAN? THAT'S RIDICULOUS! YOU'RE CRAZY!
SCOOP
IT'S TRUE, THOUGH, ISN'T IT?
MAYBE WE CAN HELP.

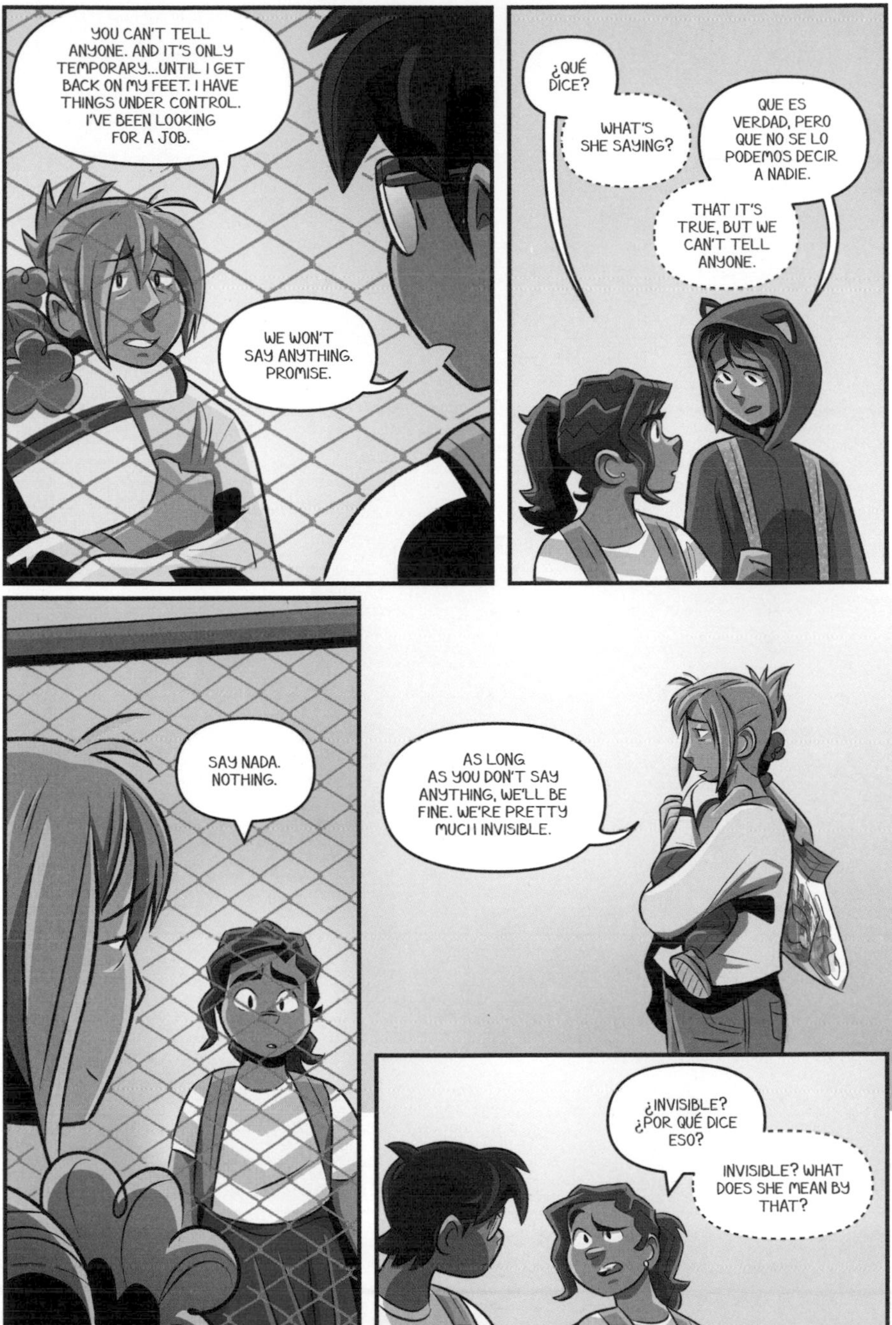
YOU CAN'T TELL ANYONE. AND IT'S ONLY TEMPORARY...UNTIL I GET BACK ON MY FEET. I HAVE THINGS UNDER CONTROL. I'VE BEEN LOOKING FOR A JOB.
WE WON'T SAY ANYTHING. PROMISE.
¿QUÉ DICE?
WHAT'S SHE SAYING?
QUE ES VERDAD, PERO QUE NO SE LO PODEMOS DECIR A NADIE.
THAT IT'S TRUE, BUT WE CAN'T TELL ANYONE.
SAY NADA. NOTHING.
AS LONG AS YOU DON'T SAY ANYTHING, WE'LL BE FINE. WE'RE PRETTY MUCH INVISIBLE.
¿INVISIBLE? ¿POR QUÉ DICE ESO?
INVISIBLE? WHAT DOES SHE MEAN BY THAT?

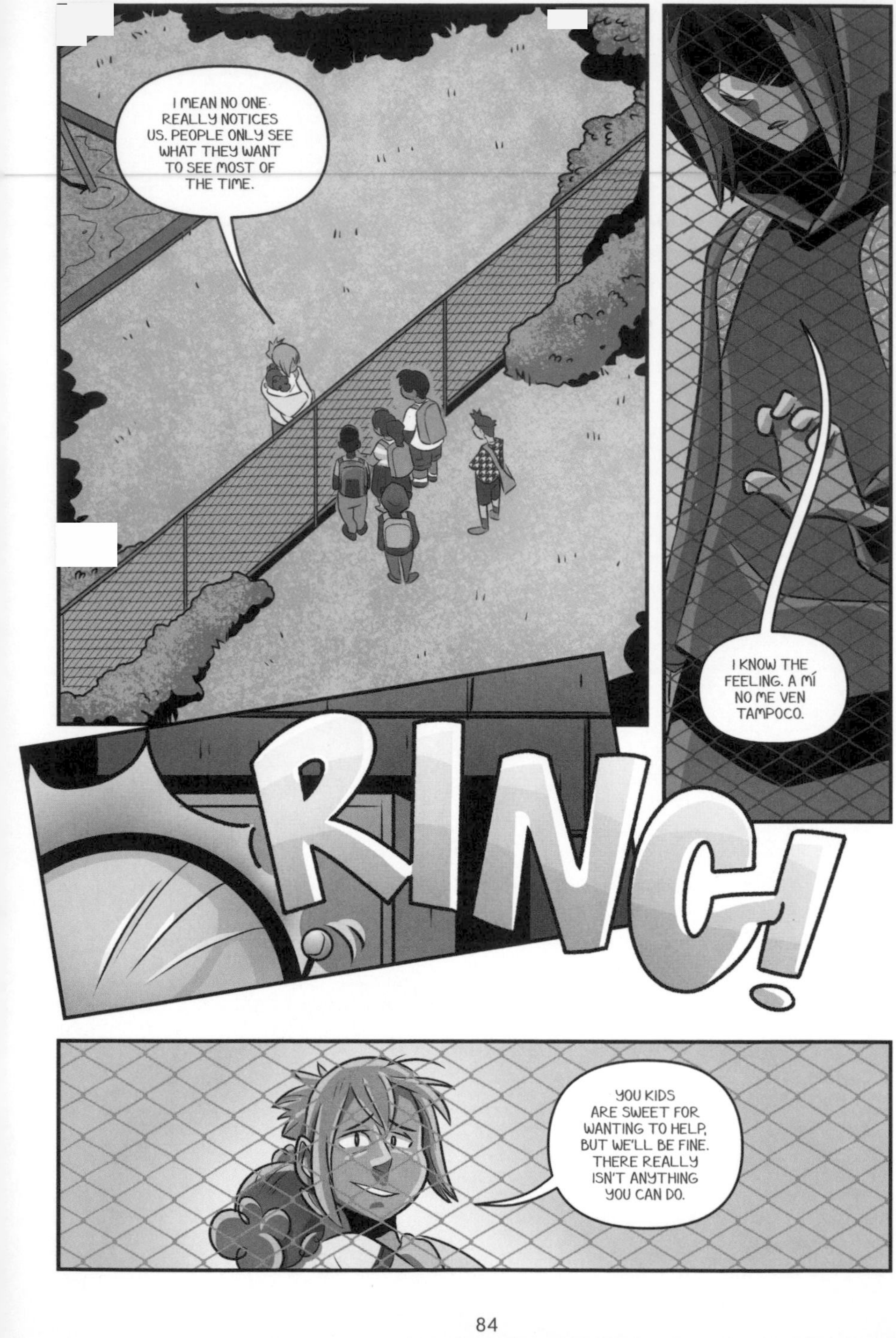
I MEAN NO ONE REALLY NOTICES US. PEOPLE ONLY SEE WHAT THEY WANT TO SEE MOST OF THE TIME.
I KNOW THE FEELING. A MÍ NO ME VEN TAMPOCO.
RING!
YOU KIDS ARE SWEET FOR WANTING TO HELP, BUT WE'LL BE FINE. THERE REALLY ISN'T ANYTHING YOU CAN DO.

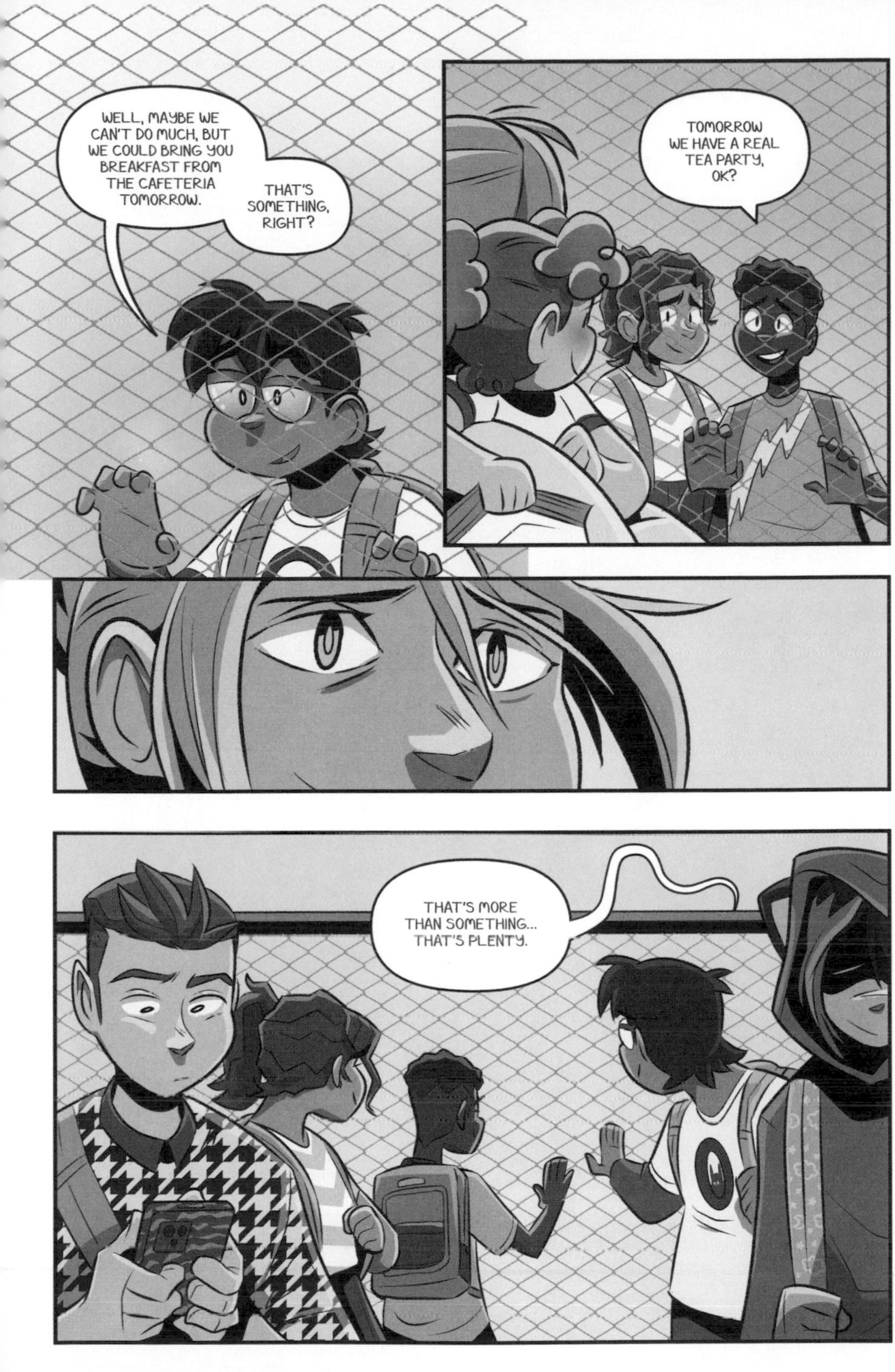
WELL, MAYBE WE CAN'T DO MUCH, BUT WE COULD BRING YOU BREAKFAST FROM THE CAFETERIA TOMORROW.
THAT'S SOMETHING, RIGHT?
TOMORROW WE HAVE A REAL TEA PARTY, OK?
THAT'S MORE THAN SOMETHING... THAT'S PLENTY.

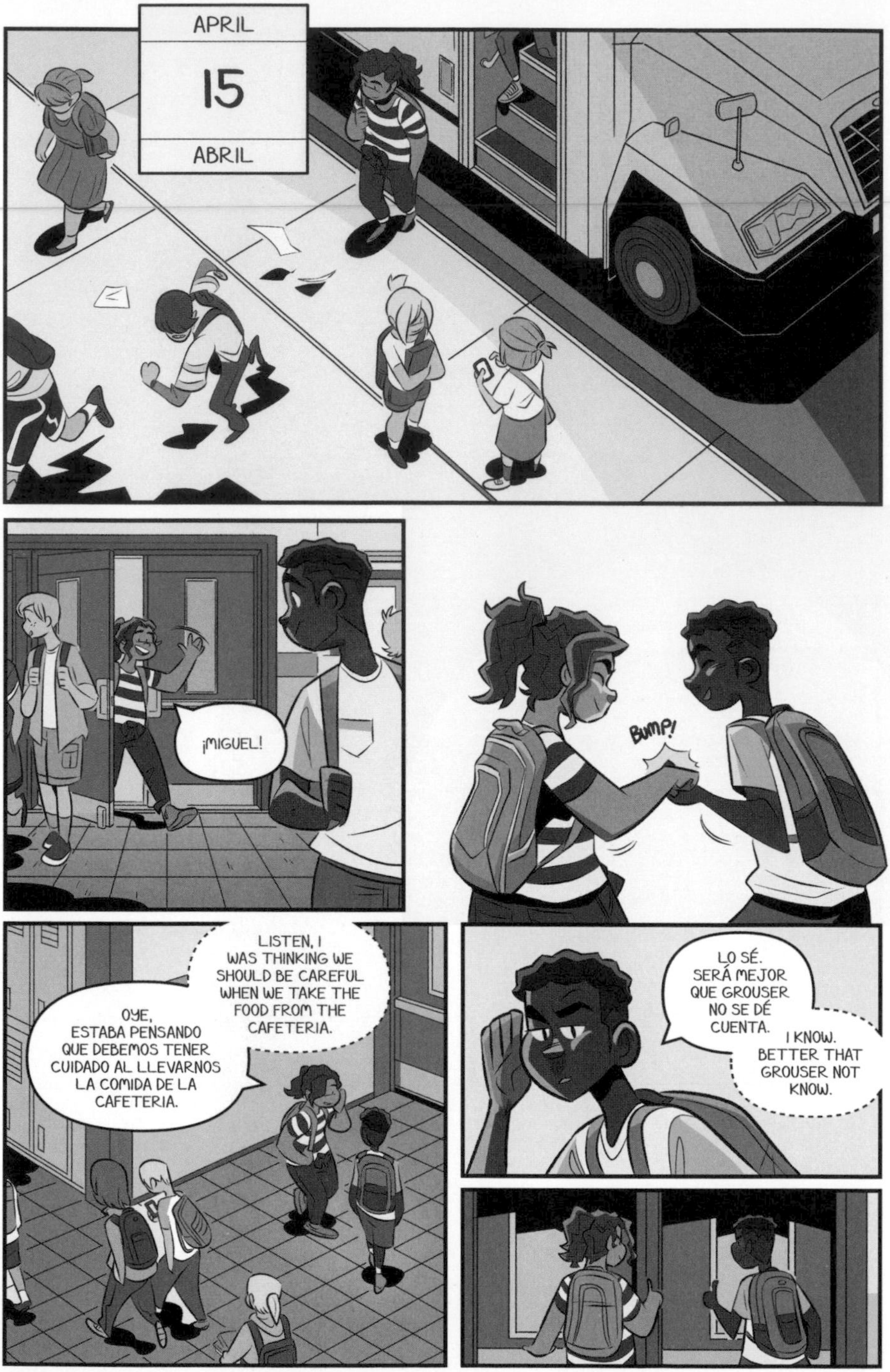
APRIL
15
ABRIL
¡MIGUEL!
BUMP!
OYE, ESTABA PENSANDO QUE DEBEMOS TENER CUIDADO AL LLEVARNOS LA COMIDA DE LA CAFETERIA.
LISTEN, I WAS THINKING WE SHOULD BE CAREFUL WHEN WE TAKE THE FOOD FROM THE CAFETERIA.
LO SÉ. SERÁ MEJOR QUE GROUSER NO SE DÉ CUENTA.
I KNOW. BETTER THAT GROUSER NOT KNOW.

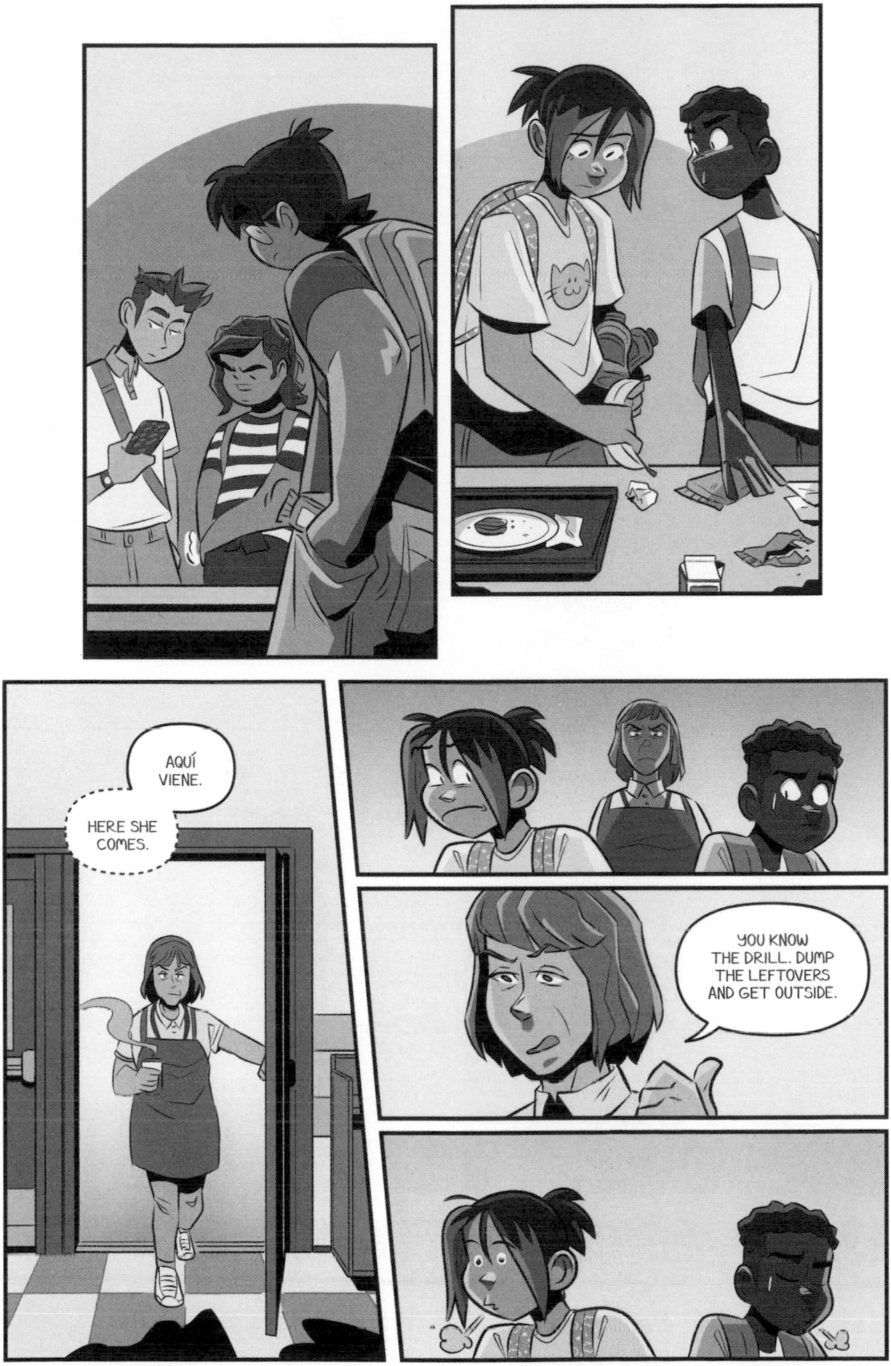
AQUÍ VIENE.
HERE SHE COMES.
YOU KNOW THE DRILL. DUMP THE LEFTOVERS AND GET OUTSIDE.

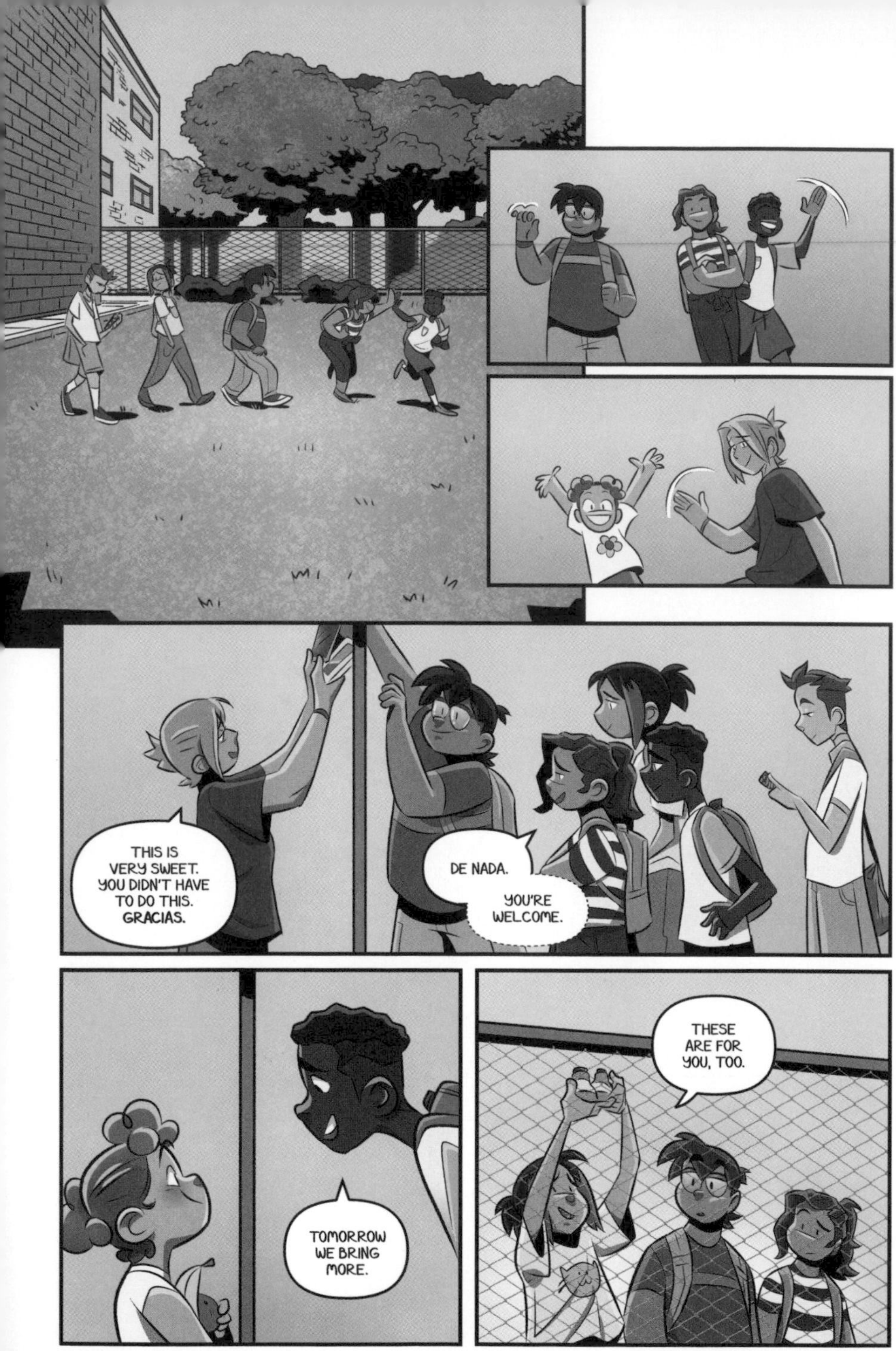
THIS IS VERY SWEET. YOU DIDN'T HAVE TO DO THIS. GRACIAS.
DE NADA.
YOU'RE WELCOME.
TOMORROW WE BRING MORE.
THESE ARE FOR YOU, TOO.

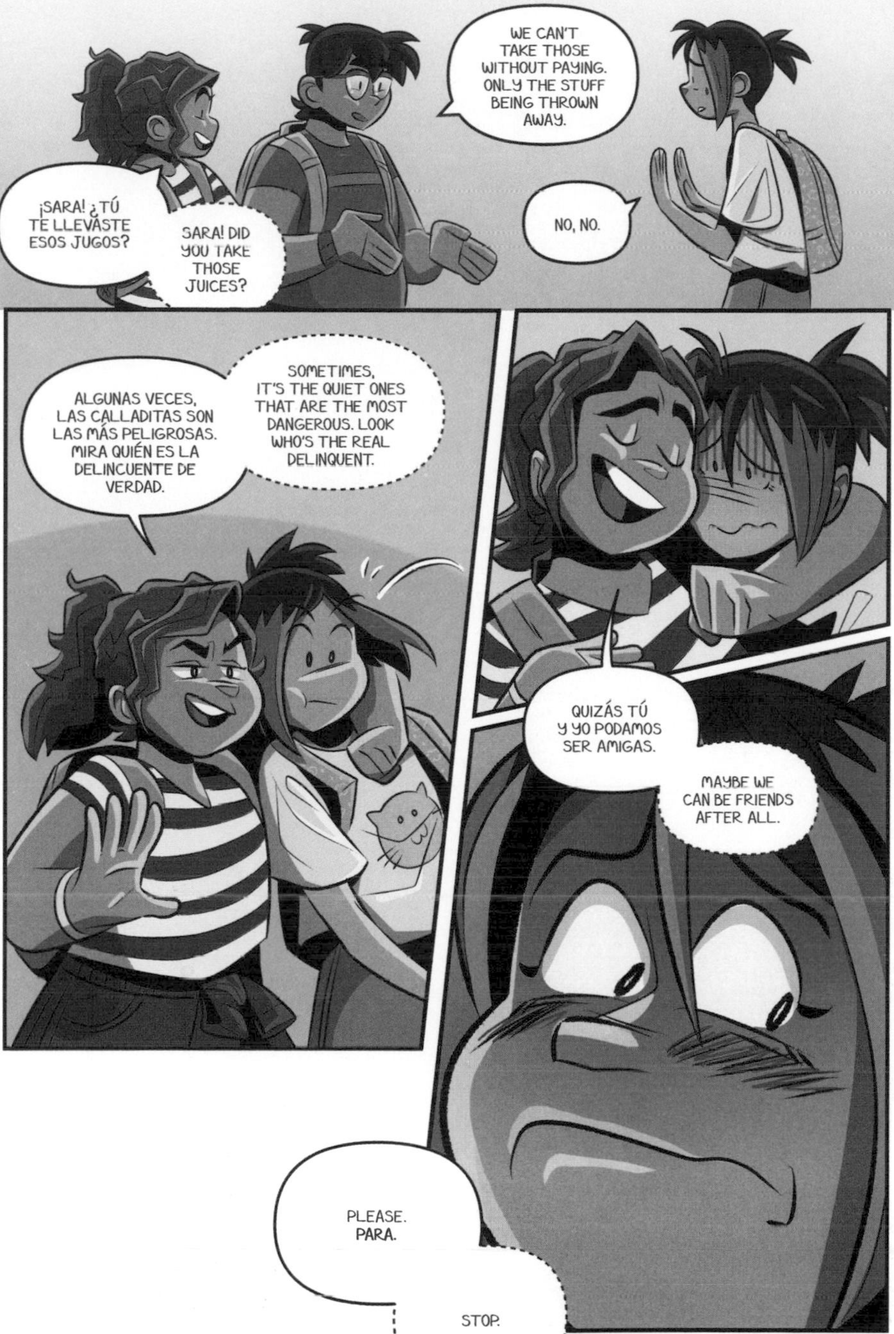
WE CAN'T TAKE THOSE WITHOUT PAYING. ONLY THE STUFF BEING THROWN AWAY.
¡SARA! ¿TÚ TE LLEVASTE ESOS JUGOS?
SARA! DID YOU TAKE THOSE JUICES?
NO, NO.
ALGUNAS VECES, LAS CALLADITAS SON LAS MÁS PELIGROSAS. MIRA QUIÉN ES LA DELINCUENTE DE VERDAD.
SOMETIMES, IT'S THE QUIET ONES THAT ARE THE MOST DANGEROUS. LOOK WHO'S THE REAL DELINQUENT.
QUIZÁS TÚ Y YO PODAMOS SER AMIGAS.
MAYBE WE CAN BE FRIENDS AFTER ALL.
PLEASE. **PARA.**
STOP.

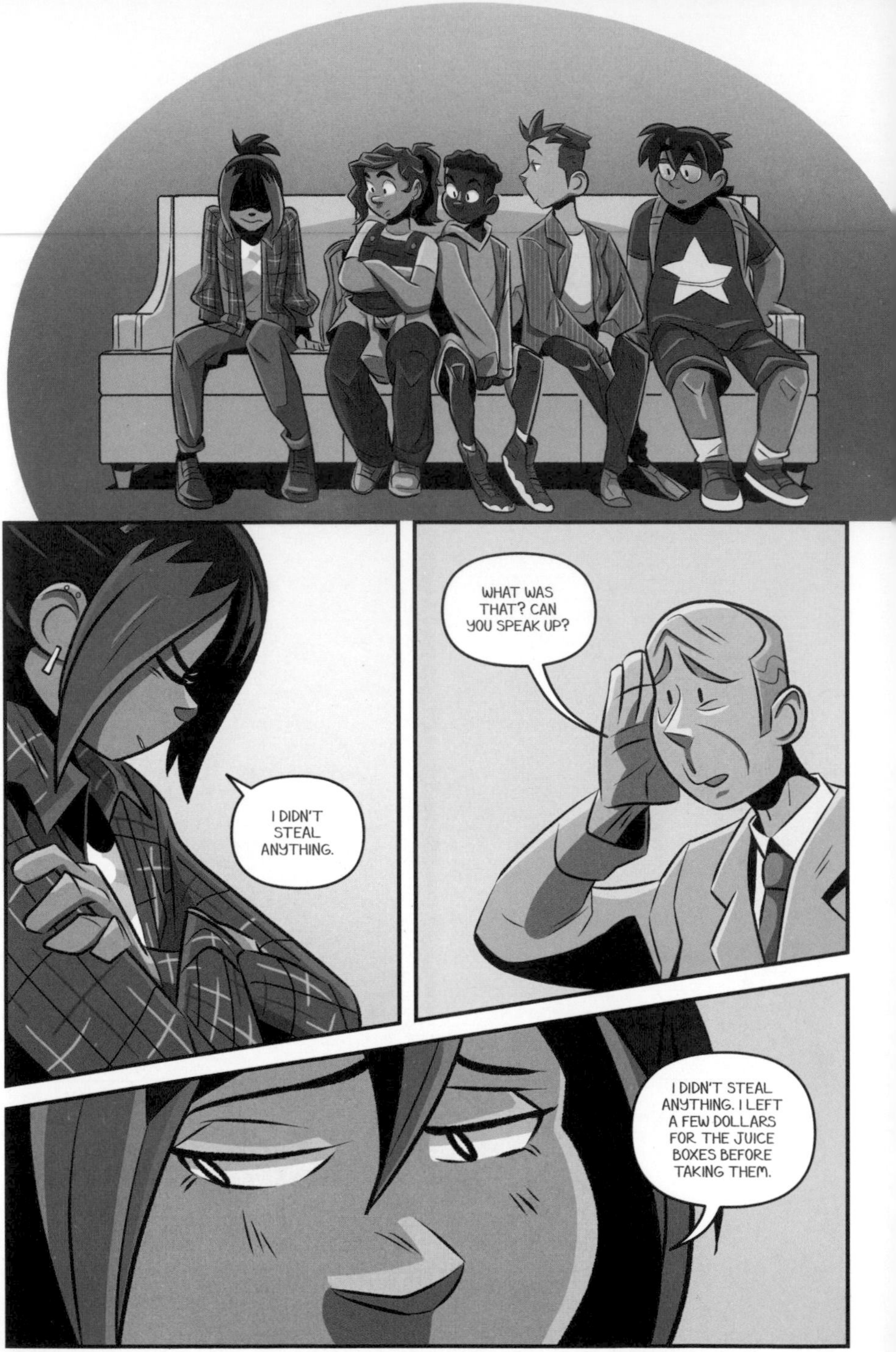
I DIDN'T
STEAL
ANYTHING.
WHAT WAS
THAT? CAN
YOU SPEAK UP?
I DIDN'T STEAL
ANYTHING. I LEFT
A FEW DOLLARS
FOR THE JUICE
BOXES BEFORE
TAKING THEM.

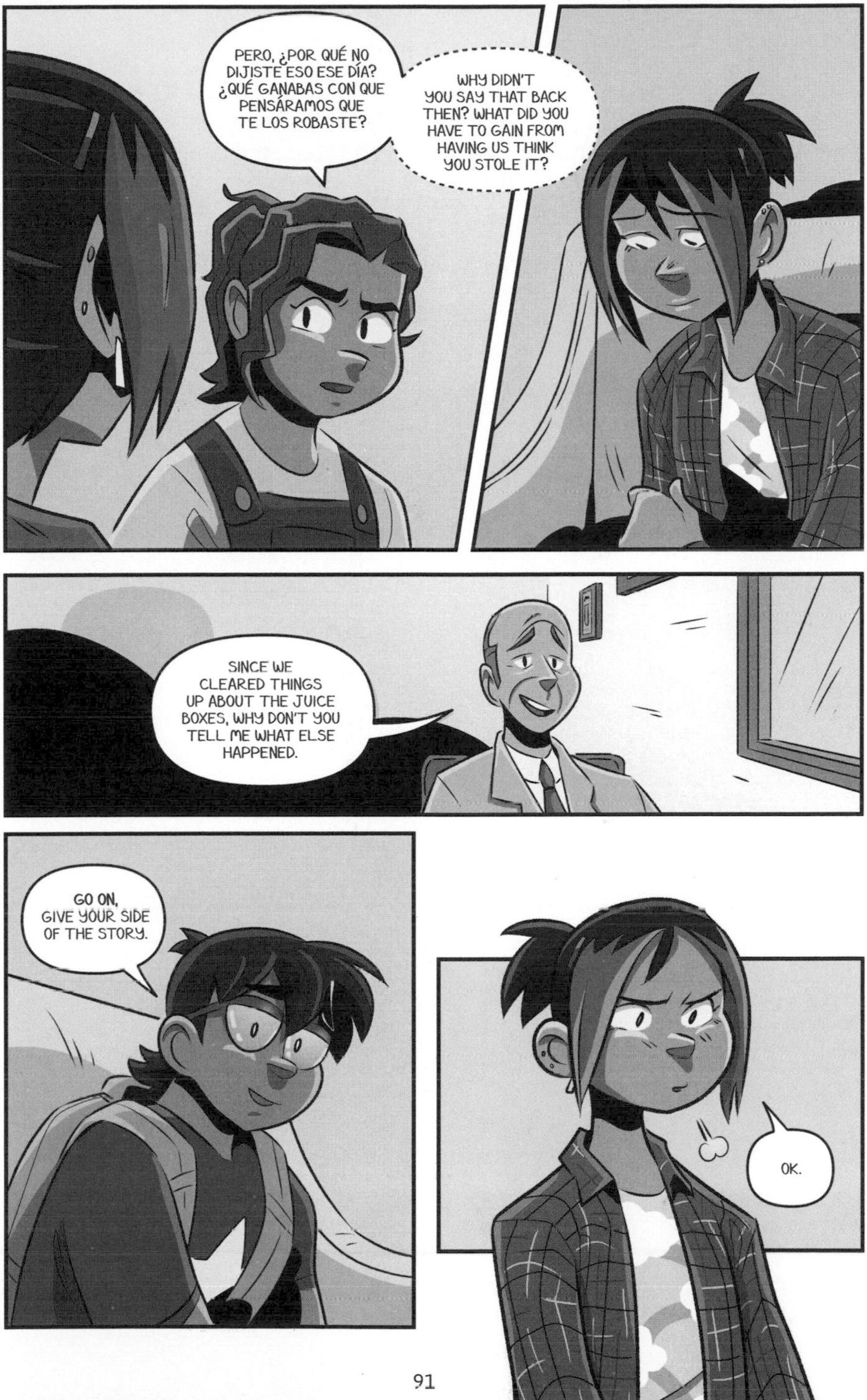
PERO, ¿POR QUÉ NO DIJISTE ESO ESE DÍA? ¿QUÉ GANABAS CON QUE PENSÁRAMOS QUE TE LOS ROBASTE?
WHY DIDN'T YOU SAY THAT BACK THEN? WHAT DID YOU HAVE TO GAIN FROM HAVING US THINK YOU STOLE IT?
SINCE WE CLEARED THINGS UP ABOUT THE JUICE BOXES, WHY DON'T YOU TELL ME WHAT ELSE HAPPENED.
GO ON, GIVE YOUR SIDE OF THE STORY.
OK.

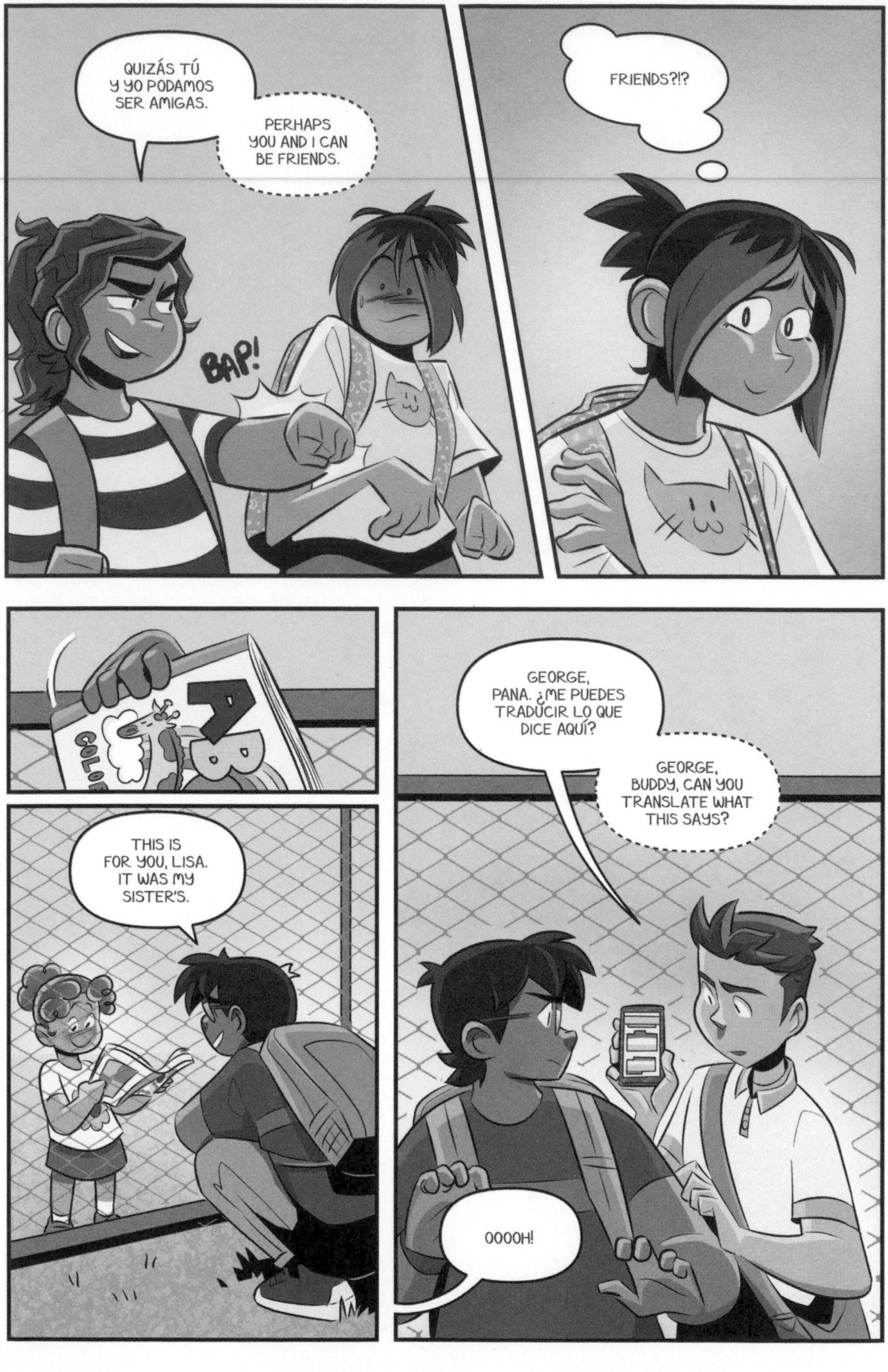
QUIZÁS TÚ Y YO PODAMOS SER AMIGAS.
PERHAPS YOU AND I CAN BE FRIENDS.
BAP!
FRIENDS?!?
THIS IS FOR YOU, LISA. IT WAS MY SISTER'S.
GEORGE, PANA. ¿ME PUEDES TRADUCIR LO QUE DICE AQUÍ?
GEORGE, BUDDY, CAN YOU TRANSLATE WHAT THIS SAYS?
OOOOH!

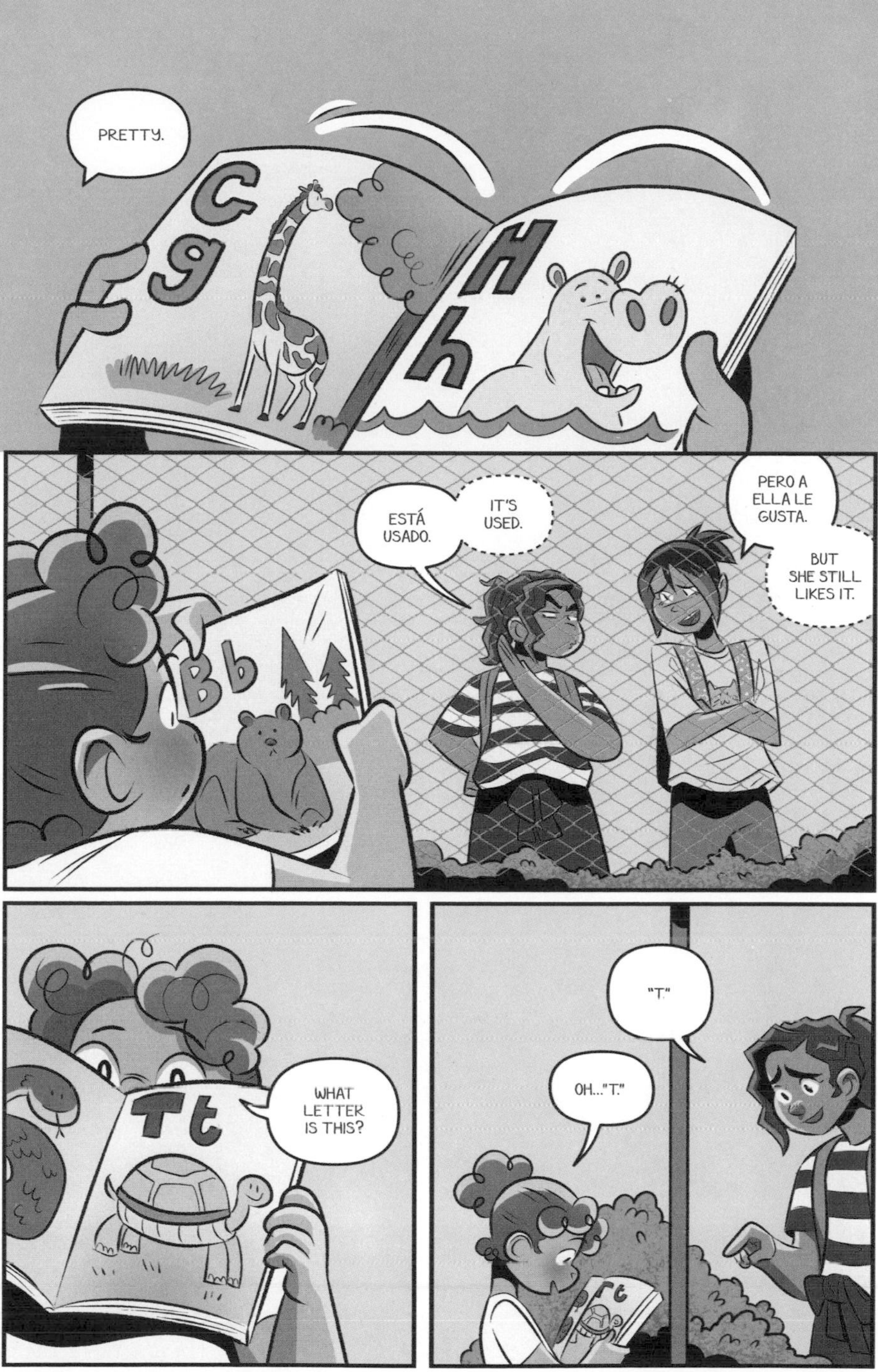

PRETTY.
ESTÁ USADO.
IT'S USED.
PERO A ELLA LE GUSTA.
BUT SHE STILL LIKES IT.
WHAT LETTER IS THIS?
"T."
OH..."T."

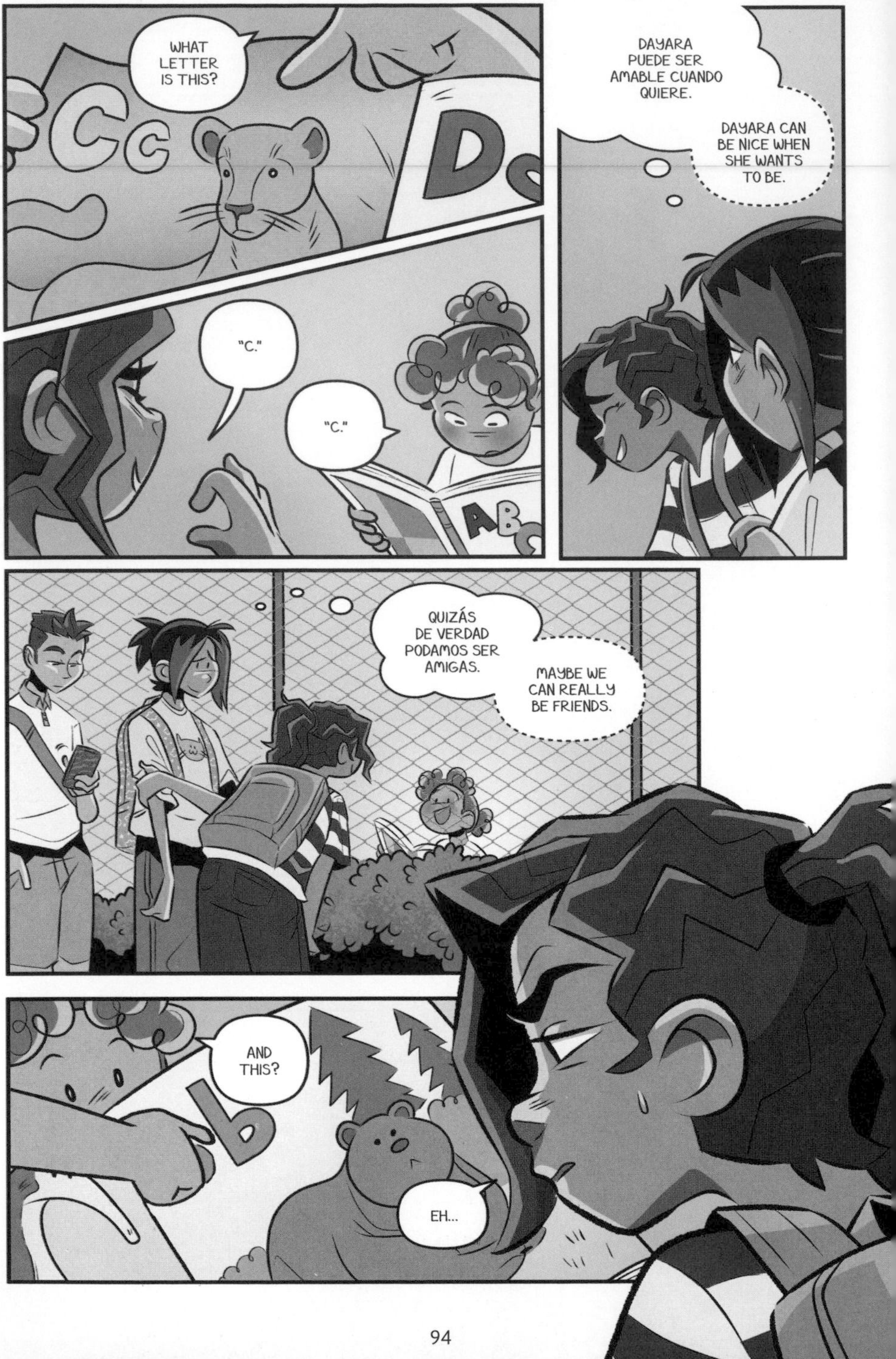
WHAT LETTER IS THIS?
Cc
D
DAYARA PUEDE SER AMABLE CUANDO QUIERE.
DAYARA CAN BE NICE WHEN SHE WANTS TO BE.
"C."
"C."
QUIZÁS DE VERDAD PODAMOS SER AMIGAS.
MAYBE WE CAN REALLY BE FRIENDS.
AND THIS?
b
EH...

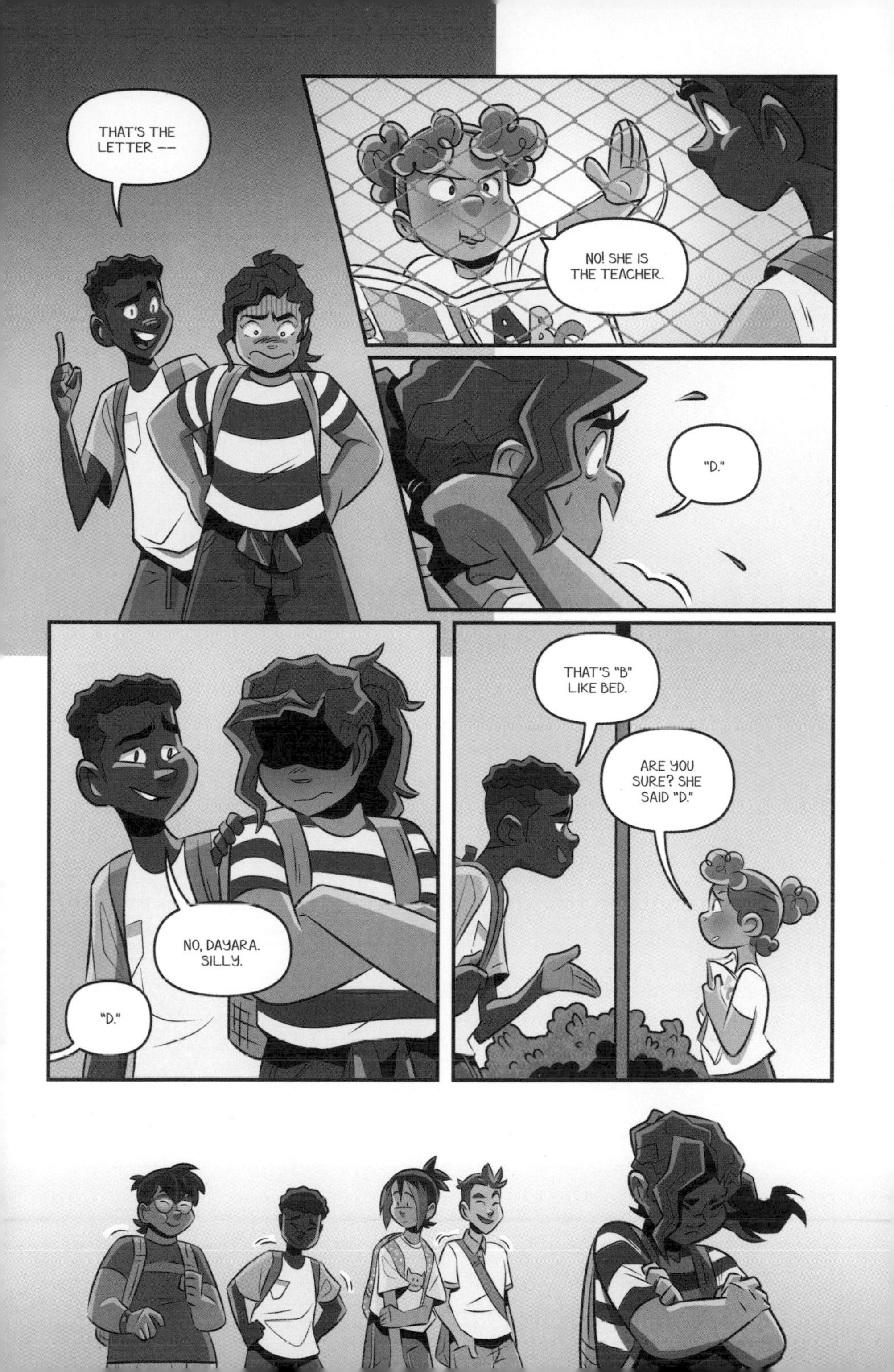
THAT'S THE LETTER --
NO! SHE IS THE TEACHER.
"D."
NO, DAYARA. SILLY.
"D."
THAT'S "B" LIKE BED.
ARE YOU SURE? SHE SAID "D."

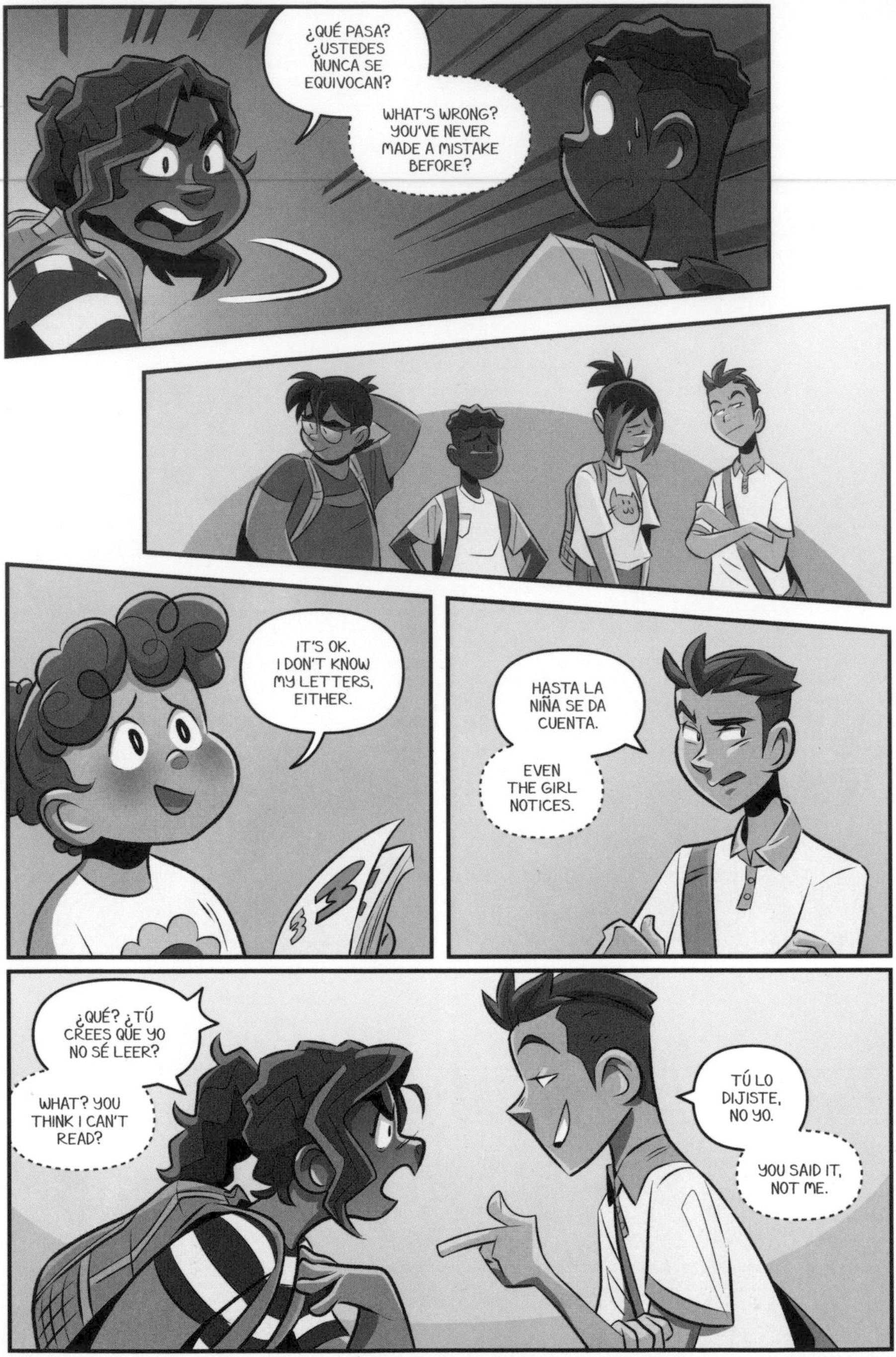
¿QUÉ PASA? ¿USTEDES NUNCA SE EQUIVOCAN?
WHAT'S WRONG? YOU'VE NEVER MADE A MISTAKE BEFORE?
IT'S OK. I DON'T KNOW MY LETTERS, EITHER.
HASTA LA NIÑA SE DA CUENTA.
EVEN THE GIRL NOTICES.
¿QUÉ? ¿TÚ CREES QUE YO NO SÉ LEER?
WHAT? YOU THINK I CAN'T READ?
TÚ LO DIJISTE, NO YO.
YOU SAID IT, NOT ME.

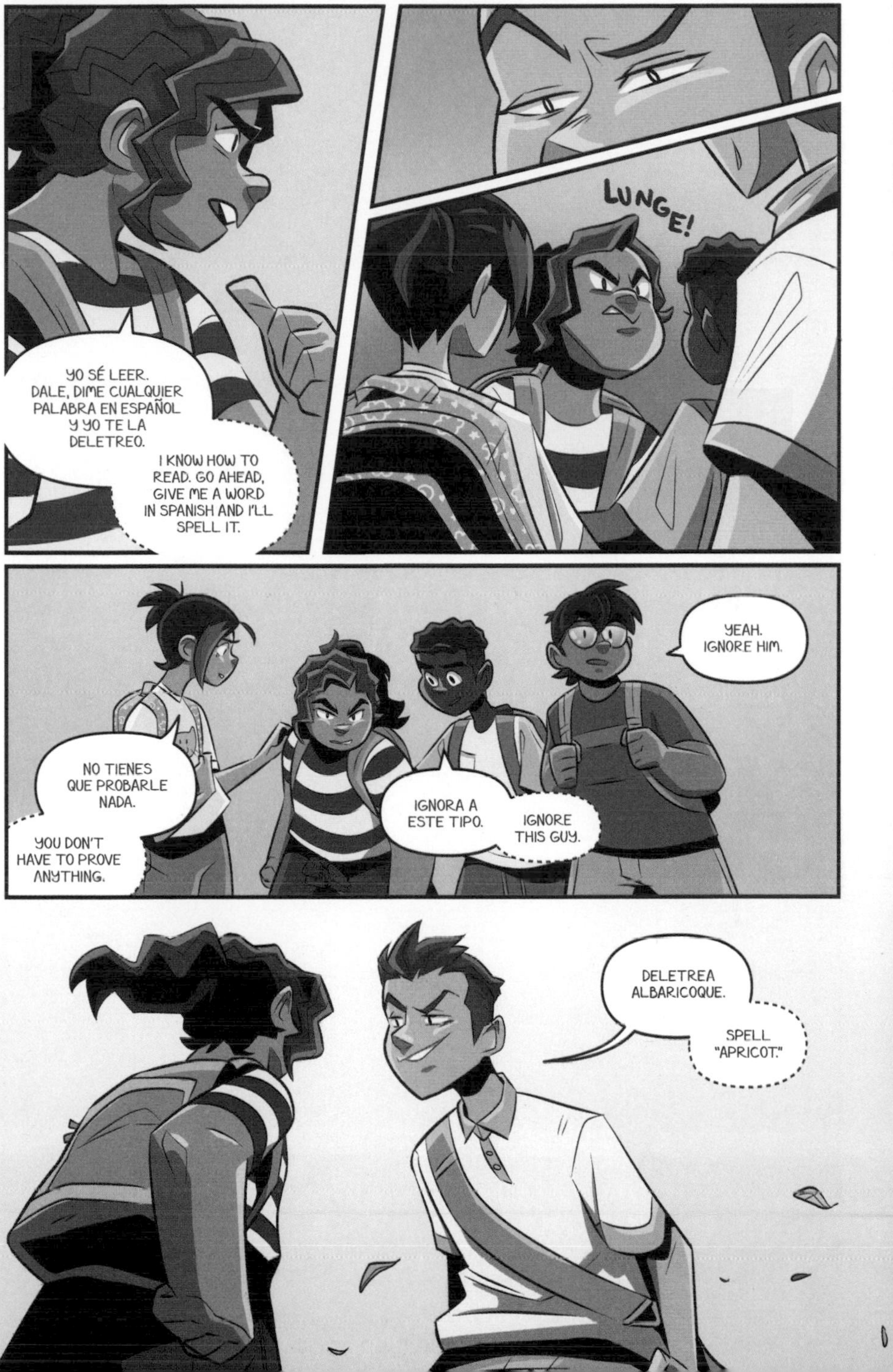
YO SÉ LEER. DALE, DIME CUALQUIER PALABRA EN ESPAÑOL Y YO TE LA DELETREO.
I KNOW HOW TO READ. GO AHEAD, GIVE ME A WORD IN SPANISH AND I'LL SPELL IT.
LUNGE!
YEAH. IGNORE HIM.
NO TIENES QUE PROBARLE NADA.
YOU DON'T HAVE TO PROVE ANYTHING.
IGNORA A ESTE TIPO.
IGNORE THIS GUY.
DELETREA ALBARICOQUE.
SPELL "APRICOT."

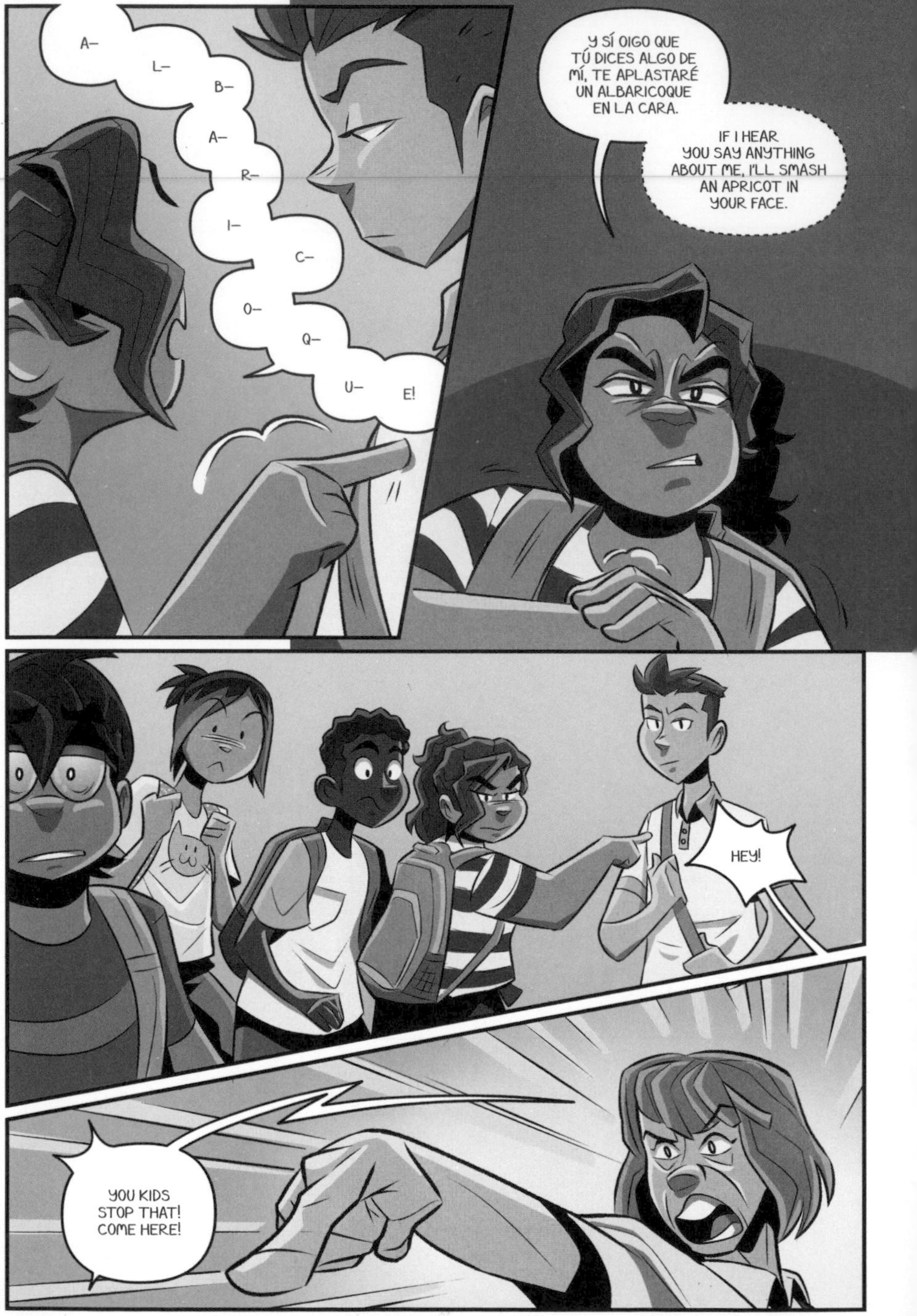
A— L— B— A— R— I— C— O— Q— U— E!
Y SÍ OIGO QUE TÚ DICES ALGO DE MÍ, TE APLASTARÉ UN ALBARICOQUE EN LA CARA.
IF I HEAR YOU SAY ANYTHING ABOUT ME, I'LL SMASH AN APRICOT IN YOUR FACE.
HEY!
YOU KIDS STOP THAT! COME HERE!

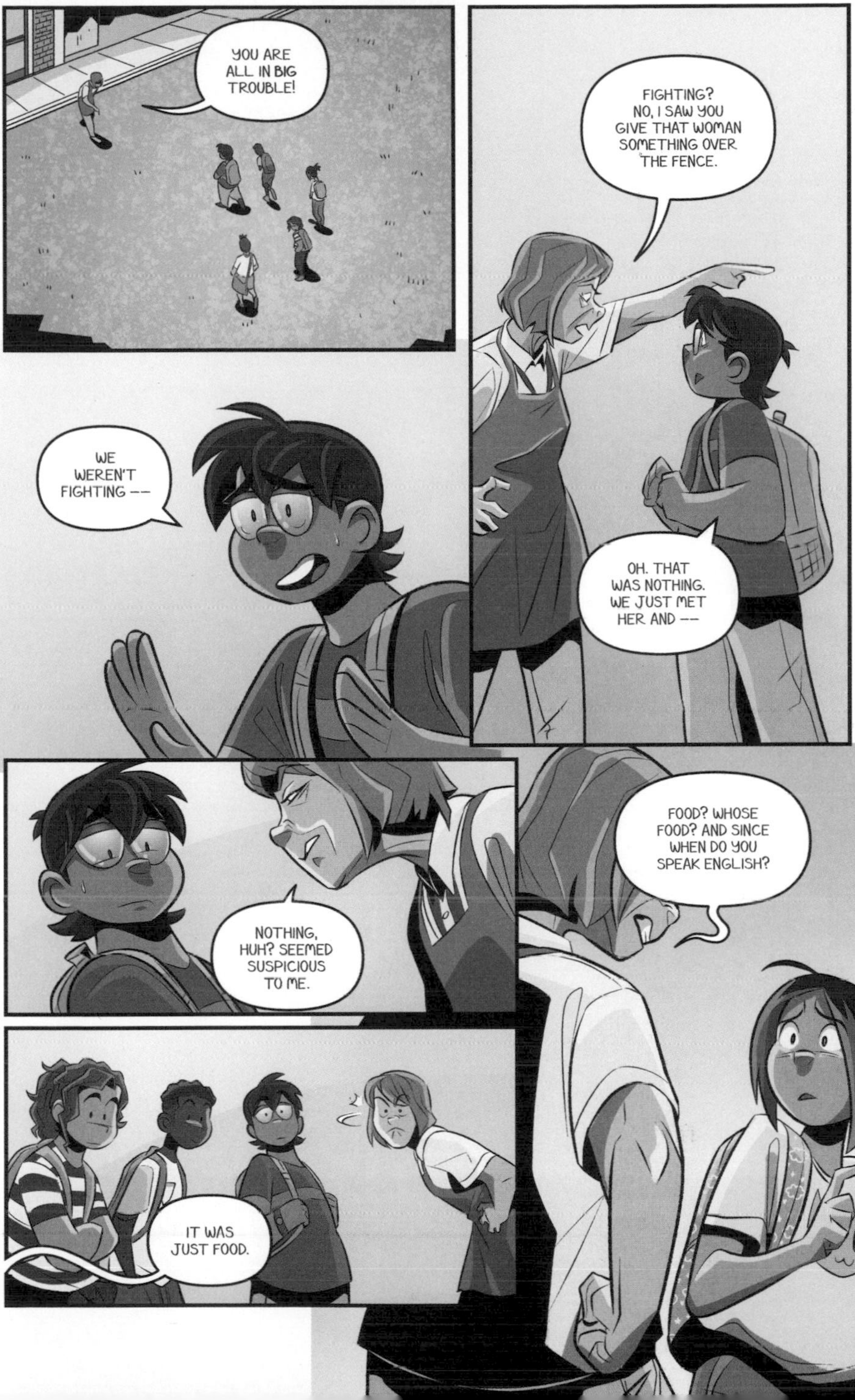
YOU ARE ALL IN BIG TROUBLE!
WE WEREN'T FIGHTING --
FIGHTING? NO, I SAW YOU GIVE THAT WOMAN SOMETHING OVER THE FENCE.
OH. THAT WAS NOTHING. WE JUST MET HER AND --
NOTHING, HUH? SEEMED SUSPICIOUS TO ME.
FOOD? WHOSE FOOD? AND SINCE WHEN DO YOU SPEAK ENGLISH?
IT WAS JUST FOOD.

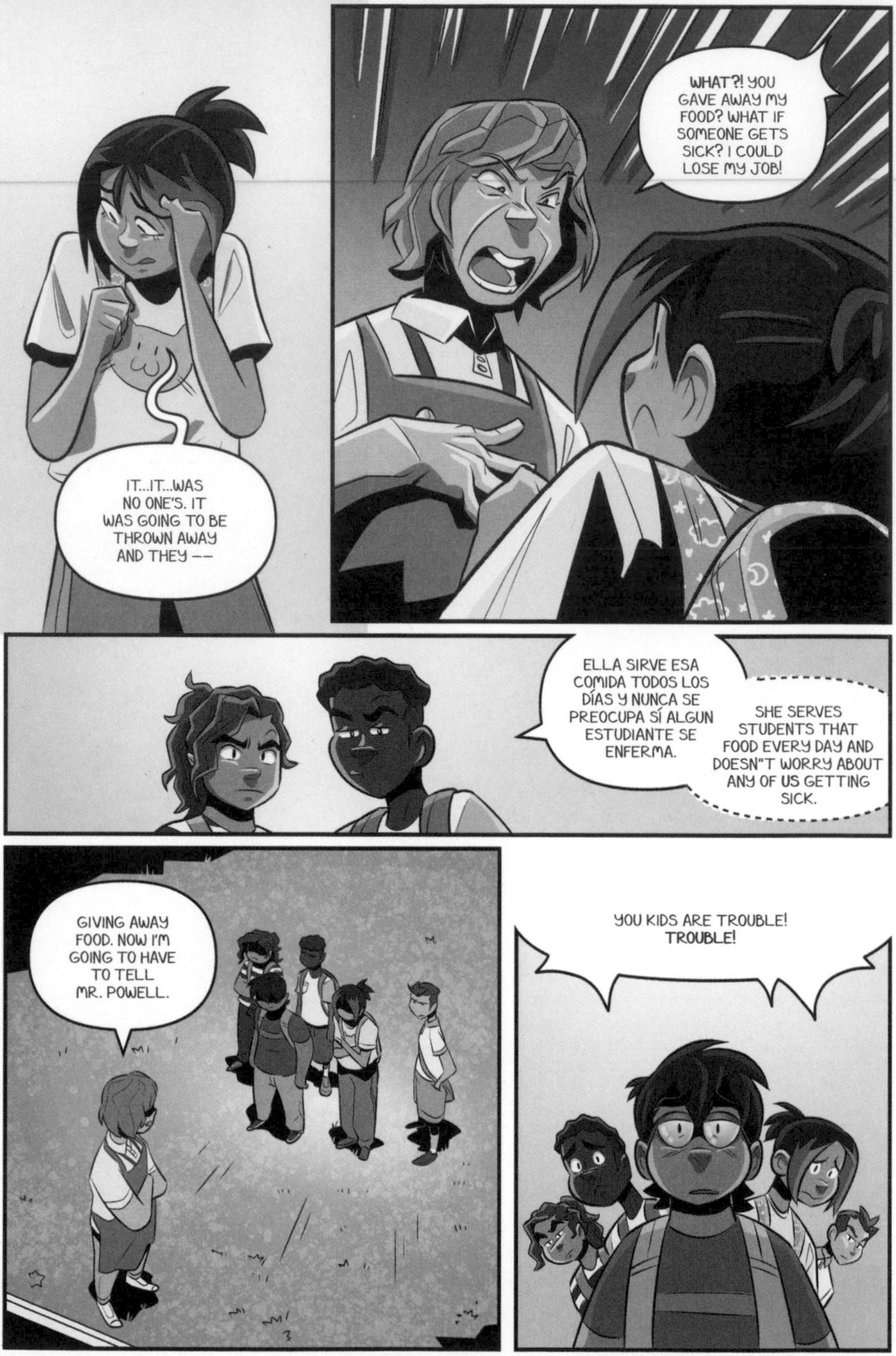
WHAT?! YOU GAVE AWAY MY FOOD? WHAT IF SOMEONE GETS SICK? I COULD LOSE MY JOB!
IT...IT...WAS NO ONE'S. IT WAS GOING TO BE THROWN AWAY AND THEY --
ELLA SIRVE ESA COMIDA TODOS LOS DÍAS Y NUNCA SE PREOCUPA SÍ ALGUN ESTUDIANTE SE ENFERMA.
SHE SERVES STUDENTS THAT FOOD EVERY DAY AND DOESN"T WORRY ABOUT ANY OF US GETTING SICK.
GIVING AWAY FOOD. NOW I'M GOING TO HAVE TO TELL MR. POWELL.
YOU KIDS ARE TROUBLE! **TROUBLE!**

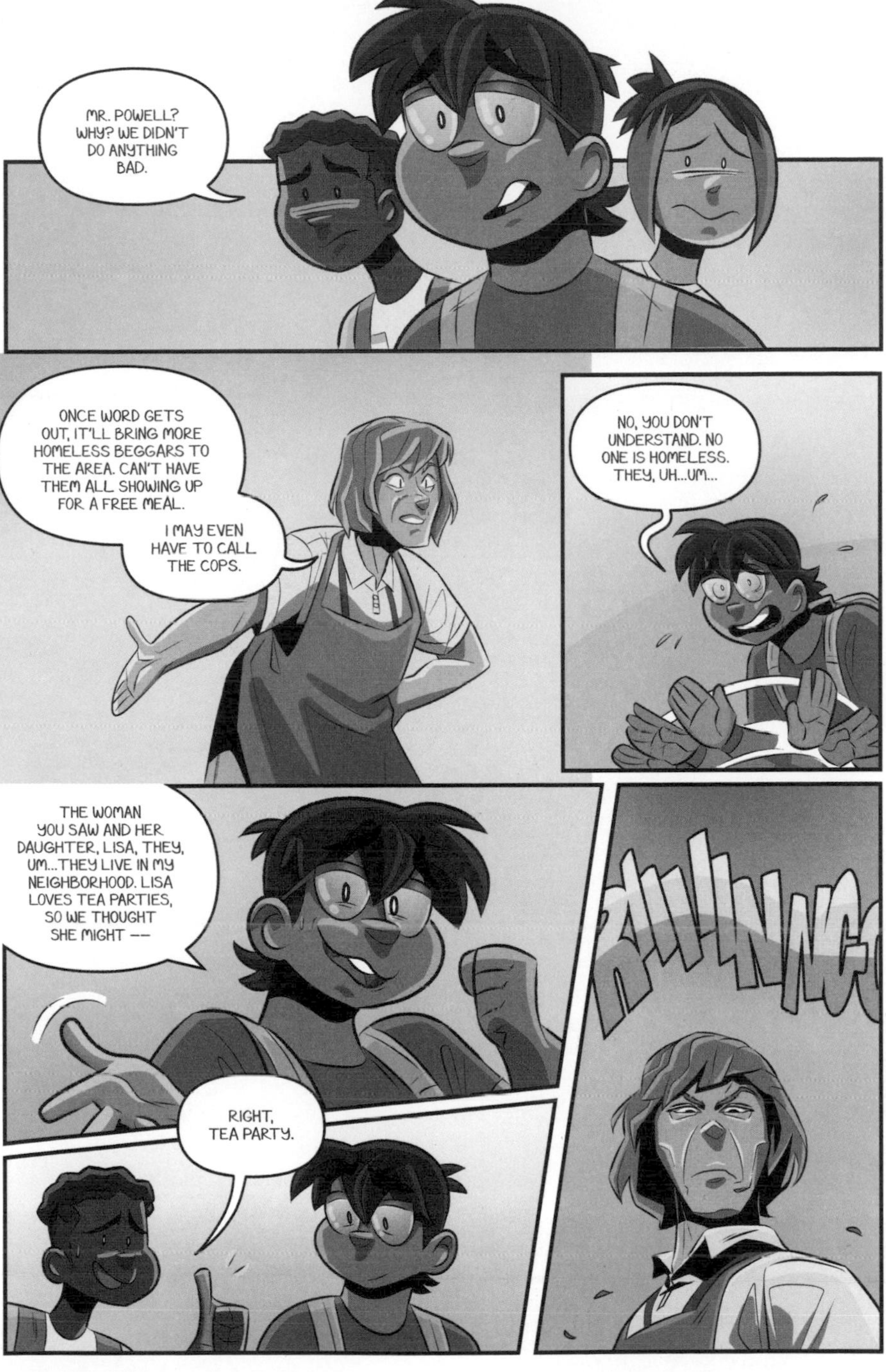
MR. POWELL? WHY? WE DIDN'T DO ANYTHING BAD.
ONCE WORD GETS OUT, IT'LL BRING MORE HOMELESS BEGGARS TO THE AREA. CAN'T HAVE THEM ALL SHOWING UP FOR A FREE MEAL.
I MAY EVEN HAVE TO CALL THE COPS.
NO, YOU DON'T UNDERSTAND. NO ONE IS HOMELESS. THEY, UH...UM...
THE WOMAN YOU SAW AND HER DAUGHTER, LISA, THEY, UM...THEY LIVE IN MY NEIGHBORHOOD. LISA LOVES TEA PARTIES, SO WE THOUGHT SHE MIGHT --
RIGHT, TEA PARTY.

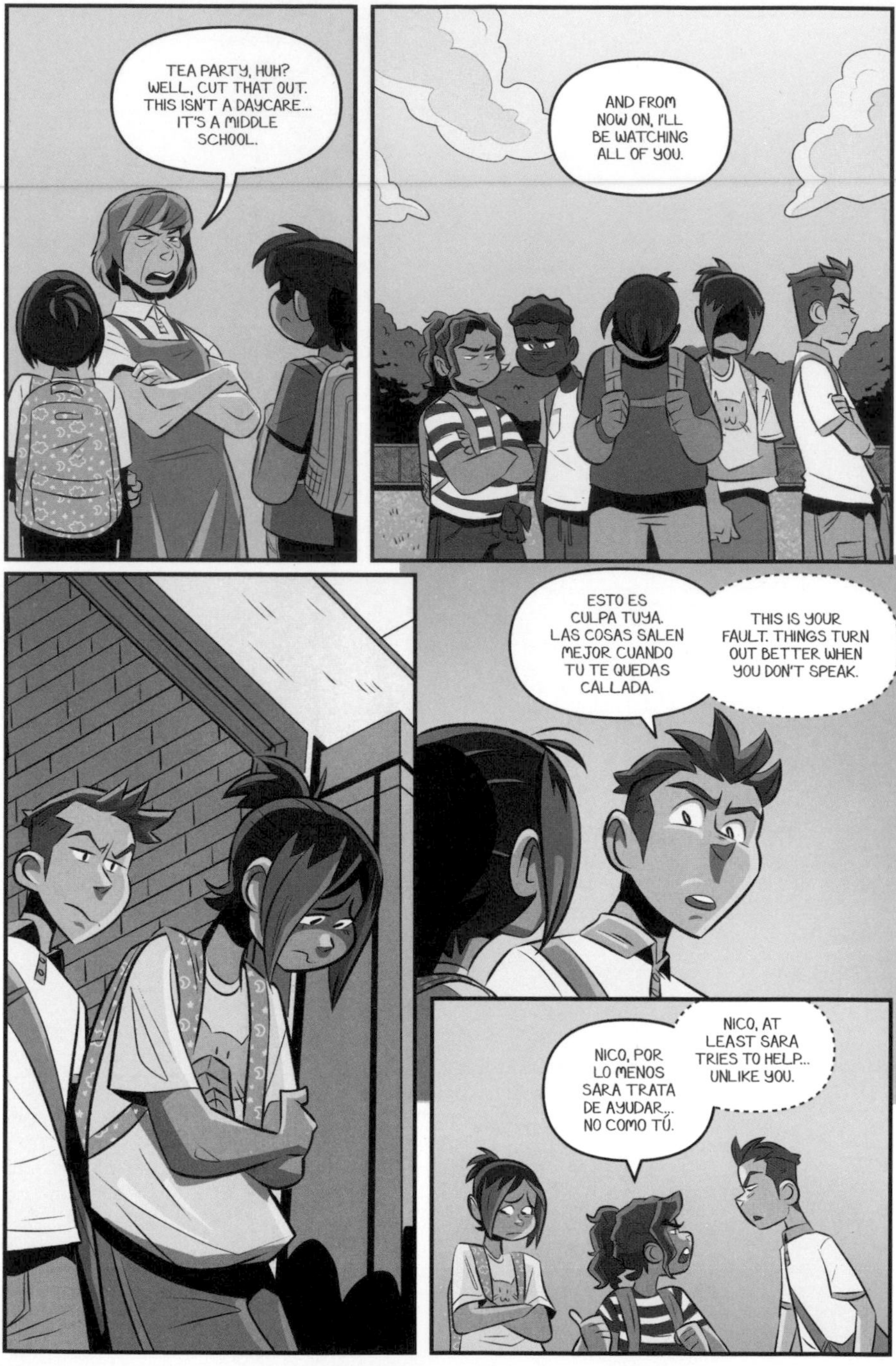
TEA PARTY, HUH? WELL, CUT THAT OUT. THIS ISN'T A DAYCARE... IT'S A MIDDLE SCHOOL.
AND FROM NOW ON, I'LL BE WATCHING ALL OF YOU.
ESTO ES CULPA TUYA. LAS COSAS SALEN MEJOR CUANDO TU TE QUEDAS CALLADA.
THIS IS YOUR FAULT. THINGS TURN OUT BETTER WHEN YOU DON'T SPEAK.
NICO, POR LO MENOS SARA TRATA DE AYUDAR... NO COMO TÚ.
NICO, AT LEAST SARA TRIES TO HELP... UNLIKE YOU.

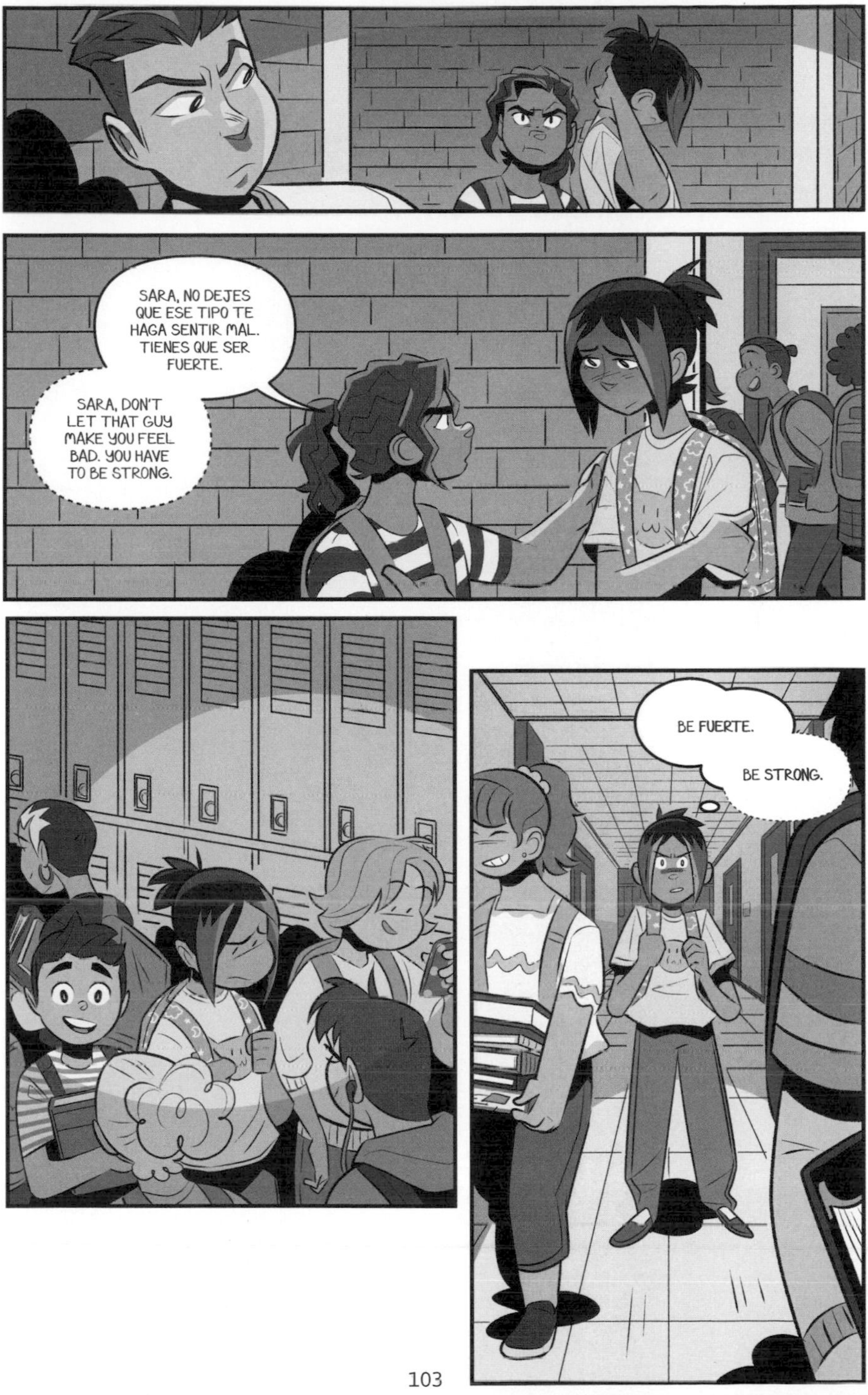
SARA, NO DEJES QUE ESE TIPO TE HAGA SENTIR MAL. TIENES QUE SER FUERTE.
SARA, DON'T LET THAT GUY MAKE YOU FEEL BAD. YOU HAVE TO BE STRONG.
BE FUERTE.
BE STRONG.

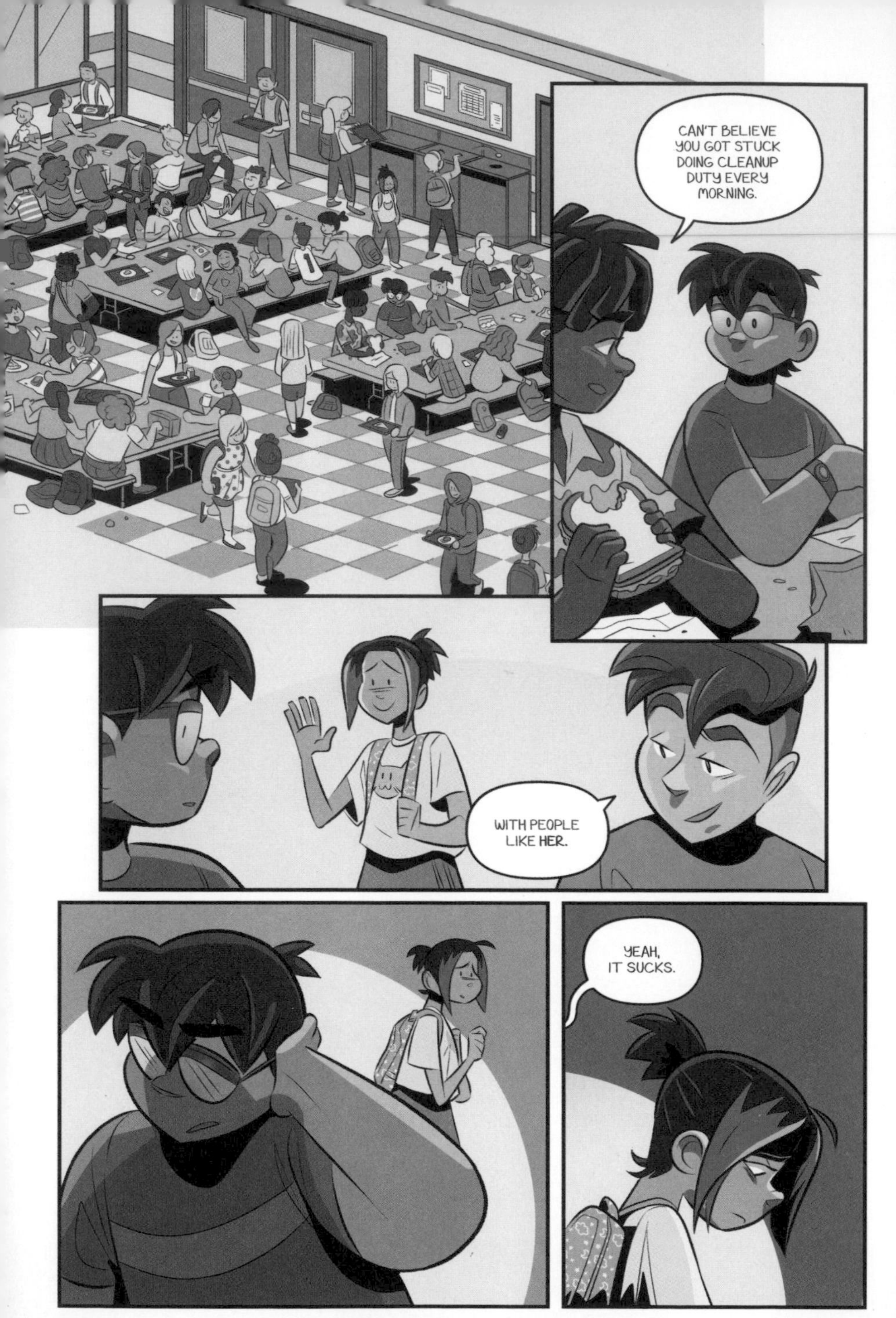
CAN'T BELIEVE YOU GOT STUCK DOING CLEANUP DUTY EVERY MORNING.
WITH PEOPLE LIKE HER.
YEAH, IT SUCKS.

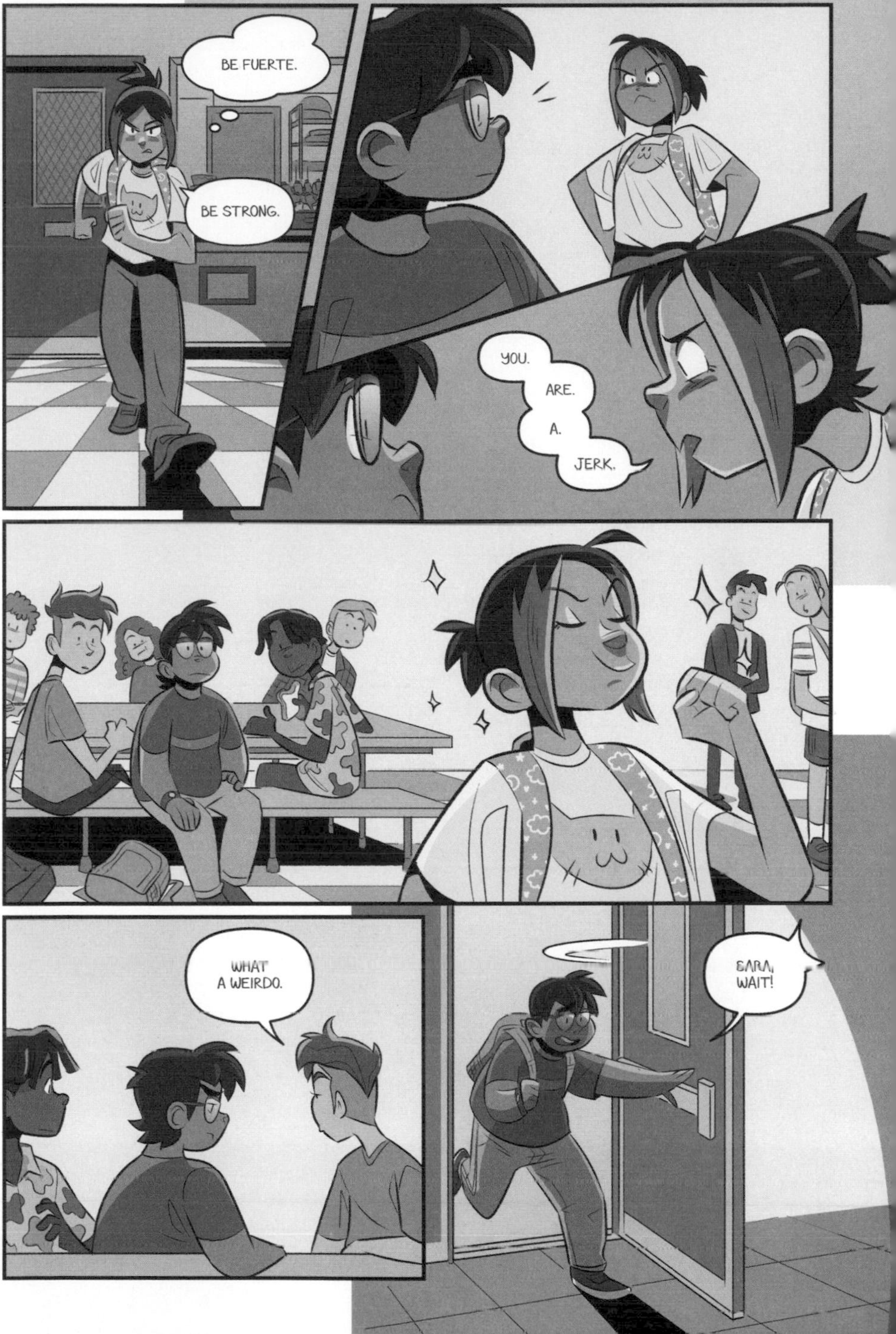
BE FUERTE.
BE STRONG.
YOU.
ARE.
A.
JERK.
WHAT A WEIRDO.
SARA, WAIT!

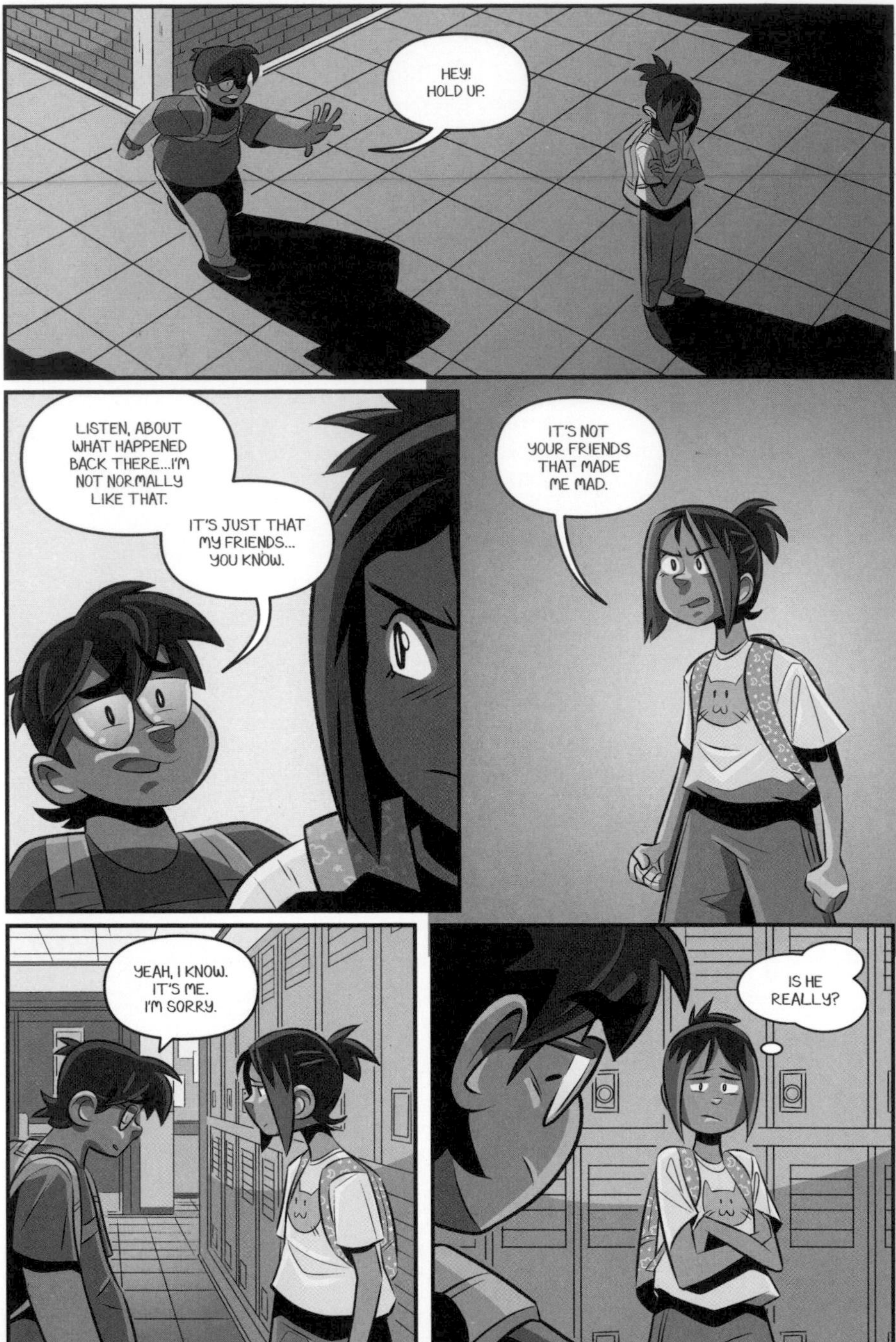
HEY! HOLD UP.
LISTEN, ABOUT WHAT HAPPENED BACK THERE...I'M NOT NORMALLY LIKE THAT.
IT'S JUST THAT MY FRIENDS... YOU KNOW.
IT'S NOT YOUR FRIENDS THAT MADE ME MAD.
YEAH, I KNOW. IT'S ME. I'M SORRY.
IS HE REALLY?

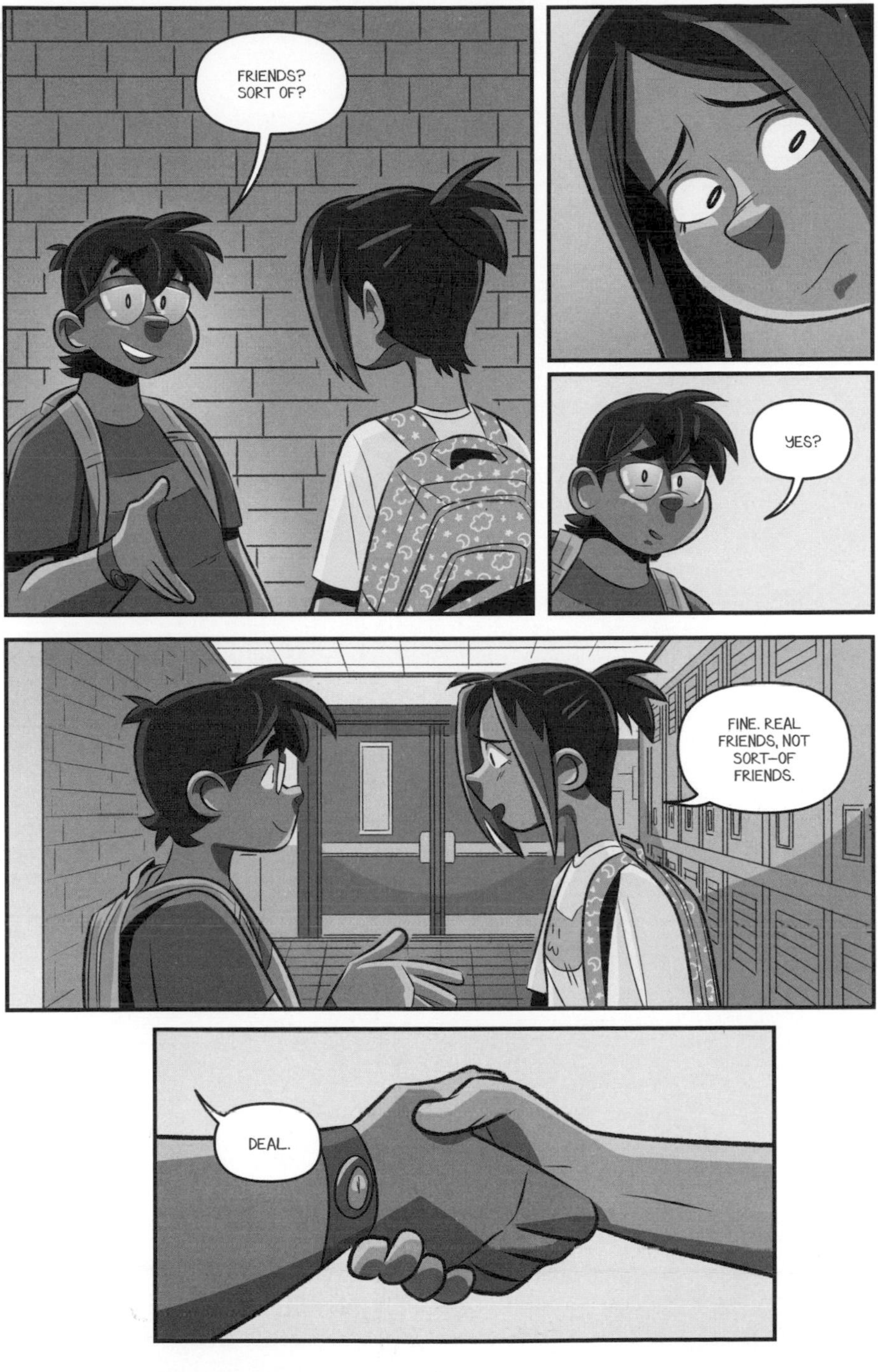
FRIENDS? SORT OF?
YES?
FINE. REAL FRIENDS, NOT SORT-OF FRIENDS.
DEAL.

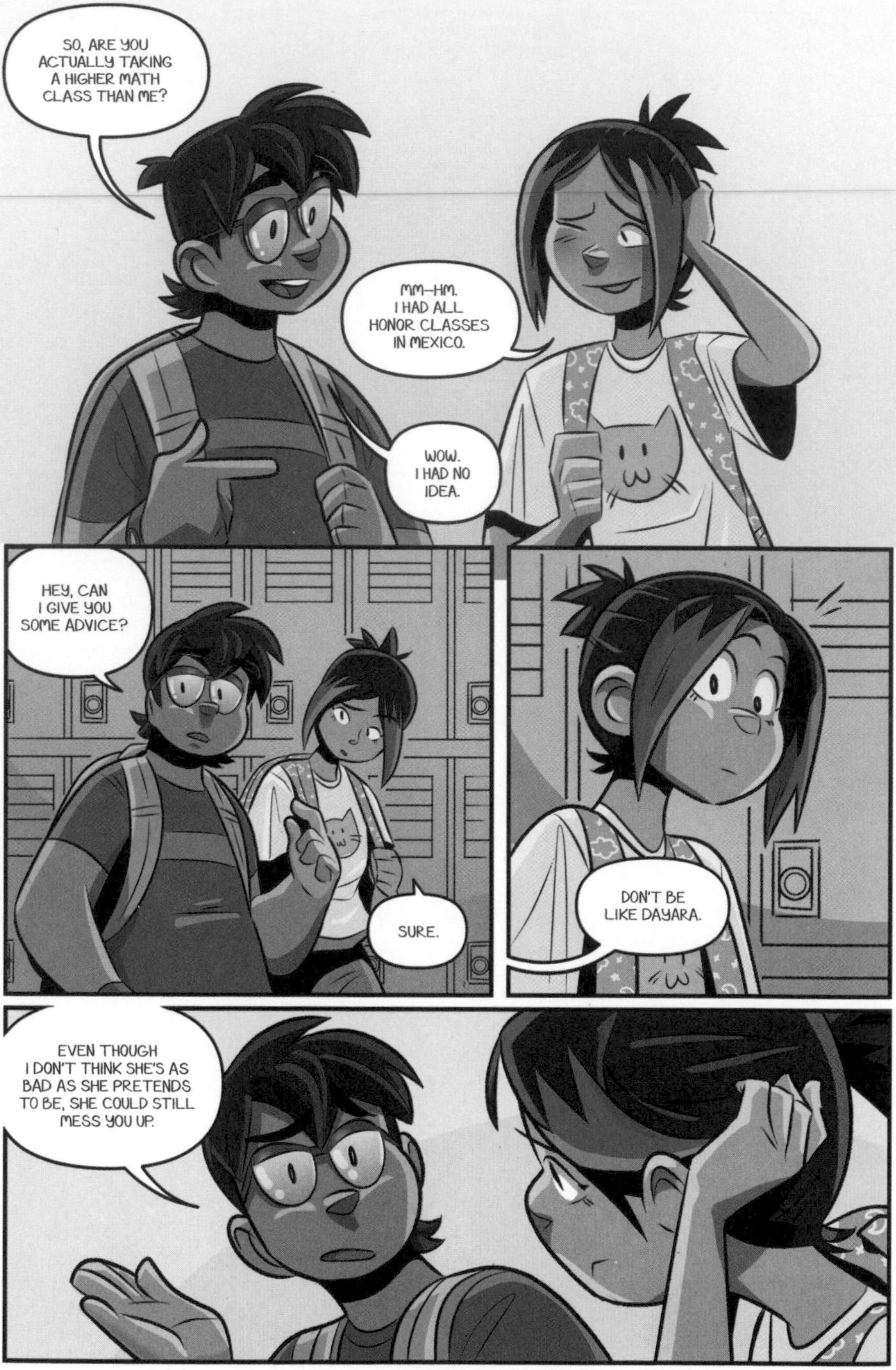
SO, ARE YOU ACTUALLY TAKING A HIGHER MATH CLASS THAN ME?
MM-HM. I HAD ALL HONOR CLASSES IN MEXICO.
WOW. I HAD NO IDEA.
HEY, CAN I GIVE YOU SOME ADVICE?
SURE.
DON'T BE LIKE DAYARA.
EVEN THOUGH I DON'T THINK SHE'S AS BAD AS SHE PRETENDS TO BE, SHE COULD STILL MESS YOU UP.

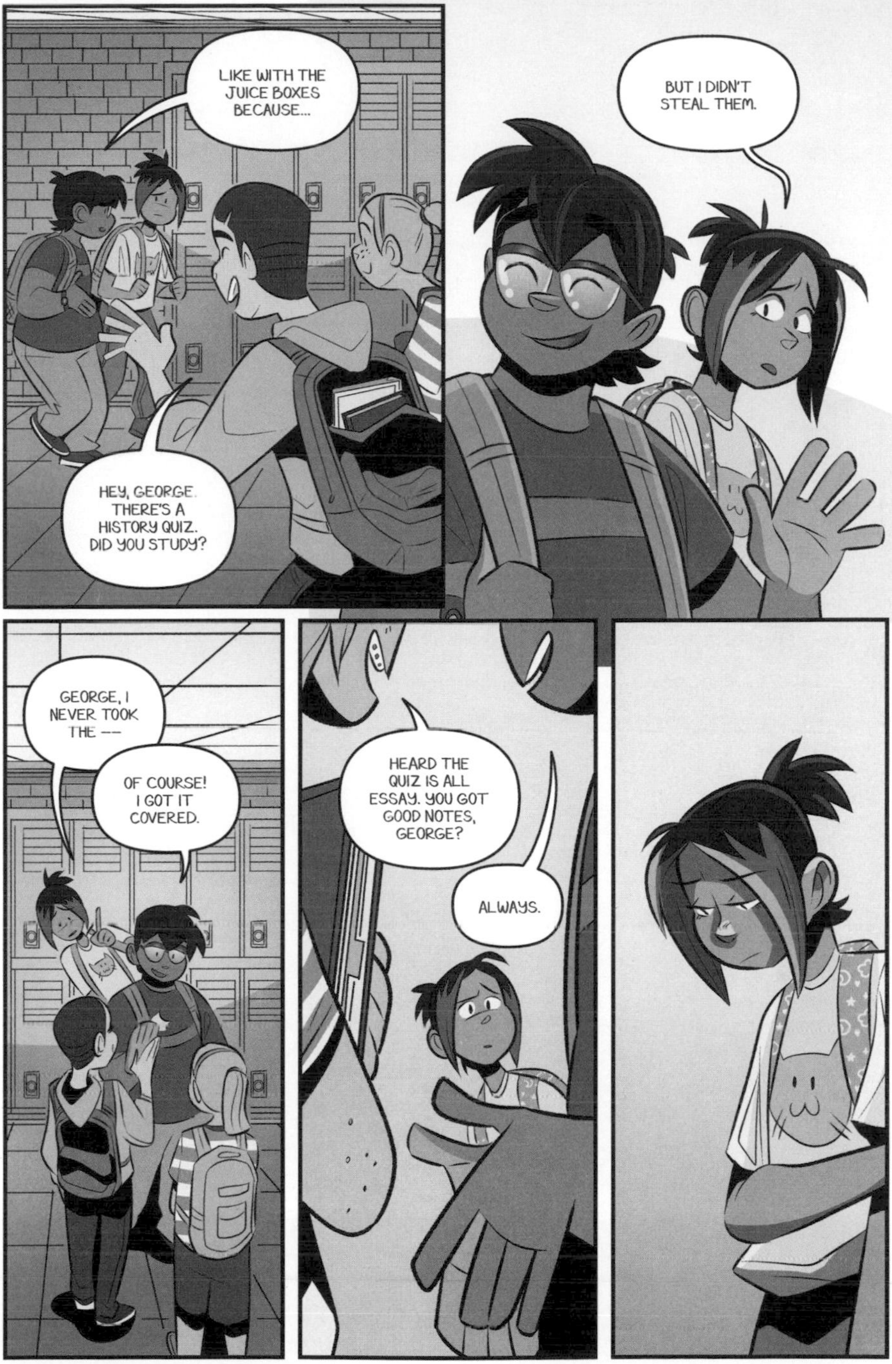
LIKE WITH THE JUICE BOXES BECAUSE...
HEY, GEORGE. THERE'S A HISTORY QUIZ. DID YOU STUDY?
BUT I DIDN'T STEAL THEM.
GEORGE, I NEVER TOOK THE --
OF COURSE! I GOT IT COVERED.
HEARD THE QUIZ IS ALL ESSAY. YOU GOT GOOD NOTES, GEORGE?
ALWAYS.

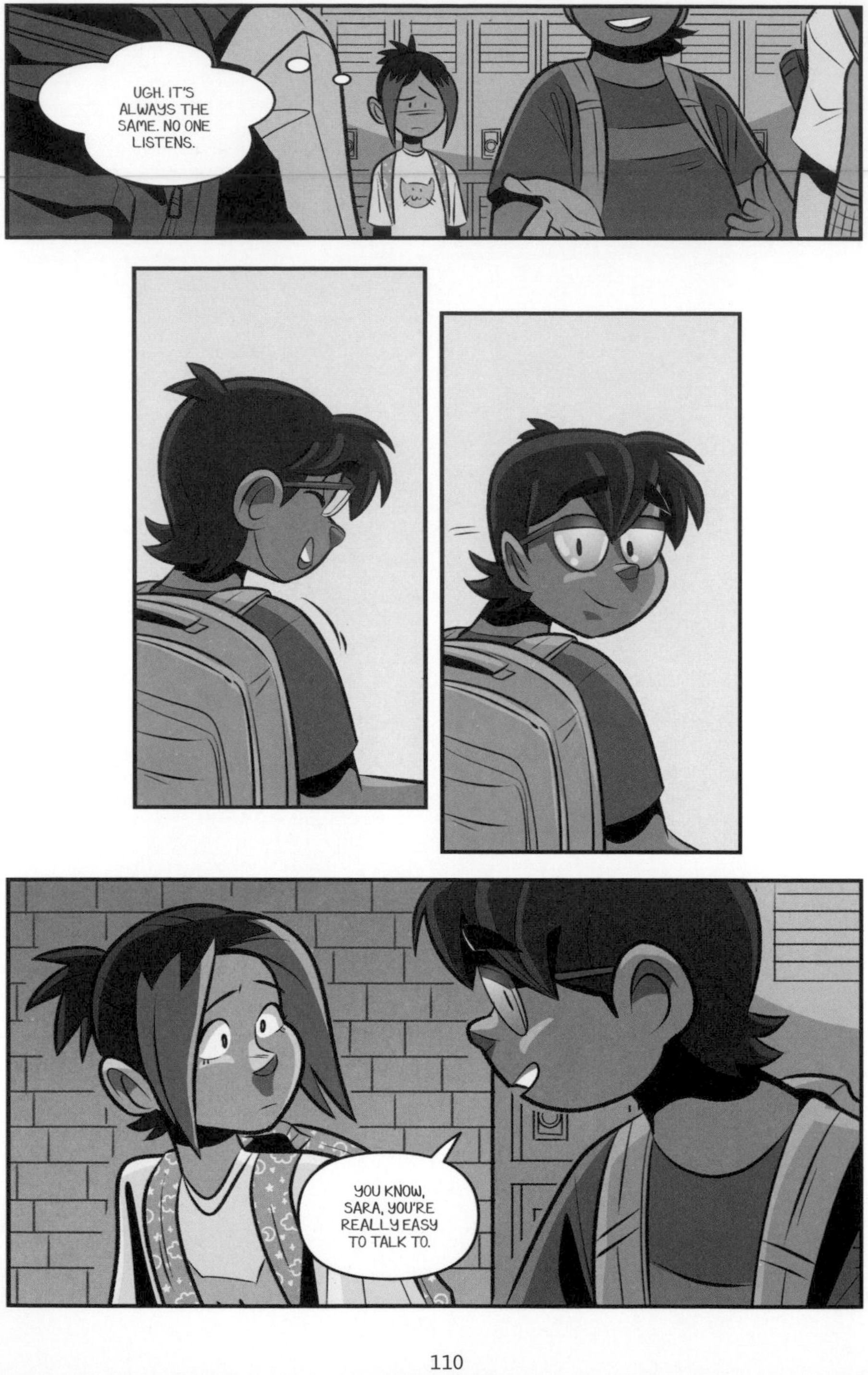
UGH. IT'S ALWAYS THE SAME. NO ONE LISTENS.
YOU KNOW, SARA, YOU'RE REALLY EASY TO TALK TO.

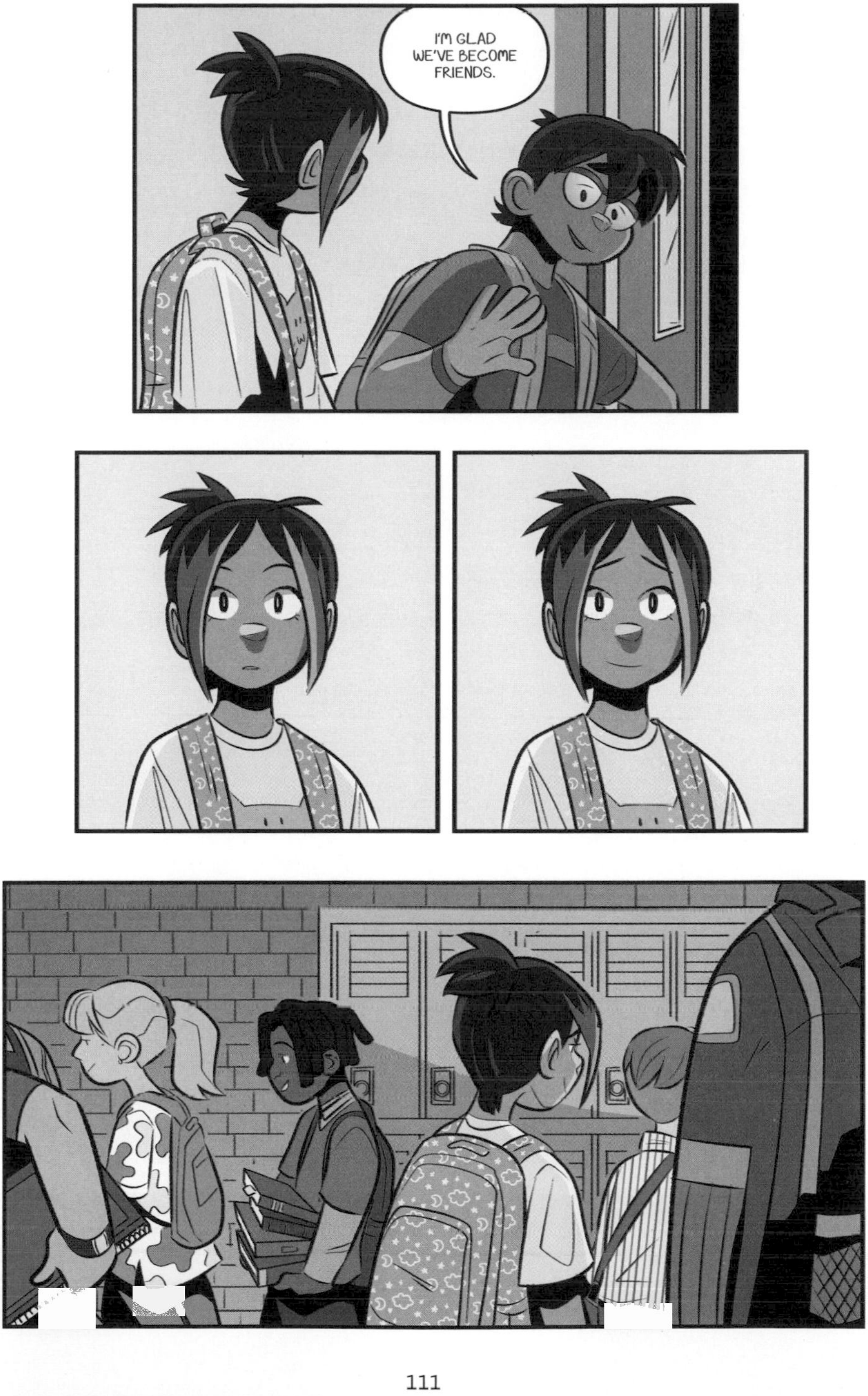
I'M GLAD WE'VE BECOME FRIENDS.

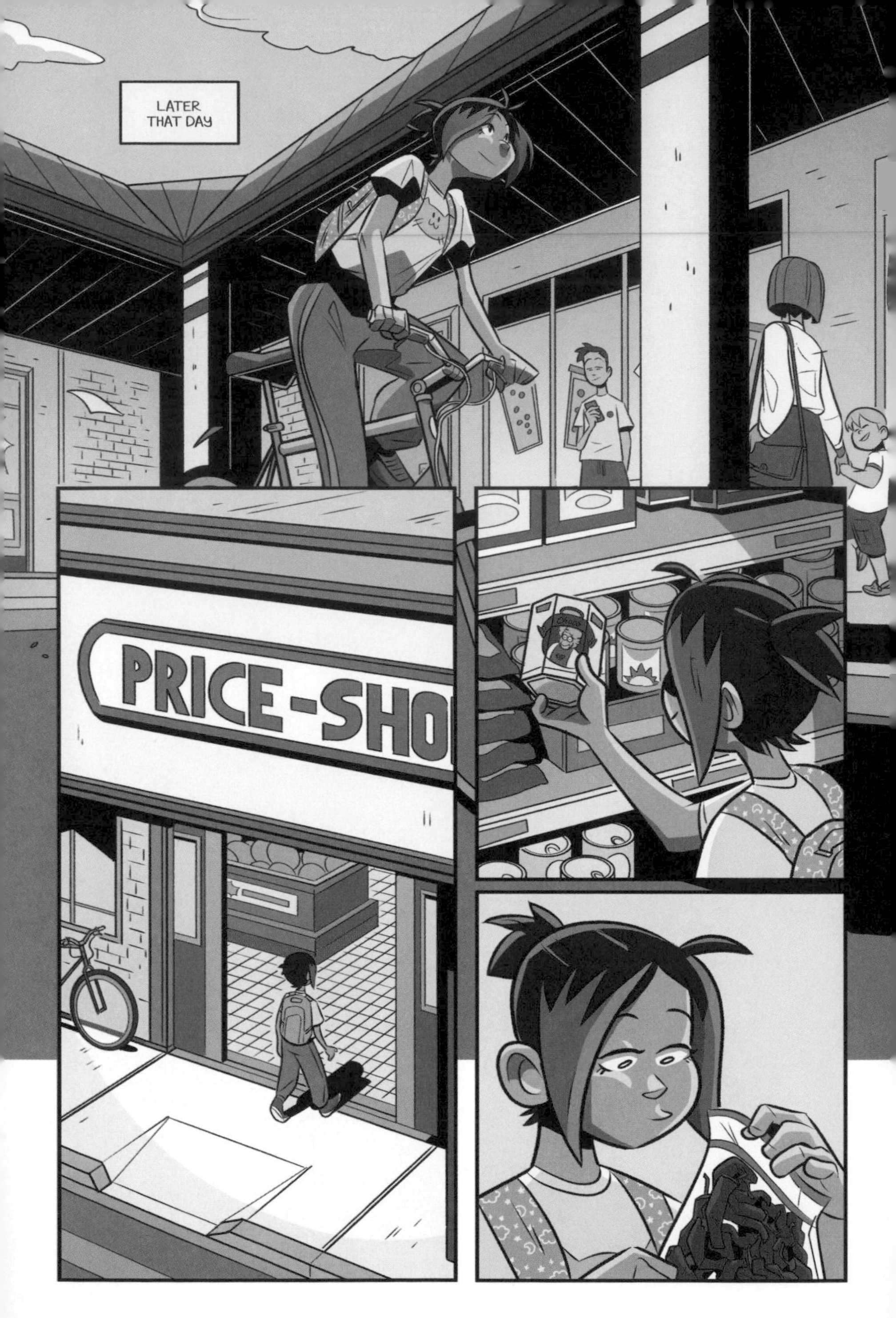
LATER THAT DAY
PRICE-SHO

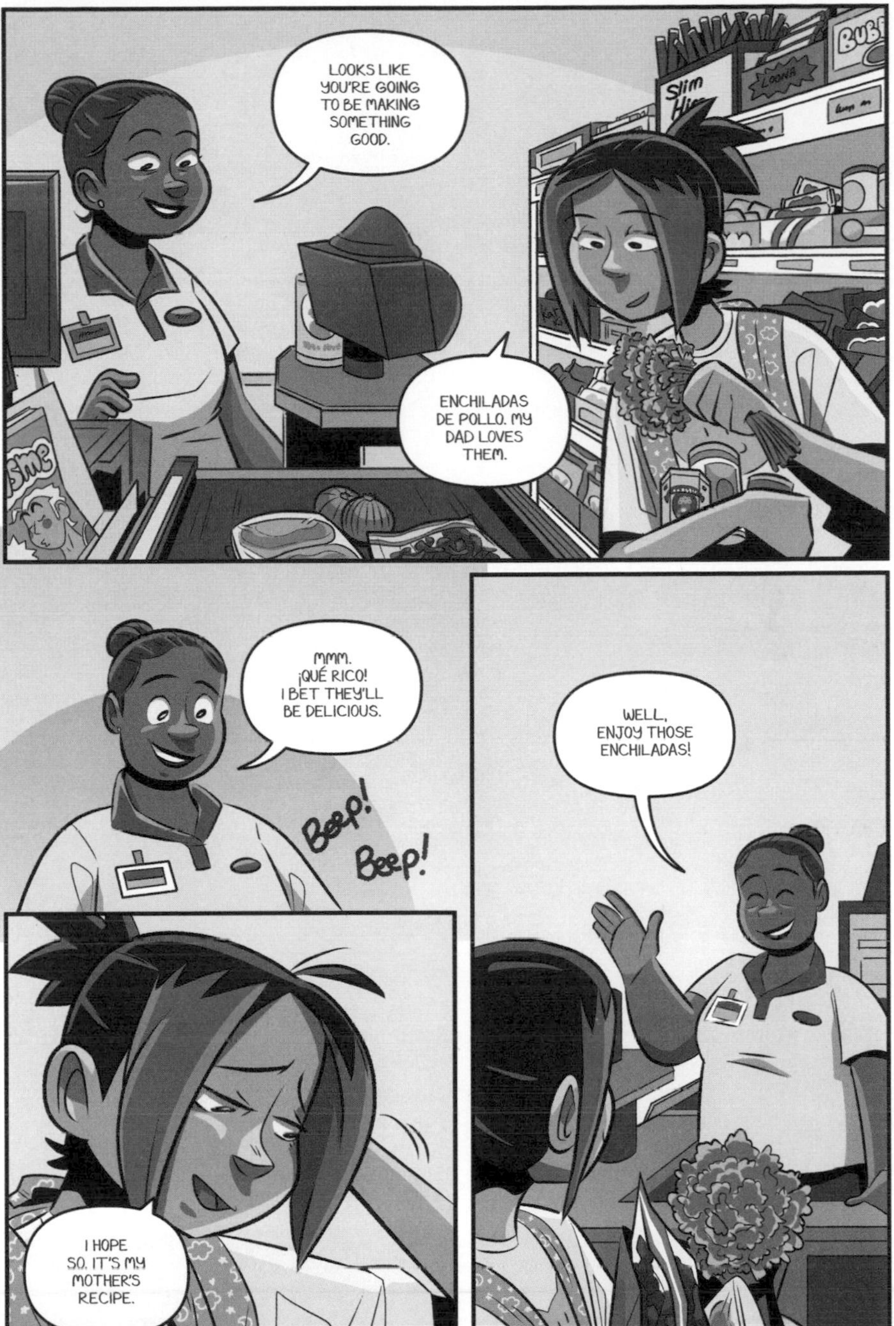
LOOKS LIKE YOU'RE GOING TO BE MAKING SOMETHING GOOD.
ENCHILADAS DE POLLO. MY DAD LOVES THEM.
MMM. ¡QUÉ RICO! I BET THEY'LL BE DELICIOUS.
Beep! Beep!
WELL, ENJOY THOSE ENCHILADAS!
I HOPE SO. IT'S MY MOTHER'S RECIPE.

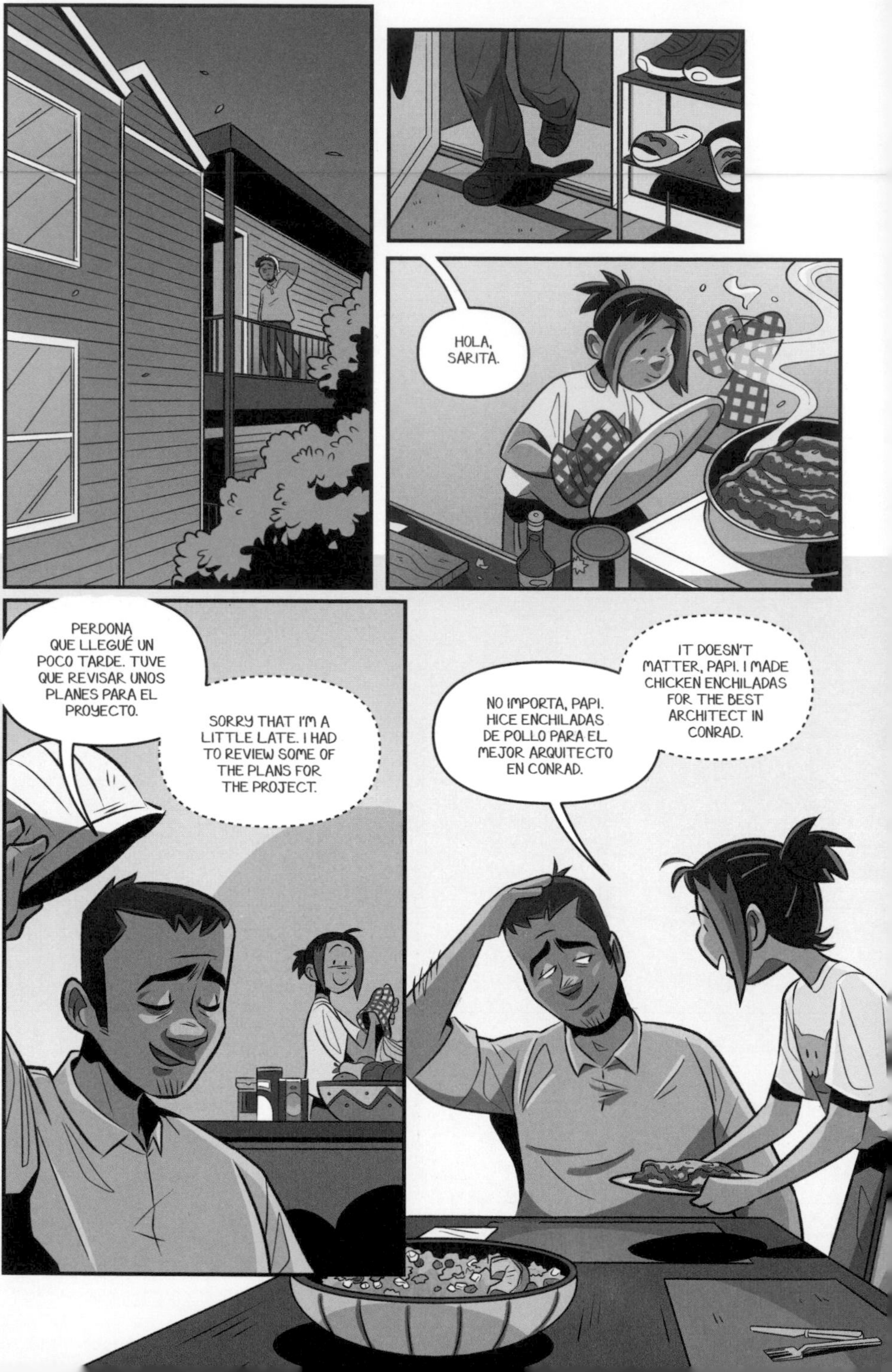
HOLA, SARITA.
PERDONA QUE LLEGUÉ UN POCO TARDE. TUVE QUE REVISAR UNOS PLANES PARA EL PROYECTO.
SORRY THAT I'M A LITTLE LATE. I HAD TO REVIEW SOME OF THE PLANS FOR THE PROJECT.
NO IMPORTA, PAPI. HICE ENCHILADAS DE POLLO PARA EL MEJOR ARQUITECTO EN CONRAD.
IT DOESN'T MATTER, PAPI. I MADE CHICKEN ENCHILADAS FOR THE BEST ARCHITECT IN CONRAD.

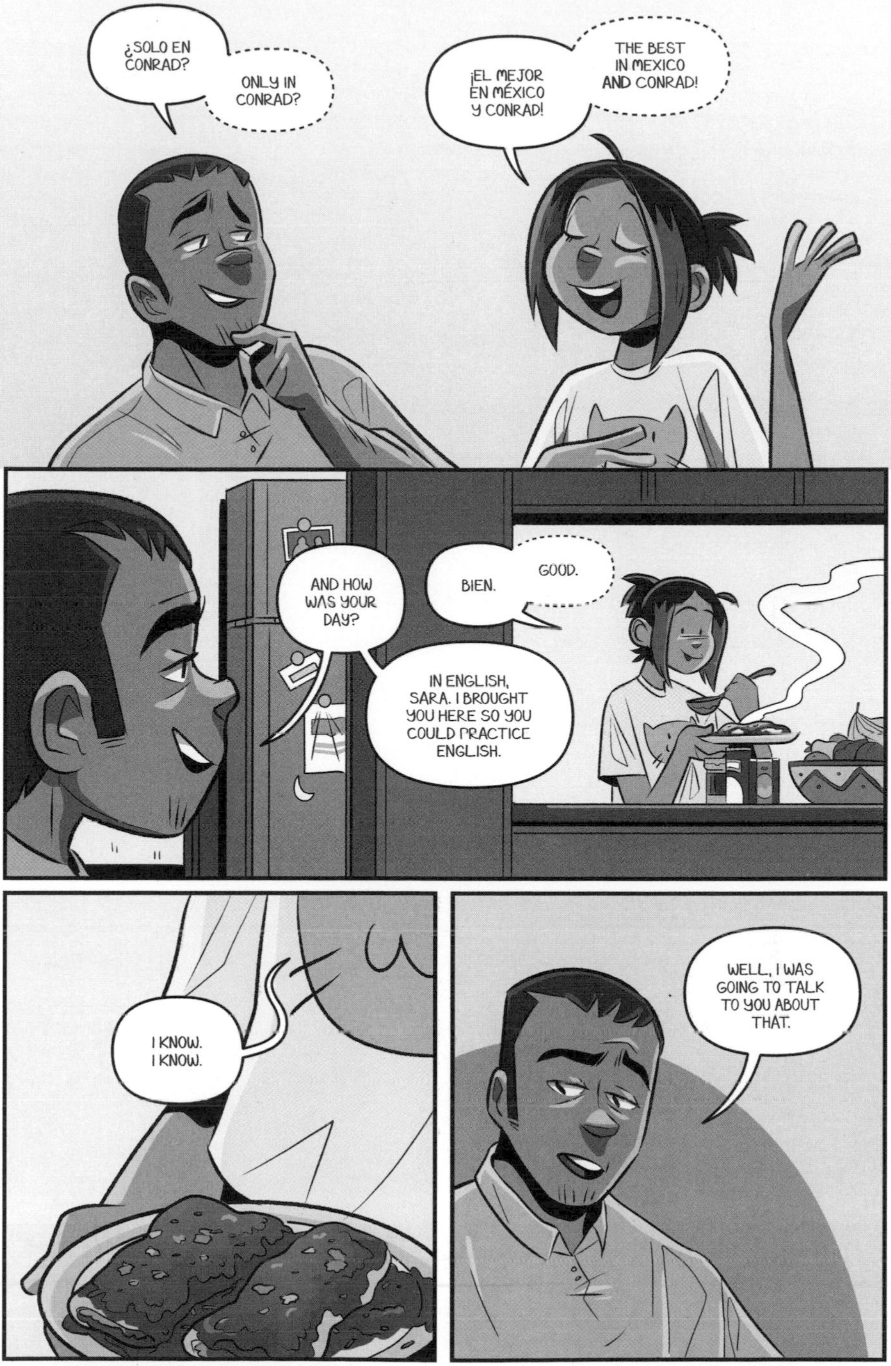
¿SOLO EN CONRAD?
ONLY IN CONRAD?
¡EL MEJOR EN MÉXICO Y CONRAD!
THE BEST IN MEXICO AND CONRAD!
AND HOW WAS YOUR DAY?
BIEN.
GOOD.
IN ENGLISH, SARA. I BROUGHT YOU HERE SO YOU COULD PRACTICE ENGLISH.
I KNOW. I KNOW.
WELL, I WAS GOING TO TALK TO YOU ABOUT THAT.

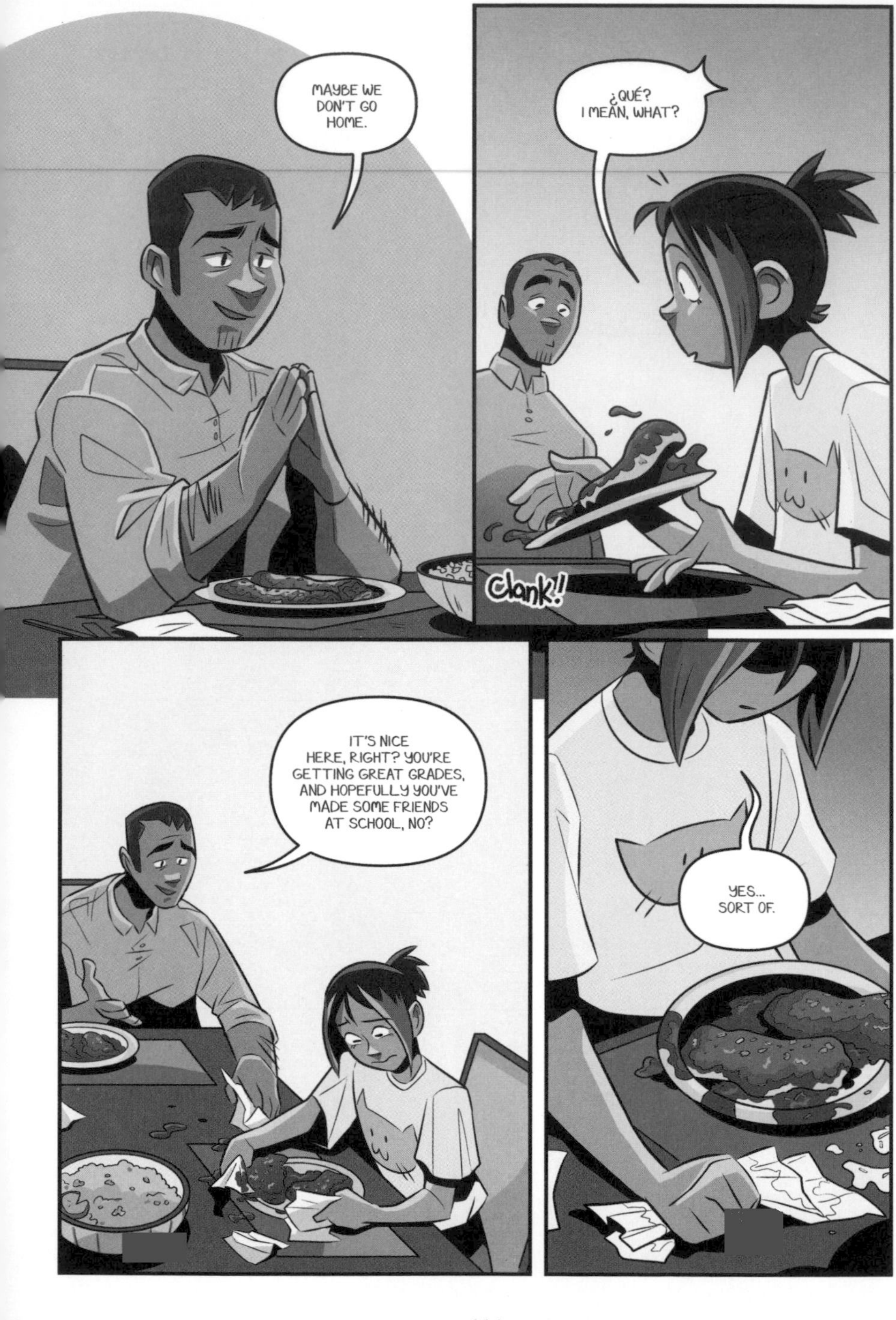
MAYBE WE DON'T GO HOME.
¿QUÉ? I MEAN, WHAT?
Clank!
IT'S NICE HERE, RIGHT? YOU'RE GETTING GREAT GRADES, AND HOPEFULLY YOU'VE MADE SOME FRIENDS AT SCHOOL, NO?
YES... SORT OF.

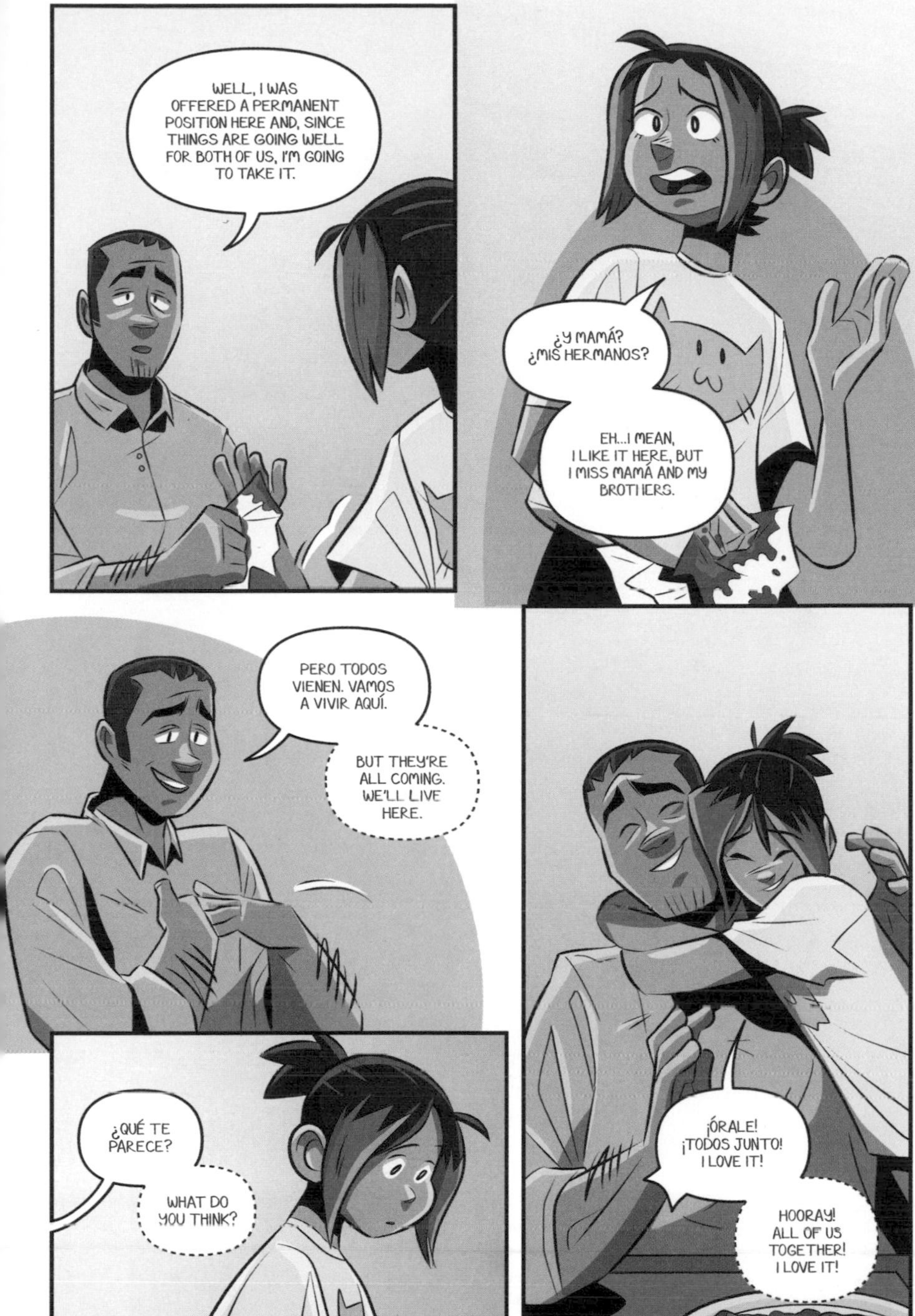
WELL, I WAS OFFERED A PERMANENT POSITION HERE AND, SINCE THINGS ARE GOING WELL FOR BOTH OF US, I'M GOING TO TAKE IT.
¿Y MAMÁ? ¿MIS HERMANOS?
EH...I MEAN, I LIKE IT HERE, BUT I MISS MAMÁ AND MY BROTHERS.
PERO TODOS VIENEN. VAMOS A VIVIR AQUÍ.
BUT THEY'RE ALL COMING. WE'LL LIVE HERE.
¿QUÉ TE PARECE?
WHAT DO YOU THINK?
¡ÓRALE! ¡TODOS JUNTO! I LOVE IT!
HOORAY! ALL OF US TOGETHER! I LOVE IT!

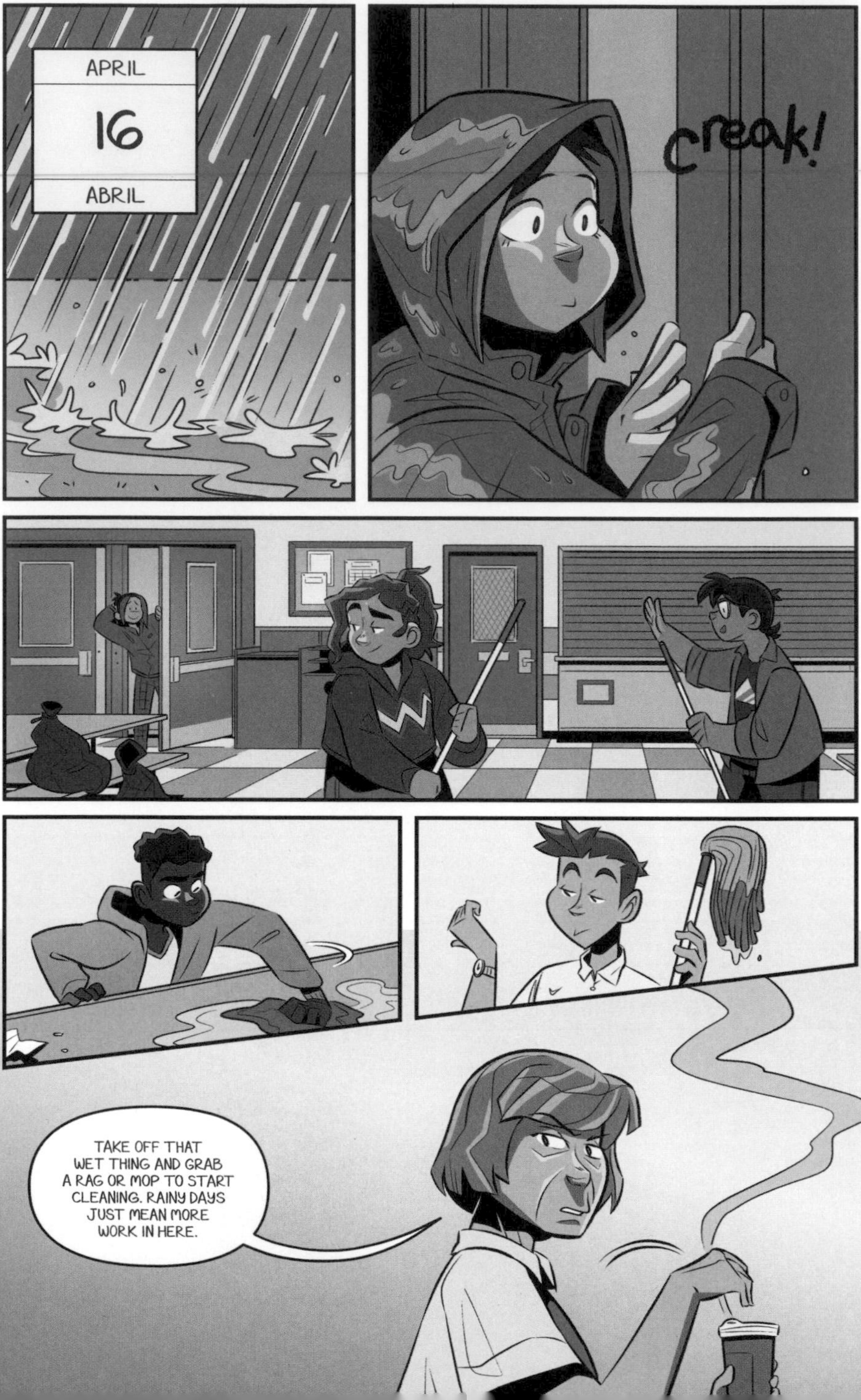
APRIL
16
ABRIL
creak!
TAKE OFF THAT WET THING AND GRAB A RAG OR MOP TO START CLEANING. RAINY DAYS JUST MEAN MORE WORK IN HERE.

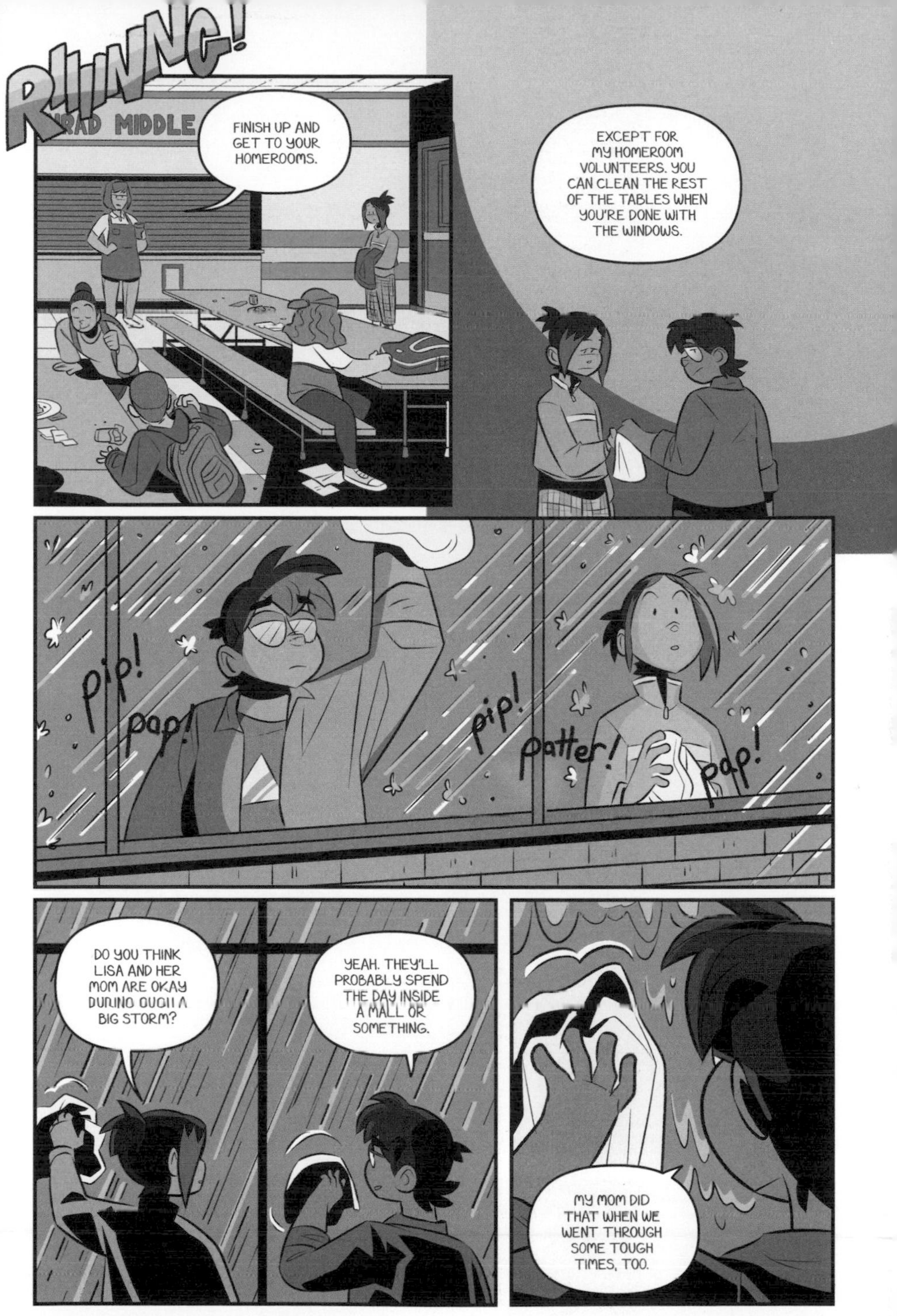
RIIIINNG!
RAD MIDDLE
FINISH UP AND GET TO YOUR HOMEROOMS.
EXCEPT FOR MY HOMEROOM VOLUNTEERS. YOU CAN CLEAN THE REST OF THE TABLES WHEN YOU'RE DONE WITH THE WINDOWS.
pip!
pap!
pip!
patter!
pap!
DO YOU THINK LISA AND HER MOM ARE OKAY DURING SUCH A BIG STORM?
YEAH. THEY'LL PROBABLY SPEND THE DAY INSIDE A MALL OR SOMETHING.
MY MOM DID THAT WHEN WE WENT THROUGH SOME TOUGH TIMES, TOO.

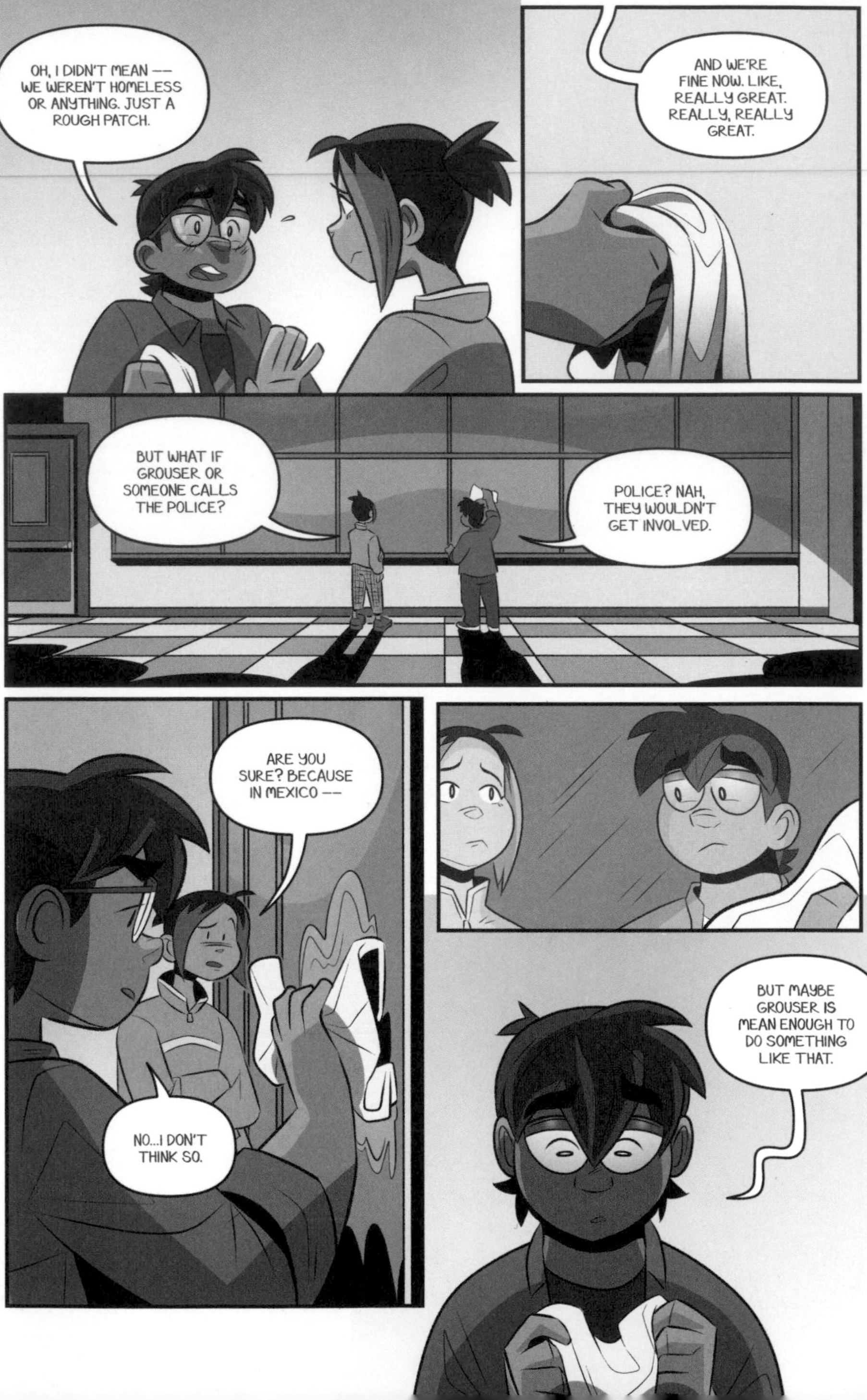
OH, I DIDN'T MEAN -- WE WEREN'T HOMELESS OR ANYTHING. JUST A ROUGH PATCH.
AND WE'RE FINE NOW. LIKE, REALLY GREAT. REALLY, REALLY GREAT.
BUT WHAT IF GROUSER OR SOMEONE CALLS THE POLICE?
POLICE? NAH, THEY WOULDN'T GET INVOLVED.
ARE YOU SURE? BECAUSE IN MEXICO --
NO...I DON'T THINK SO.
BUT MAYBE GROUSER IS MEAN ENOUGH TO DO SOMETHING LIKE THAT.

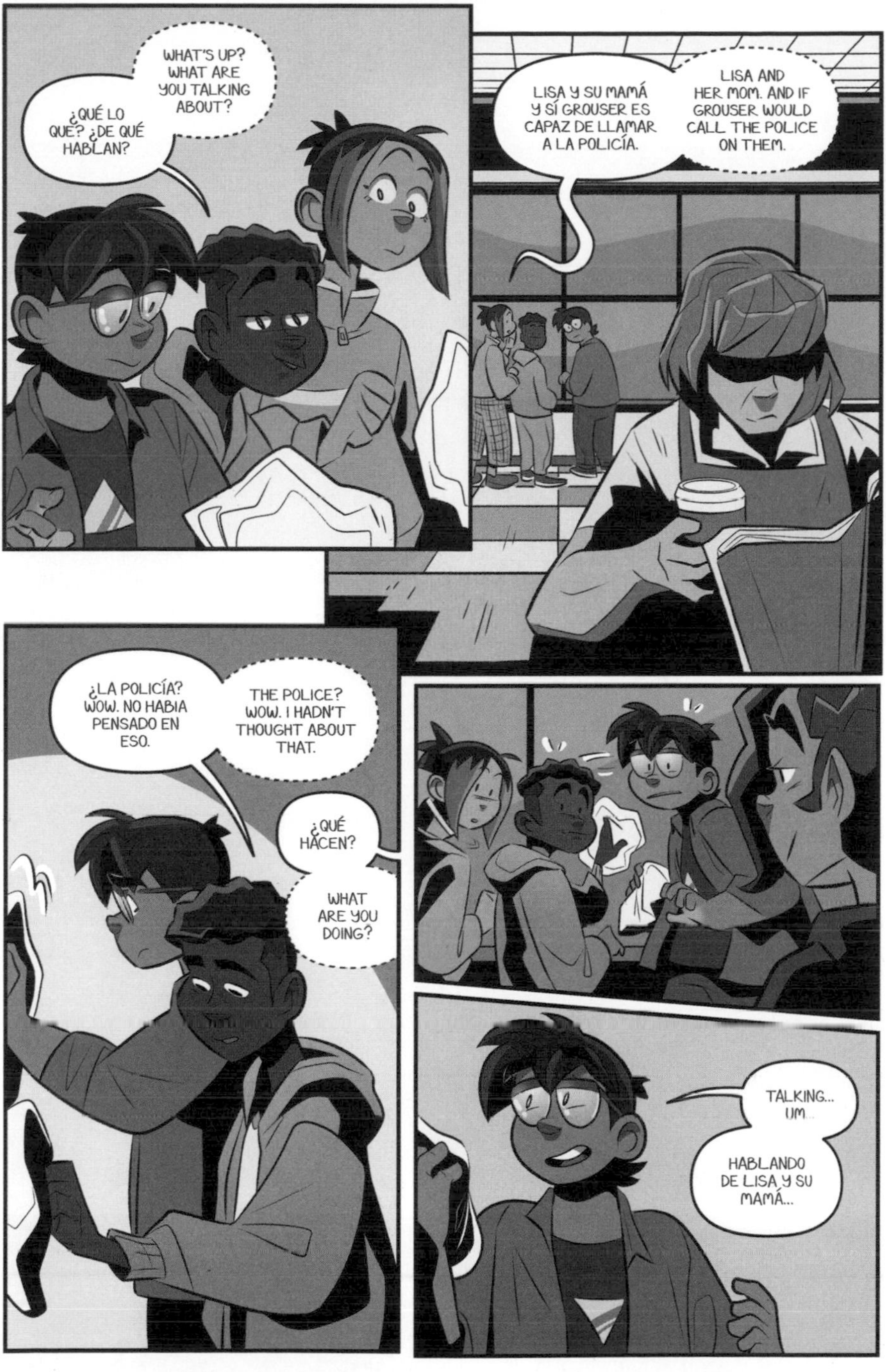
¿QUÉ LO QUE? ¿DE QUÉ HABLAN?
WHAT'S UP? WHAT ARE YOU TALKING ABOUT?
LISA Y SU MAMÁ Y SÍ GROUSER ES CAPAZ DE LLAMAR A LA POLICÍA.
LISA AND HER MOM. AND IF GROUSER WOULD CALL THE POLICE ON THEM.
¿LA POLICÍA? WOW. NO HABIA PENSADO EN ESO.
THE POLICE? WOW. I HADN'T THOUGHT ABOUT THAT.
¿QUÉ HACEN?
WHAT ARE YOU DOING?
TALKING... UM...
HABLANDO DE LISA Y SU MAMÁ...

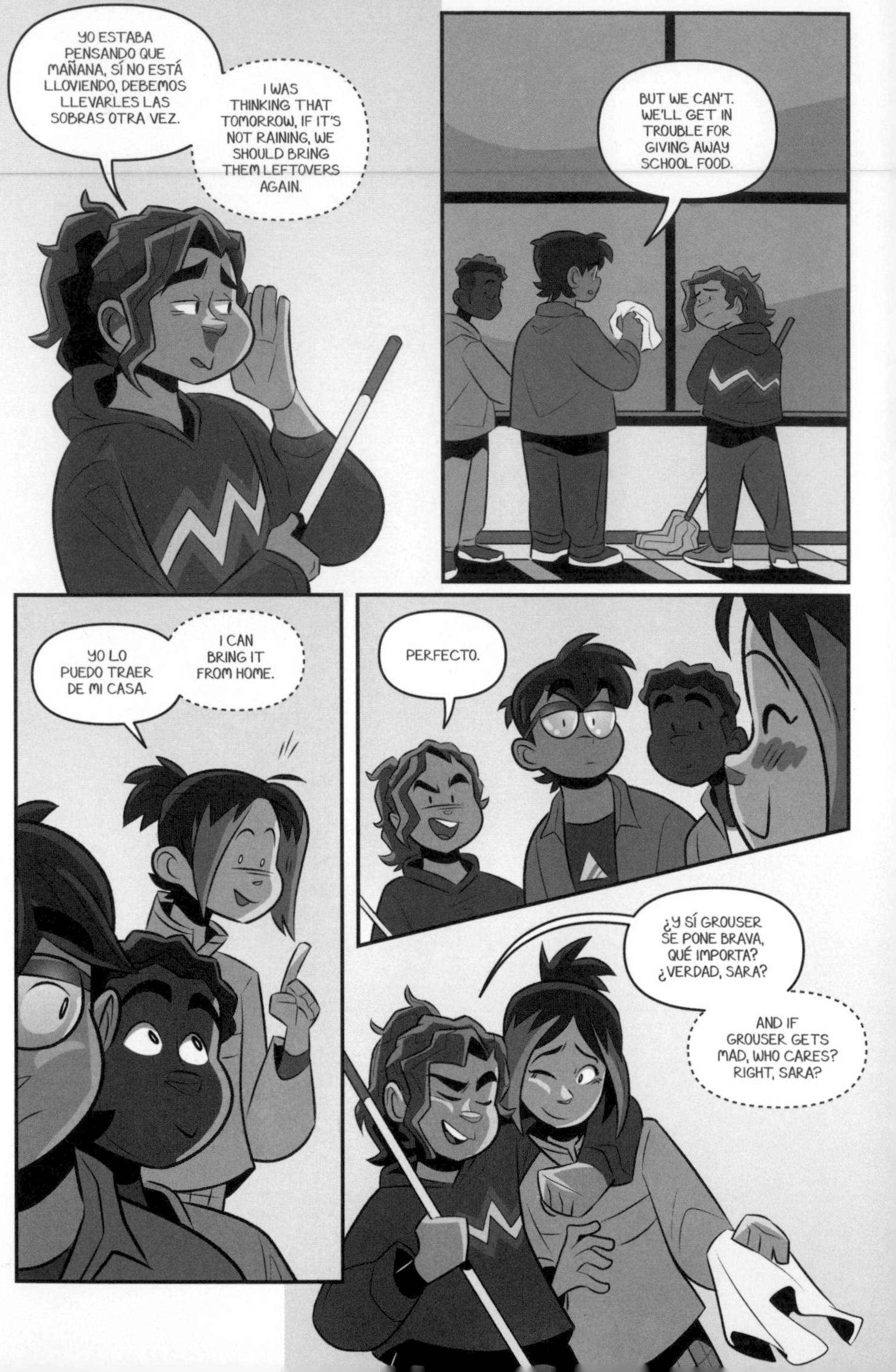
YO ESTABA PENSANDO QUE MAÑANA, SÍ NO ESTÁ LLOVIENDO, DEBEMOS LLEVARLES LAS SOBRAS OTRA VEZ.
I WAS THINKING THAT TOMORROW, IF IT'S NOT RAINING, WE SHOULD BRING THEM LEFTOVERS AGAIN.
BUT WE CAN'T. WE'LL GET IN TROUBLE FOR GIVING AWAY SCHOOL FOOD.
YO LO PUEDO TRAER DE MI CASA.
I CAN BRING IT FROM HOME.
PERFECTO.
¿Y SÍ GROUSER SE PONE BRAVA, QUÉ IMPORTA? ¿VERDAD, SARA?
AND IF GROUSER GETS MAD, WHO CARES? RIGHT, SARA?

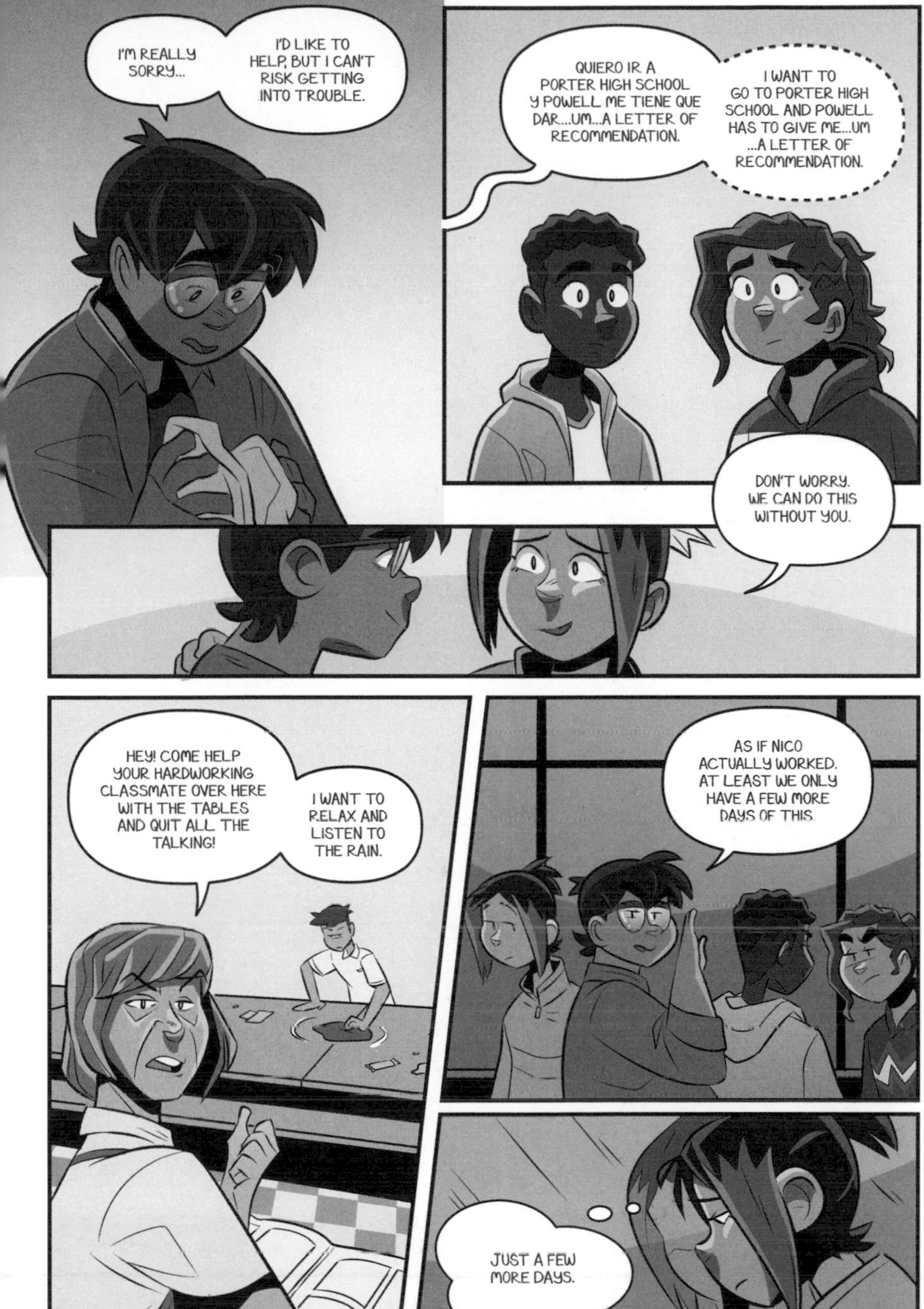
I'M REALLY SORRY...
I'D LIKE TO HELP, BUT I CAN'T RISK GETTING INTO TROUBLE.
QUIERO IR A PORTER HIGH SCHOOL Y POWELL ME TIENE QUE DAR...UM...A LETTER OF RECOMMENDATION.
I WANT TO GO TO PORTER HIGH SCHOOL AND POWELL HAS TO GIVE ME...UM ...A LETTER OF RECOMMENDATION.
DON'T WORRY. WE CAN DO THIS WITHOUT YOU.
HEY! COME HELP YOUR HARDWORKING CLASSMATE OVER HERE WITH THE TABLES AND QUIT ALL THE TALKING!
I WANT TO RELAX AND LISTEN TO THE RAIN.
AS IF NICO ACTUALLY WORKED. AT LEAST WE ONLY HAVE A FEW MORE DAYS OF THIS.
JUST A FEW MORE DAYS.

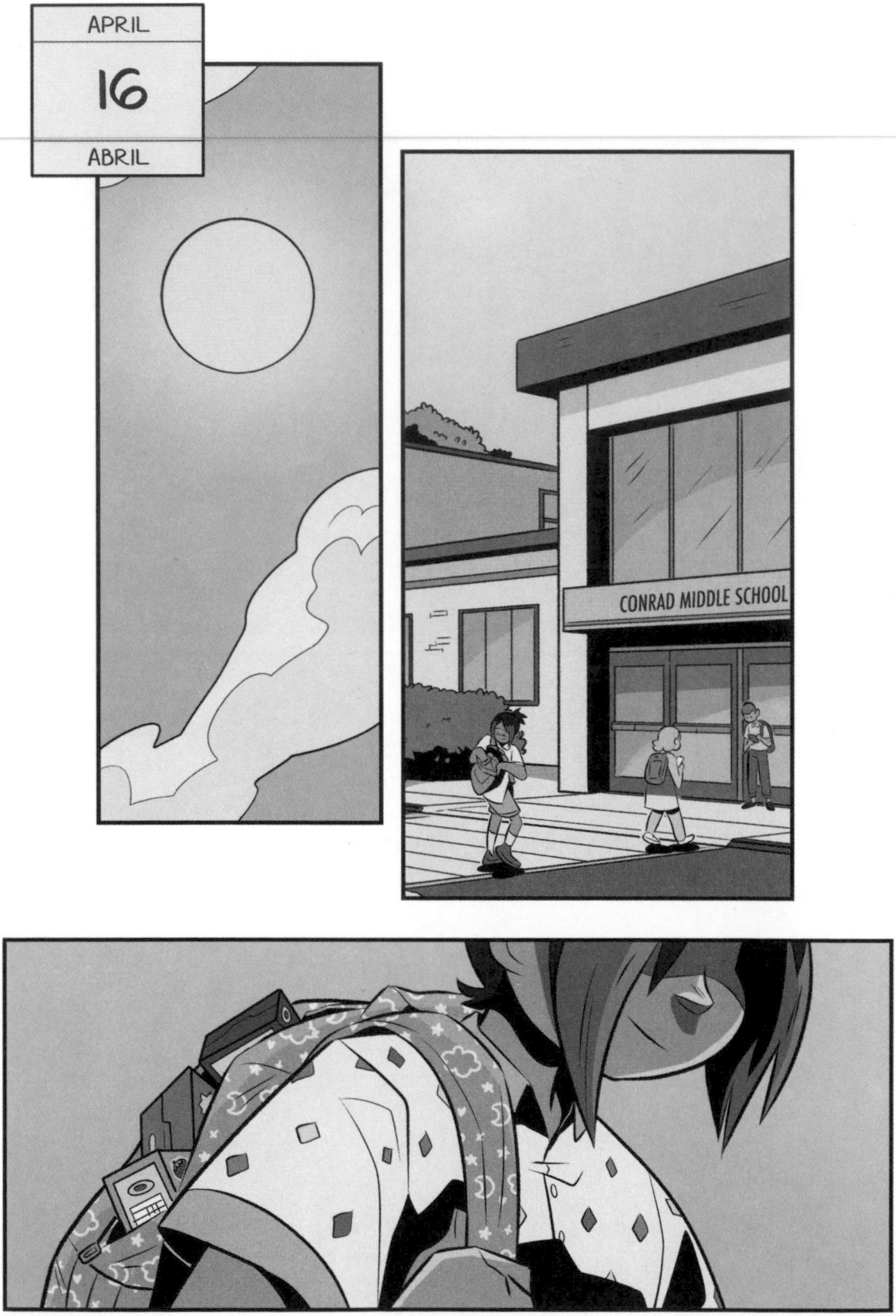
APRIL
16
ABRIL
CONRAD MIDDLE SCHOOL

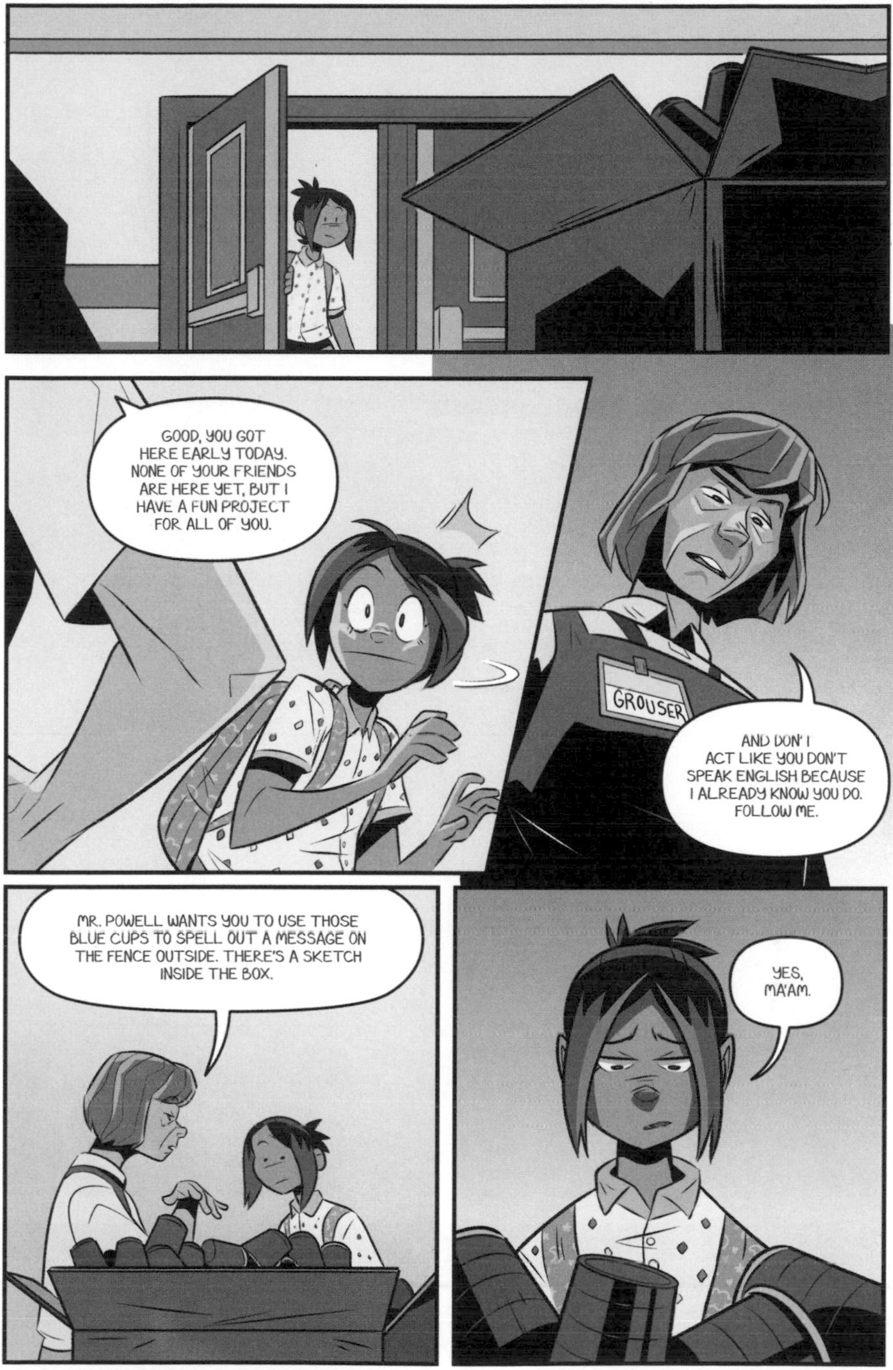
GOOD, YOU GOT HERE EARLY TODAY. NONE OF YOUR FRIENDS ARE HERE YET, BUT I HAVE A FUN PROJECT FOR ALL OF YOU.
GROUSER
AND DON'T ACT LIKE YOU DON'T SPEAK ENGLISH BECAUSE I ALREADY KNOW YOU DO. FOLLOW ME.
MR. POWELL WANTS YOU TO USE THOSE BLUE CUPS TO SPELL OUT A MESSAGE ON THE FENCE OUTSIDE. THERE'S A SKETCH INSIDE THE BOX.
YES, MA'AM.

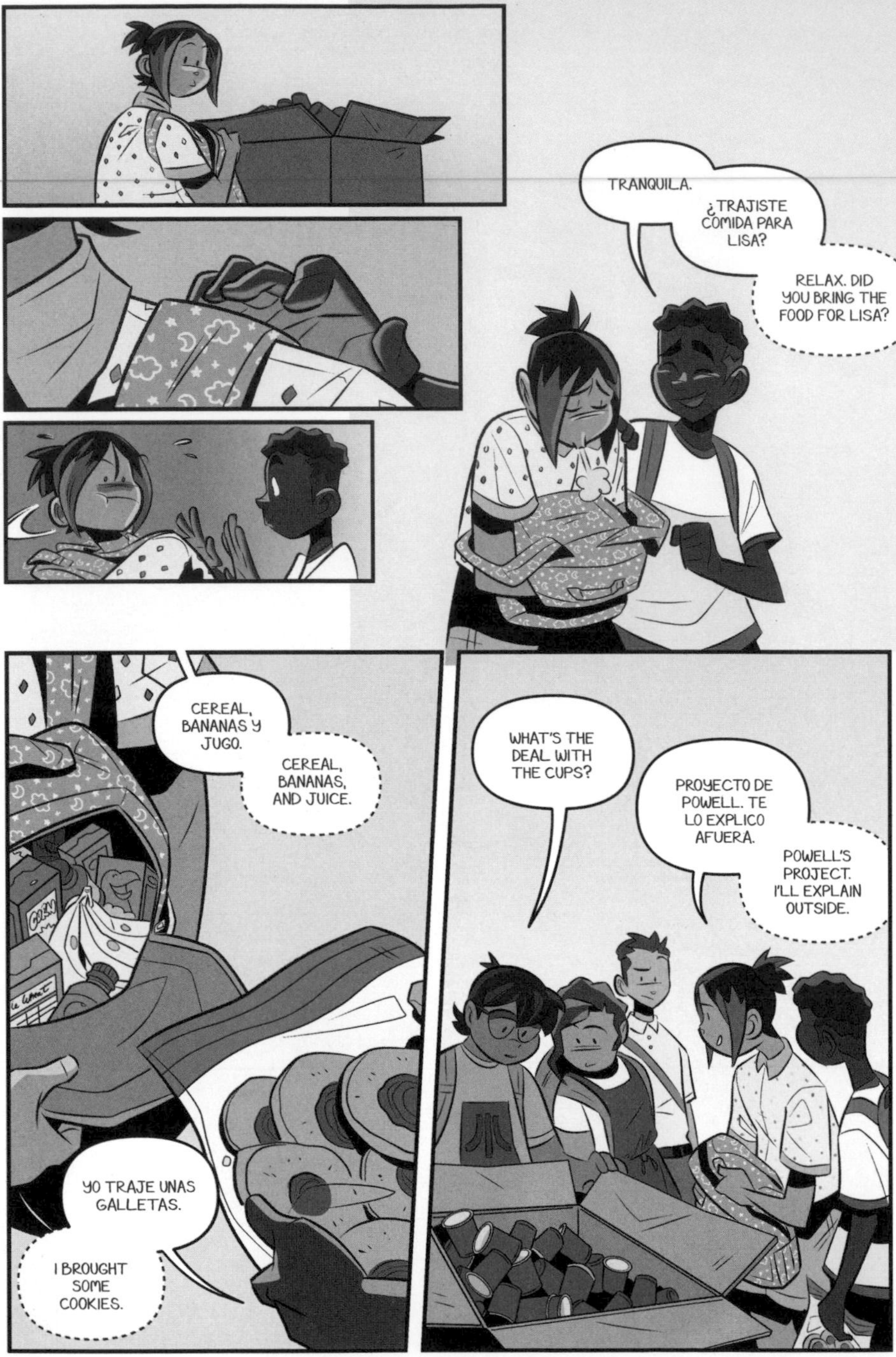
TRANQUILA.
¿TRAJISTE COMIDA PARA LISA?
RELAX. DID YOU BRING THE FOOD FOR LISA?
CEREAL, BANANAS Y JUGO.
CEREAL, BANANAS, AND JUICE.
YO TRAJE UNAS GALLETAS.
I BROUGHT SOME COOKIES.
WHAT'S THE DEAL WITH THE CUPS?
PROYECTO DE POWELL. TE LO EXPLICO AFUERA.
POWELL'S PROJECT. I'LL EXPLAIN OUTSIDE.

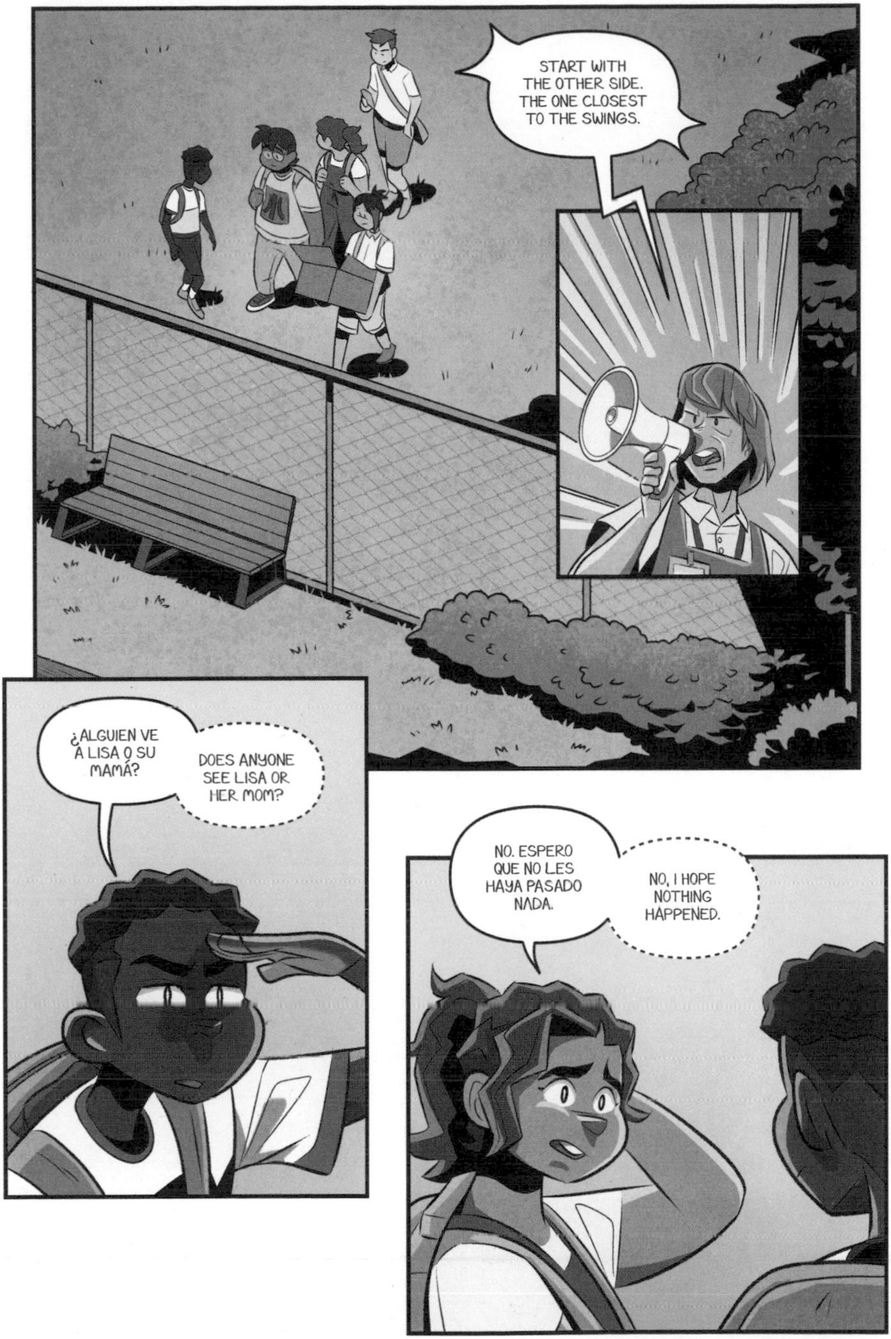
START WITH THE OTHER SIDE. THE ONE CLOSEST TO THE SWINGS.
¿ALGUIEN VE A LISA O SU MAMÁ?
DOES ANYONE SEE LISA OR HER MOM?
NO. ESPERO QUE NO LES HAYA PASADO NADA.
NO, I HOPE NOTHING HAPPENED.

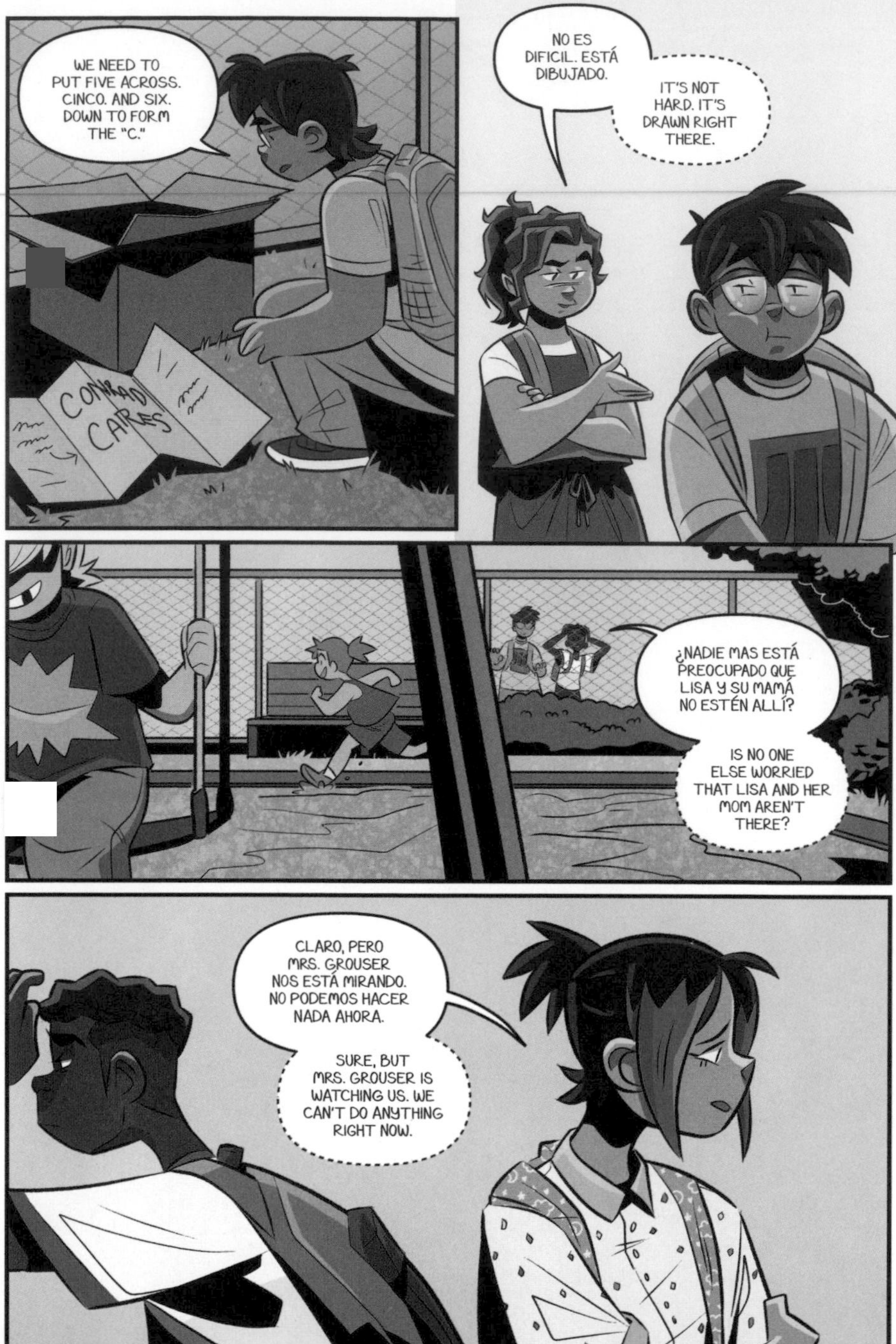
WE NEED TO PUT FIVE ACROSS. CINCO. AND SIX. DOWN TO FORM THE "C."
CONRAD CARES
NO ES DIFICIL. ESTÁ DIBUJADO.
IT'S NOT HARD. IT'S DRAWN RIGHT THERE.
¿NADIE MAS ESTÁ PREOCUPADO QUE LISA Y SU MAMÁ NO ESTÉN ALLÍ?
IS NO ONE ELSE WORRIED THAT LISA AND HER MOM AREN'T THERE?
CLARO, PERO MRS. GROUSER NOS ESTÁ MIRANDO. NO PODEMOS HACER NADA AHORA.
SURE, BUT MRS. GROUSER IS WATCHING US. WE CAN'T DO ANYTHING RIGHT NOW.

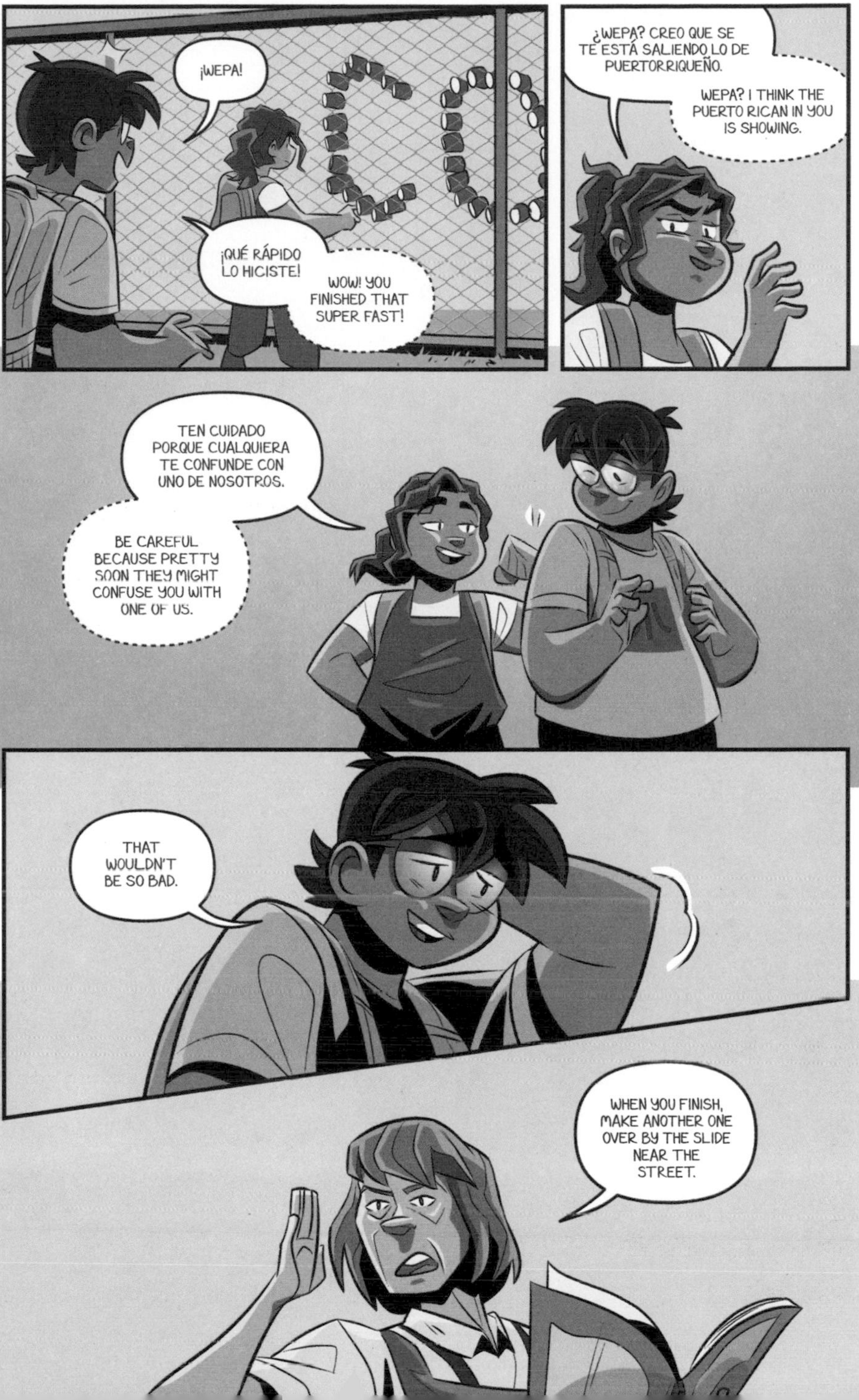
¡WEPA!
¡QUÉ RÁPIDO LO HICISTE!
WOW! YOU FINISHED THAT SUPER FAST!
¿WEPA? CREO QUE SE TE ESTÁ SALIENDO LO DE PUERTORRIQUEÑO.
WEPA? I THINK THE PUERTO RICAN IN YOU IS SHOWING.
TEN CUIDADO PORQUE CUALQUIERA TE CONFUNDE CON UNO DE NOSOTROS.
BE CAREFUL BECAUSE PRETTY SOON THEY MIGHT CONFUSE YOU WITH ONE OF US.
THAT WOULDN'T BE SO BAD.
WHEN YOU FINISH, MAKE ANOTHER ONE OVER BY THE SLIDE NEAR THE STREET.

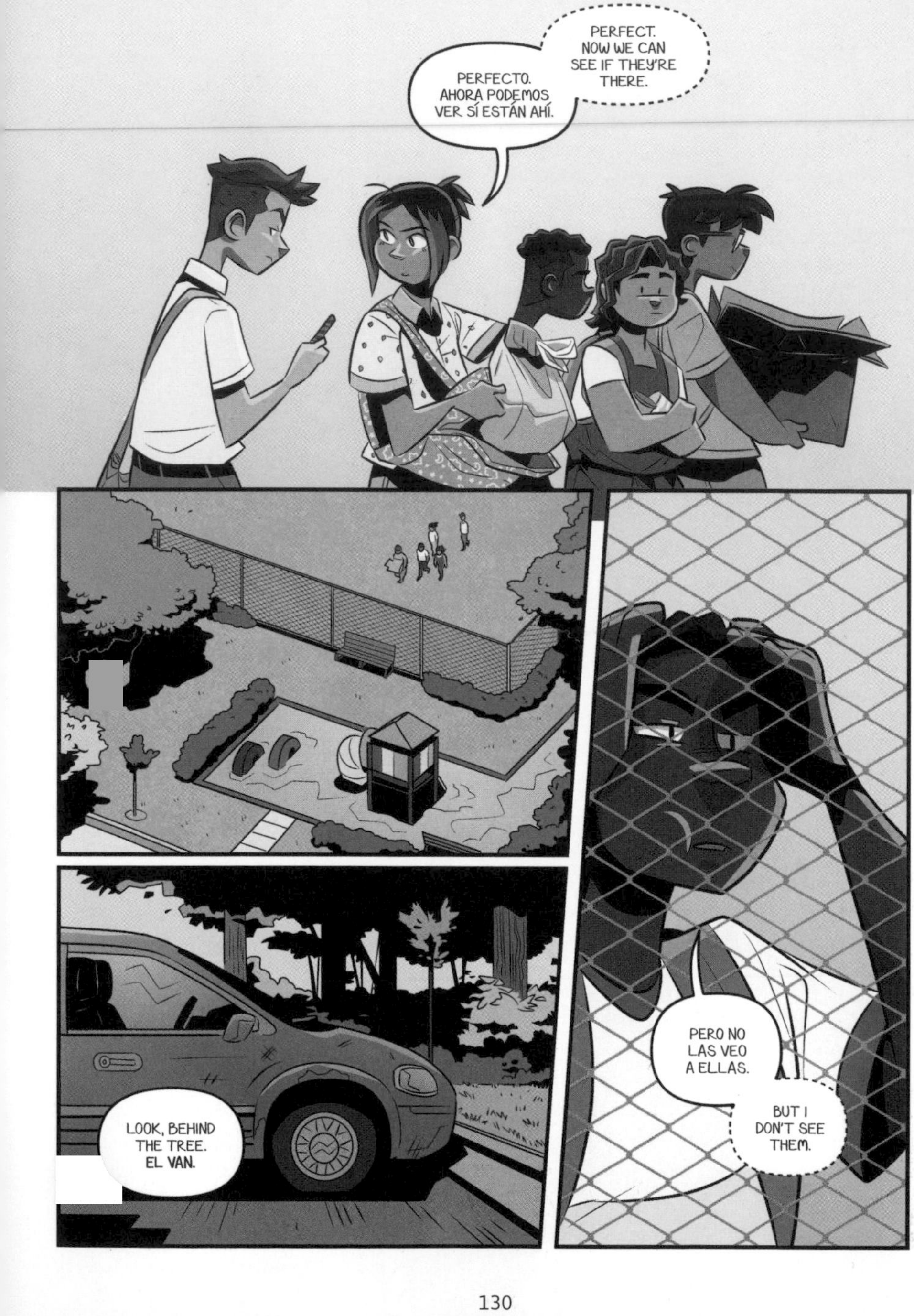
PERFECTO. AHORA PODEMOS VER SÍ ESTÁN AHÍ.
PERFECT. NOW WE CAN SEE IF THEY'RE THERE.
LOOK, BEHIND THE TREE. EL VAN.
PERO NO LAS VEO A ELLAS.
BUT I DON'T SEE THEM.

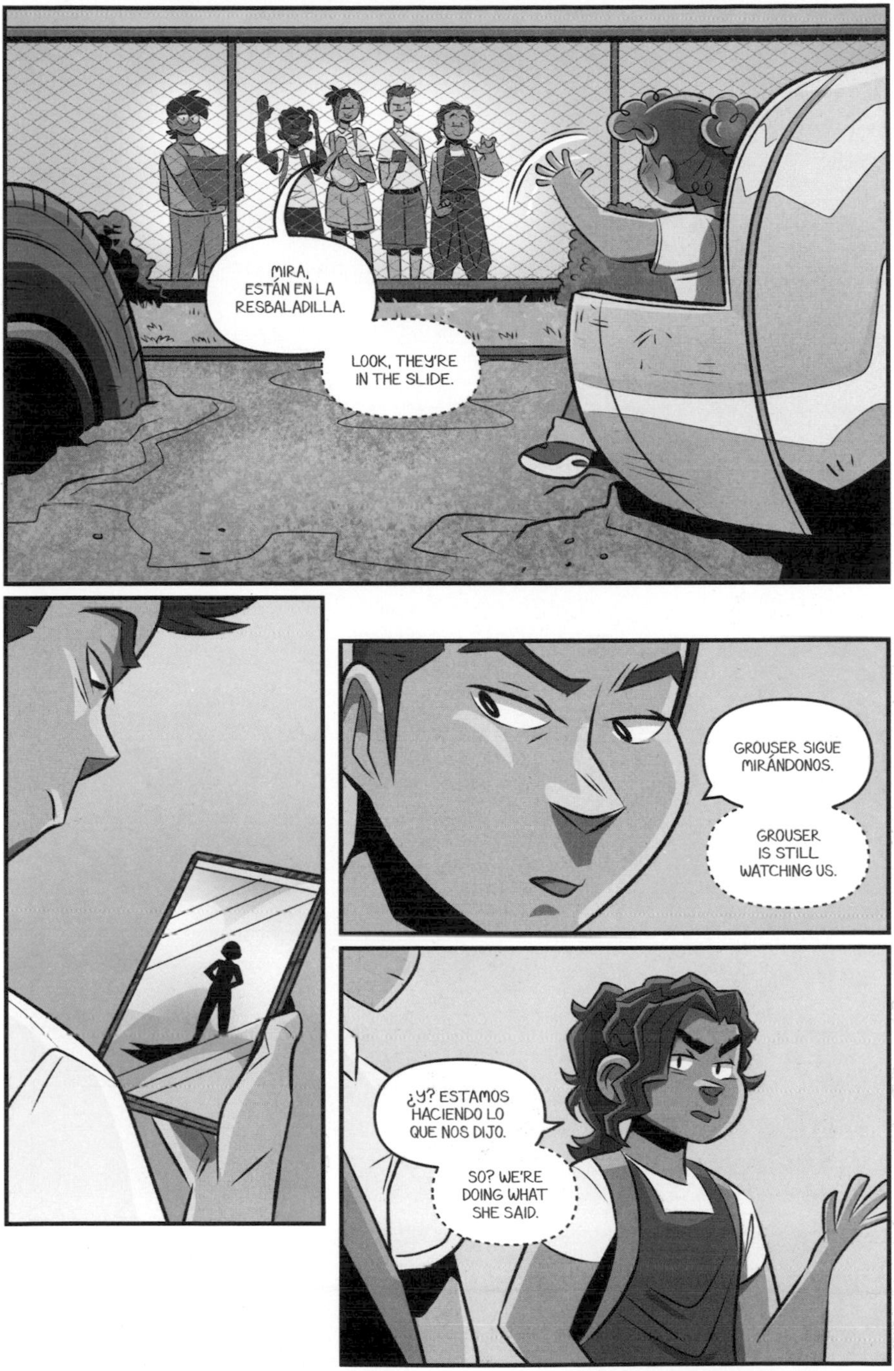
MIRA, ESTÁN EN LA RESBALADILLA.
LOOK, THEY'RE IN THE SLIDE.
GROUSER SIGUE MIRÁNDONOS.
GROUSER IS STILL WATCHING US.
¿Y? ESTAMOS HACIENDO LO QUE NOS DIJO.
SO? WE'RE DOING WHAT SHE SAID.

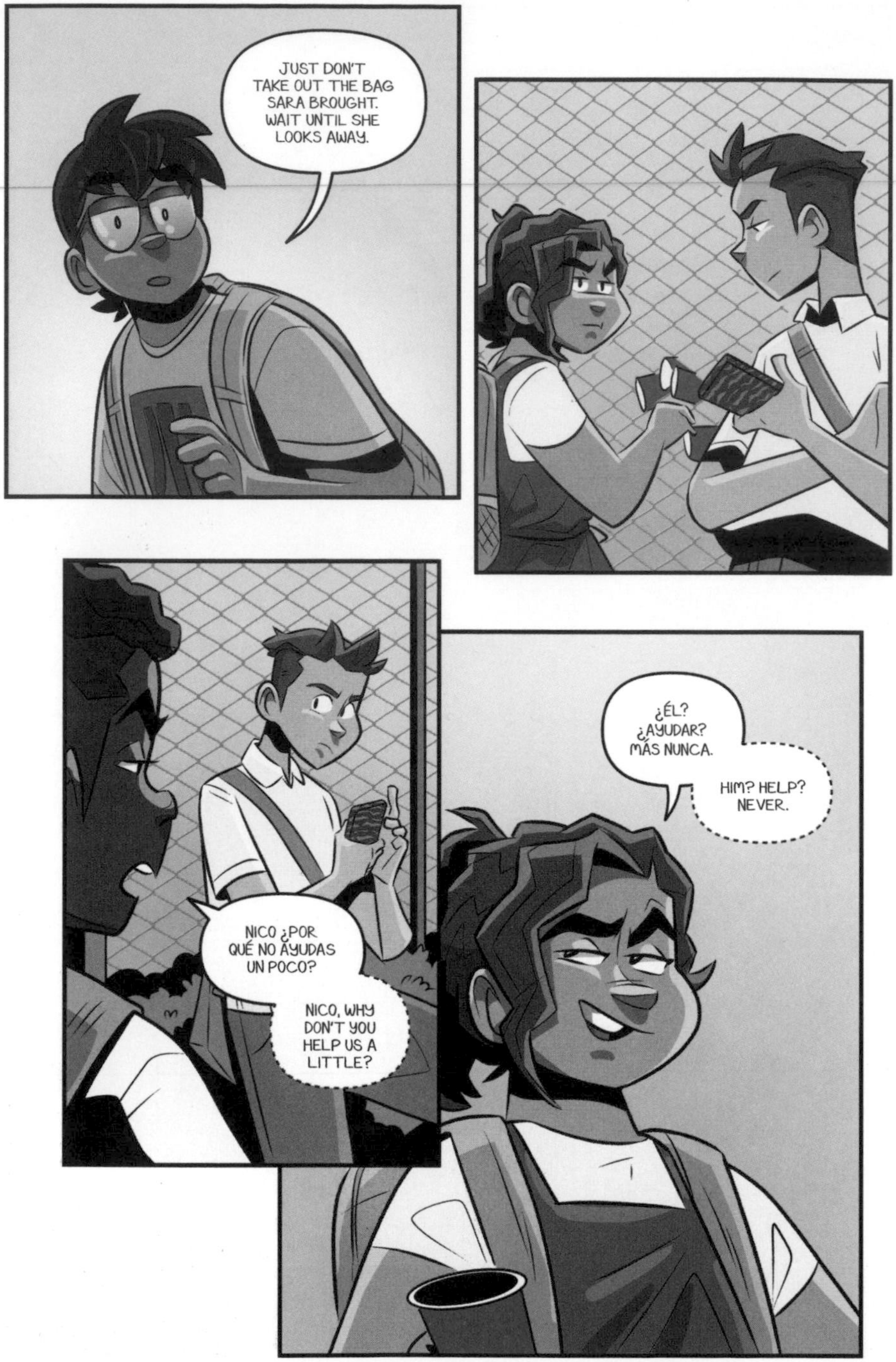
JUST DON'T TAKE OUT THE BAG SARA BROUGHT. WAIT UNTIL SHE LOOKS AWAY.
NICO ¿POR QUÉ NO AYUDAS UN POCO?
NICO, WHY DON'T YOU HELP US A LITTLE?
¿ÉL? ¿AYUDAR? MÁS NUNCA.
HIM? HELP? NEVER.

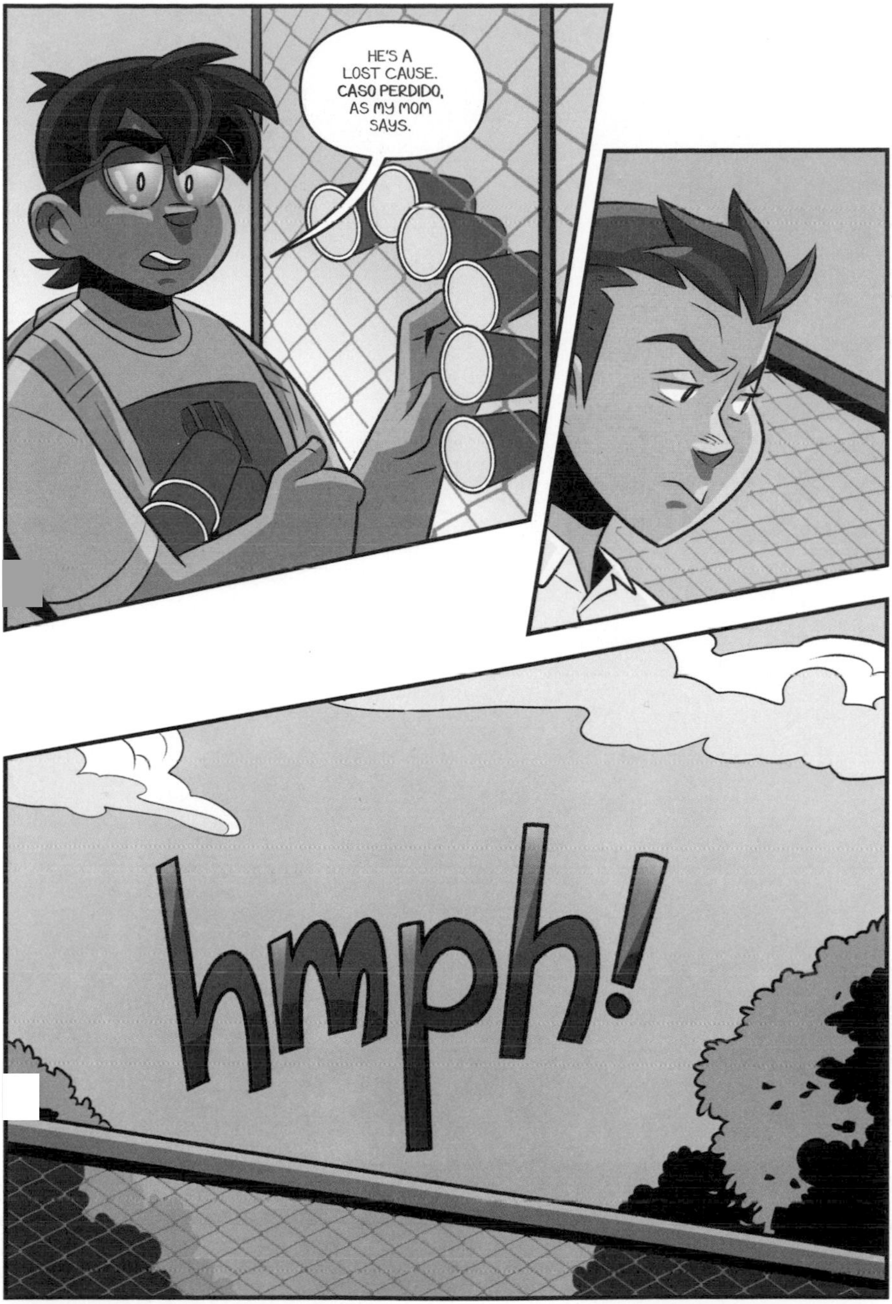
HE'S A LOST CAUSE. **CASO PERDIDO,** AS MY MOM SAYS.
hmph!

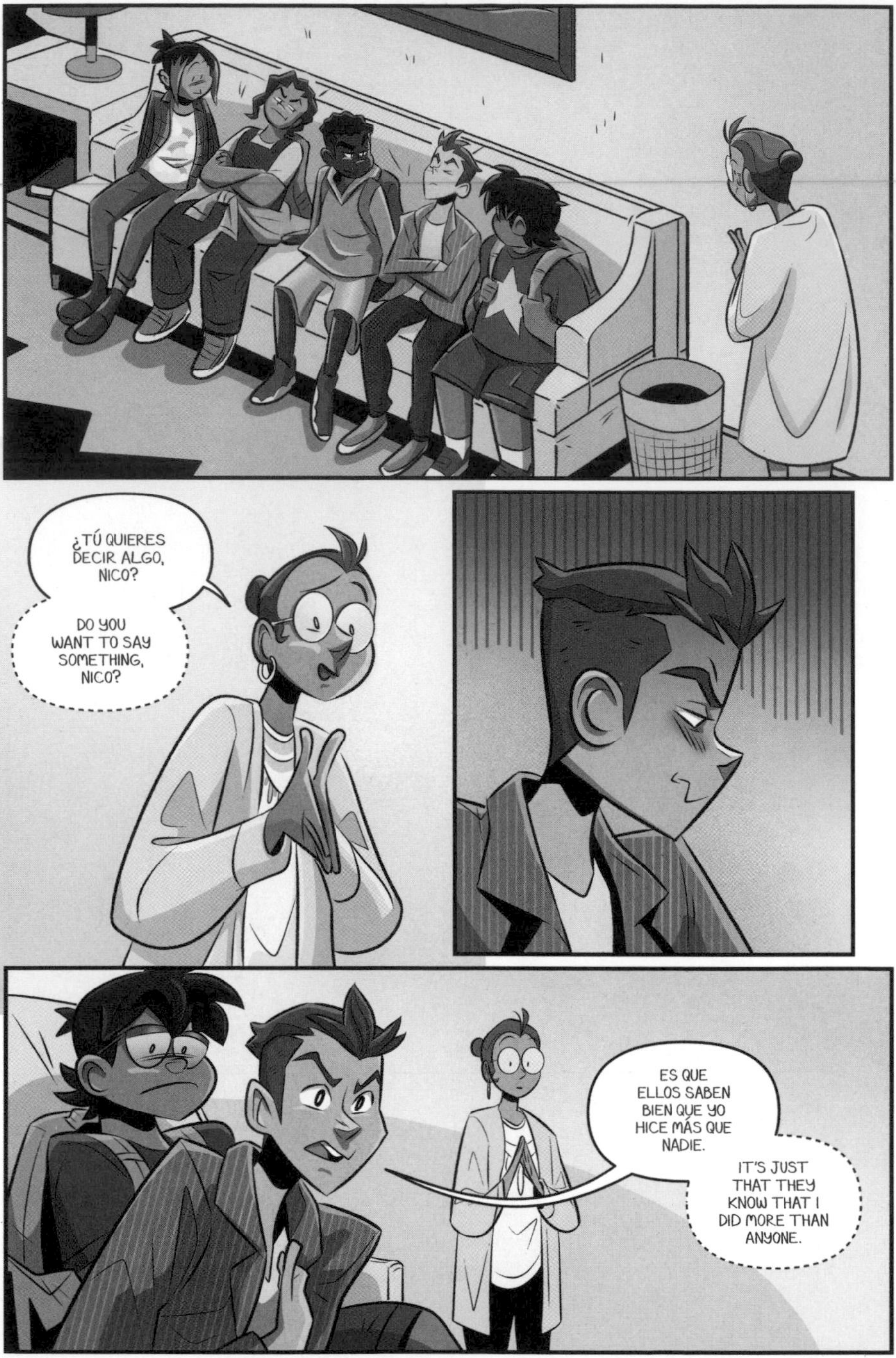
¿TÚ QUIERES DECIR ALGO, NICO?
DO YOU WANT TO SAY SOMETHING, NICO?
ES QUE ELLOS SABEN BIEN QUE YO HICE MÁS QUE NADIE.
IT'S JUST THAT THEY KNOW THAT I DID MORE THAN ANYONE.

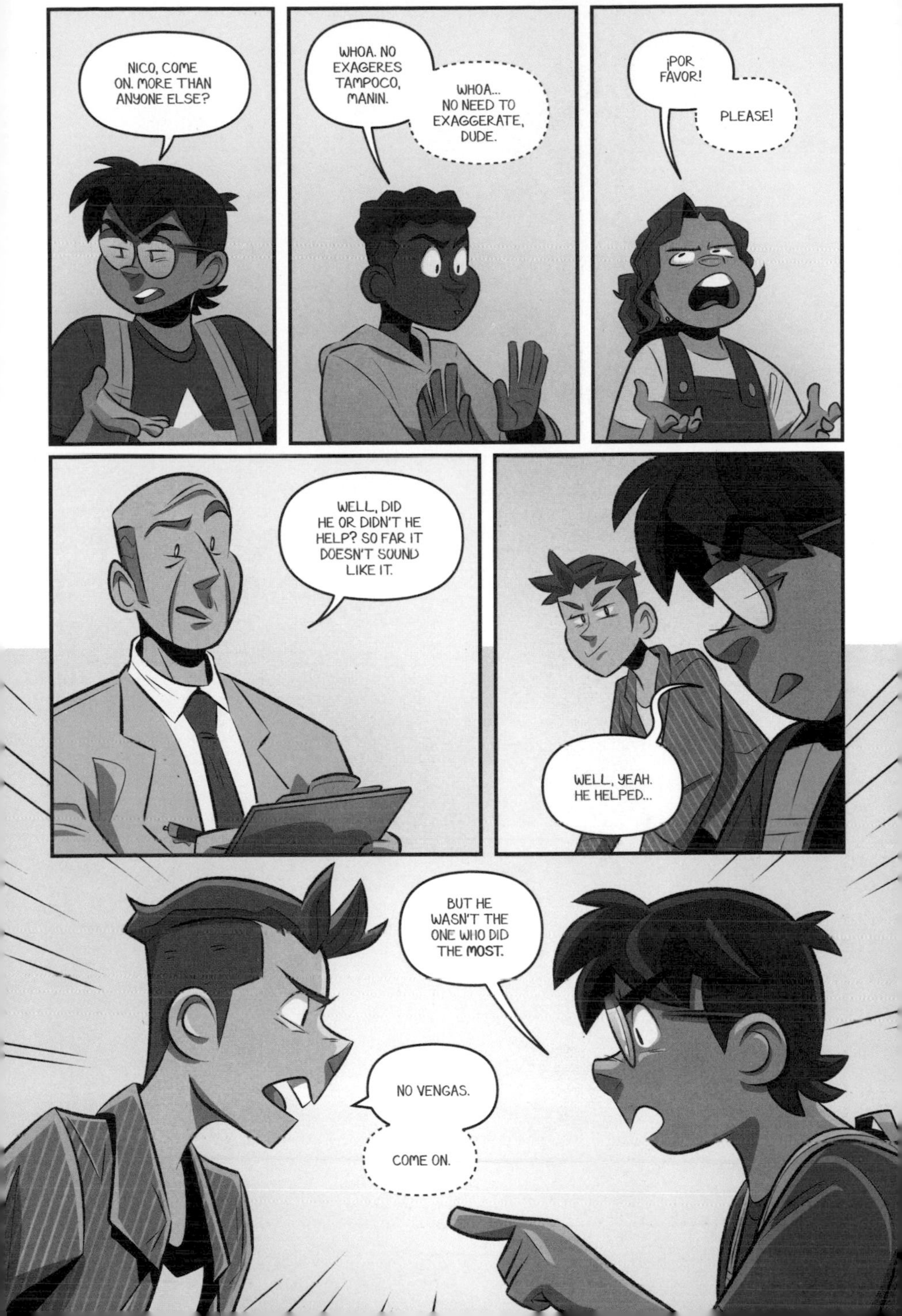
NICO, COME ON. MORE THAN ANYONE ELSE?
WHOA. NO EXAGERES TAMPOCO, MANIN.
WHOA... NO NEED TO EXAGGERATE, DUDE.
¡POR FAVOR!
PLEASE!
WELL, DID HE OR DIDN'T HE HELP? SO FAR IT DOESN'T SOUND LIKE IT.
WELL, YEAH. HE HELPED...
BUT HE WASN'T THE ONE WHO DID THE MOST.
NO VENGAS.
COME ON.

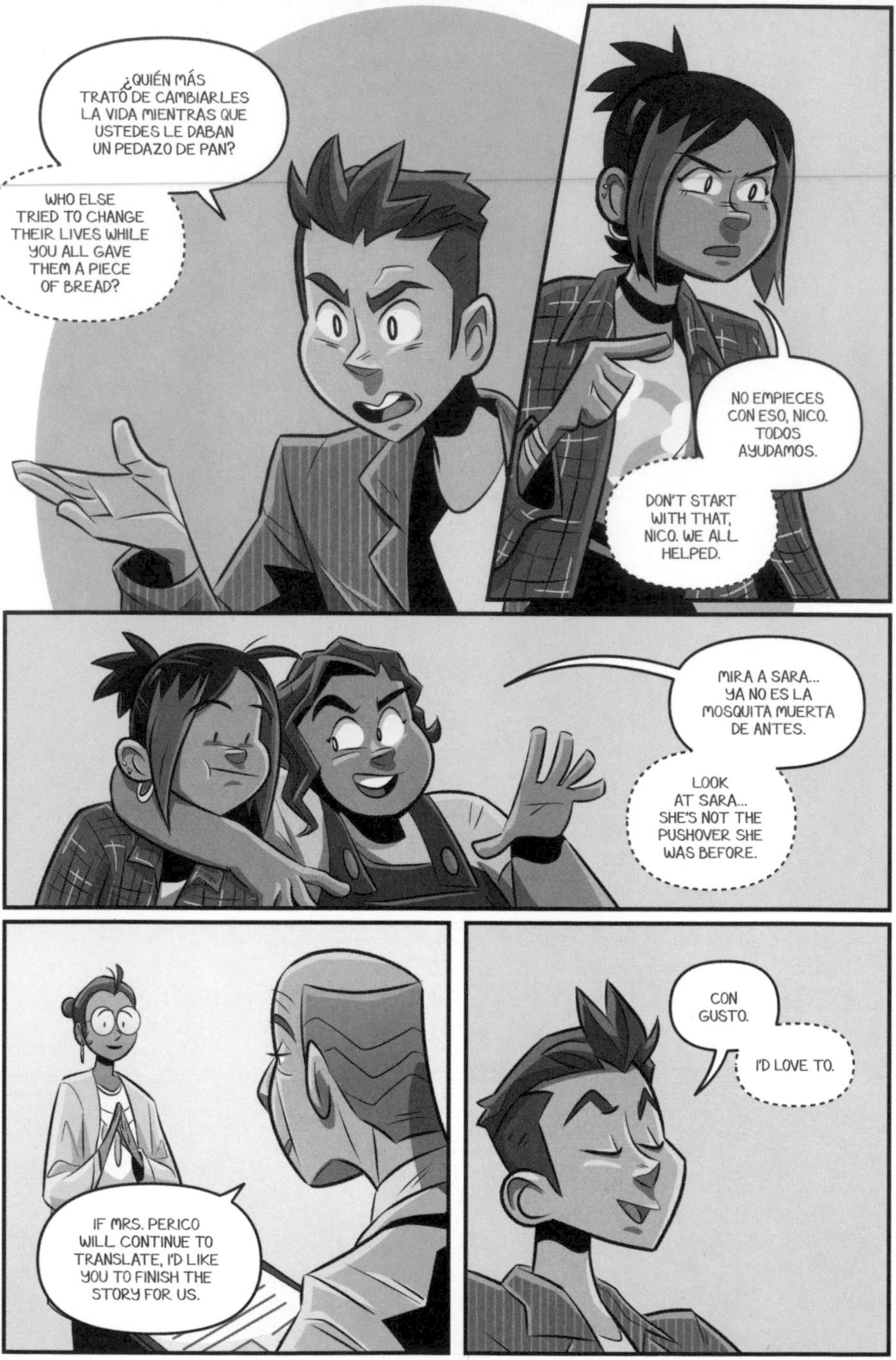
¿QUIÉN MÁS TRATÓ DE CAMBIARLES LA VIDA MIENTRAS QUE USTEDES LE DABAN UN PEDAZO DE PAN?
WHO ELSE TRIED TO CHANGE THEIR LIVES WHILE YOU ALL GAVE THEM A PIECE OF BREAD?
NO EMPIECES CON ESO, NICO. TODOS AYUDAMOS.
DON'T START WITH THAT, NICO. WE ALL HELPED.
MIRA A SARA... YA NO ES LA MOSQUITA MUERTA DE ANTES.
LOOK AT SARA... SHE'S NOT THE PUSHOVER SHE WAS BEFORE.
IF MRS. PERICO WILL CONTINUE TO TRANSLATE, I'D LIKE YOU TO FINISH THE STORY FOR US.
CON GUSTO.
I'D LOVE TO.

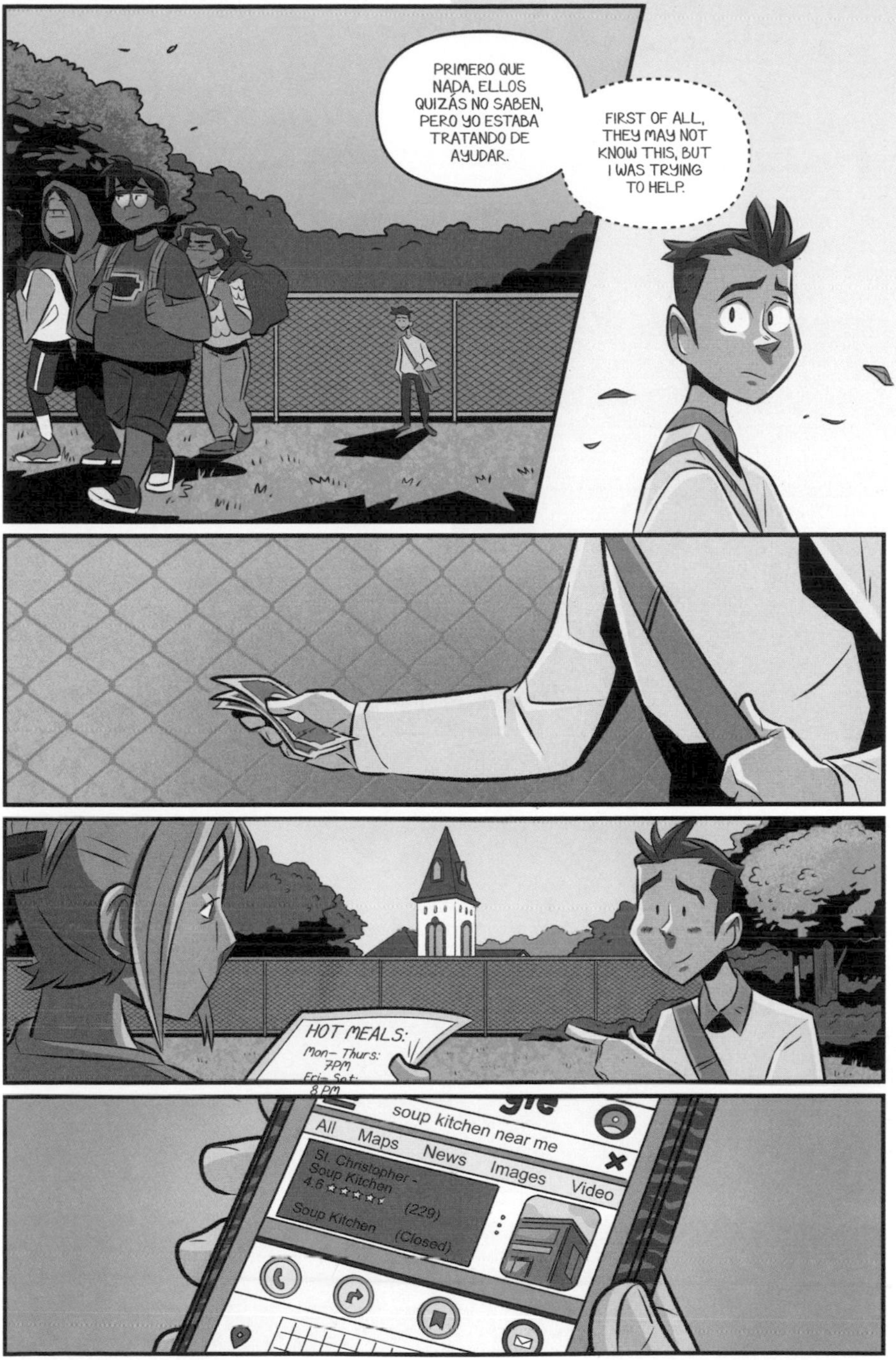
PRIMERO QUE NADA, ELLOS QUIZÁS NO SABEN, PERO YO ESTABA TRATANDO DE AYUDAR.
FIRST OF ALL, THEY MAY NOT KNOW THIS, BUT I WAS TRYING TO HELP.
HOT MEALS:
Mon– Thurs: 7PM
Fri– Sat: 8PM
soup kitchen near me
All Maps News Images Video
St. Christopher - Soup Kitchen
4.6 ★★★★★ (229)
Soup Kitchen (Closed)

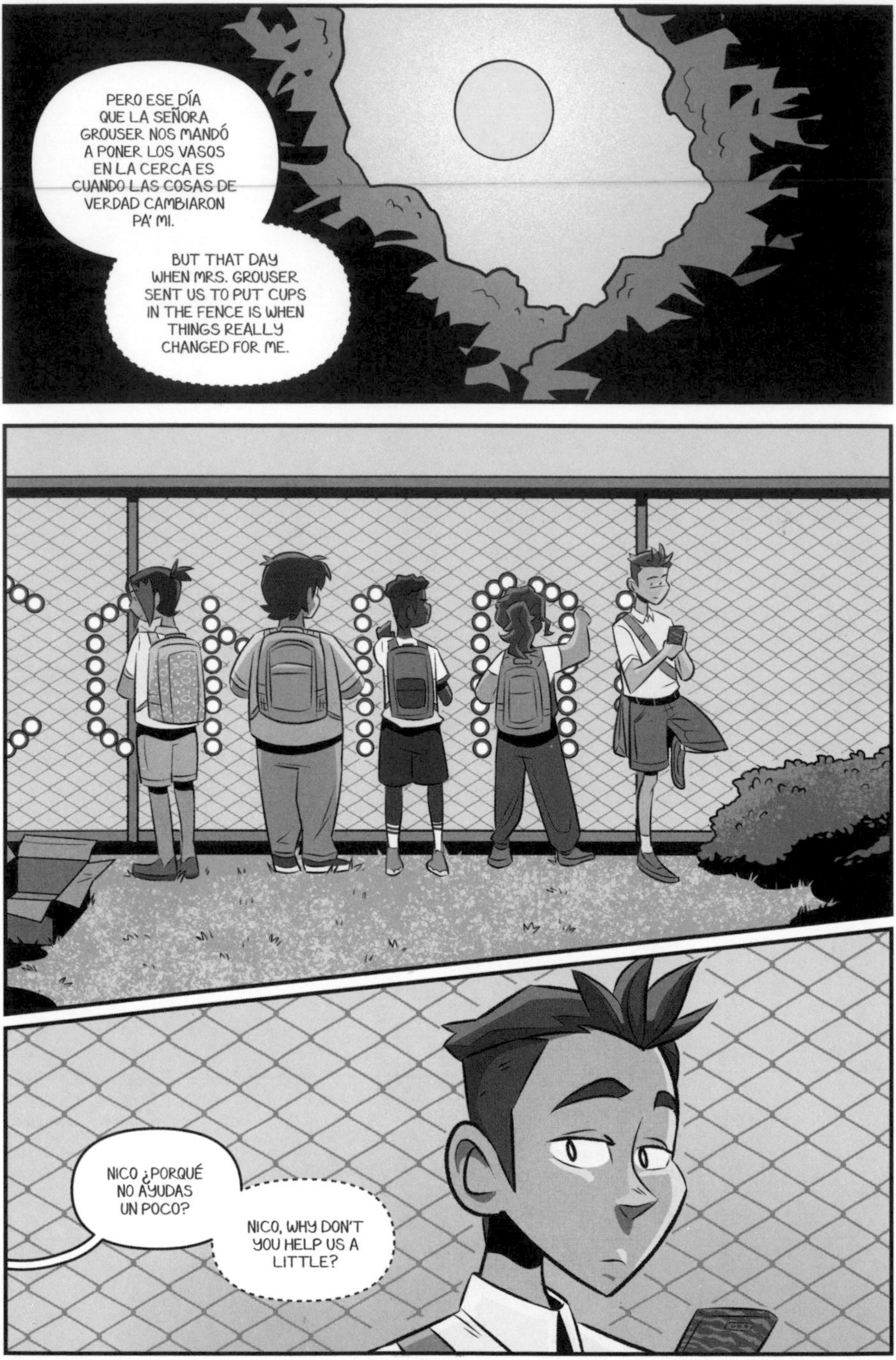
PERO ESE DÍA QUE LA SEÑORA GROUSER NOS MANDÓ A PONER LOS VASOS EN LA CERCA ES CUANDO LAS COSAS DE VERDAD CAMBIARON PA' MI.
BUT THAT DAY WHEN MRS. GROUSER SENT US TO PUT CUPS IN THE FENCE IS WHEN THINGS REALLY CHANGED FOR ME.
NICO ¿PORQUÉ NO AYUDAS UN POCO?
NICO, WHY DON'T YOU HELP US A LITTLE?

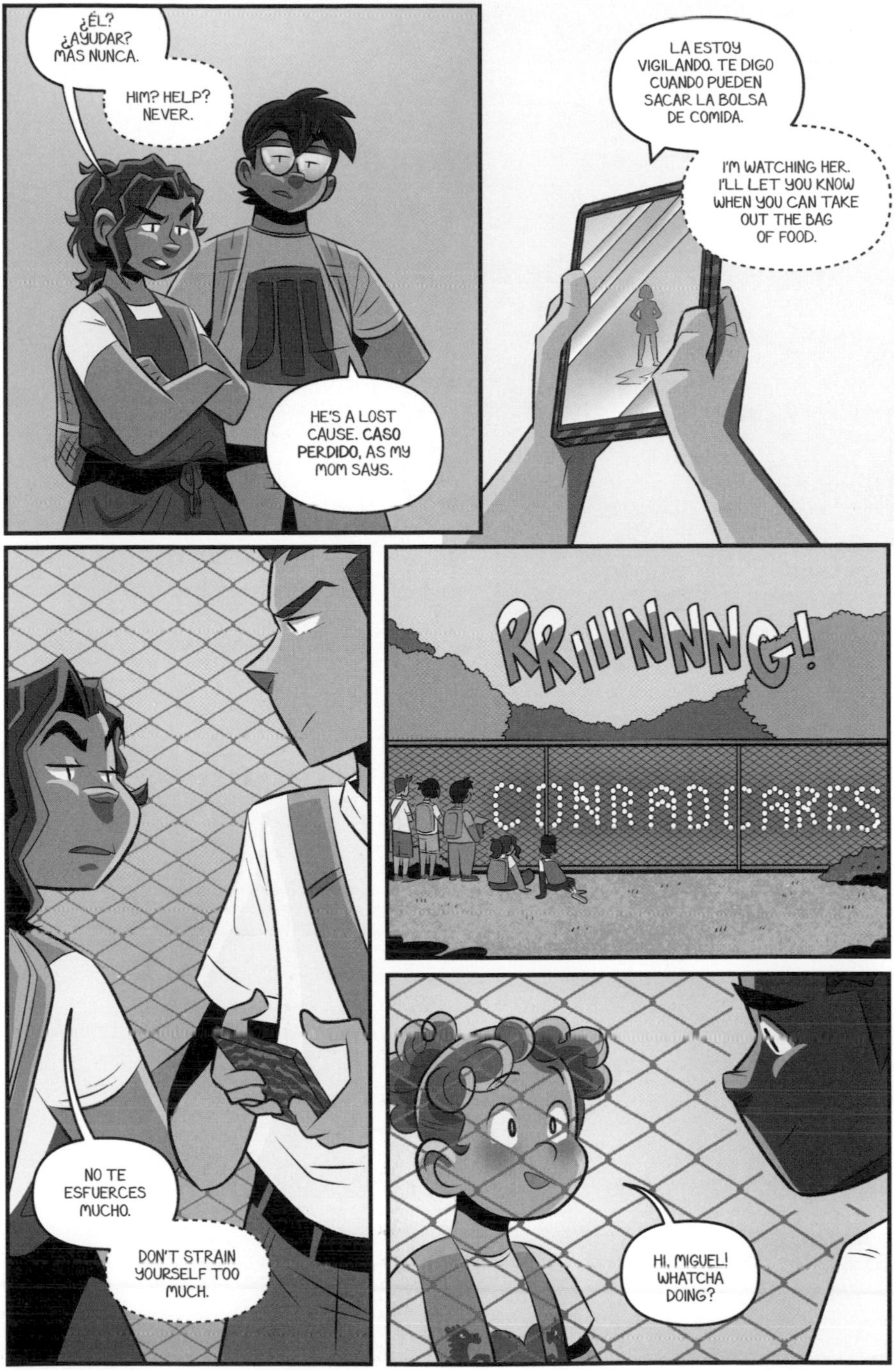
¿ÉL? ¿AYUDAR? MÁS NUNCA.
HIM? HELP? NEVER.
LA ESTOY VIGILANDO. TE DIGO CUANDO PUEDEN SACAR LA BOLSA DE COMIDA.
I'M WATCHING HER. I'LL LET YOU KNOW WHEN YOU CAN TAKE OUT THE BAG OF FOOD.
HE'S A LOST CAUSE. CASO PERDIDO, AS MY MOM SAYS.
RRIIINNNG!
CONRADCARES
NO TE ESFUERCES MUCHO.
DON'T STRAIN YOURSELF TOO MUCH.
HI, MIGUEL! WHATCHA DOING?

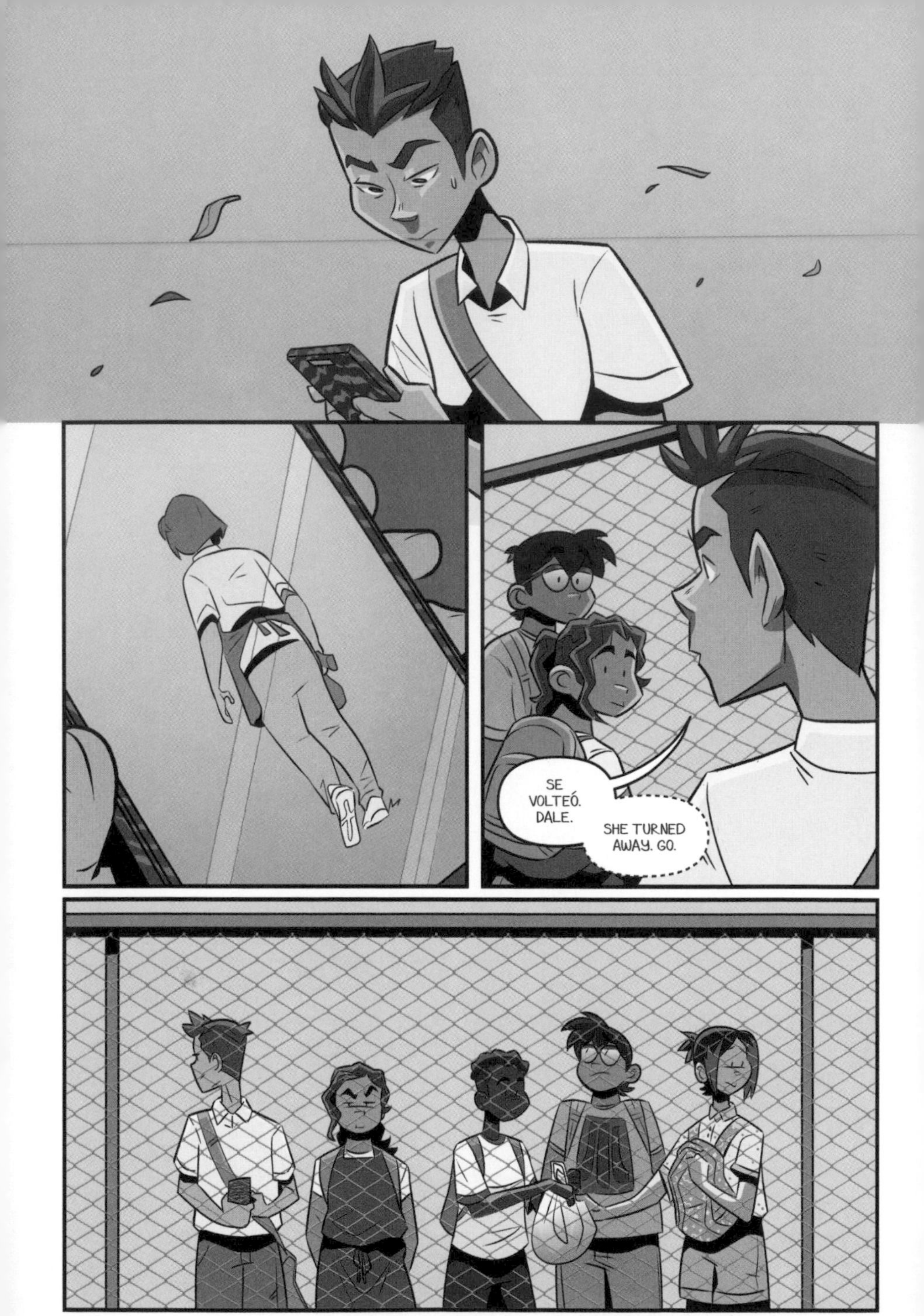
SE VOLTEÓ. DALE.
SHE TURNED AWAY. GO.

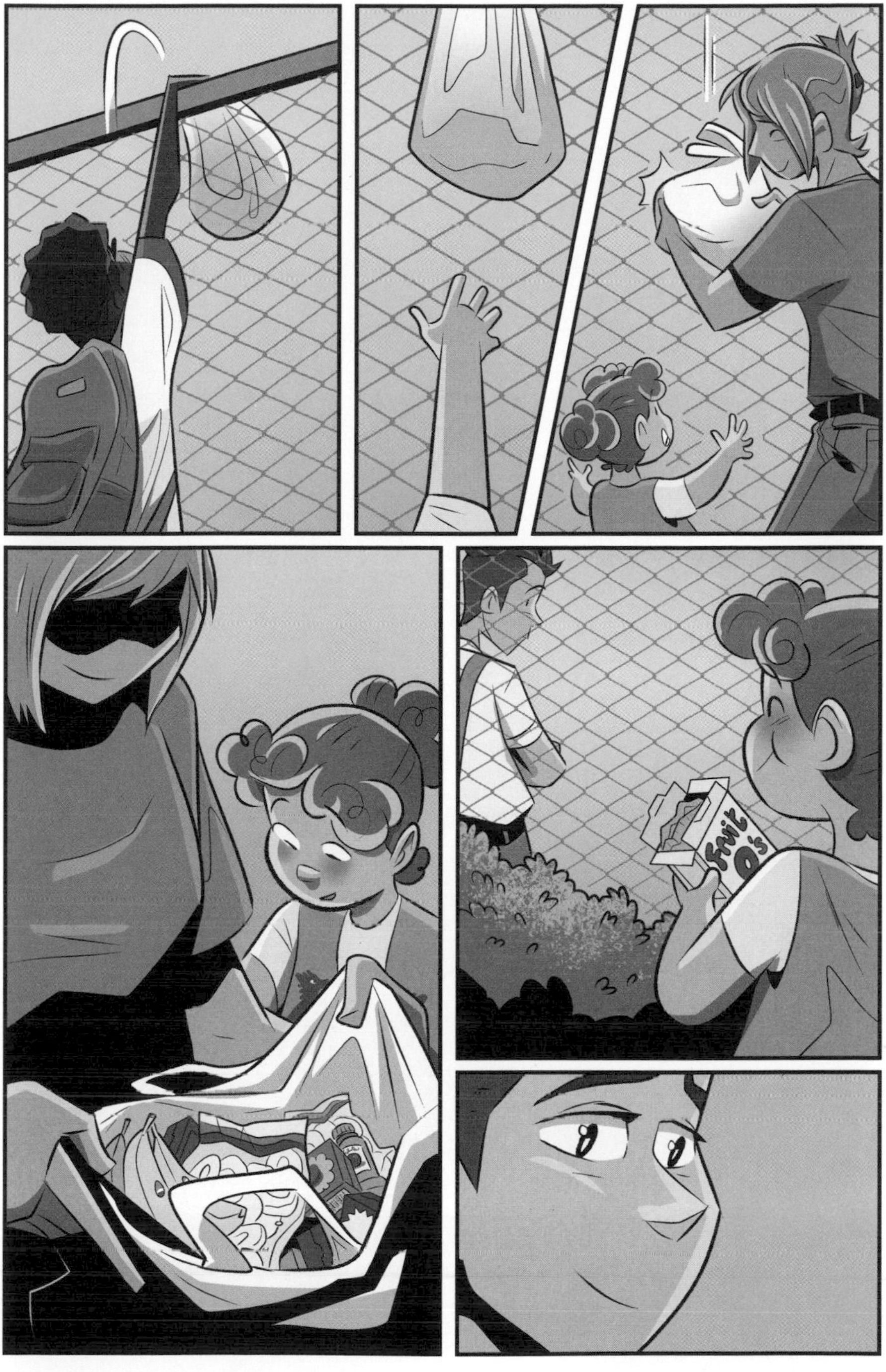
fruit
O's

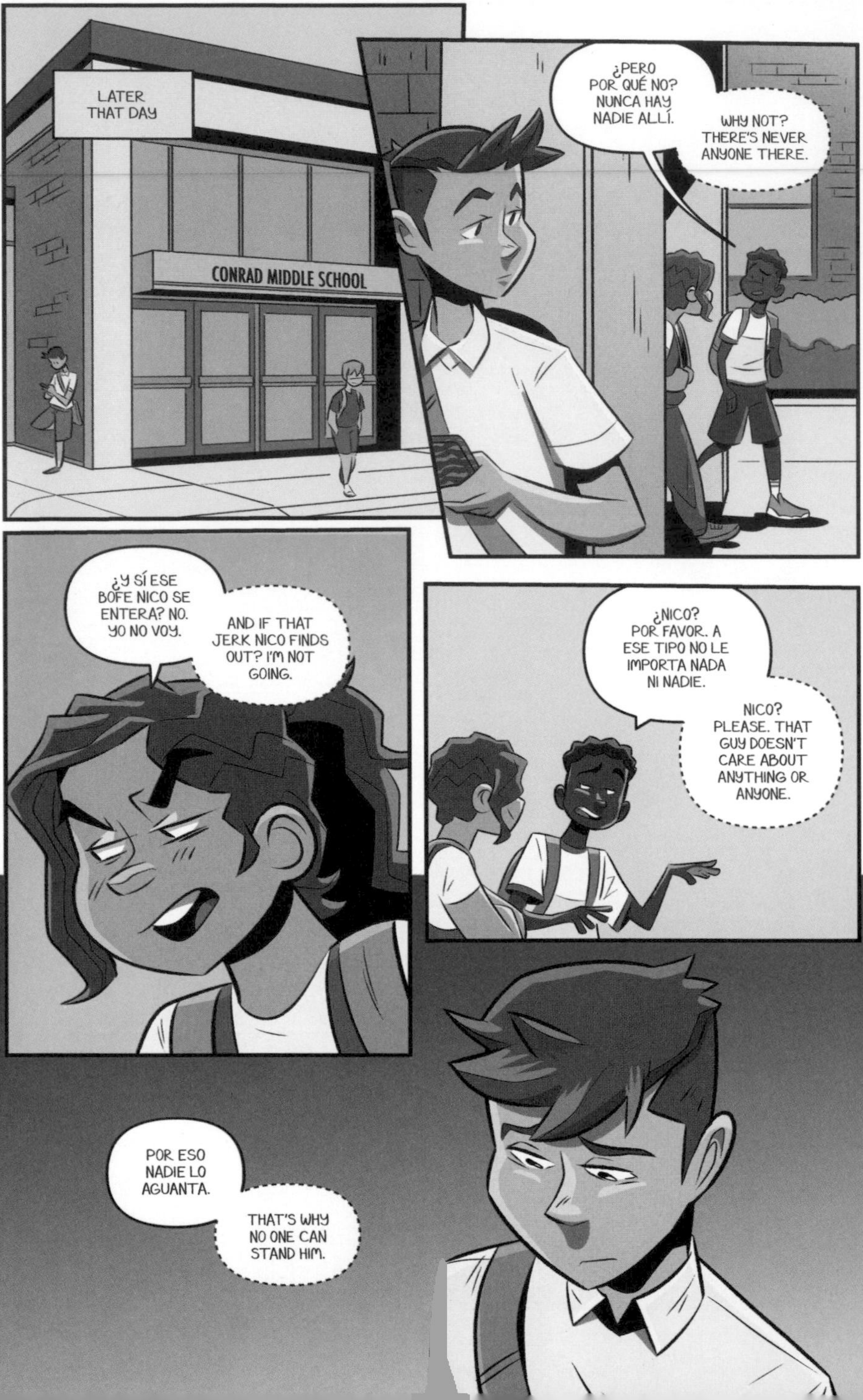
LATER THAT DAY
CONRAD MIDDLE SCHOOL
¿PERO POR QUÉ NO? NUNCA HAY NADIE ALLÍ.
WHY NOT? THERE'S NEVER ANYONE THERE.
¿Y SÍ ESE BOFE NICO SE ENTERA? NO. YO NO VOY.
AND IF THAT JERK NICO FINDS OUT? I'M NOT GOING.
¿NICO? POR FAVOR. A ESE TIPO NO LE IMPORTA NADA NI NADIE.
NICO? PLEASE. THAT GUY DOESN'T CARE ABOUT ANYTHING OR ANYONE.
POR ESO NADIE LO AGUANTA.
THAT'S WHY NO ONE CAN STAND HIM.

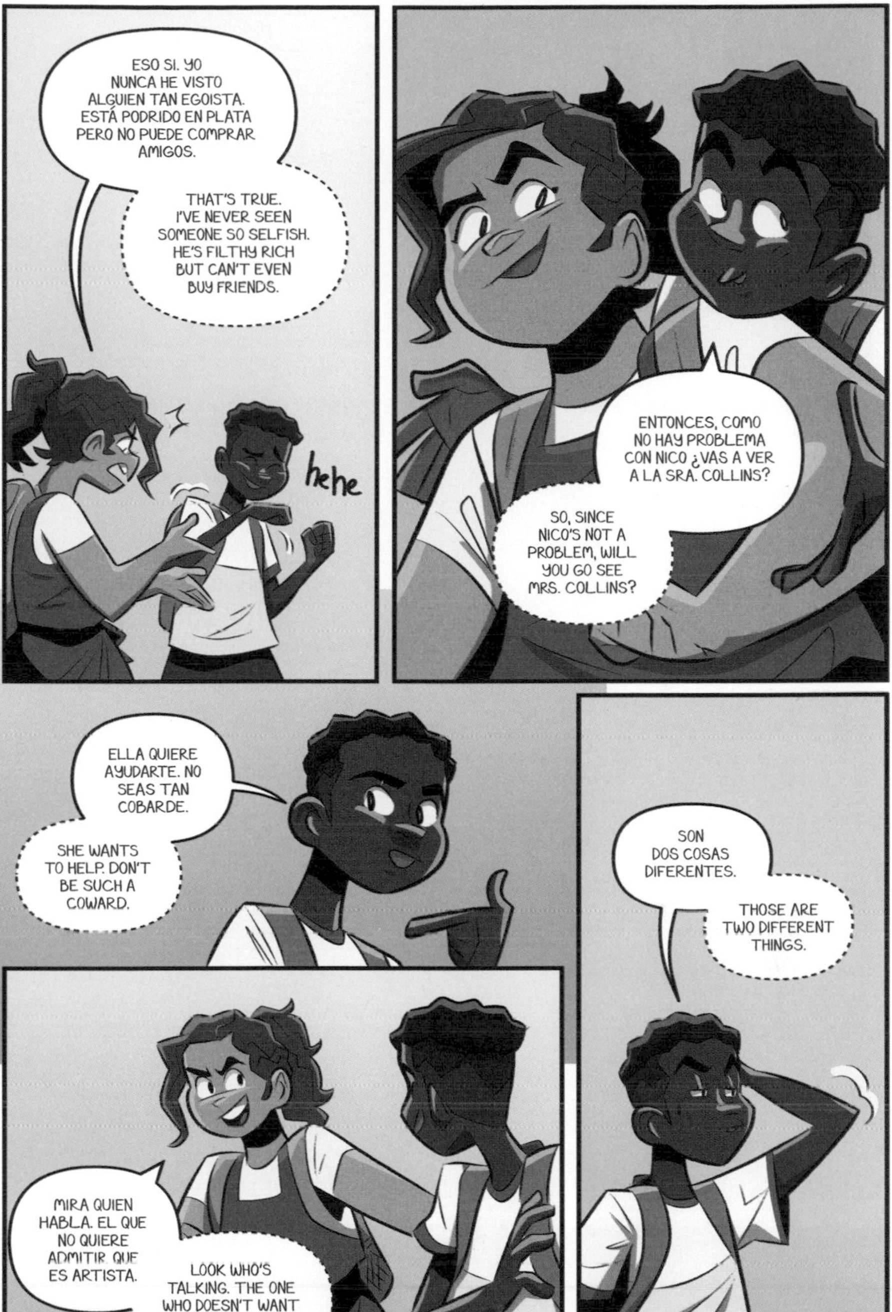
ESO SI. YO NUNCA HE VISTO ALGUIEN TAN EGOISTA. ESTÁ PODRIDO EN PLATA PERO NO PUEDE COMPRAR AMIGOS.
THAT'S TRUE. I'VE NEVER SEEN SOMEONE SO SELFISH. HE'S FILTHY RICH BUT CAN'T EVEN BUY FRIENDS.
hehe
ENTONCES, COMO NO HAY PROBLEMA CON NICO ¿VAS A VER A LA SRA. COLLINS?
SO, SINCE NICO'S NOT A PROBLEM, WILL YOU GO SEE MRS. COLLINS?
ELLA QUIERE AYUDARTE. NO SEAS TAN COBARDE.
SHE WANTS TO HELP. DON'T BE SUCH A COWARD.
SON DOS COSAS DIFERENTES.
THOSE ARE TWO DIFFERENT THINGS.
MIRA QUIEN HABLA. EL QUE NO QUIERE ADMITIR QUE ES ARTISTA.
LOOK WHO'S TALKING. THE ONE WHO DOESN'T WANT TO ADMIT HE'S AN ARTIST.

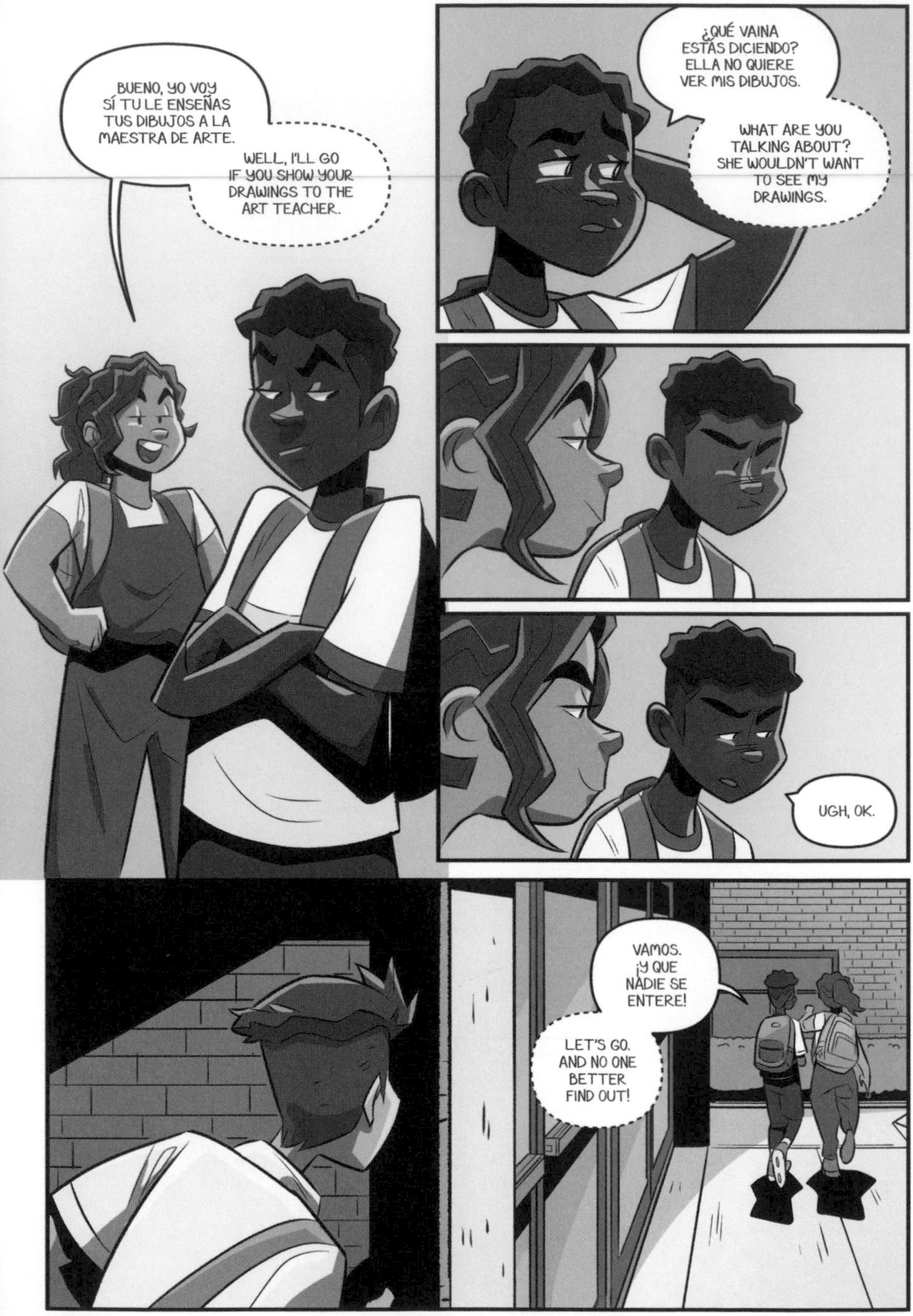
BUENO, YO VOY SÍ TU LE ENSEÑAS TUS DIBUJOS A LA MAESTRA DE ARTE.
WELL, I'LL GO IF YOU SHOW YOUR DRAWINGS TO THE ART TEACHER.
¿QUÉ VAINA ESTÁS DICIENDO? ELLA NO QUIERE VER MIS DIBUJOS.
WHAT ARE YOU TALKING ABOUT? SHE WOULDN'T WANT TO SEE MY DRAWINGS.
UGH, OK.
VAMOS. ¡Y QUE NADIE SE ENTERE!
LET'S GO. AND NO ONE BETTER FIND OUT!

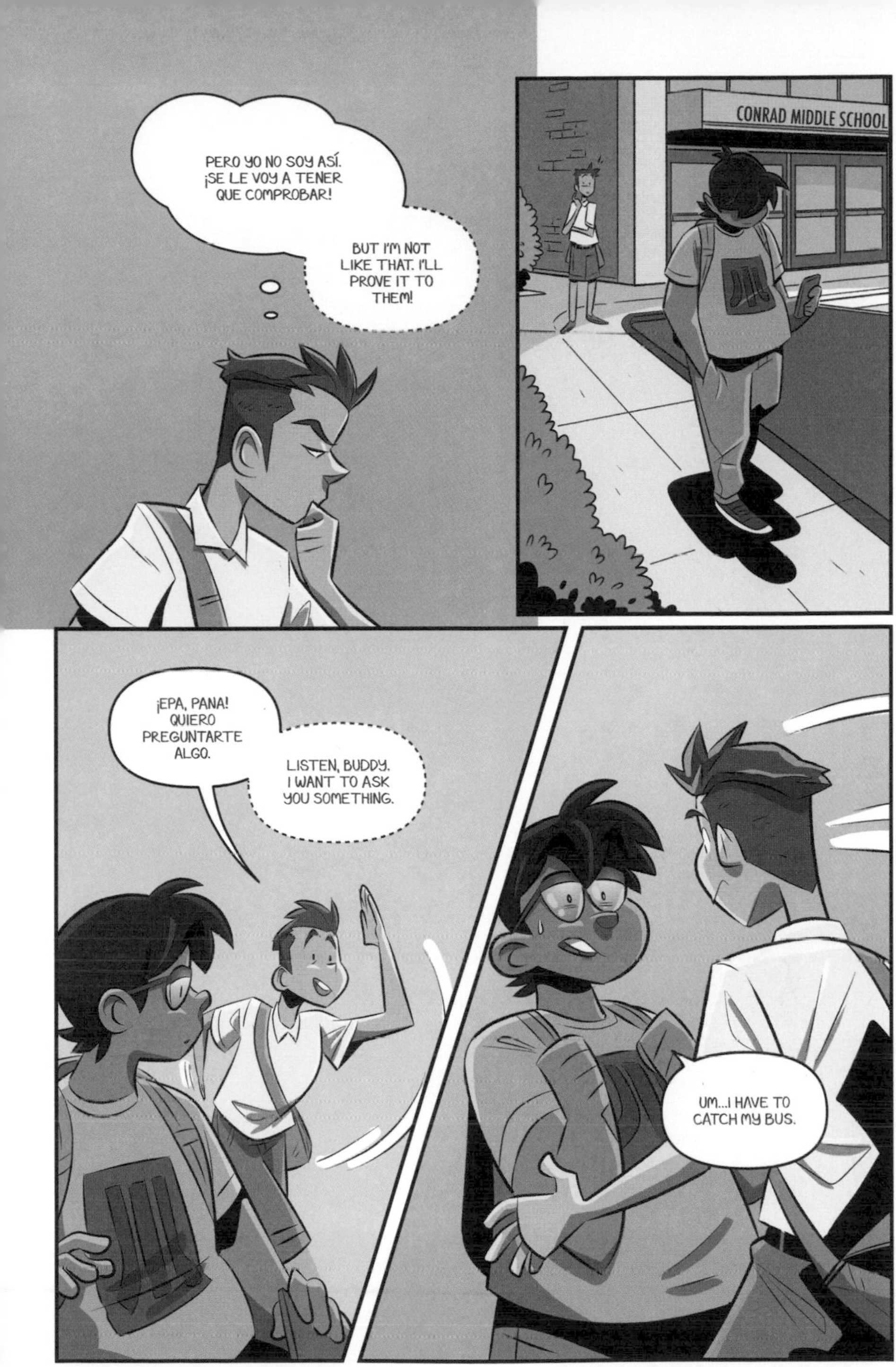
PERO YO NO SOY ASÍ. ¡SE LE VOY A TENER QUE COMPROBAR!
BUT I'M NOT LIKE THAT. I'LL PROVE IT TO THEM!
CONRAD MIDDLE SCHOOL
¡EPA, PANA! QUIERO PREGUNTARTE ALGO.
LISTEN, BUDDY. I WANT TO ASK YOU SOMETHING.
UM...I HAVE TO CATCH MY BUS.

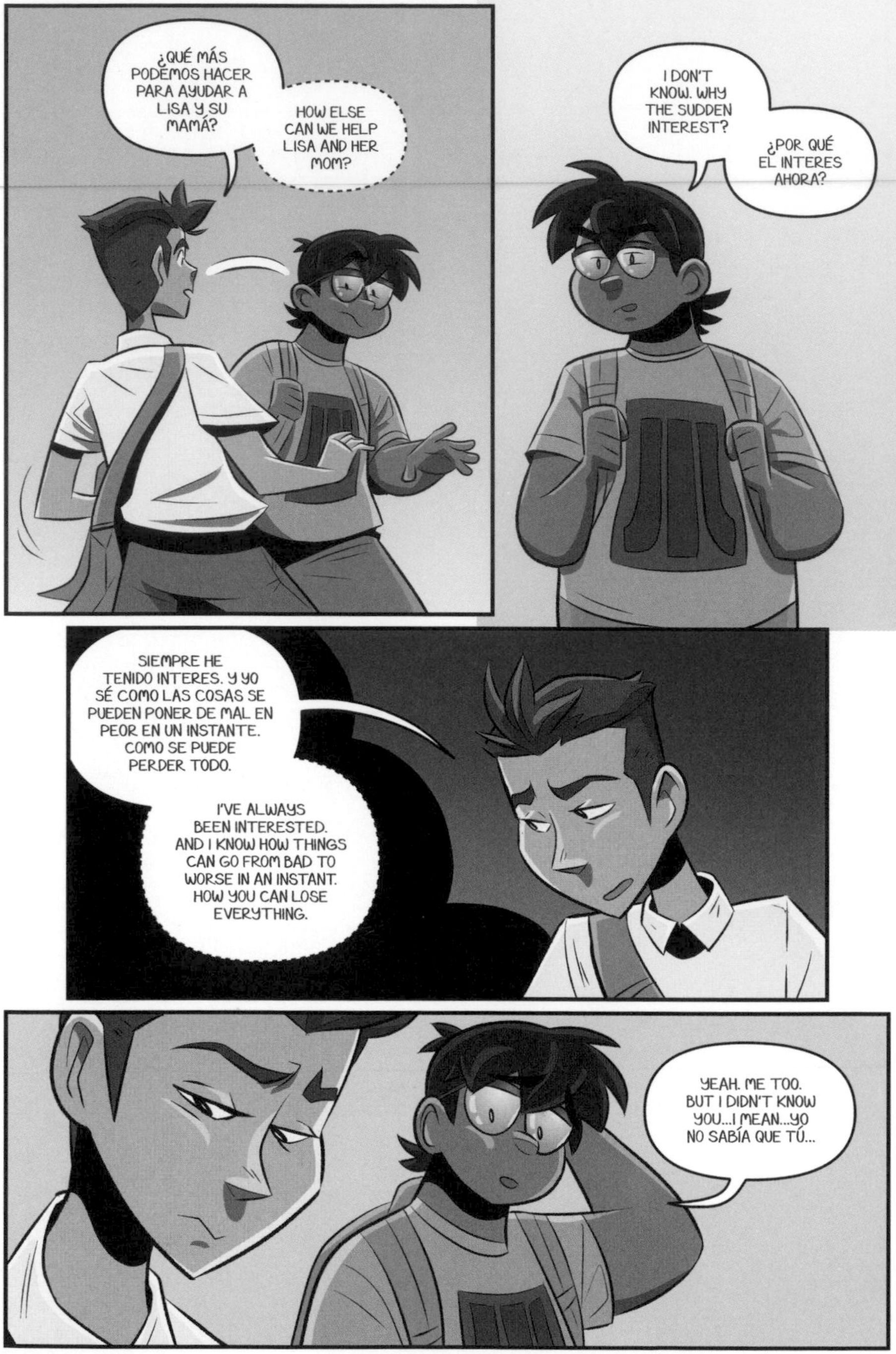
¿QUÉ MÁS PODEMOS HACER PARA AYUDAR A LISA Y SU MAMÁ?
HOW ELSE CAN WE HELP LISA AND HER MOM?
I DON'T KNOW. WHY THE SUDDEN INTEREST?
¿POR QUÉ EL INTERES AHORA?
SIEMPRE HE TENIDO INTERES. Y YO SÉ COMO LAS COSAS SE PUEDEN PONER DE MAL EN PEOR EN UN INSTANTE. COMO SE PUEDE PERDER TODO.
I'VE ALWAYS BEEN INTERESTED. AND I KNOW HOW THINGS CAN GO FROM BAD TO WORSE IN AN INSTANT. HOW YOU CAN LOSE EVERYTHING.
YEAH. ME TOO. BUT I DIDN'T KNOW YOU...I MEAN...YO NO SABÍA QUE TÚ...

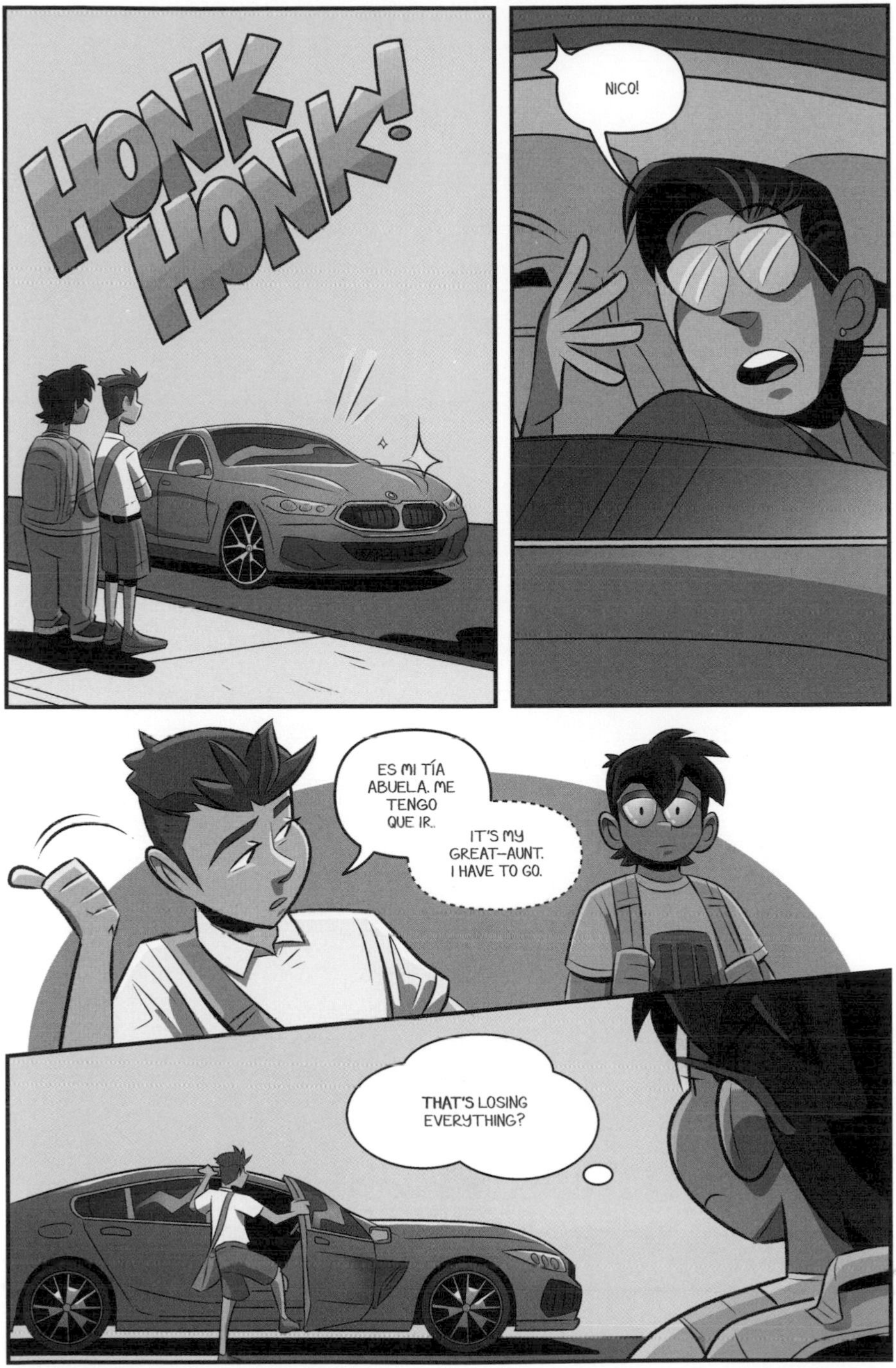
HONK HONK!
NICO!
ES MI TÍA ABUELA. ME TENGO QUE IR..
IT'S MY GREAT-AUNT. I HAVE TO GO.
THAT'S LOSING EVERYTHING?

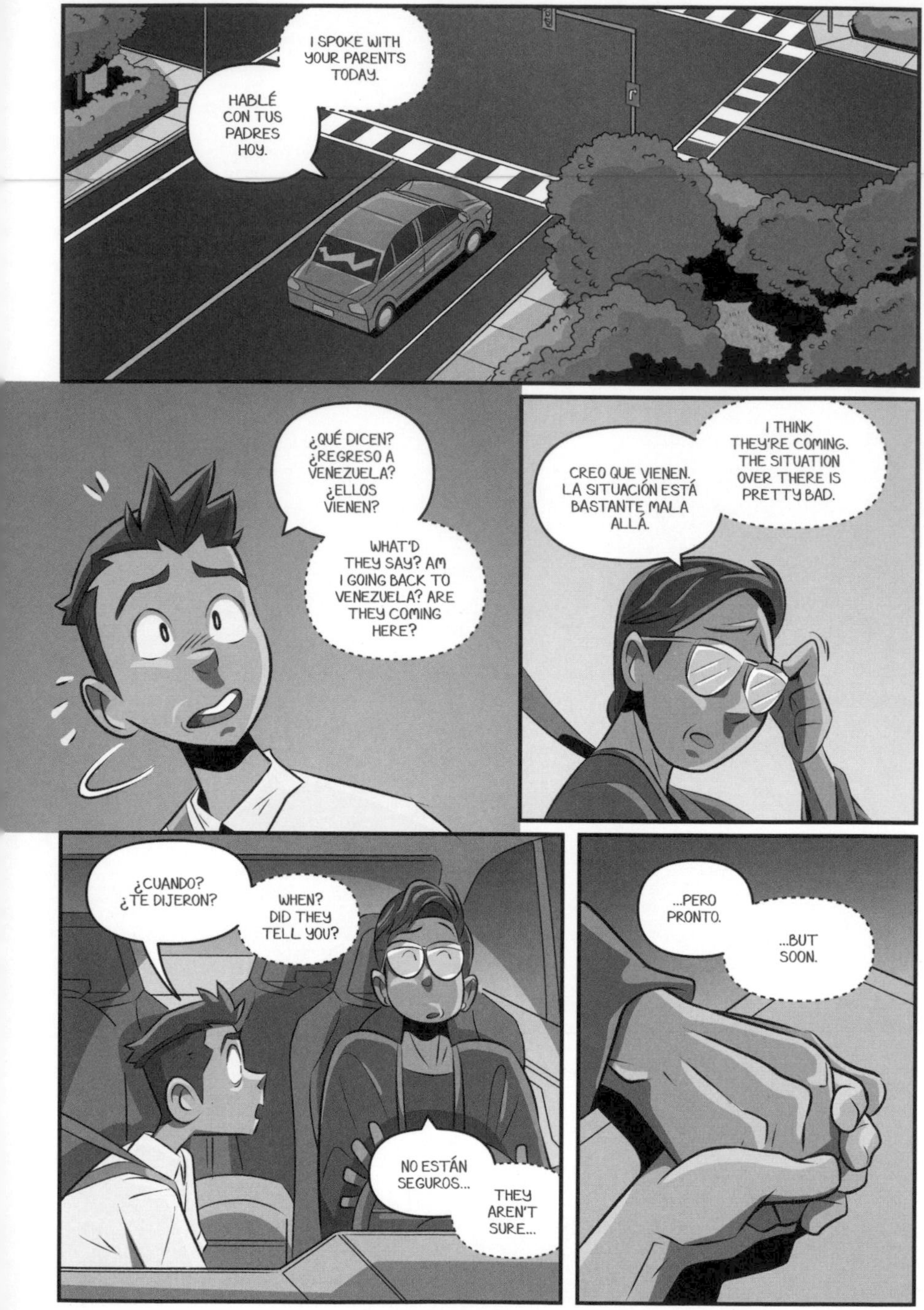
HABLÉ CON TUS PADRES HOY.
I SPOKE WITH YOUR PARENTS TODAY.
¿QUÉ DICEN? ¿REGRESO A VENEZUELA? ¿ELLOS VIENEN?
WHAT'D THEY SAY? AM I GOING BACK TO VENEZUELA? ARE THEY COMING HERE?
CREO QUE VIENEN. LA SITUACIÓN ESTÁ BASTANTE MALA ALLÁ.
I THINK THEY'RE COMING. THE SITUATION OVER THERE IS PRETTY BAD.
¿CUANDO? ¿TE DIJERON?
WHEN? DID THEY TELL YOU?
NO ESTÁN SEGUROS...
THEY AREN'T SURE...
...PERO PRONTO.
...BUT SOON.

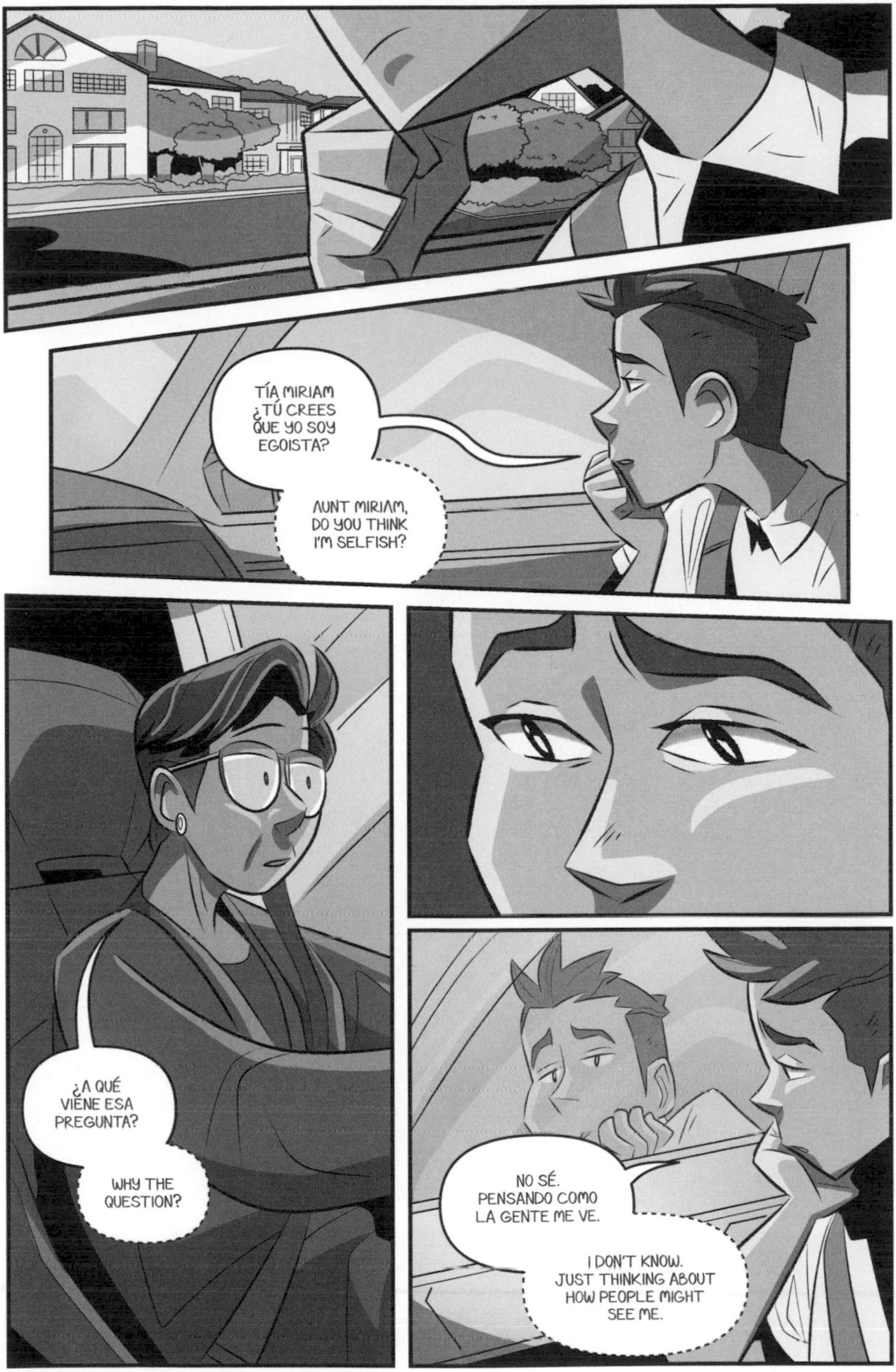

TÍA MIRIAM ¿TÚ CREES QUE YO SOY EGOISTA?
AUNT MIRIAM, DO YOU THINK I'M SELFISH?
¿A QUÉ VIENE ESA PREGUNTA?
WHY THE QUESTION?
NO SÉ. PENSANDO COMO LA GENTE ME VE.
I DON'T KNOW. JUST THINKING ABOUT HOW PEOPLE MIGHT SEE ME.

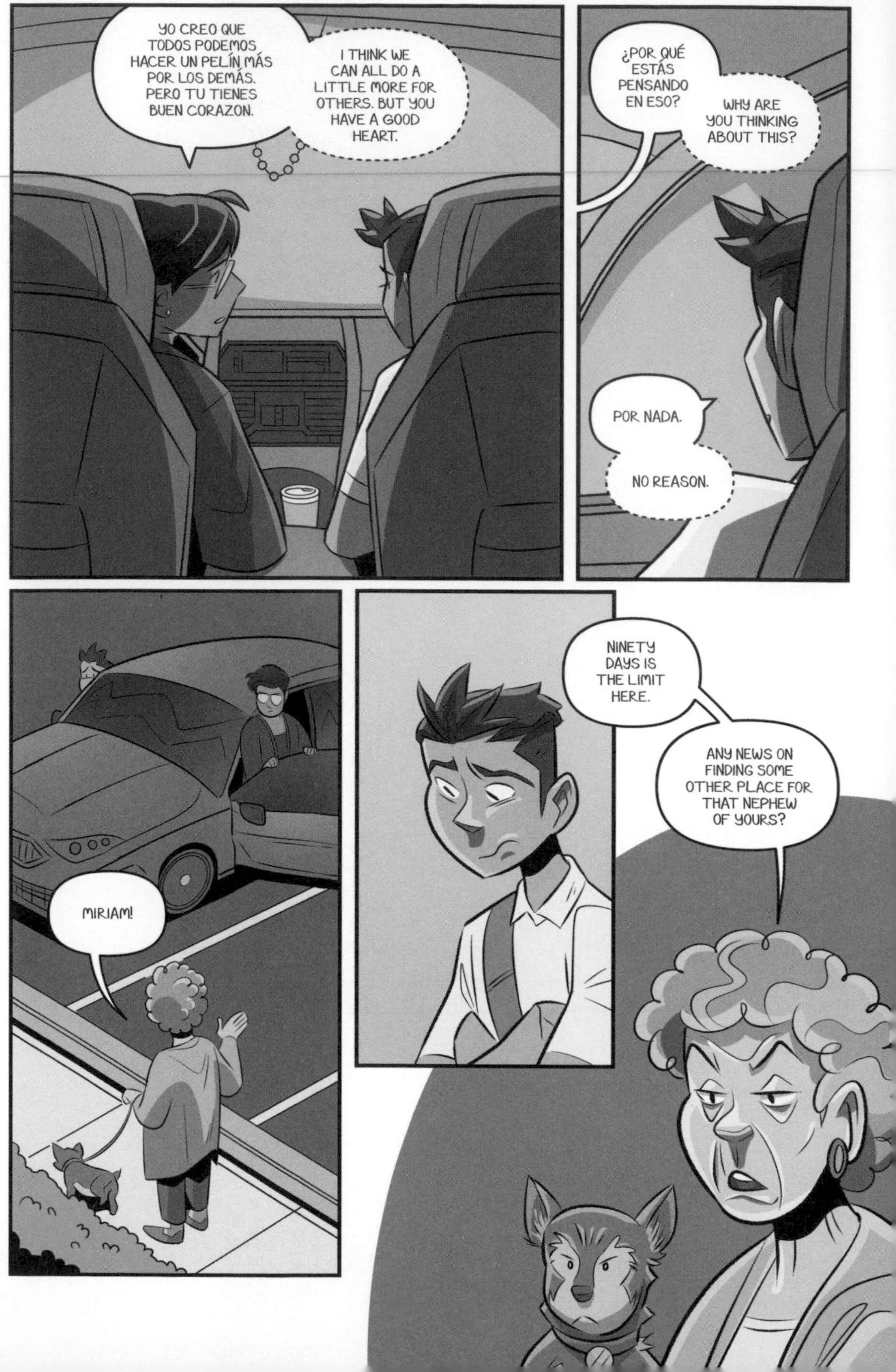
YO CREO QUE TODOS PODEMOS HACER UN PELÍN MÁS POR LOS DEMÁS. PERO TU TIENES BUEN CORAZON.
I THINK WE CAN ALL DO A LITTLE MORE FOR OTHERS. BUT YOU HAVE A GOOD HEART.
¿POR QUÉ ESTÁS PENSANDO EN ESO?
WHY ARE YOU THINKING ABOUT THIS?
POR NADA.
NO REASON.
MIRIAM!
NINETY DAYS IS THE LIMIT HERE.
ANY NEWS ON FINDING SOME OTHER PLACE FOR THAT NEPHEW OF YOURS?

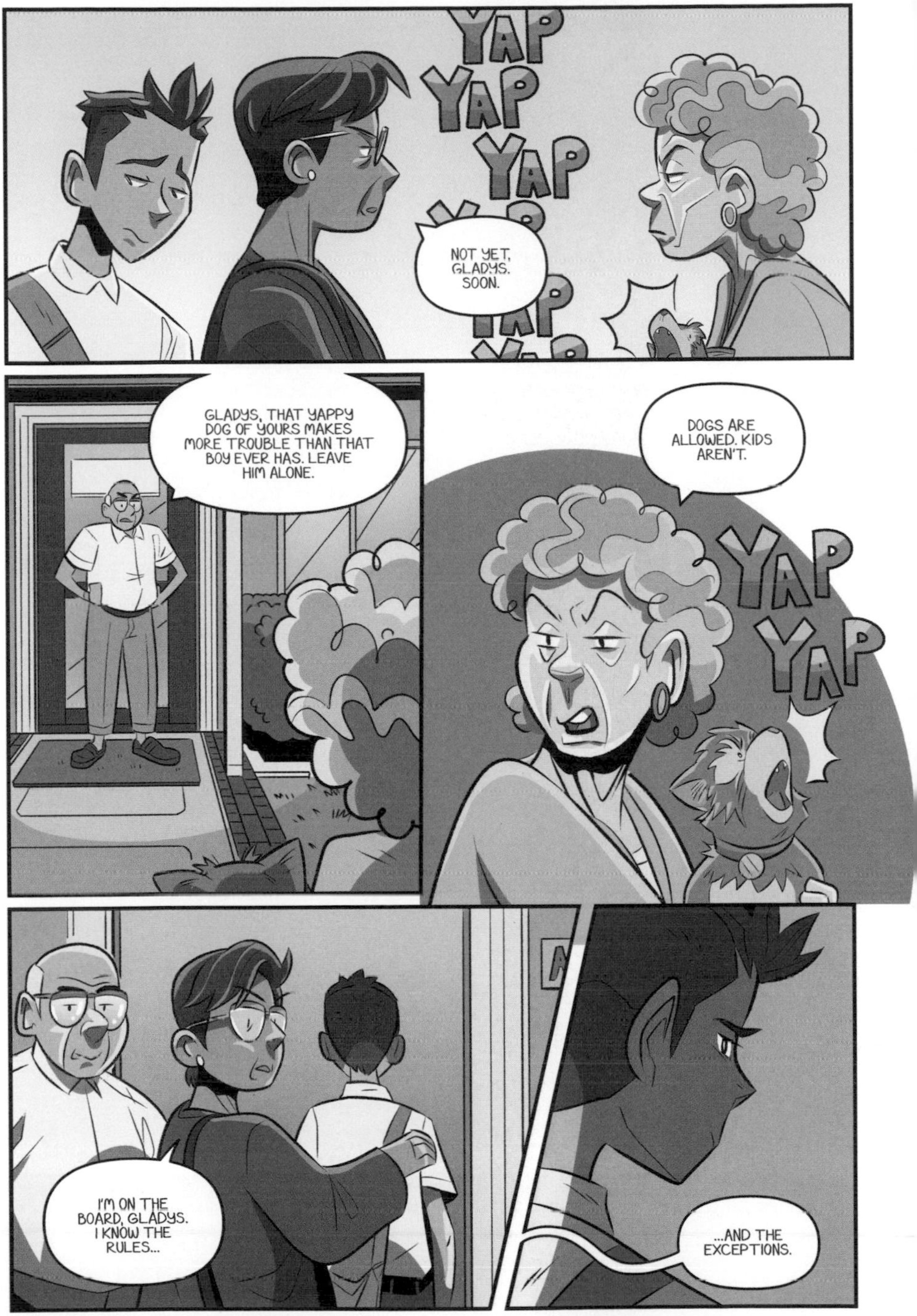
YAP
YAP
YAP
NOT YET, GLADYS. SOON.
GLADYS, THAT YAPPY DOG OF YOURS MAKES MORE TROUBLE THAN THAT BOY EVER HAS. LEAVE HIM ALONE.
DOGS ARE ALLOWED. KIDS AREN'T.
YAP
YAP
I'M ON THE BOARD, GLADYS. I KNOW THE RULES...
...AND THE EXCEPTIONS.

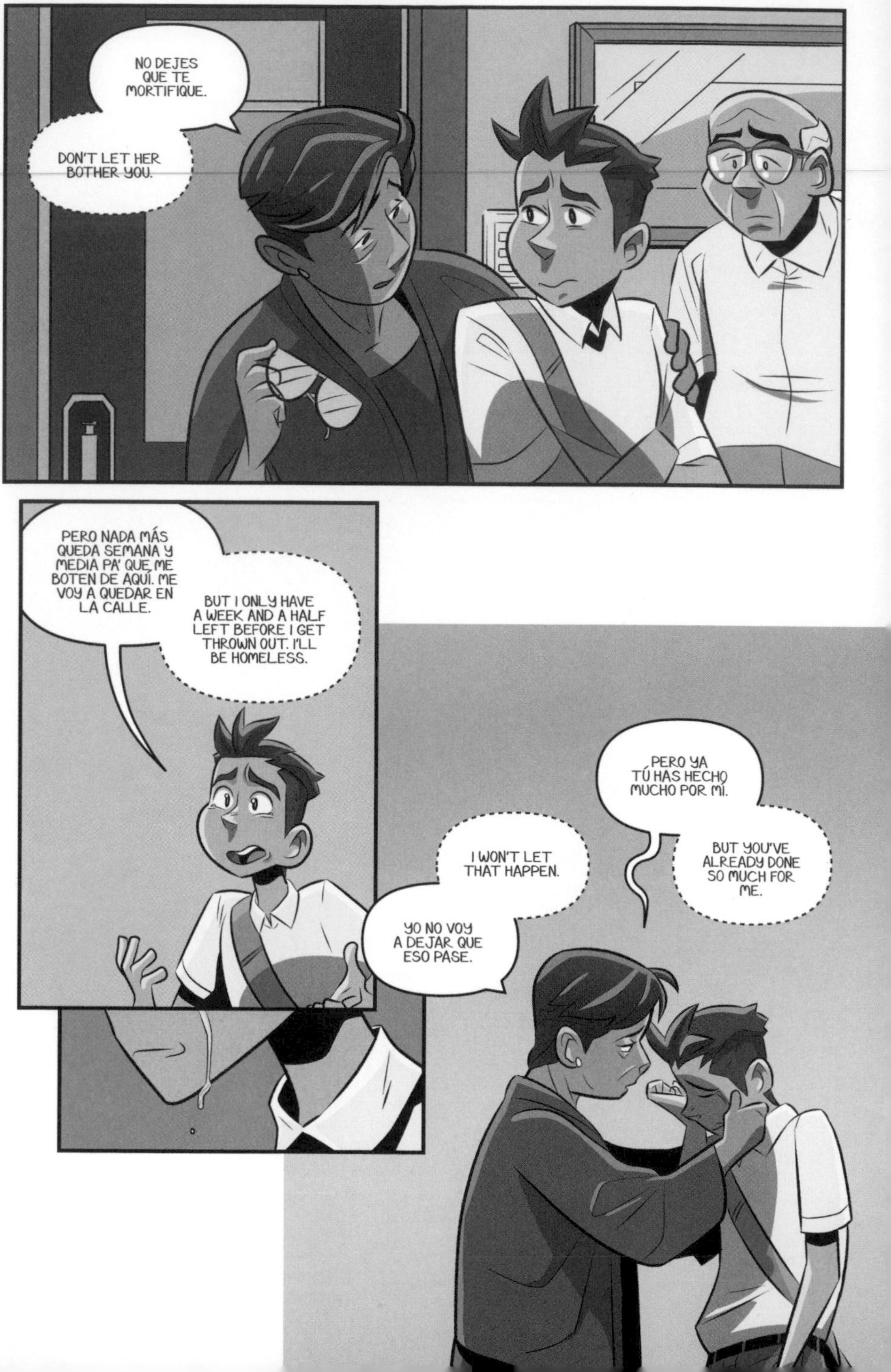
NO DEJES QUE TE MORTIFIQUE.
DON'T LET HER BOTHER YOU.
PERO NADA MÁS QUEDA SEMANA Y MEDIA PA' QUE ME BOTEN DE AQUÍ. ME VOY A QUEDAR EN LA CALLE.
BUT I ONLY HAVE A WEEK AND A HALF LEFT BEFORE I GET THROWN OUT. I'LL BE HOMELESS.
YO NO VOY A DEJAR QUE ESO PASE.
I WON'T LET THAT HAPPEN.
PERO YA TÚ HAS HECHO MUCHO POR MÍ.
BUT YOU'VE ALREADY DONE SO MUCH FOR ME.

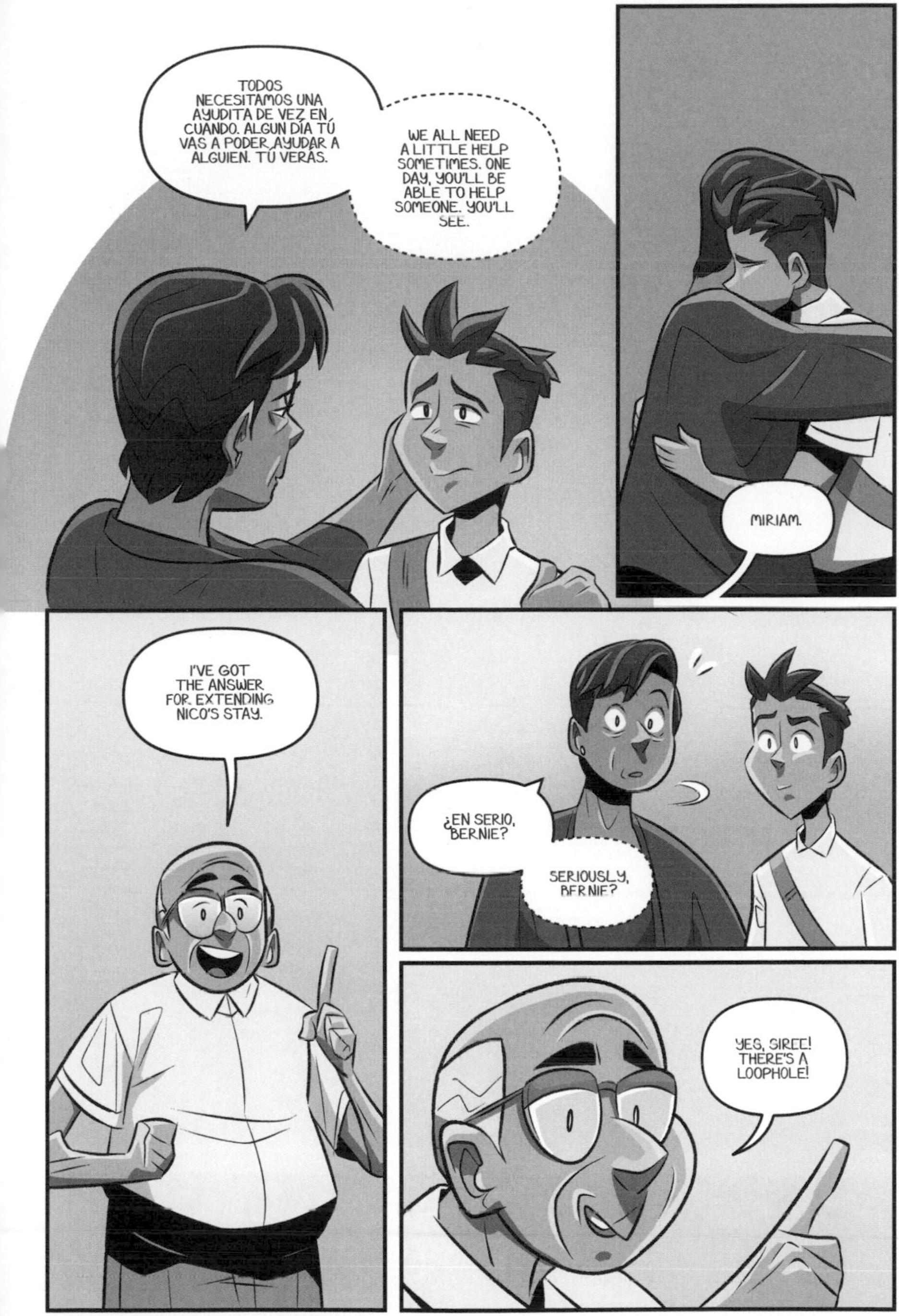
TODOS NECESITAMOS UNA AYUDITA DE VEZ EN CUANDO. ALGUN DÍA TÚ VAS A PODER AYUDAR A ALGUIEN. TÚ VERÁS.
WE ALL NEED A LITTLE HELP SOMETIMES. ONE DAY, YOU'LL BE ABLE TO HELP SOMEONE. YOU'LL SEE.
MIRIAM.
I'VE GOT THE ANSWER FOR EXTENDING NICO'S STAY.
¿EN SERIO, BERNIE?
SERIOUSLY, BERNIE?
YES, SIREE! THERE'S A LOOPHOLE!

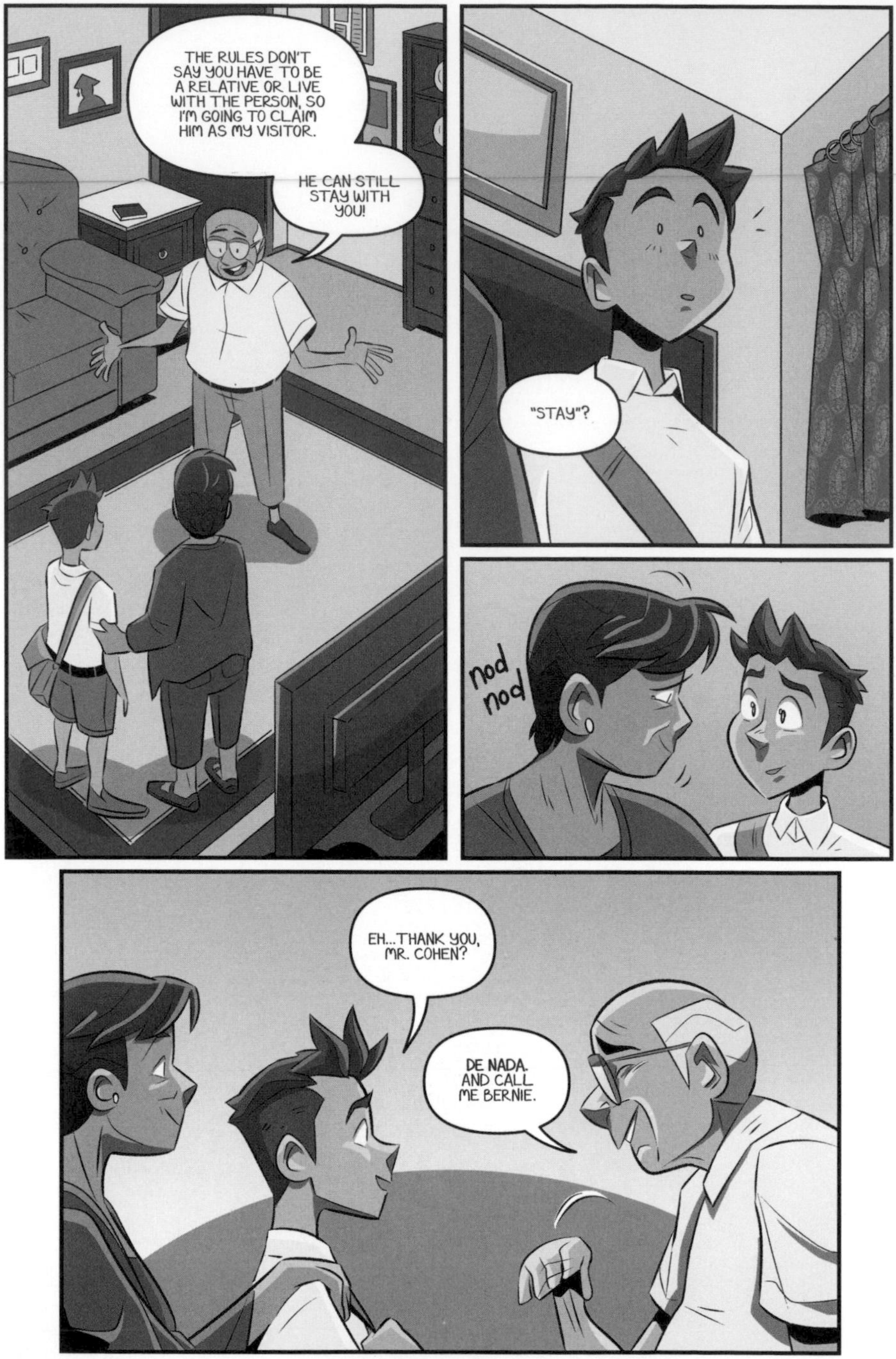
THE RULES DON'T SAY YOU HAVE TO BE A RELATIVE OR LIVE WITH THE PERSON, SO I'M GOING TO CLAIM HIM AS MY VISITOR.
HE CAN STILL STAY WITH YOU!
"STAY"?
nod nod
EH...THANK YOU, MR. COHEN?
DE NADA. AND CALL ME BERNIE.

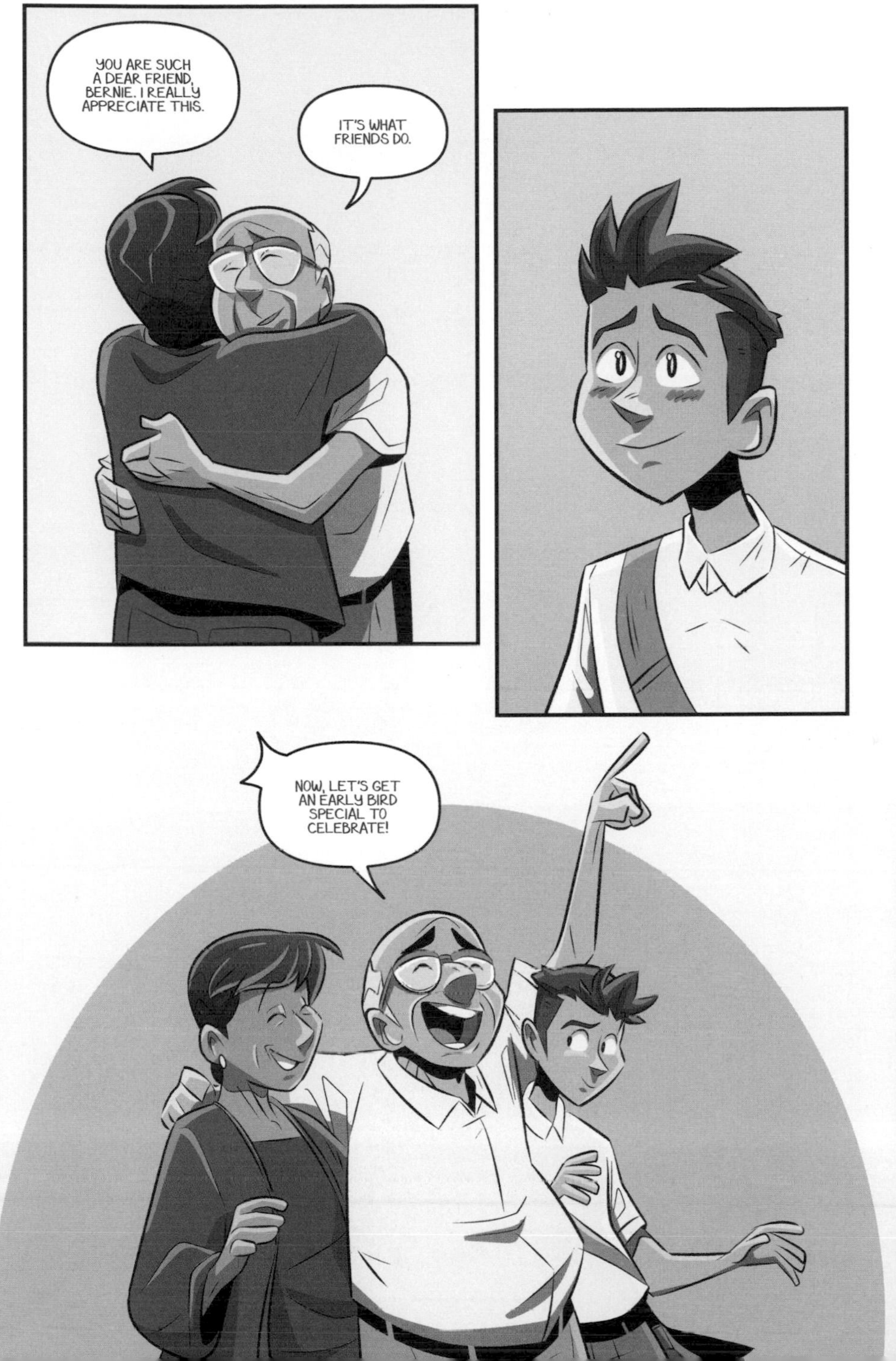
YOU ARE SUCH A DEAR FRIEND, BERNIE. I REALLY APPRECIATE THIS.
IT'S WHAT FRIENDS DO.
NOW, LET'S GET AN EARLY BIRD SPECIAL TO CELEBRATE!

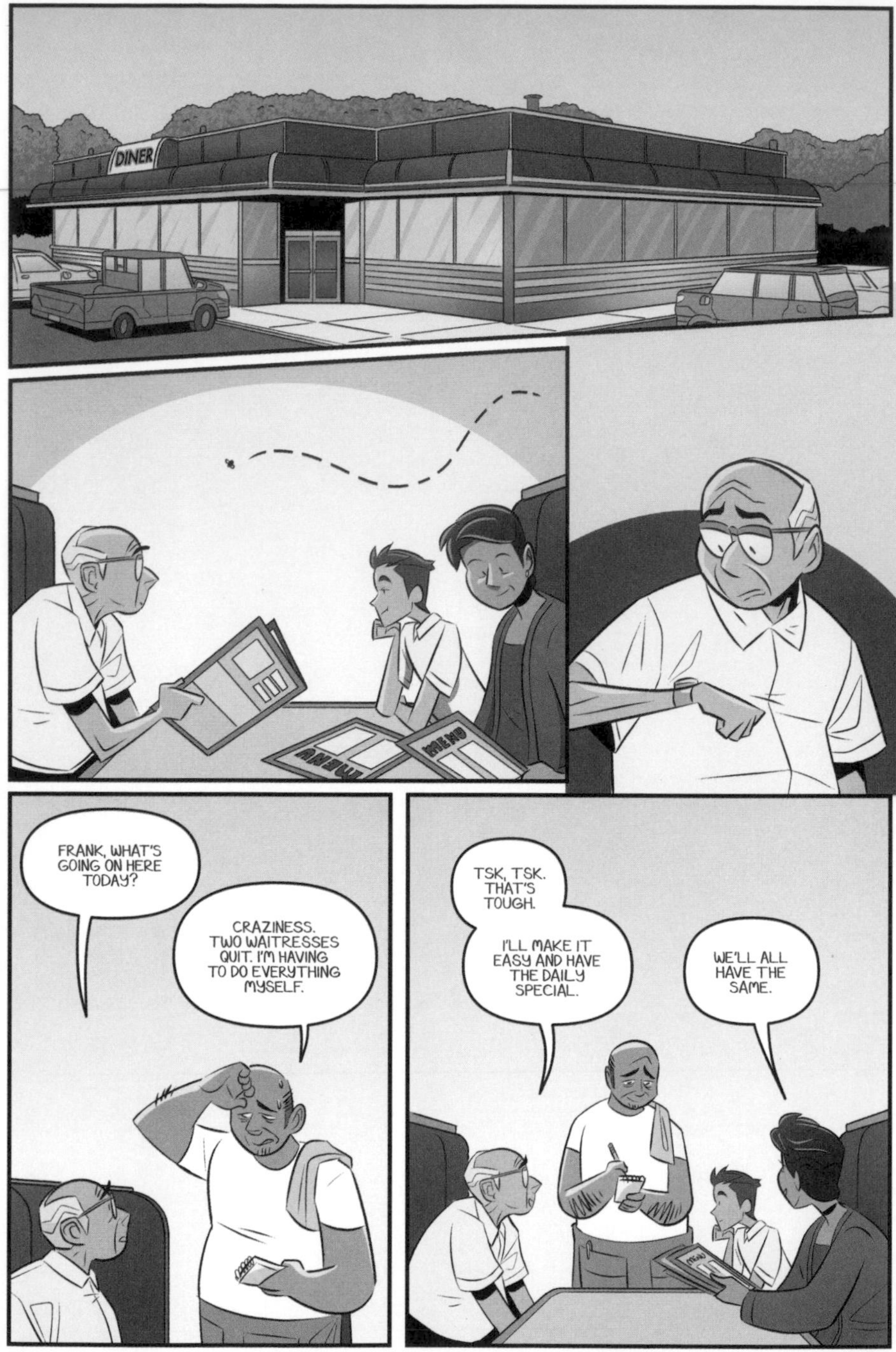
DINER
MENU
MENU
FRANK, WHAT'S GOING ON HERE TODAY?
CRAZINESS. TWO WAITRESSES QUIT. I'M HAVING TO DO EVERYTHING MYSELF.
TSK, TSK. THAT'S TOUGH.
I'LL MAKE IT EASY AND HAVE THE DAILY SPECIAL.
WE'LL ALL HAVE THE SAME.

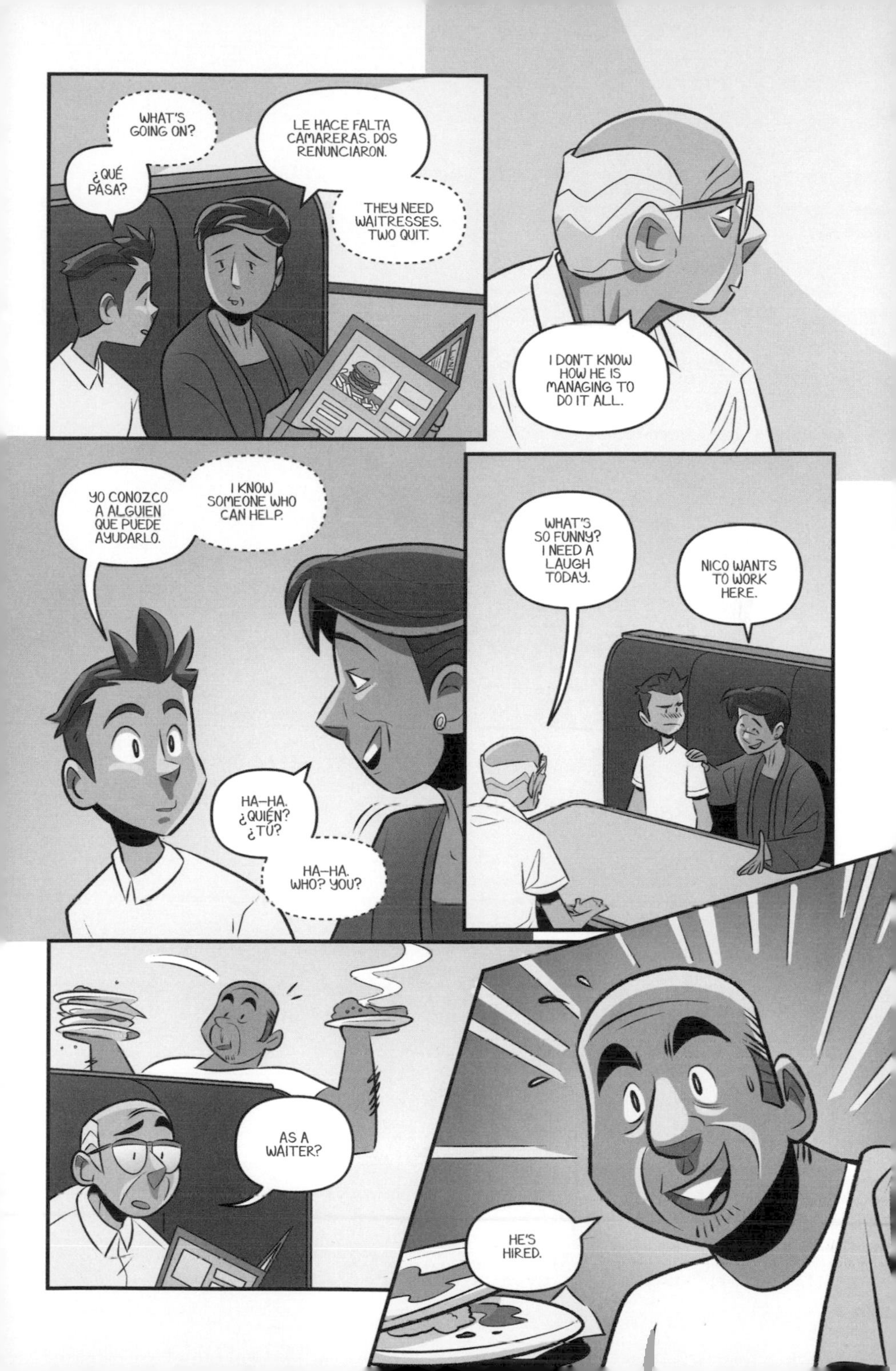
¿QUÉ PASA?
WHAT'S GOING ON?
LE HACE FALTA CAMARERAS. DOS RENUNCIARON.
THEY NEED WAITRESSES. TWO QUIT.
I DON'T KNOW HOW HE IS MANAGING TO DO IT ALL.
YO CONOZCO A ALGUIEN QUE PUEDE AYUDARLO.
I KNOW SOMEONE WHO CAN HELP.
HA-HA. ¿QUIÉN? ¿TÚ?
HA-HA. WHO? YOU?
WHAT'S SO FUNNY? I NEED A LAUGH TODAY.
NICO WANTS TO WORK HERE.
AS A WAITER?
HE'S HIRED.

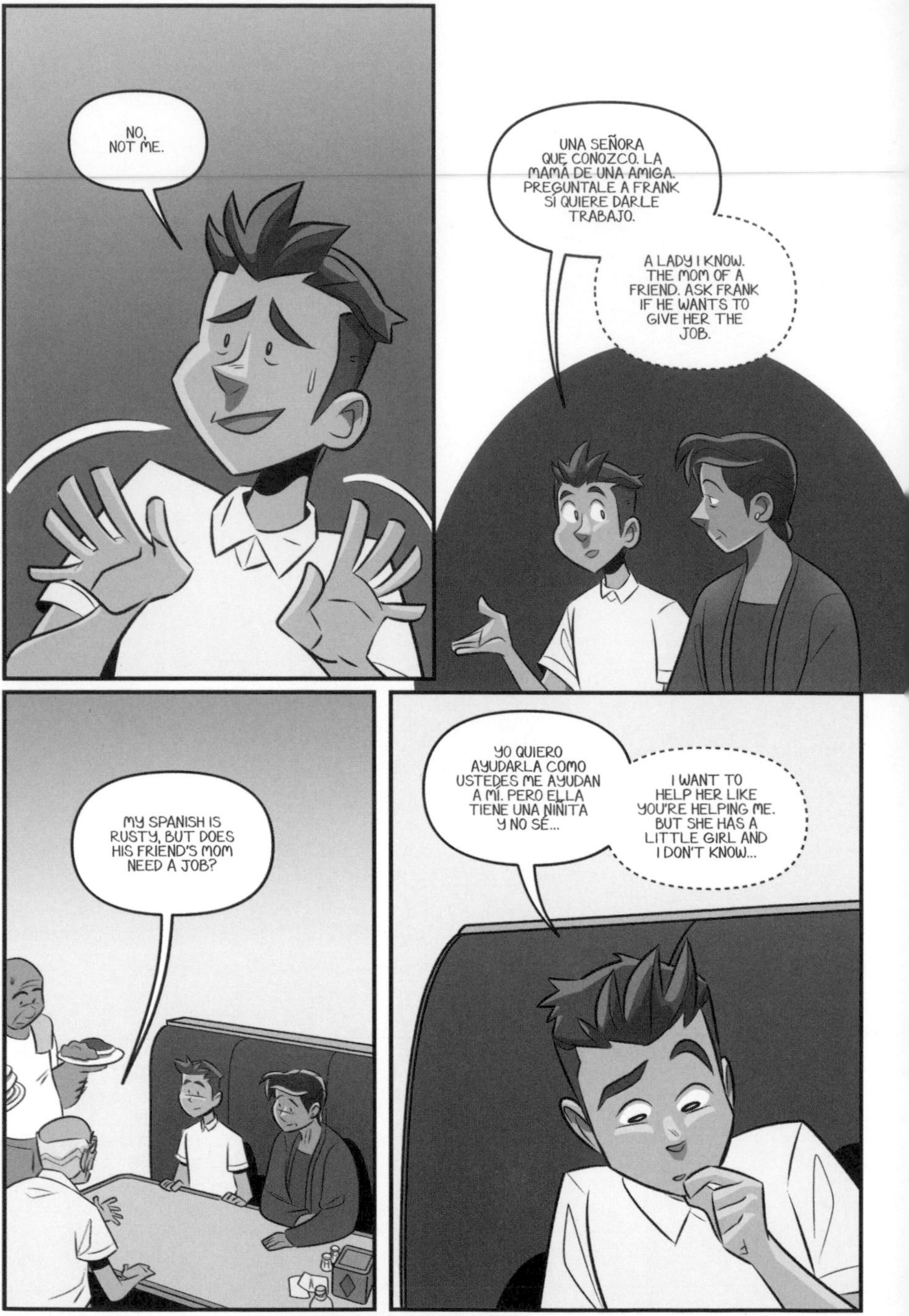
NO, NOT ME.
UNA SEÑORA QUE CONOZCO. LA MAMÁ DE UNA AMIGA. PREGUNTALE A FRANK SÍ QUIERE DARLE TRABAJO.
A LADY I KNOW. THE MOM OF A FRIEND. ASK FRANK IF HE WANTS TO GIVE HER THE JOB.
MY SPANISH IS RUSTY, BUT DOES HIS FRIEND'S MOM NEED A JOB?
YO QUIERO AYUDARLA COMO USTEDES ME AYUDAN A MÍ. PERO ELLA TIENE UNA NIÑITA Y NO SÉ...
I WANT TO HELP HER LIKE YOU'RE HELPING ME. BUT SHE HAS A LITTLE GIRL AND I DON'T KNOW...

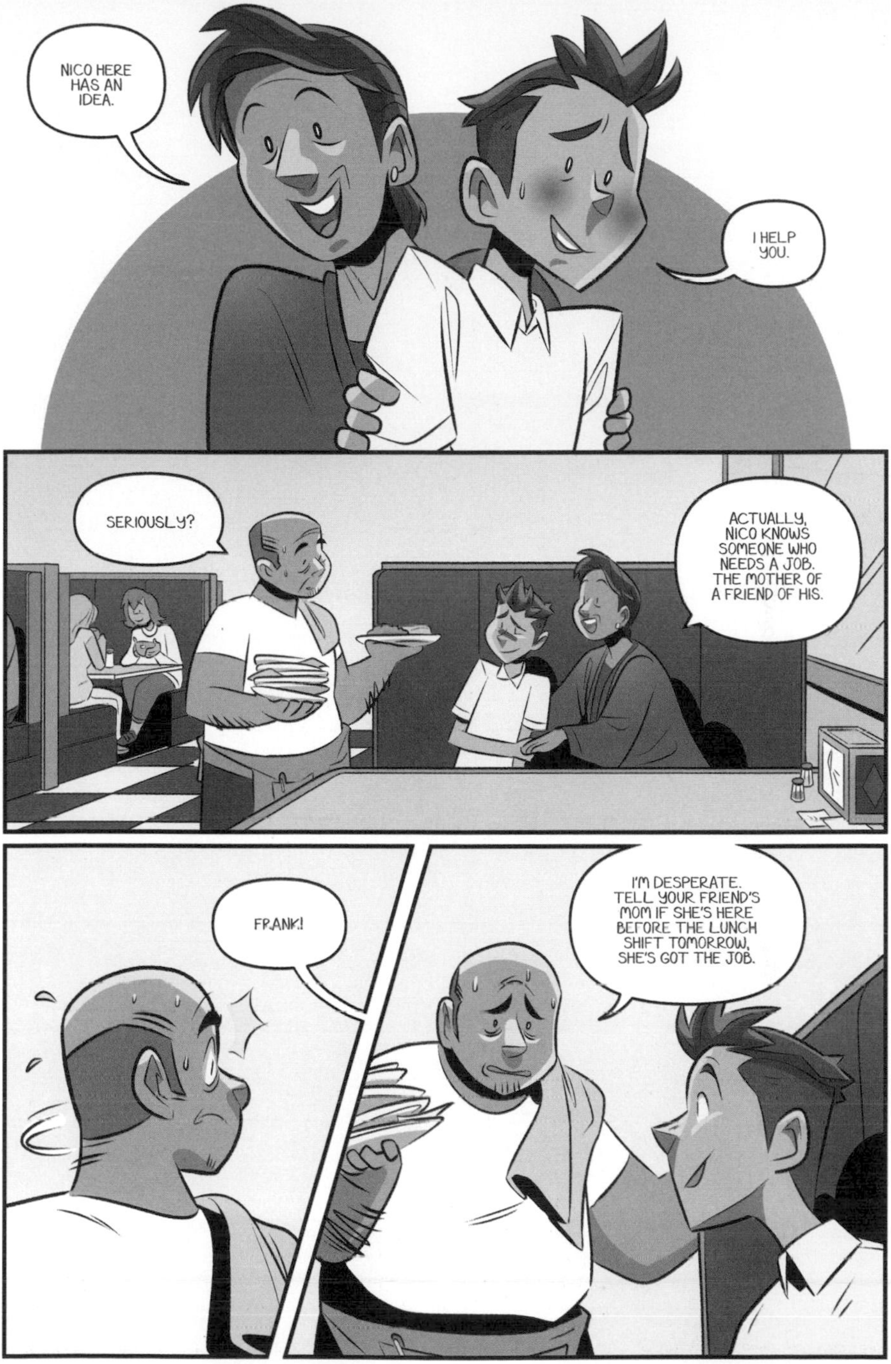
NICO HERE HAS AN IDEA.
I HELP YOU.
SERIOUSLY?
ACTUALLY, NICO KNOWS SOMEONE WHO NEEDS A JOB. THE MOTHER OF A FRIEND OF HIS.
FRANK!
I'M DESPERATE. TELL YOUR FRIEND'S MOM IF SHE'S HERE BEFORE THE LUNCH SHIFT TOMORROW, SHE'S GOT THE JOB.

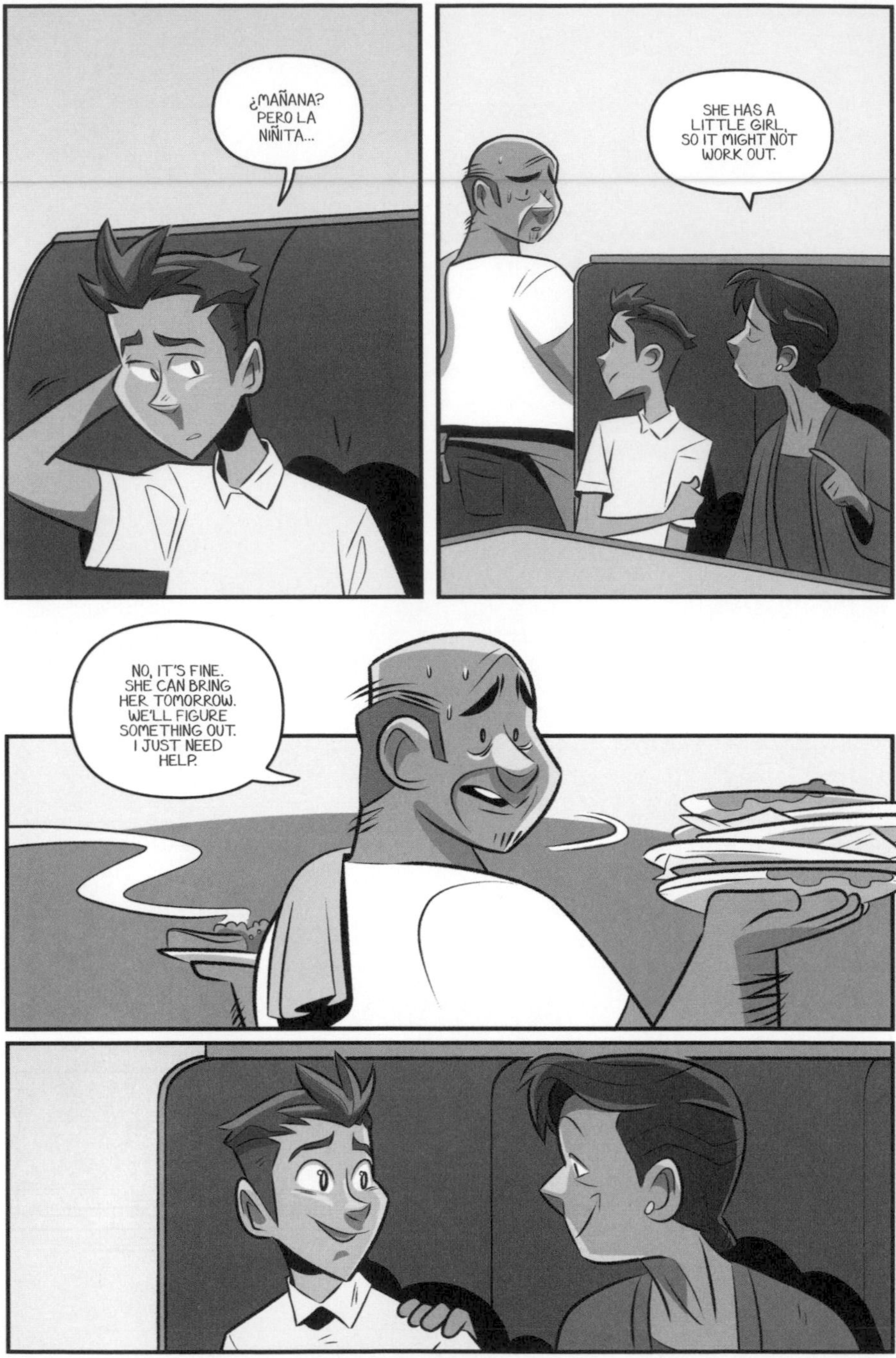
¿MAÑANA? PERO LA NIÑITA...
SHE HAS A LITTLE GIRL, SO IT MIGHT NOT WORK OUT.
NO, IT'S FINE. SHE CAN BRING HER TOMORROW. WE'LL FIGURE SOMETHING OUT. I JUST NEED HELP.

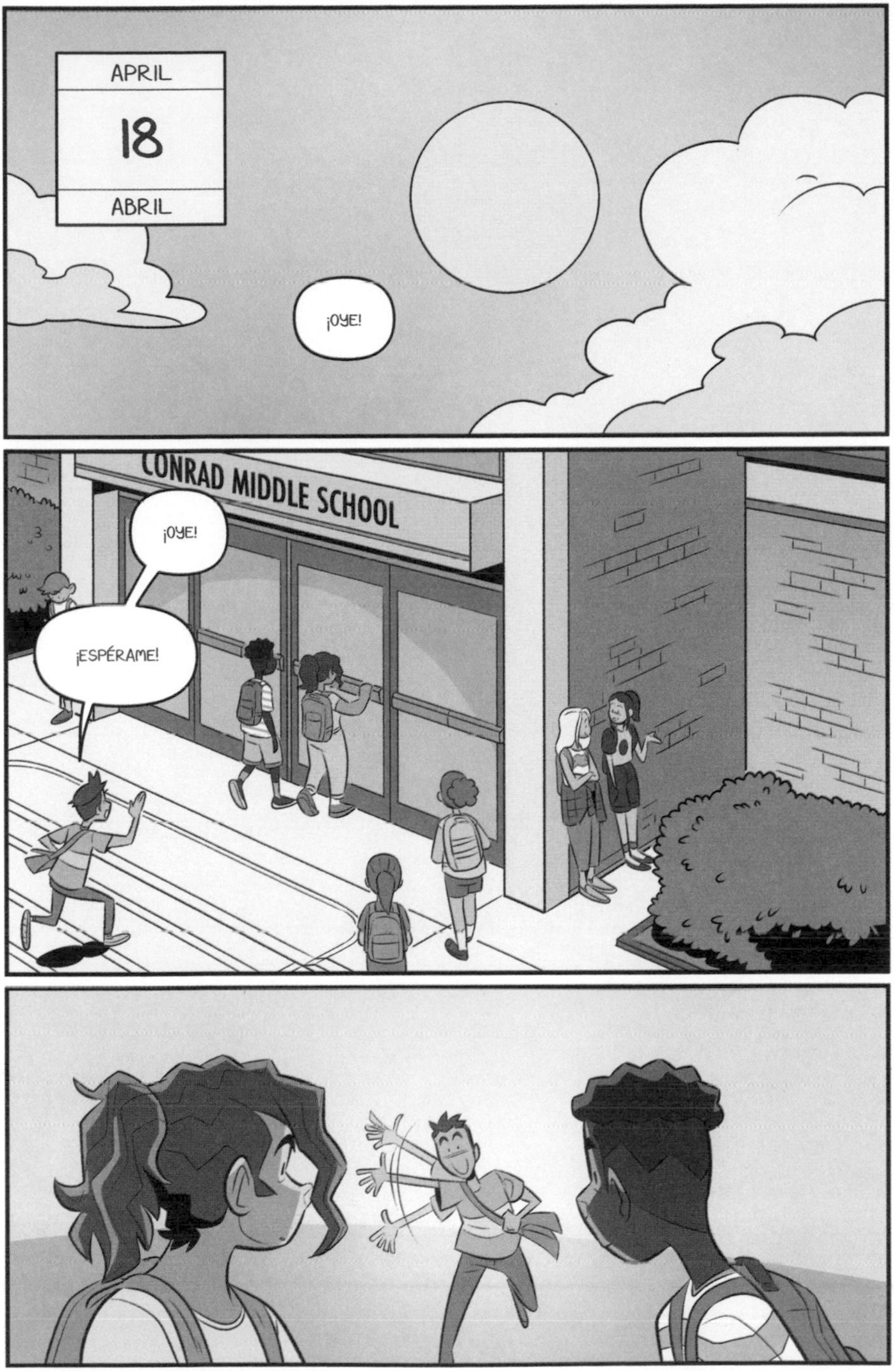
APRIL
18
ABRIL
¡OYE!
CONRAD MIDDLE SCHOOL
¡OYE!
¡ESPÉRAME!

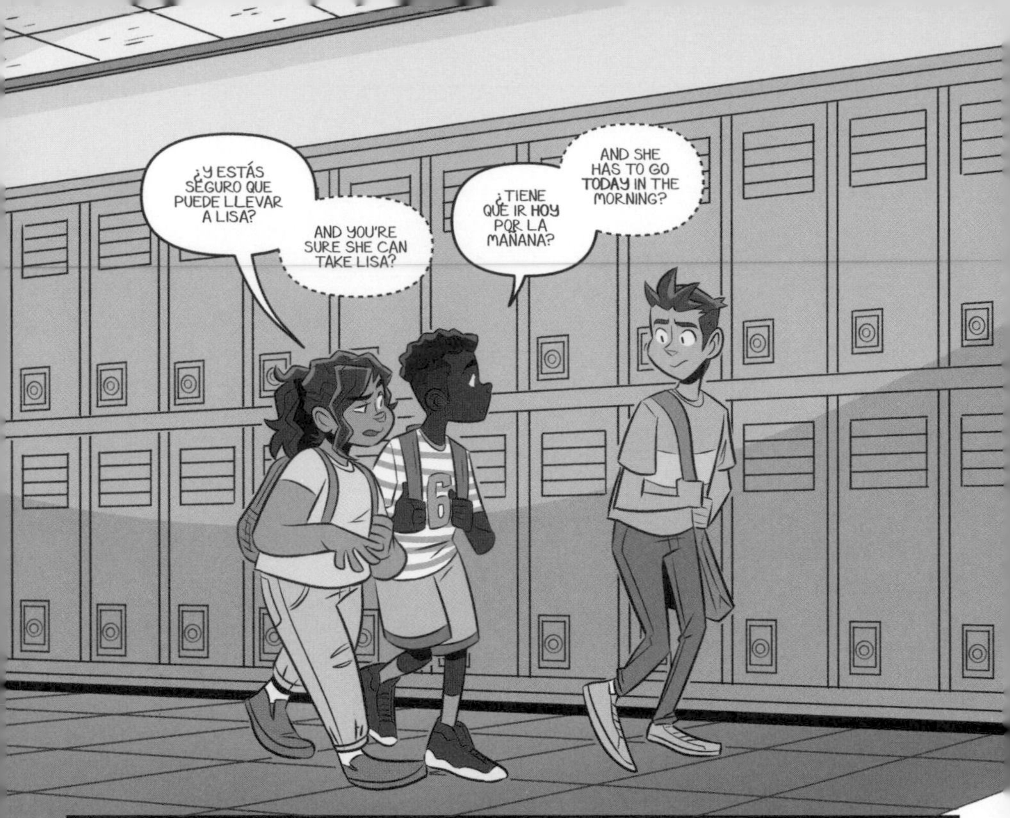
¿Y ESTÁS SEGURO QUE PUEDE LLEVAR A LISA?
AND YOU'RE SURE SHE CAN TAKE LISA?
¿TIENE QUE IR HOY POR LA MAÑANA?
AND SHE HAS TO GO TODAY IN THE MORNING?

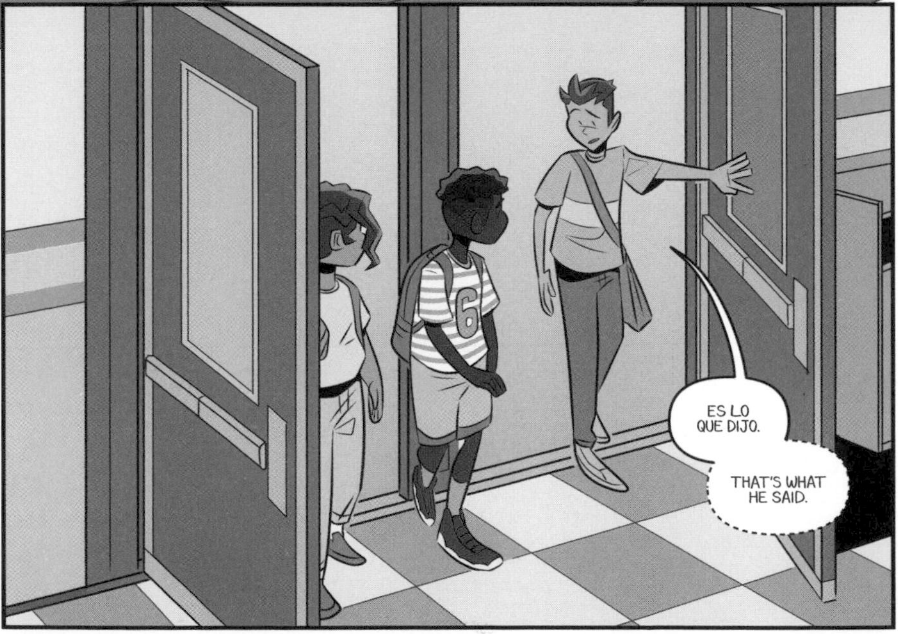
ES LO QUE DIJO.
THAT'S WHAT HE SAID.

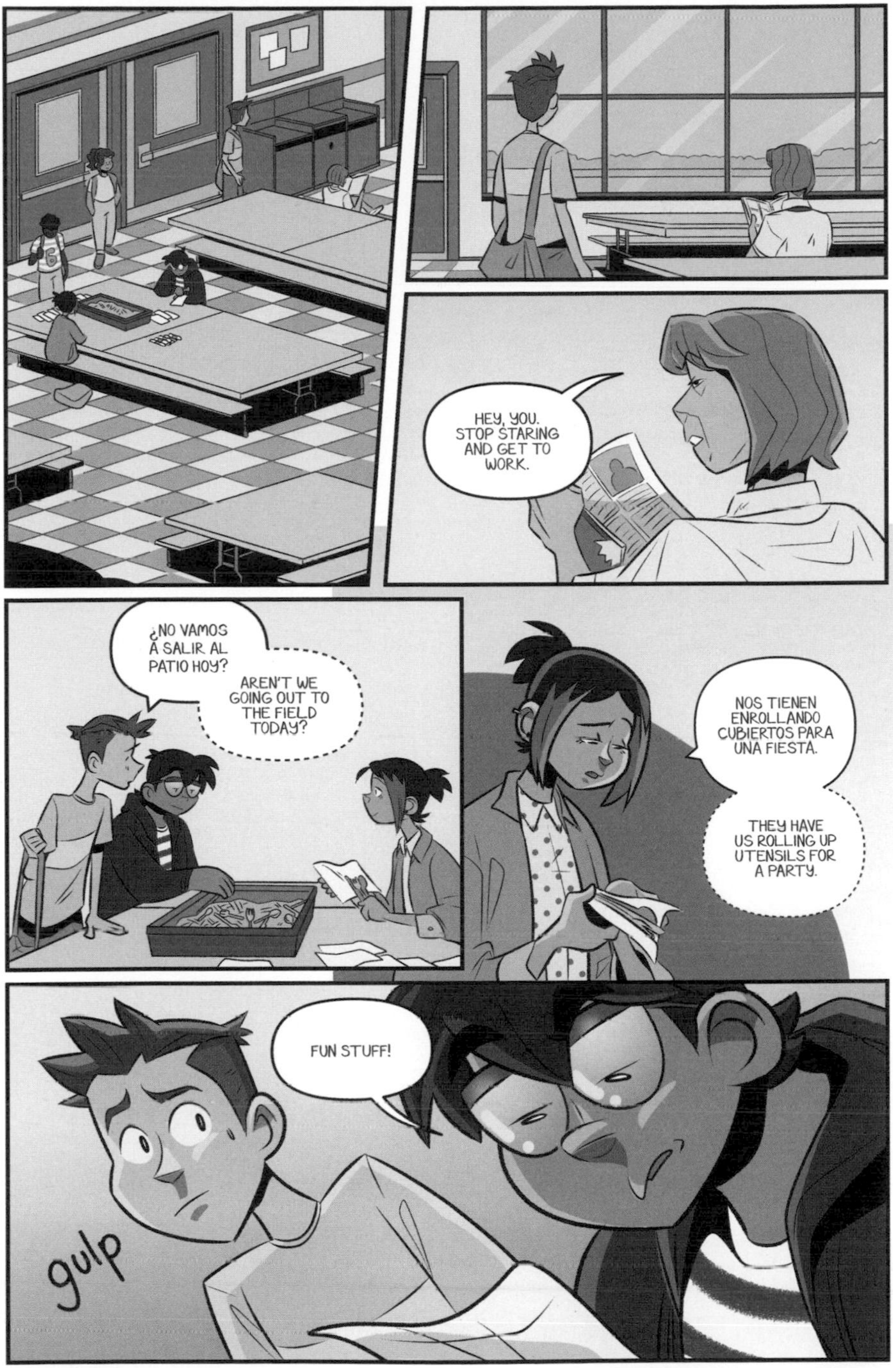
HEY, YOU. STOP STARING AND GET TO WORK.
¿NO VAMOS A SALIR AL PATIO HOY?
AREN'T WE GOING OUT TO THE FIELD TODAY?
NOS TIENEN ENROLLANDO CUBIERTOS PARA UNA FIESTA.
THEY HAVE US ROLLING UP UTENSILS FOR A PARTY.
FUN STUFF!
gulp

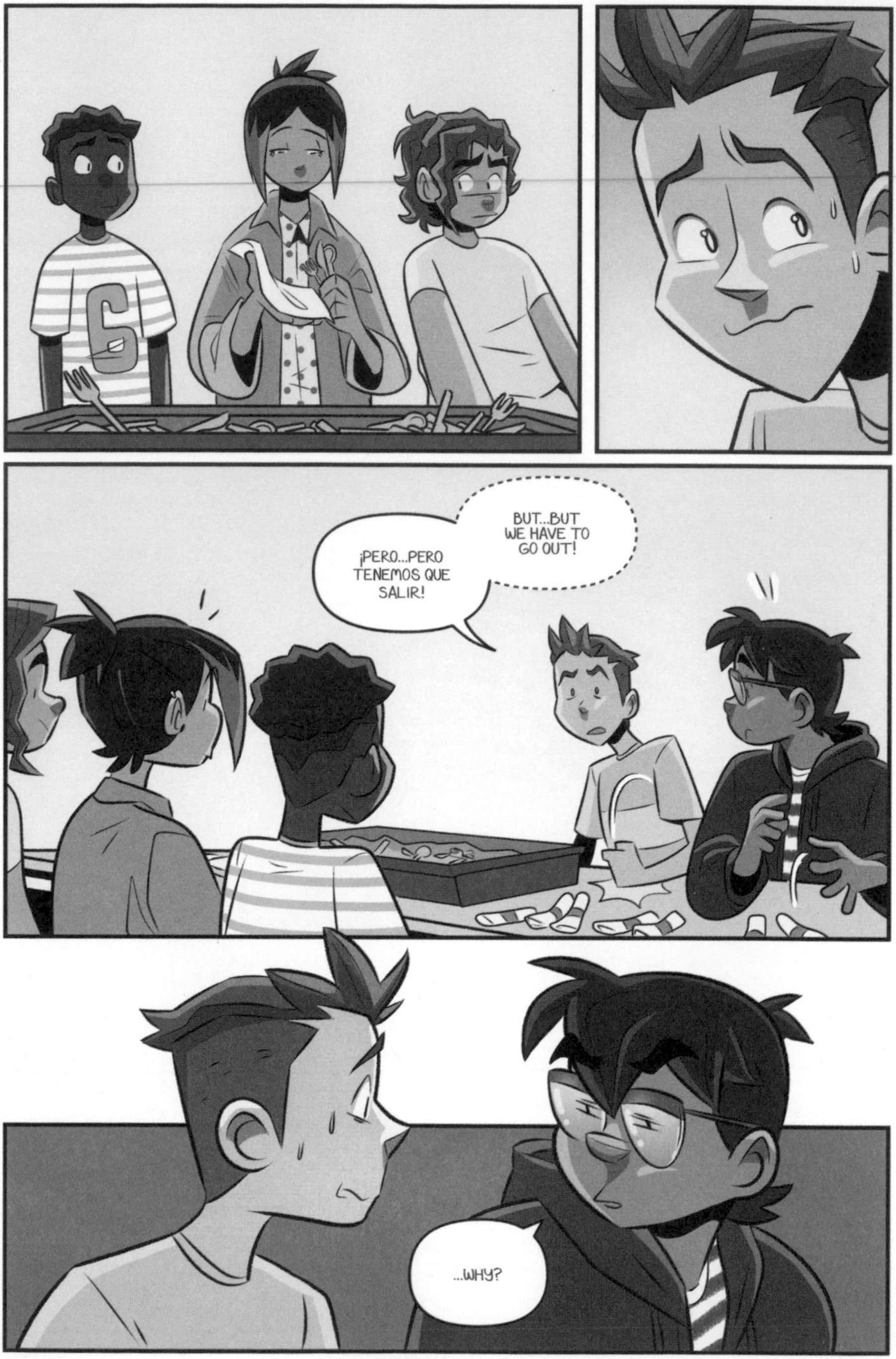

¡PERO...PERO TENEMOS QUE SALIR!
BUT...BUT WE HAVE TO GO OUT!
...WHY?

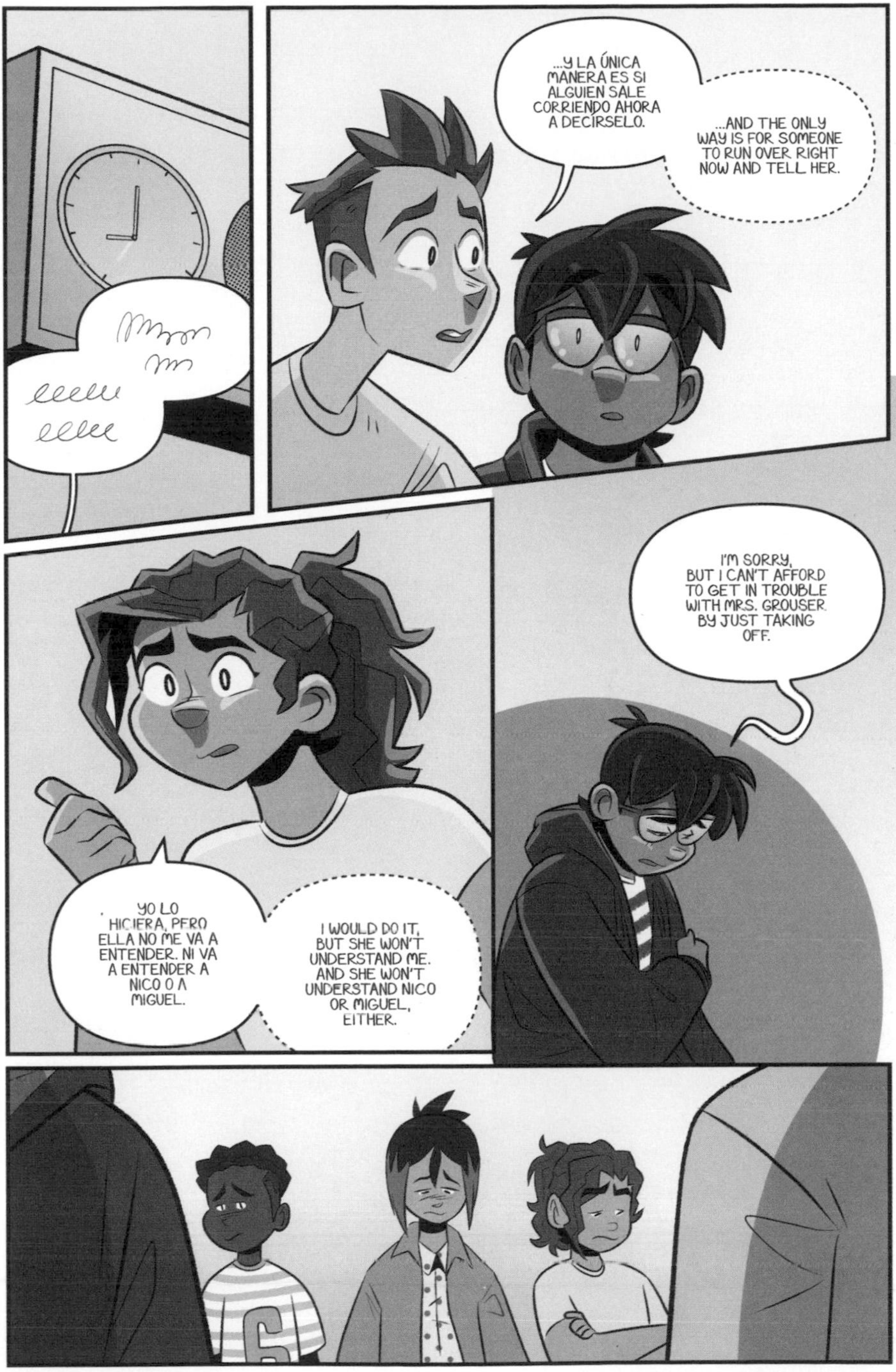
...Y LA ÚNICA MANERA ES SI ALGUIEN SALE CORRIENDO AHORA A DECIRSELO.
...AND THE ONLY WAY IS FOR SOMEONE TO RUN OVER RIGHT NOW AND TELL HER.
I'M SORRY, BUT I CAN'T AFFORD TO GET IN TROUBLE WITH MRS. GROUSER BY JUST TAKING OFF.
YO LO HICIERA, PERO ELLA NO ME VA A ENTENDER. NI VA A ENTENDER A NICO O A MIGUEL.
I WOULD DO IT, BUT SHE WON'T UNDERSTAND ME. AND SHE WON'T UNDERSTAND NICO OR MIGUEL, EITHER.

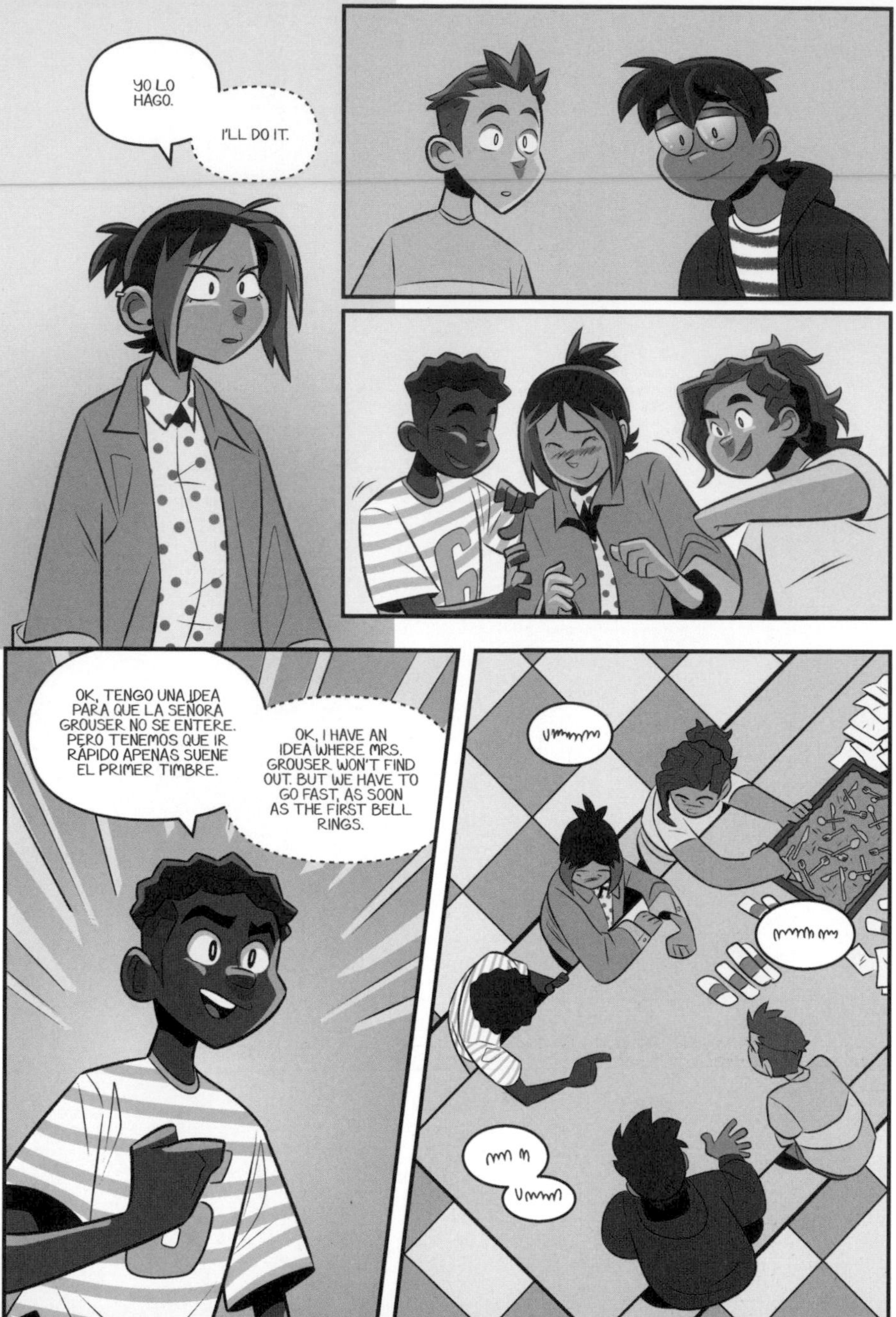
YO LO HAGO.
I'LL DO IT.
OK, TENGO UNA IDEA PARA QUE LA SEÑORA GROUSER NO SE ENTERE. PERO TENEMOS QUE IR RÁPIDO APENAS SUENE EL PRIMER TIMBRE.
OK, I HAVE AN IDEA WHERE MRS. GROUSER WON'T FIND OUT. BUT WE HAVE TO GO FAST, AS SOON AS THE FIRST BELL RINGS.

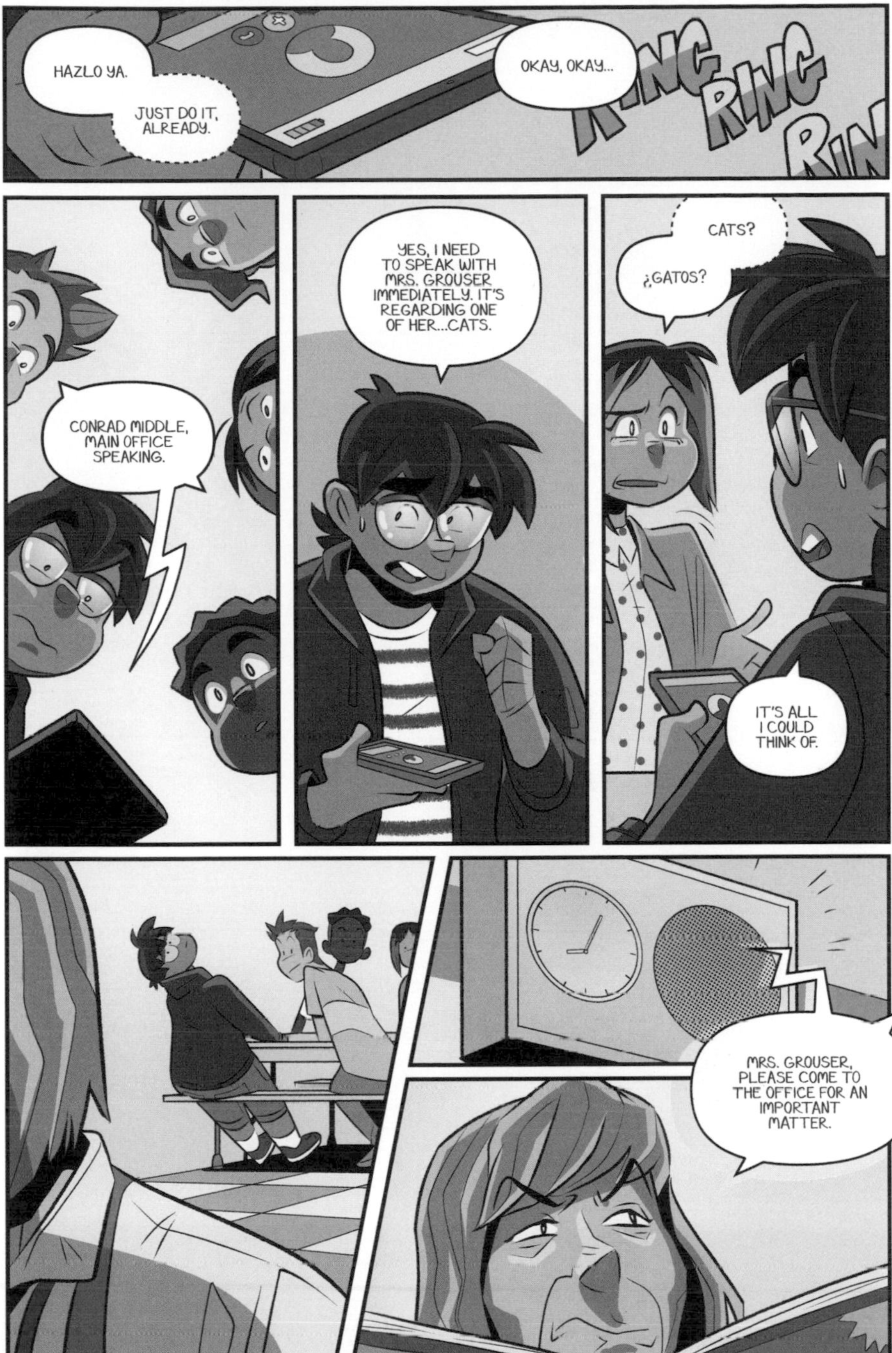
HAZLO YA.
JUST DO IT, ALREADY.
OKAY, OKAY...
RING RING RIN
CONRAD MIDDLE, MAIN OFFICE SPEAKING.
YES, I NEED TO SPEAK WITH MRS. GROUSER IMMEDIATELY. IT'S REGARDING ONE OF HER...CATS.
¿GATOS?
CATS?
IT'S ALL I COULD THINK OF.
MRS. GROUSER, PLEASE COME TO THE OFFICE FOR AN IMPORTANT MATTER.

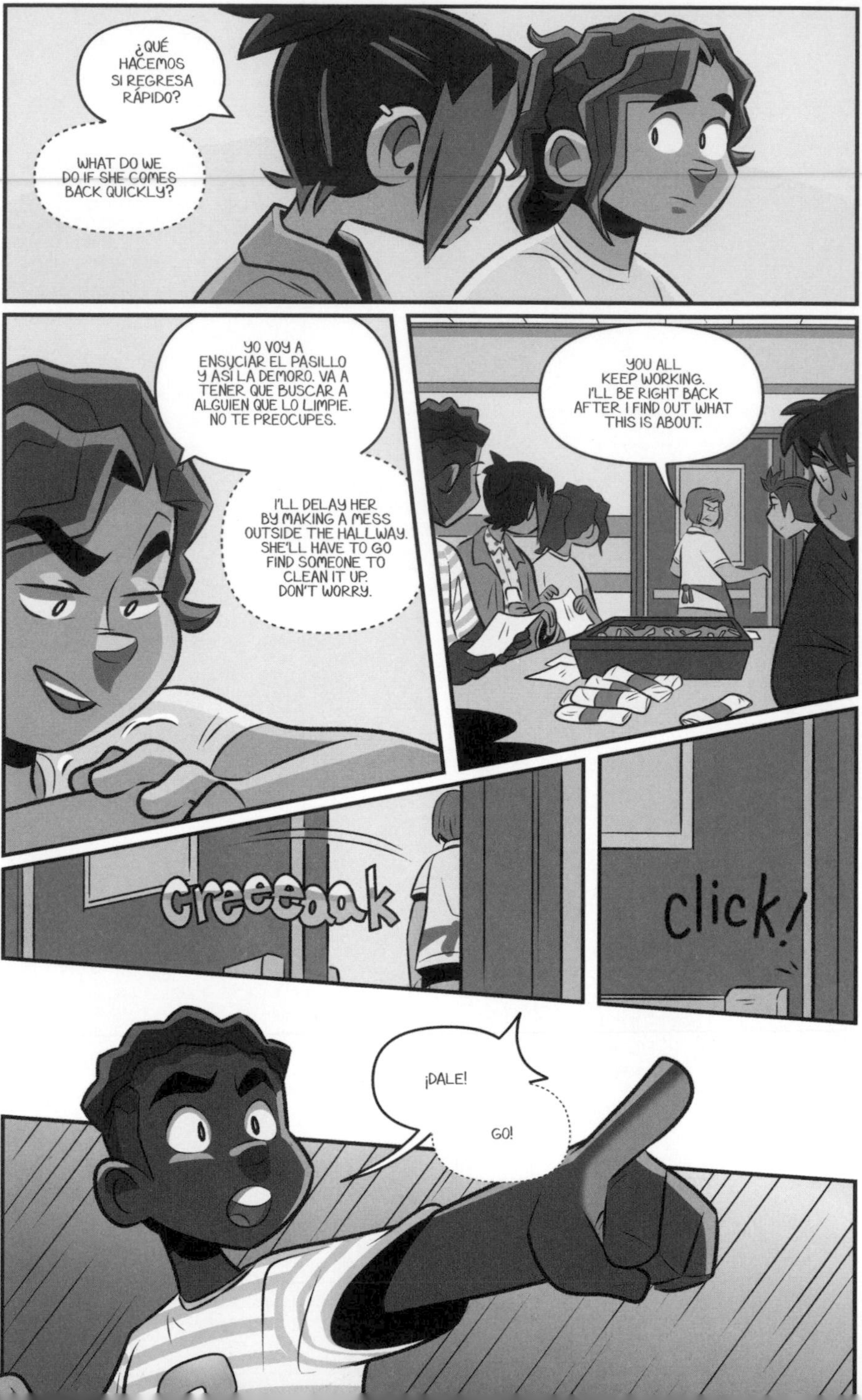
¿QUÉ HACEMOS SI REGRESA RÁPIDO?
WHAT DO WE DO IF SHE COMES BACK QUICKLY?
YO VOY A ENSUCIAR EL PASILLO Y ASÍ LA DEMORO. VA A TENER QUE BUSCAR A ALGUIEN QUE LO LIMPIE. NO TE PREOCUPES.
I'LL DELAY HER BY MAKING A MESS OUTSIDE THE HALLWAY. SHE'LL HAVE TO GO FIND SOMEONE TO CLEAN IT UP. DON'T WORRY.
YOU ALL KEEP WORKING. I'LL BE RIGHT BACK AFTER I FIND OUT WHAT THIS IS ABOUT.
creeeaak
click!
¡DALE!
GO!

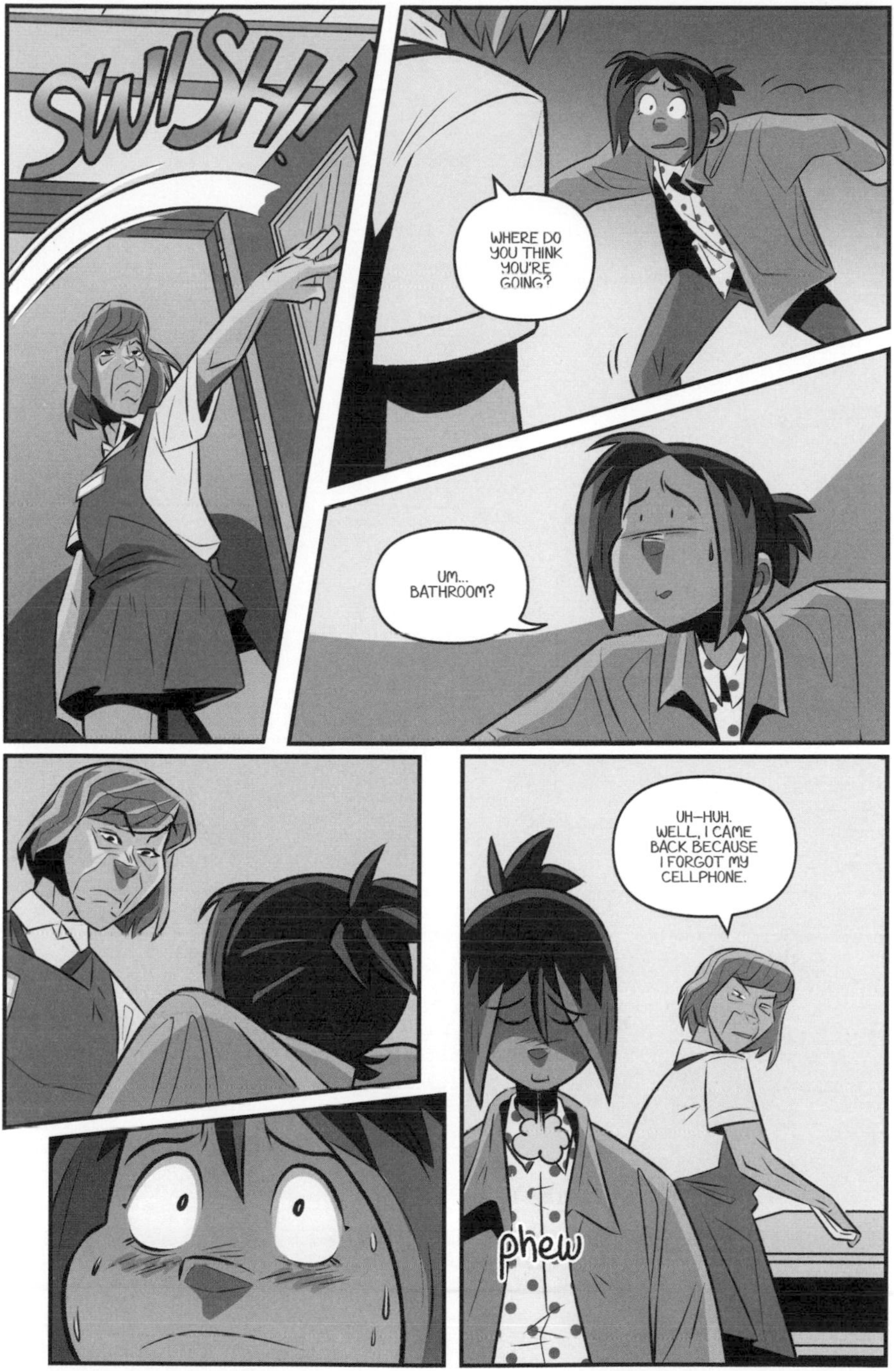
SWISH!
WHERE DO YOU THINK YOU'RE GOING?
UM... BATHROOM?
UH-HUH. WELL, I CAME BACK BECAUSE I FORGOT MY CELLPHONE.
phew

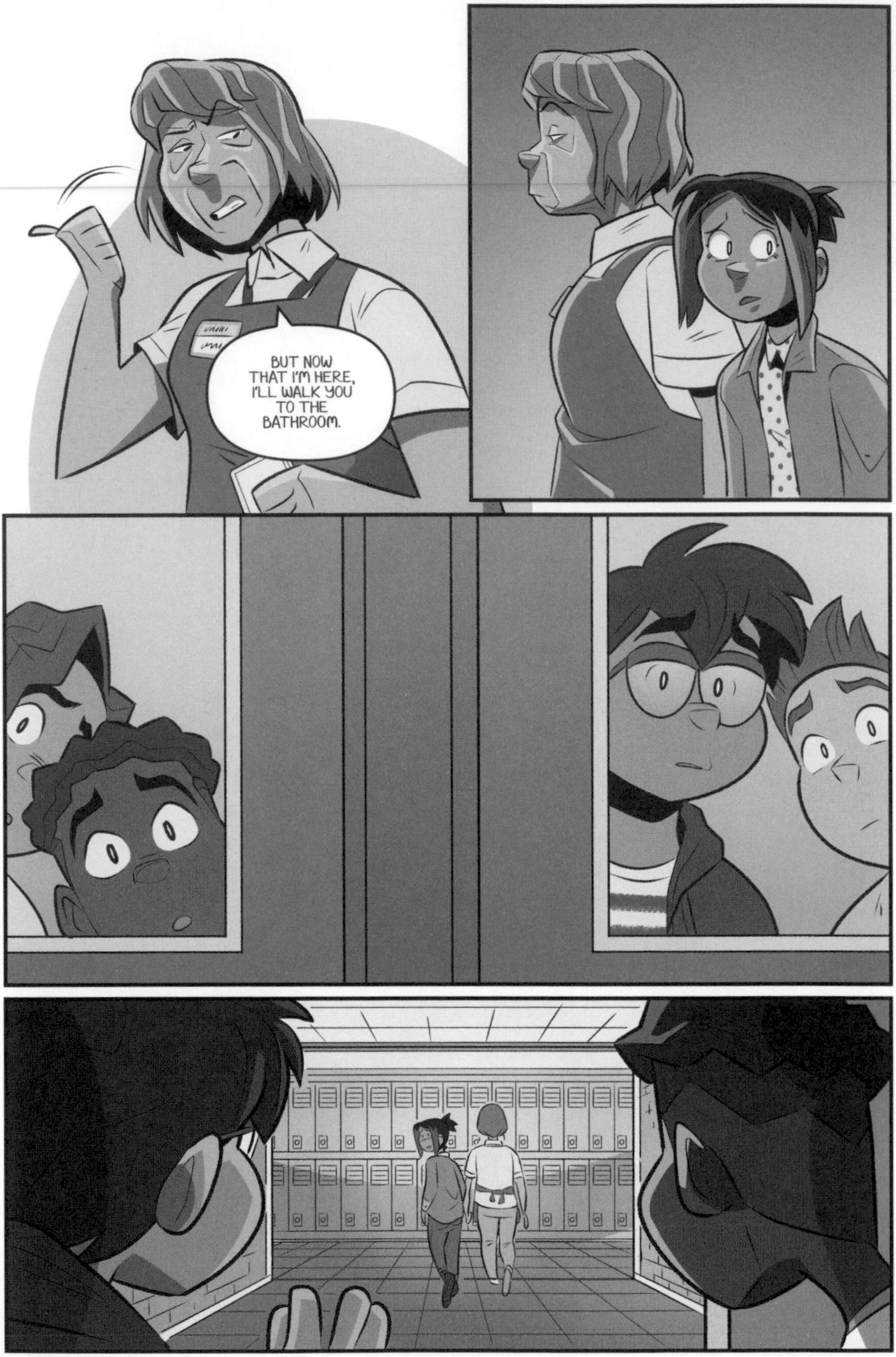
BUT NOW THAT I'M HERE, I'LL WALK YOU TO THE BATHROOM.

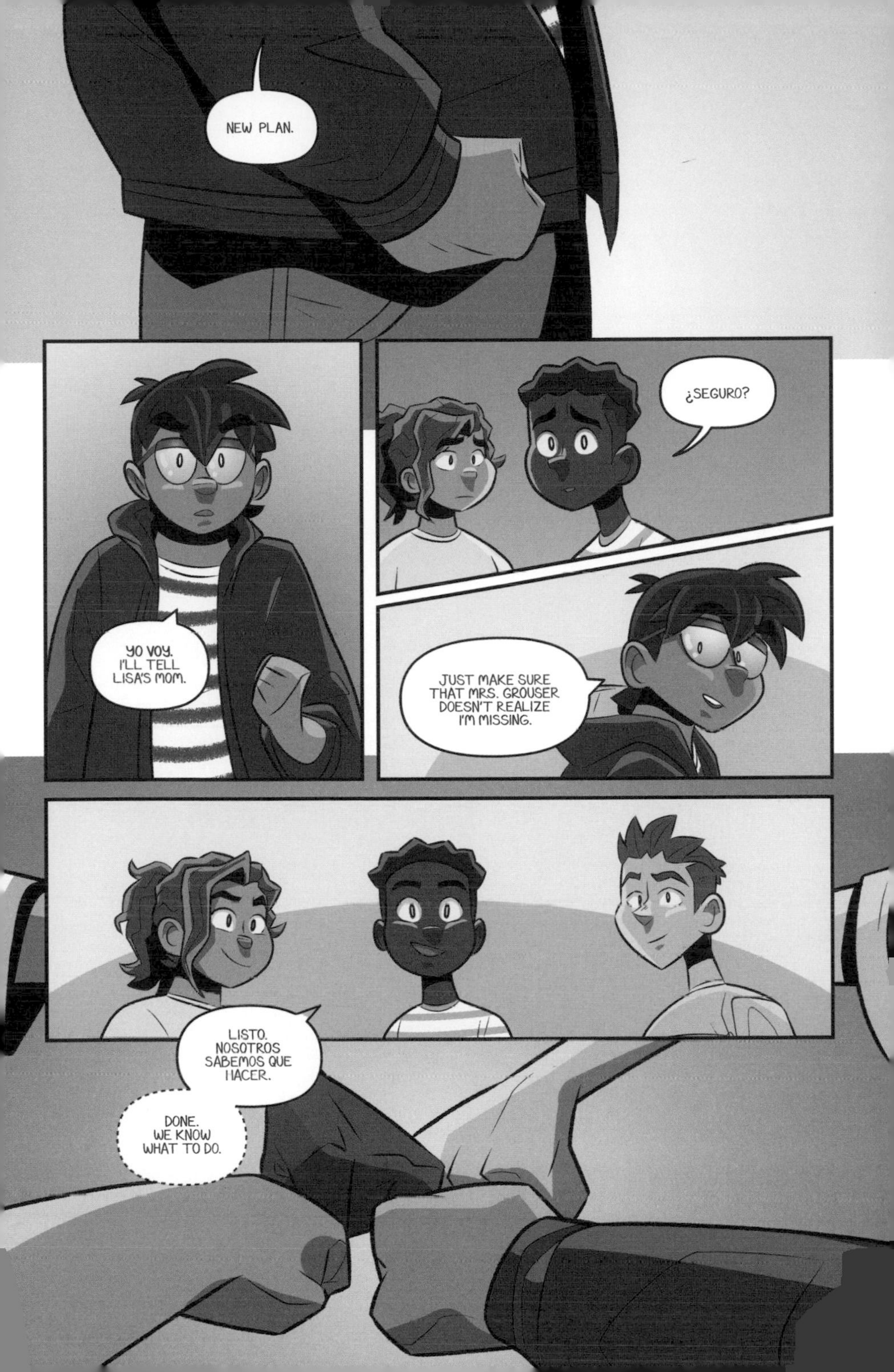
NEW PLAN.
YO VOY. I'LL TELL LISA'S MOM.
¿SEGURO?
JUST MAKE SURE THAT MRS. GROUSER DOESN'T REALIZE I'M MISSING.
LISTO. NOSOTROS SABEMOS QUE HACER.
DONE. WE KNOW WHAT TO DO.

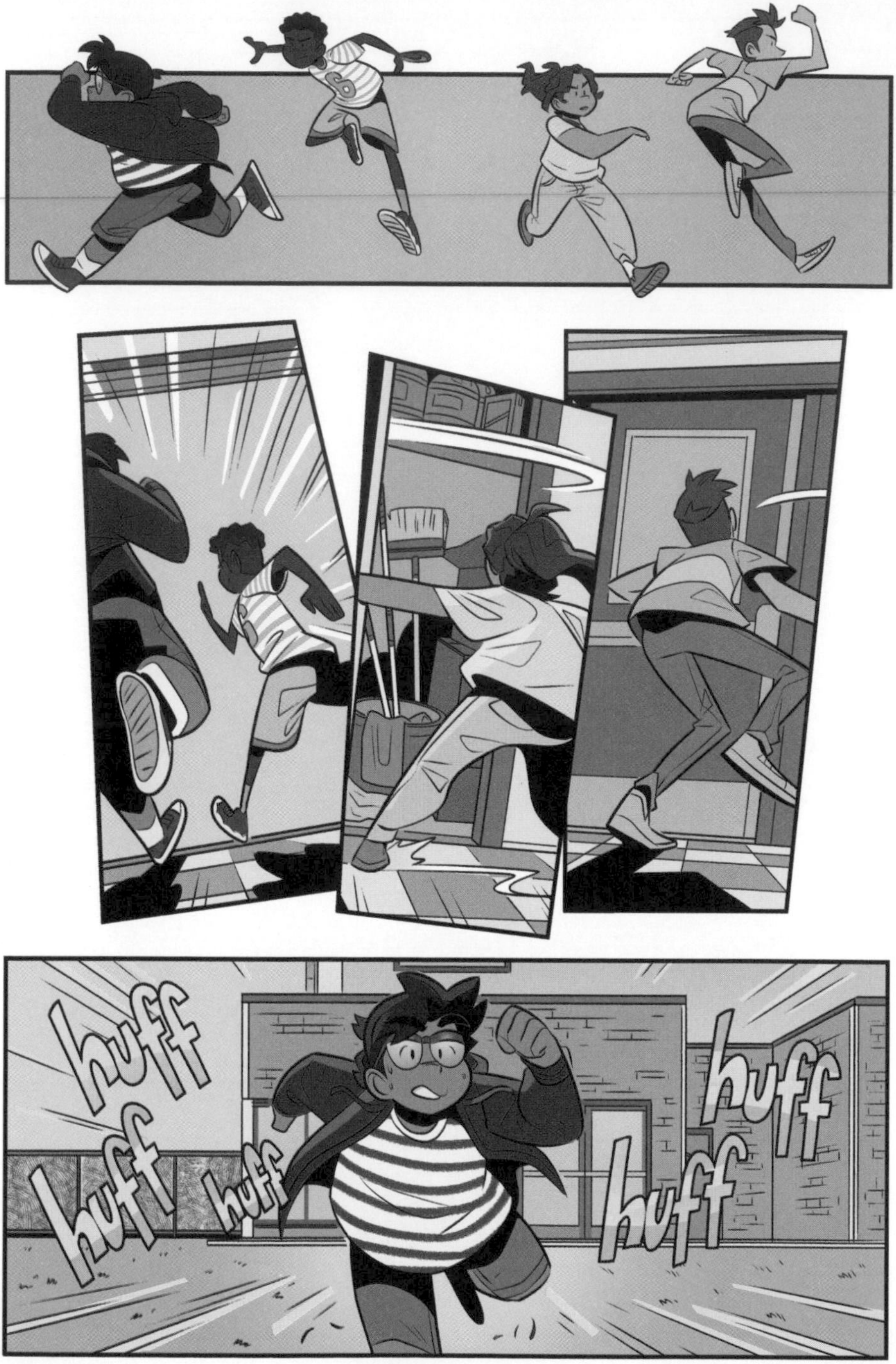
huff
huff
huff
huff
huff

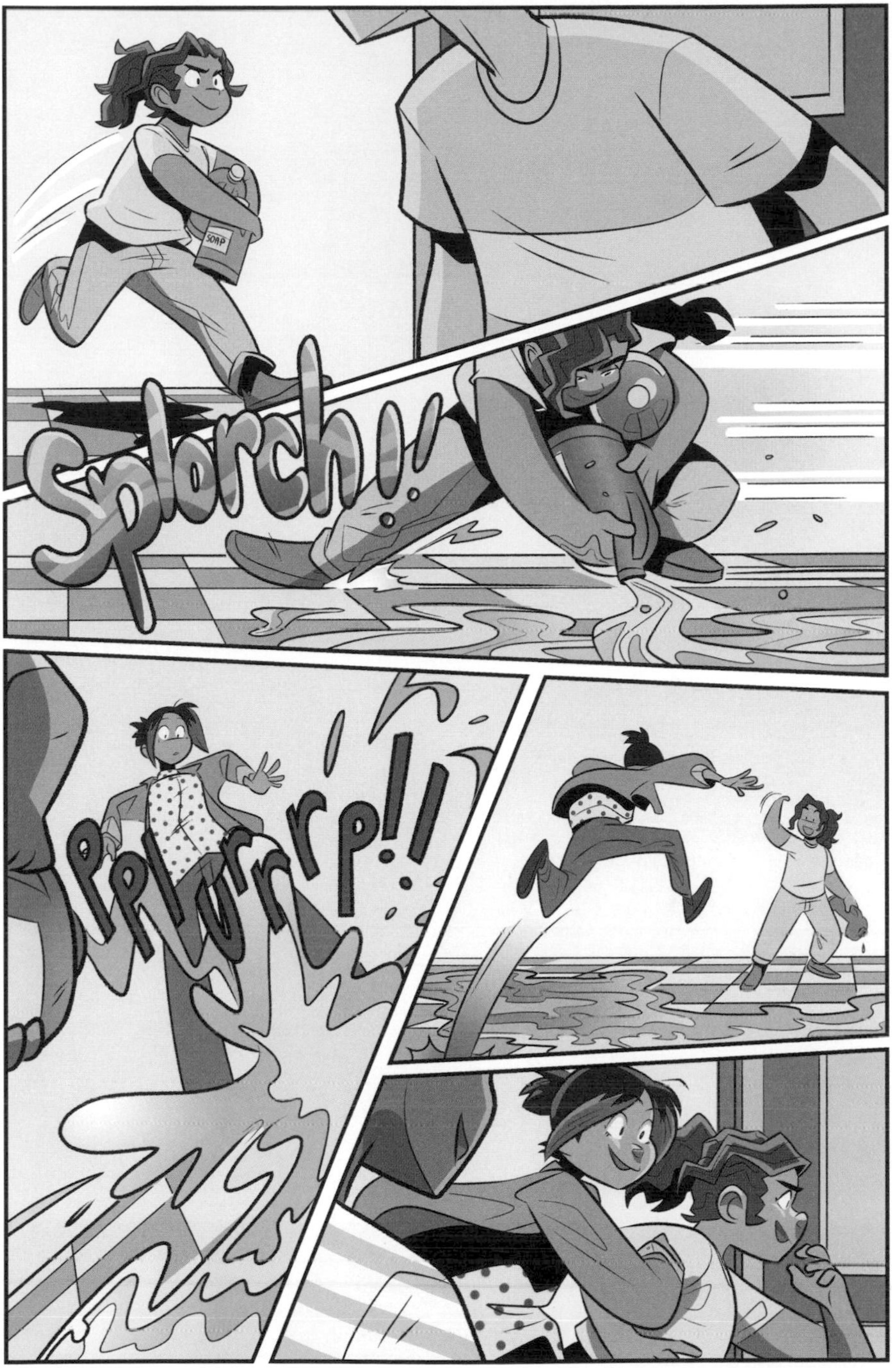

SOAP
Splorch!!
Pplurrrp!!!

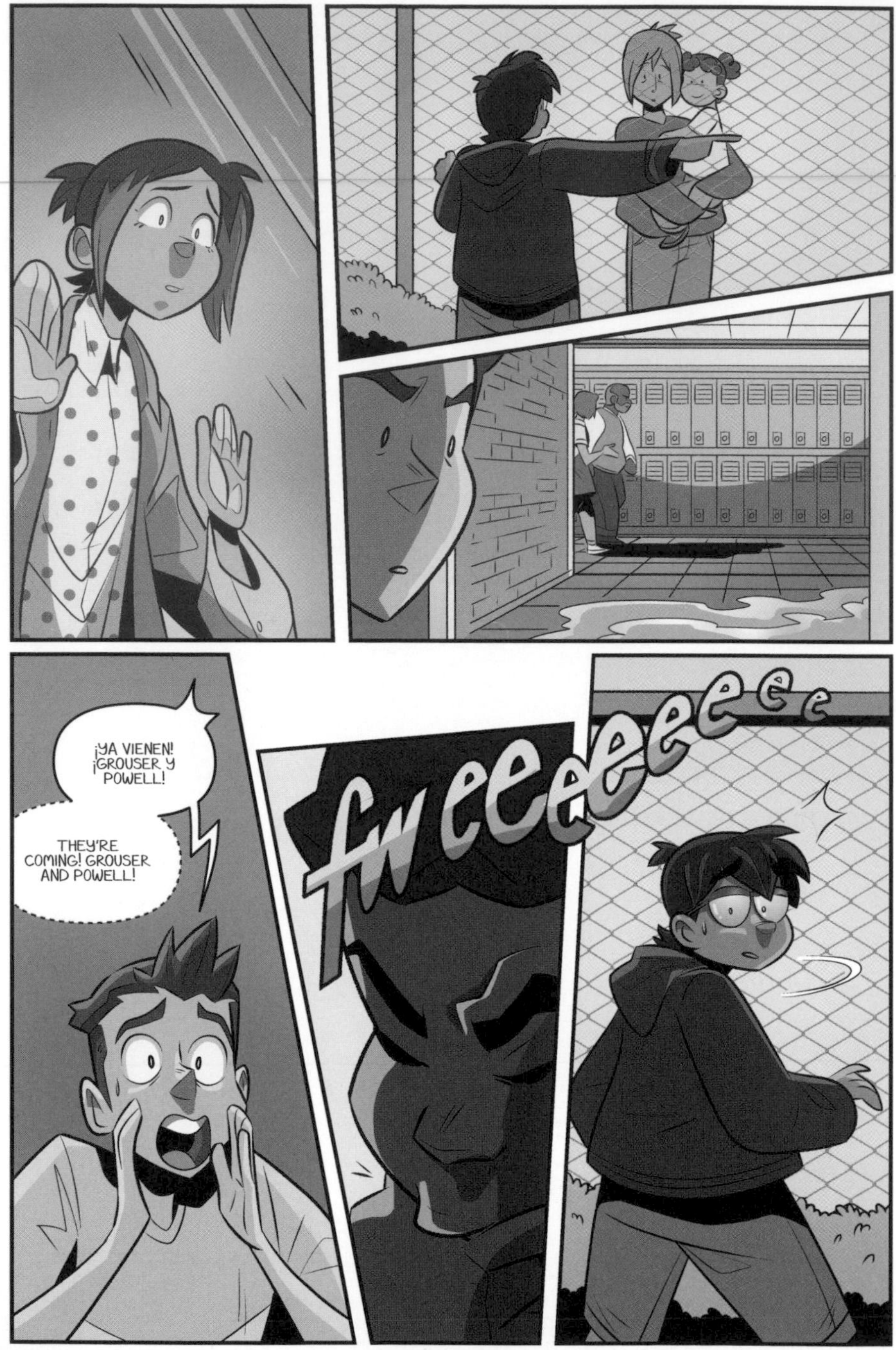
¡YA VIENEN! ¡GROUSER Y POWELL!
THEY'RE COMING! GROUSER AND POWELL!
FWEEEEEEEEe

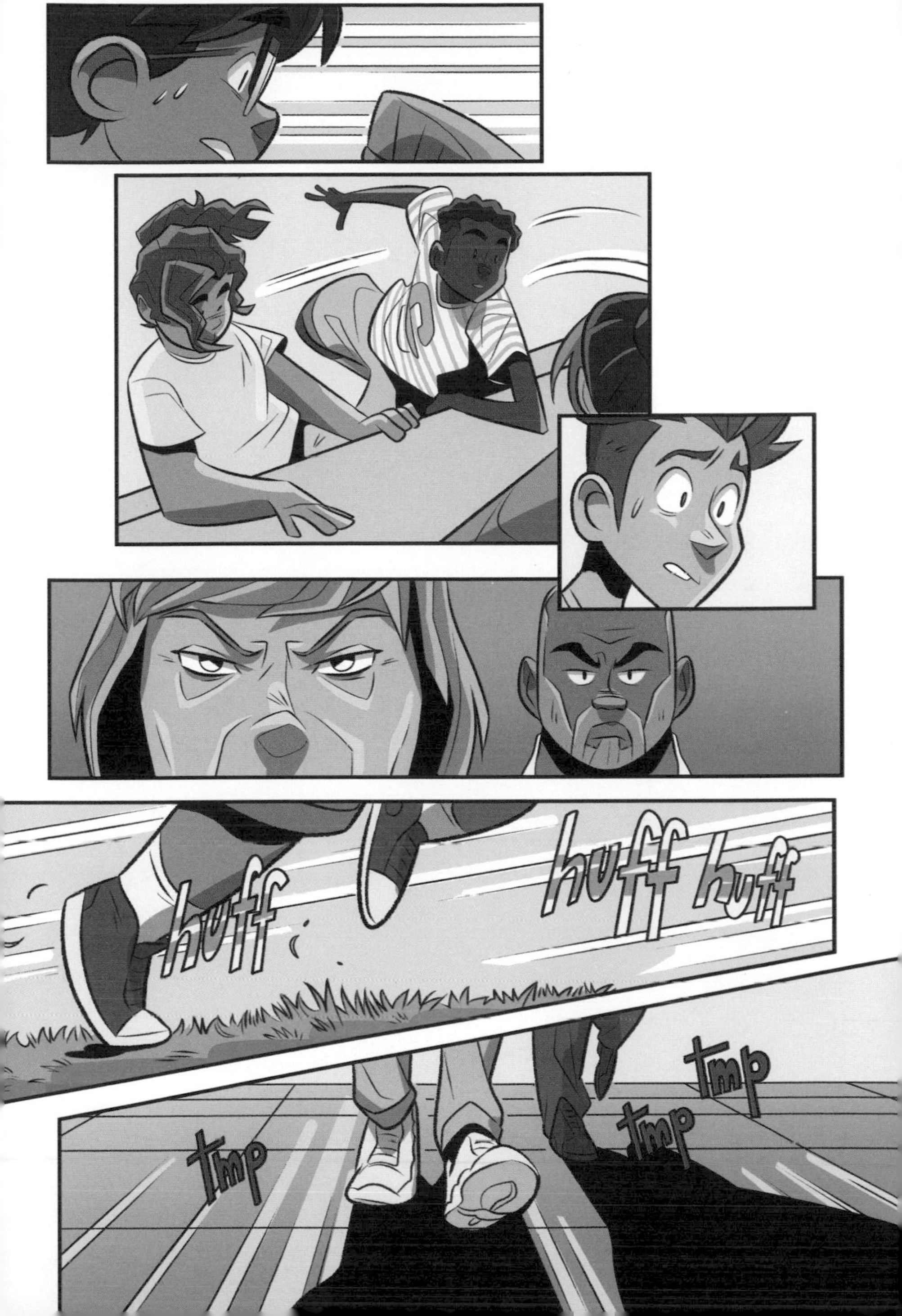
huff
huff huff
tmp
tmp
tmp

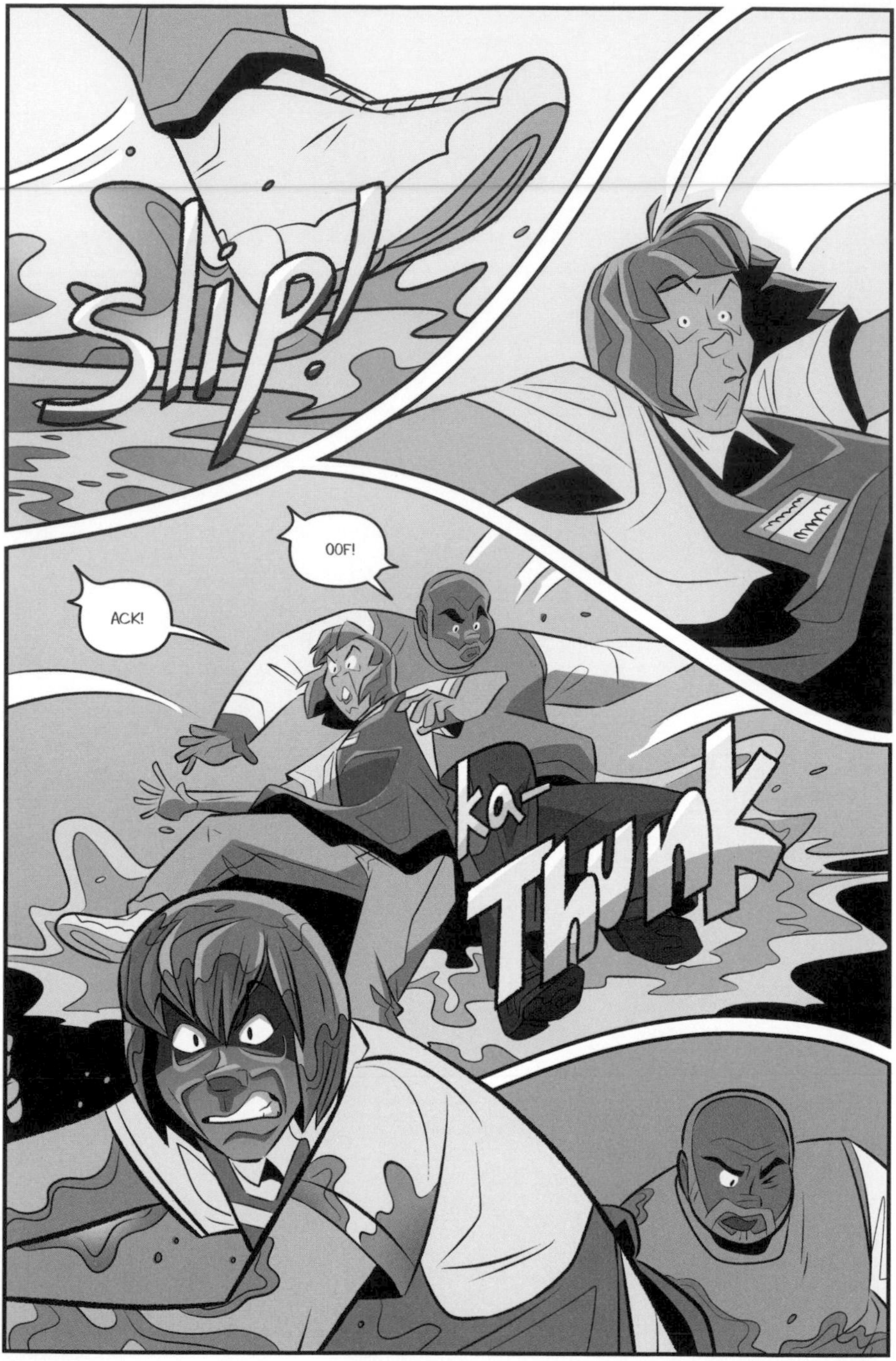
SLIP!
OOF!
ACK!
KA-THUNK

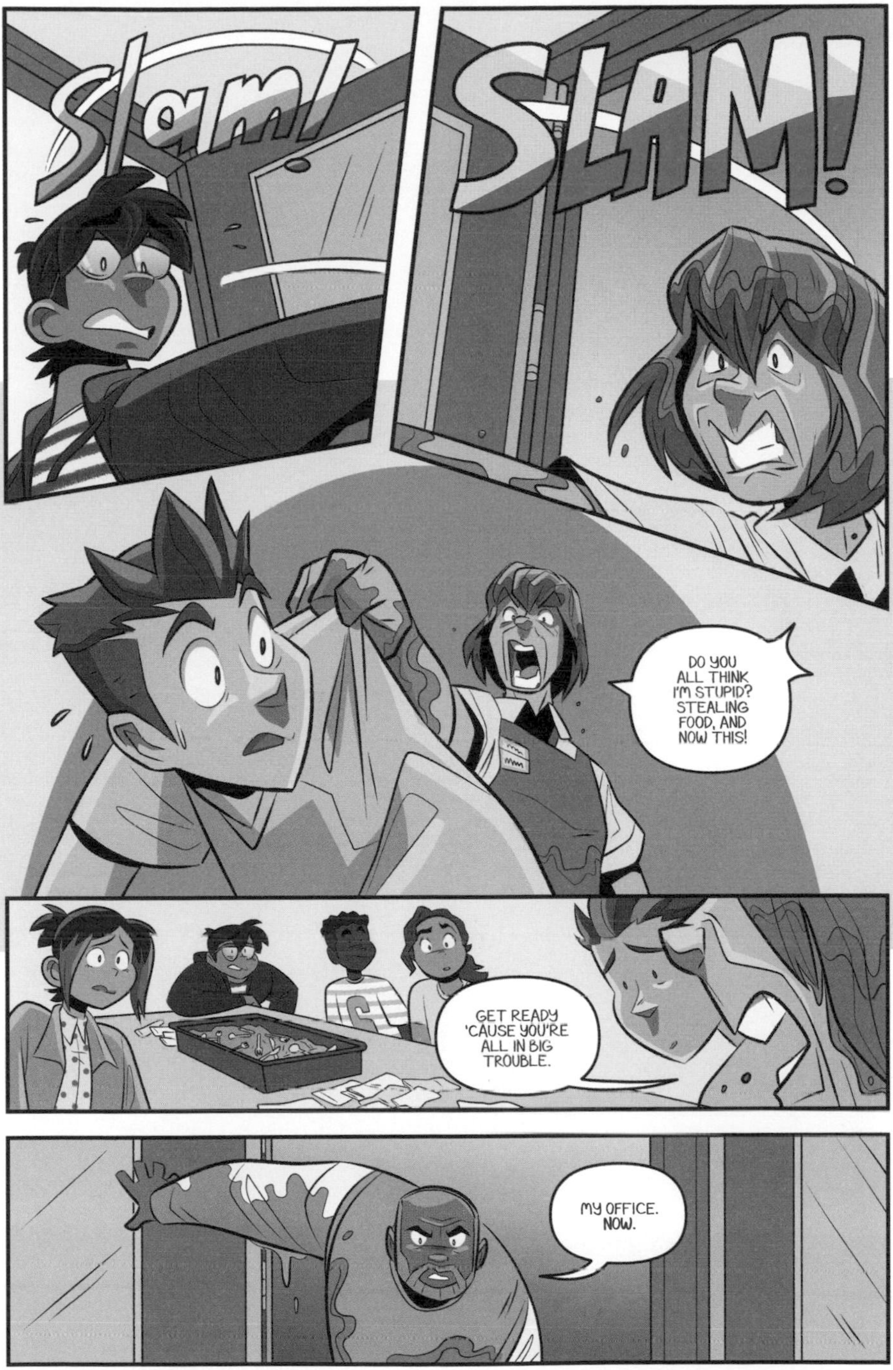
Slam!
SLAM!
DO YOU ALL THINK I'M STUPID? STEALING FOOD, AND NOW THIS!
GET READY 'CAUSE YOU'RE ALL IN BIG TROUBLE.
MY OFFICE. NOW.

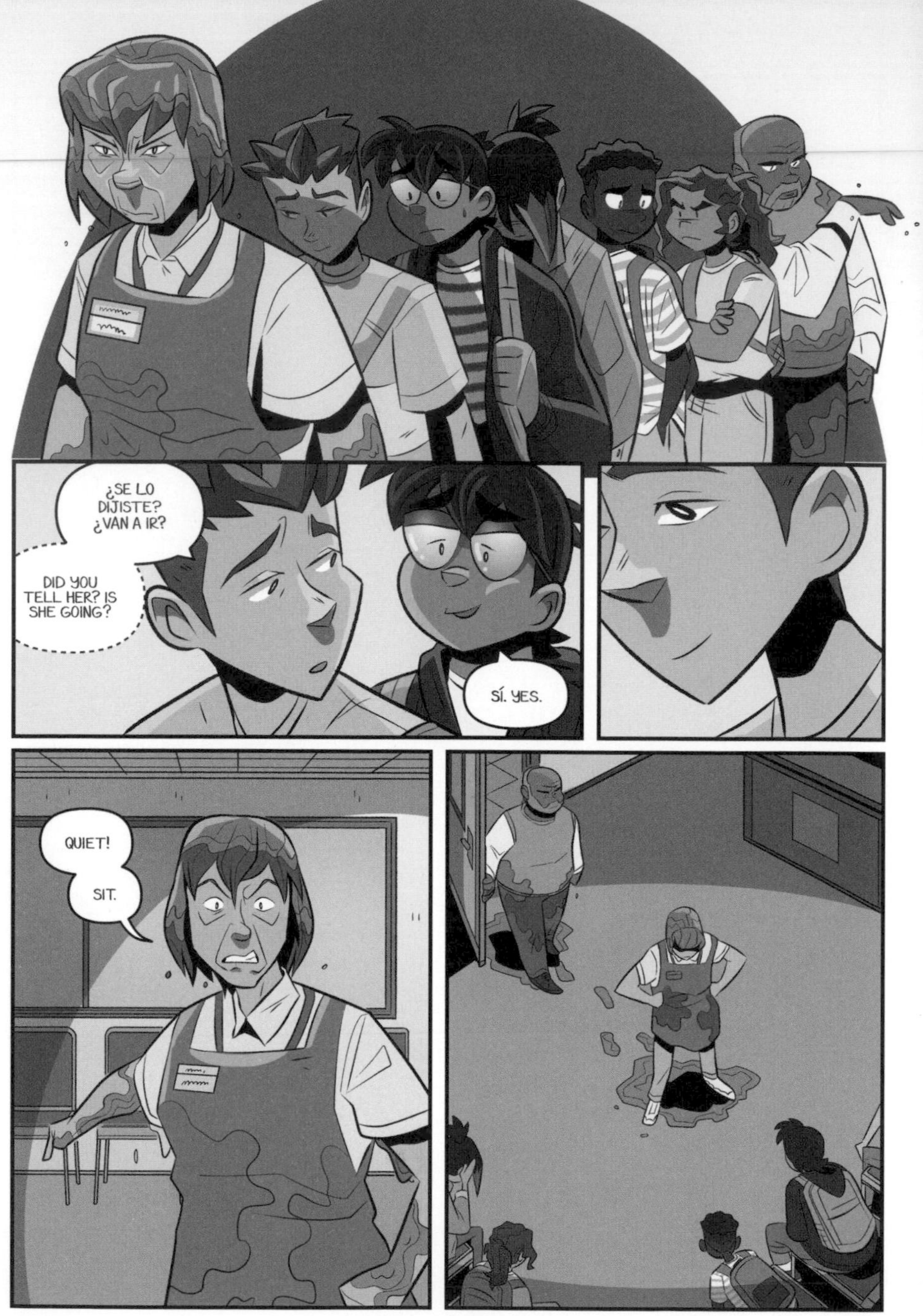
¿SE LO DIJISTE? ¿VAN A IR?
DID YOU TELL HER? IS SHE GOING?
SÍ. YES.
QUIET!
SIT.

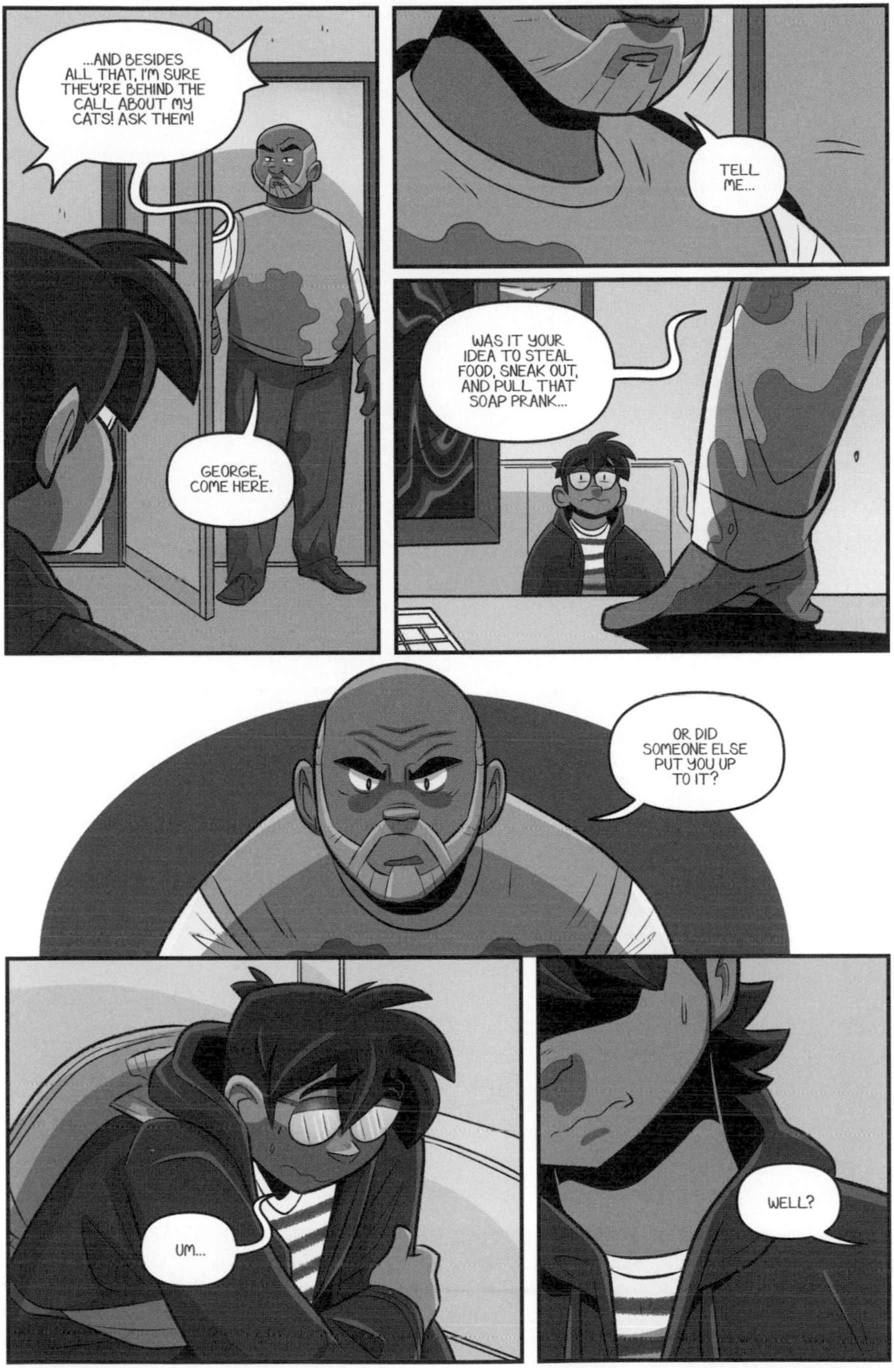
...AND BESIDES ALL THAT, I'M SURE THEY'RE BEHIND THE CALL ABOUT MY CATS! ASK THEM!
GEORGE, COME HERE.
TELL ME...
WAS IT YOUR IDEA TO STEAL FOOD, SNEAK OUT, AND PULL THAT SOAP PRANK...
OR DID SOMEONE ELSE PUT YOU UP TO IT?
UM...
WELL?

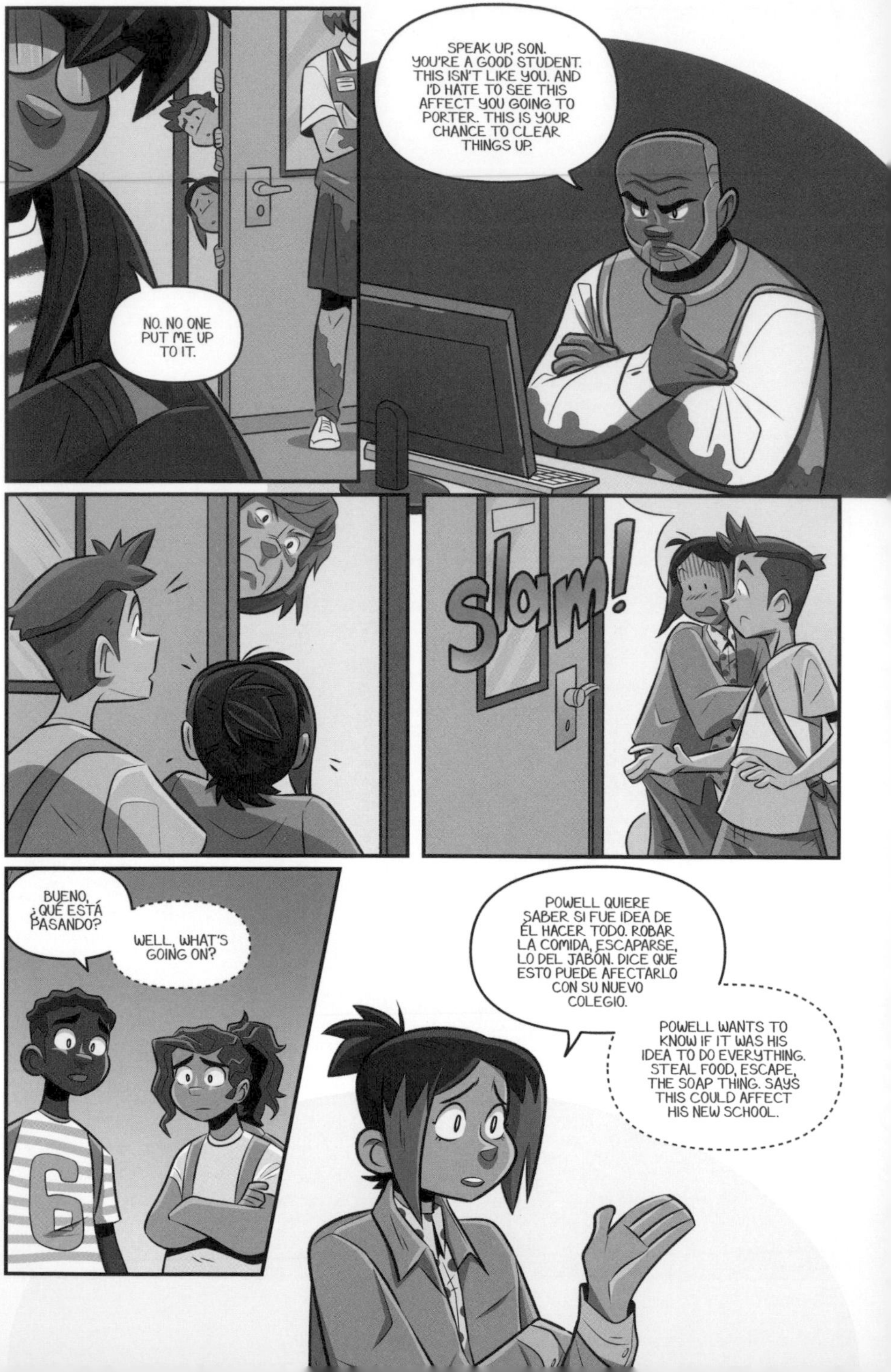
NO. NO ONE PUT ME UP TO IT.
SPEAK UP, SON. YOU'RE A GOOD STUDENT. THIS ISN'T LIKE YOU. AND I'D HATE TO SEE THIS AFFECT YOU GOING TO PORTER. THIS IS YOUR CHANCE TO CLEAR THINGS UP.
SLAM!
BUENO, ¿QUÉ ESTÁ PASANDO?
WELL, WHAT'S GOING ON?
POWELL QUIERE SABER SI FUE IDEA DE ÉL HACER TODO. ROBAR LA COMIDA, ESCAPARSE, LO DEL JABÓN. DICE QUE ESTO PUEDE AFECTARLO CON SU NUEVO COLEGIO.
POWELL WANTS TO KNOW IF IT WAS HIS IDEA TO DO EVERYTHING. STEAL FOOD, ESCAPE, THE SOAP THING. SAYS THIS COULD AFFECT HIS NEW SCHOOL.

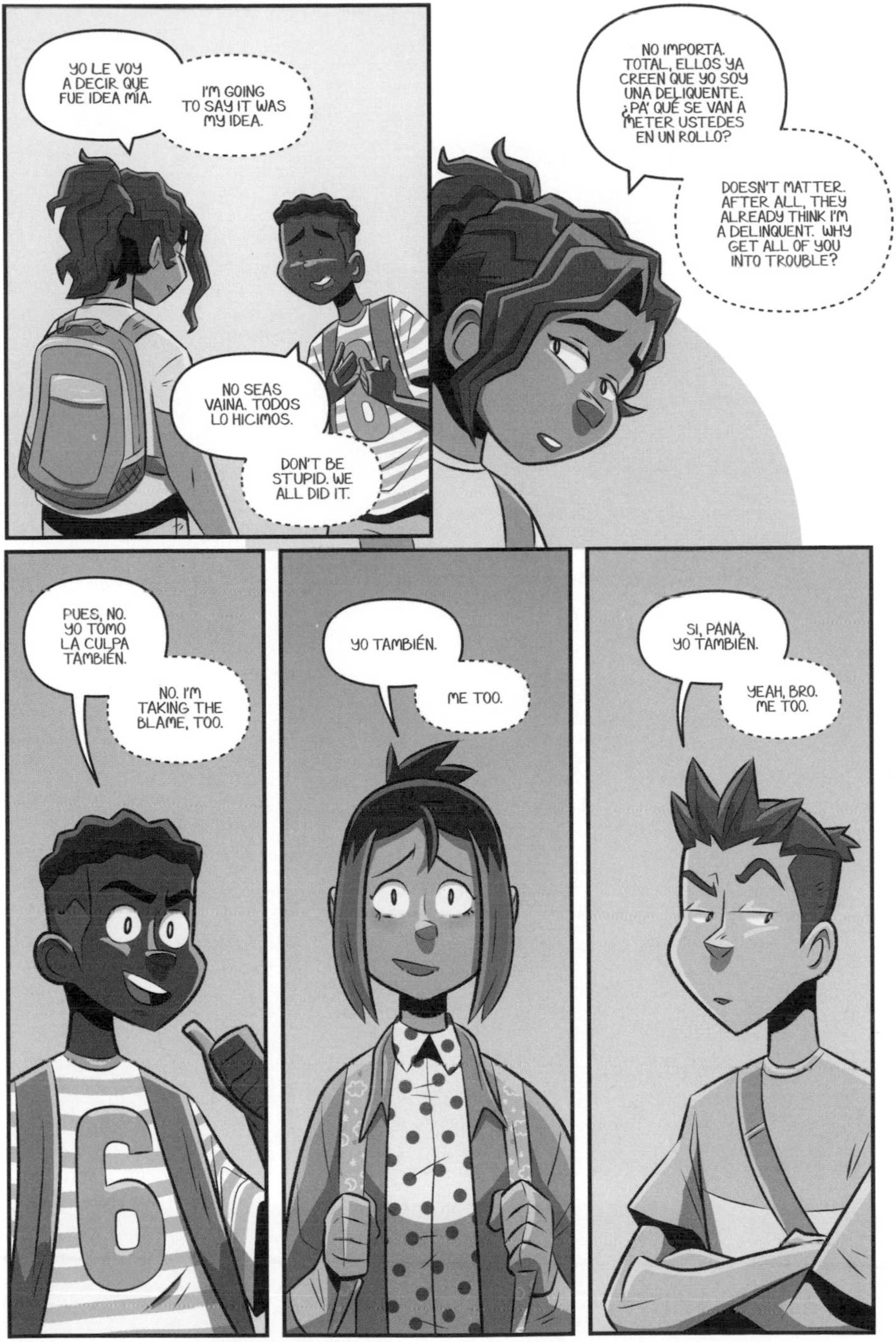
YO LE VOY A DECIR QUE FUE IDEA MIA.
I'M GOING TO SAY IT WAS MY IDEA.
NO SEAS VAINA. TODOS LO HICIMOS.
DON'T BE STUPID. WE ALL DID IT.
NO IMPORTA. TOTAL, ELLOS YA CREEN QUE YO SOY UNA DELIQUENTE. ¿PA' QUÉ SE VAN A METER USTEDES EN UN ROLLO?
DOESN'T MATTER. AFTER ALL, THEY ALREADY THINK I'M A DELINQUENT. WHY GET ALL OF YOU INTO TROUBLE?
PUES, NO. YO TOMO LA CULPA TAMBIÉN.
NO. I'M TAKING THE BLAME, TOO.
YO TAMBIÉN.
ME TOO.
SI, PANA, YO TAMBIÉN.
YEAH, BRO. ME TOO.

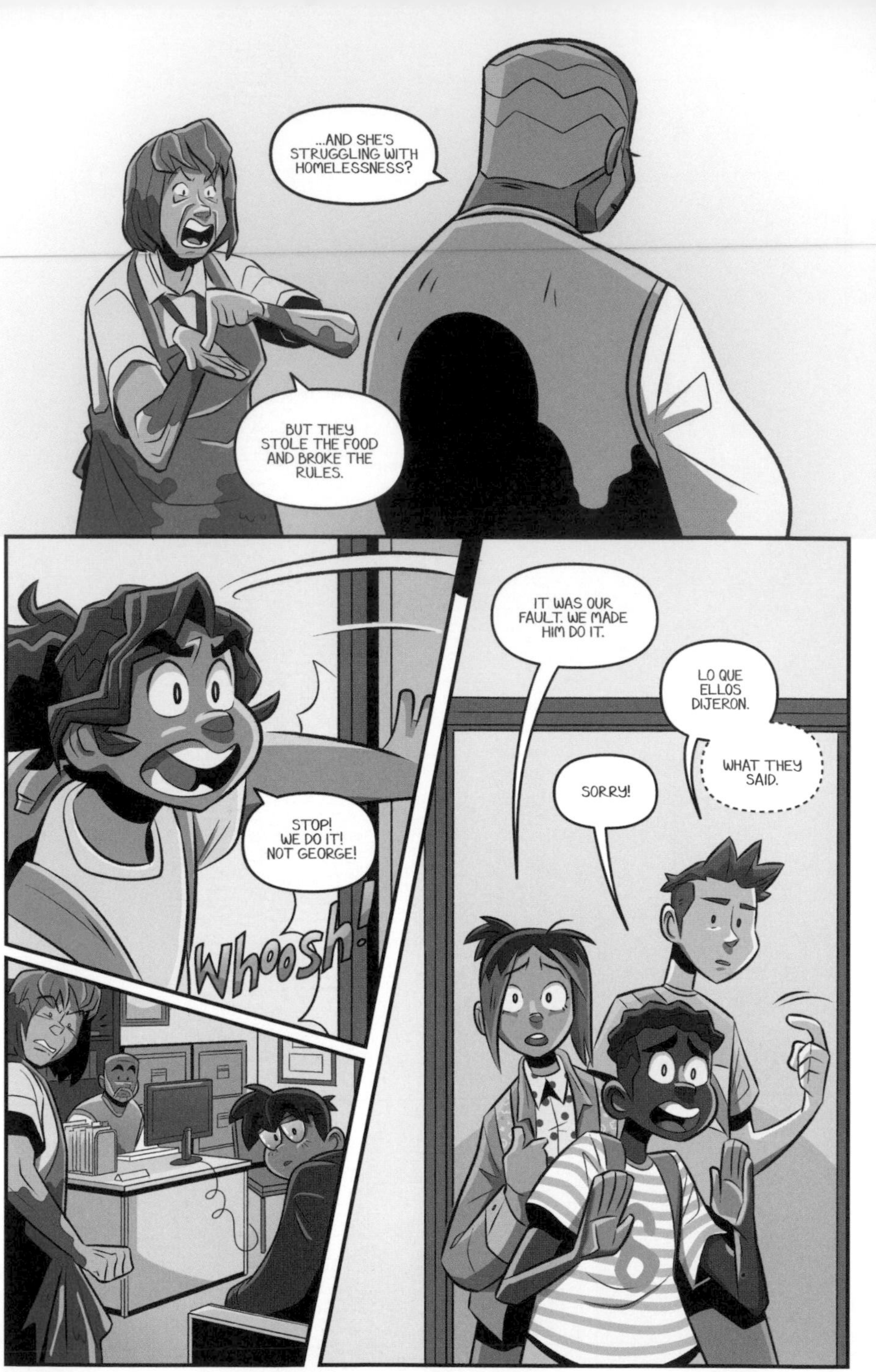
...AND SHE'S STRUGGLING WITH HOMELESSNESS?
BUT THEY STOLE THE FOOD AND BROKE THE RULES.
STOP! WE DO IT! NOT GEORGE!
Whoosh!
IT WAS OUR FAULT. WE MADE HIM DO IT.
LO QUE ELLOS DIJERON.
SORRY!
WHAT THEY SAID.

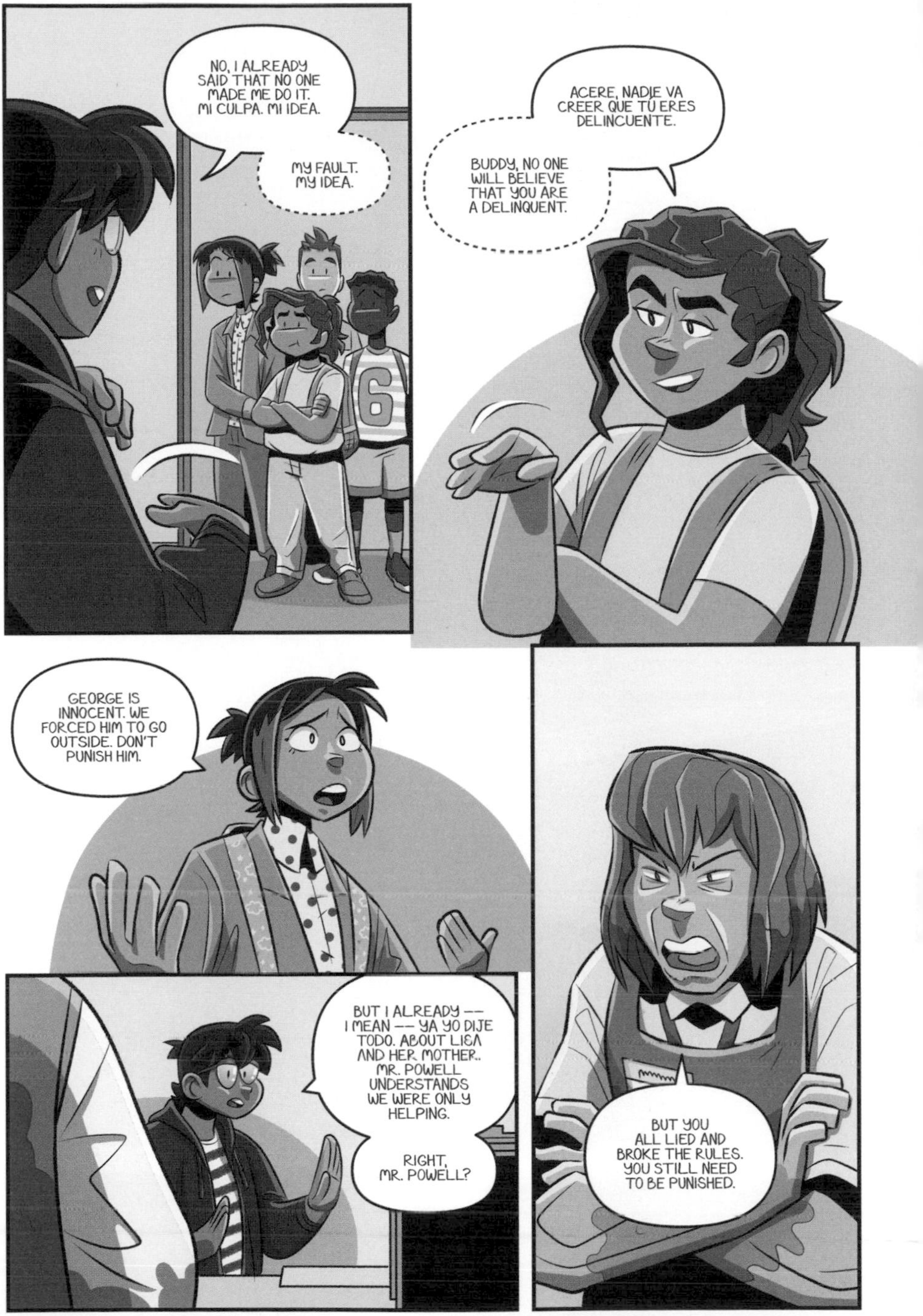
NO, I ALREADY SAID THAT NO ONE MADE ME DO IT. MI CULPA. MI IDEA.
MY FAULT. MY IDEA.
ACERE, NADIE VA CREER QUE TÚ ERES DELINCUENTE.
BUDDY, NO ONE WILL BELIEVE THAT YOU ARE A DELINQUENT.
GEORGE IS INNOCENT. WE FORCED HIM TO GO OUTSIDE. DON'T PUNISH HIM.
BUT I ALREADY -- I MEAN -- YA YO DIJE TODO. ABOUT LISA AND HER MOTHER.. MR. POWELL UNDERSTANDS WE WERE ONLY HELPING.
RIGHT, MR. POWELL?
BUT YOU ALL LIED AND BROKE THE RULES. YOU STILL NEED TO BE PUNISHED.

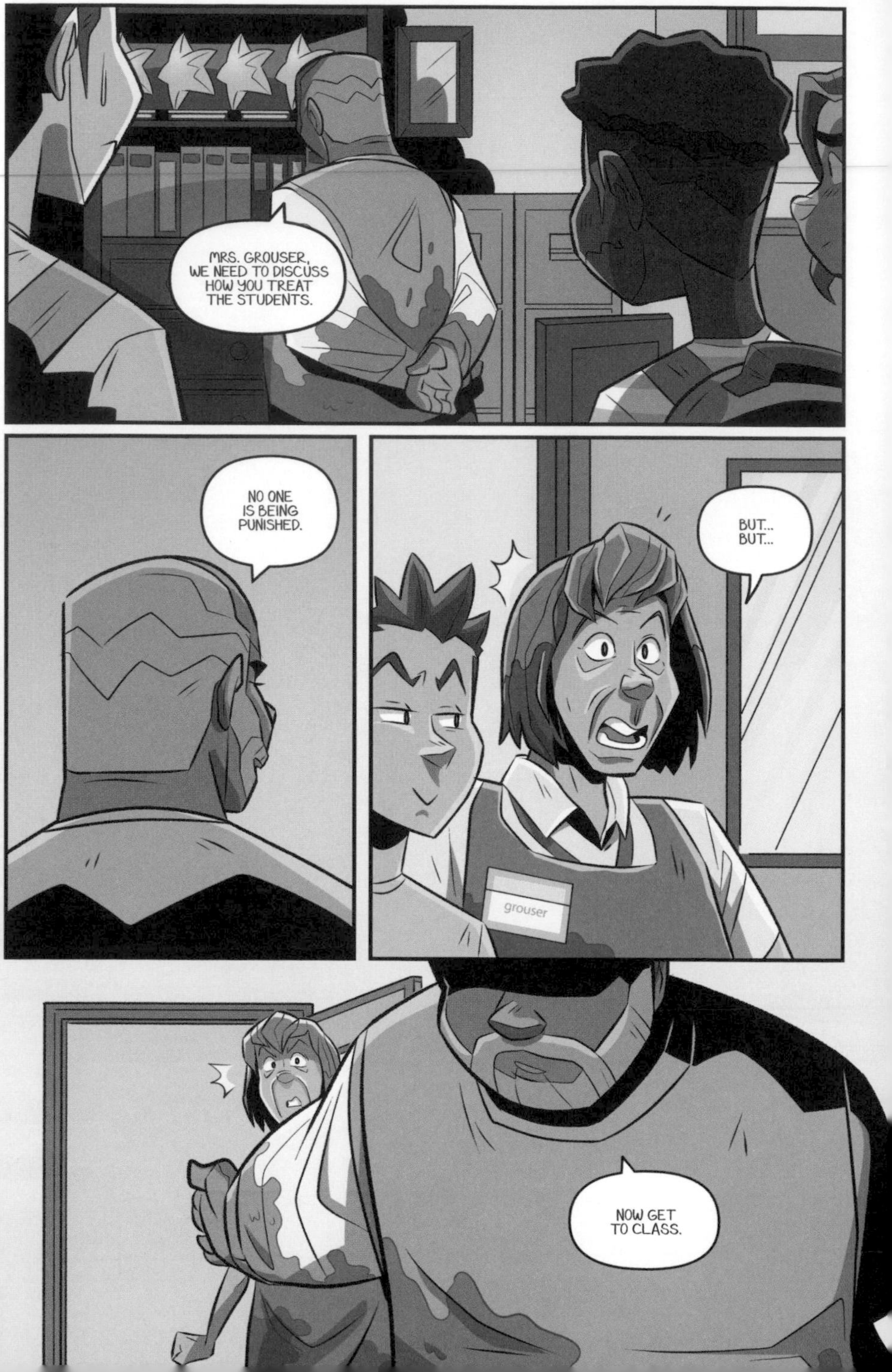
MRS. GROUSER, WE NEED TO DISCUSS HOW YOU TREAT THE STUDENTS.
NO ONE IS BEING PUNISHED.
BUT... BUT...
grouser
NOW GET TO CLASS.

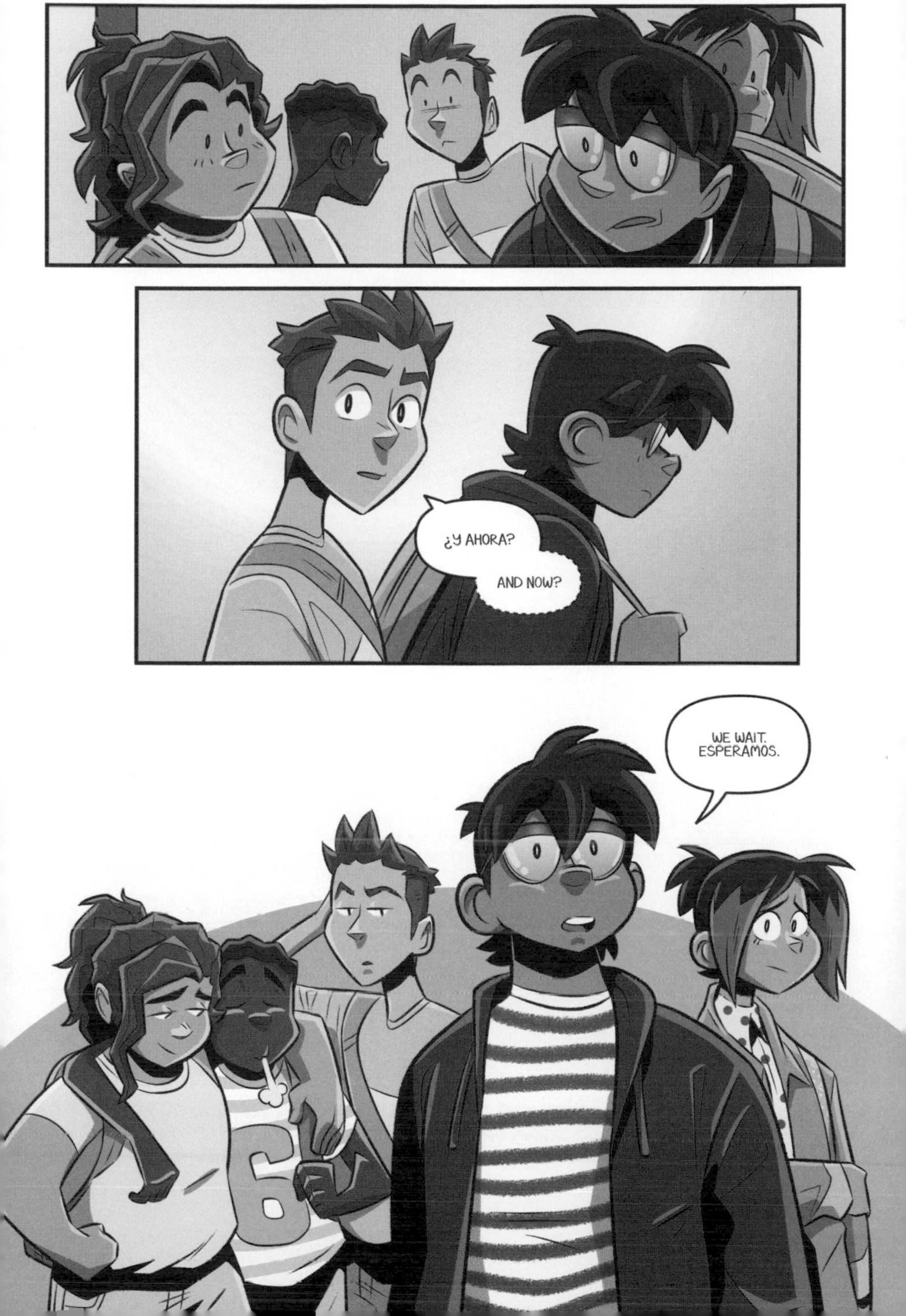
¿Y AHORA?
AND NOW?
WE WAIT.
ESPERAMOS.

APRIL
19
ABRIL

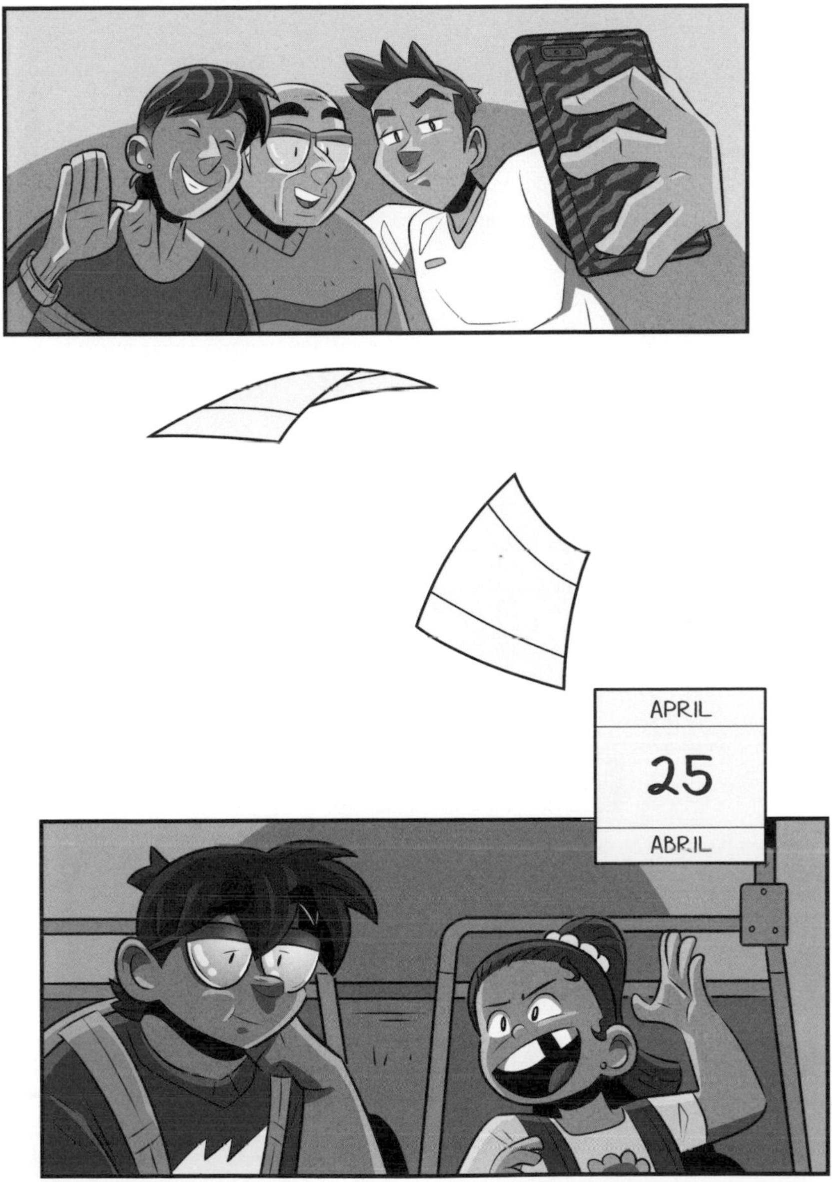
APRIL
25
ABRIL

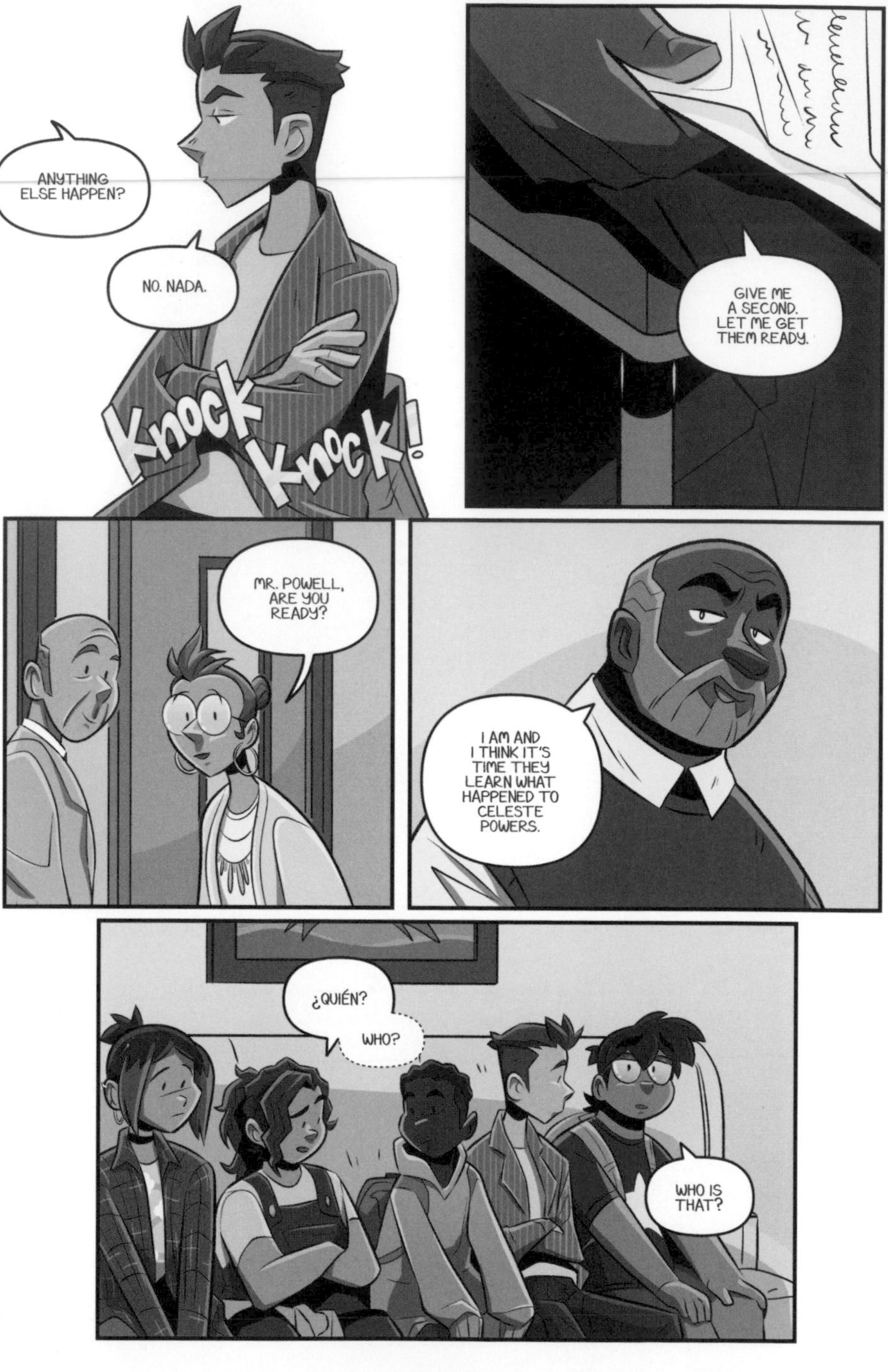
ANYTHING ELSE HAPPEN?
NO. NADA.
KNOCK KNOCK!
GIVE ME A SECOND. LET ME GET THEM READY.
MR. POWELL, ARE YOU READY?
I AM AND I THINK IT'S TIME THEY LEARN WHAT HAPPENED TO CELESTE POWERS.
¿QUIÉN?
WHO?
WHO IS THAT?

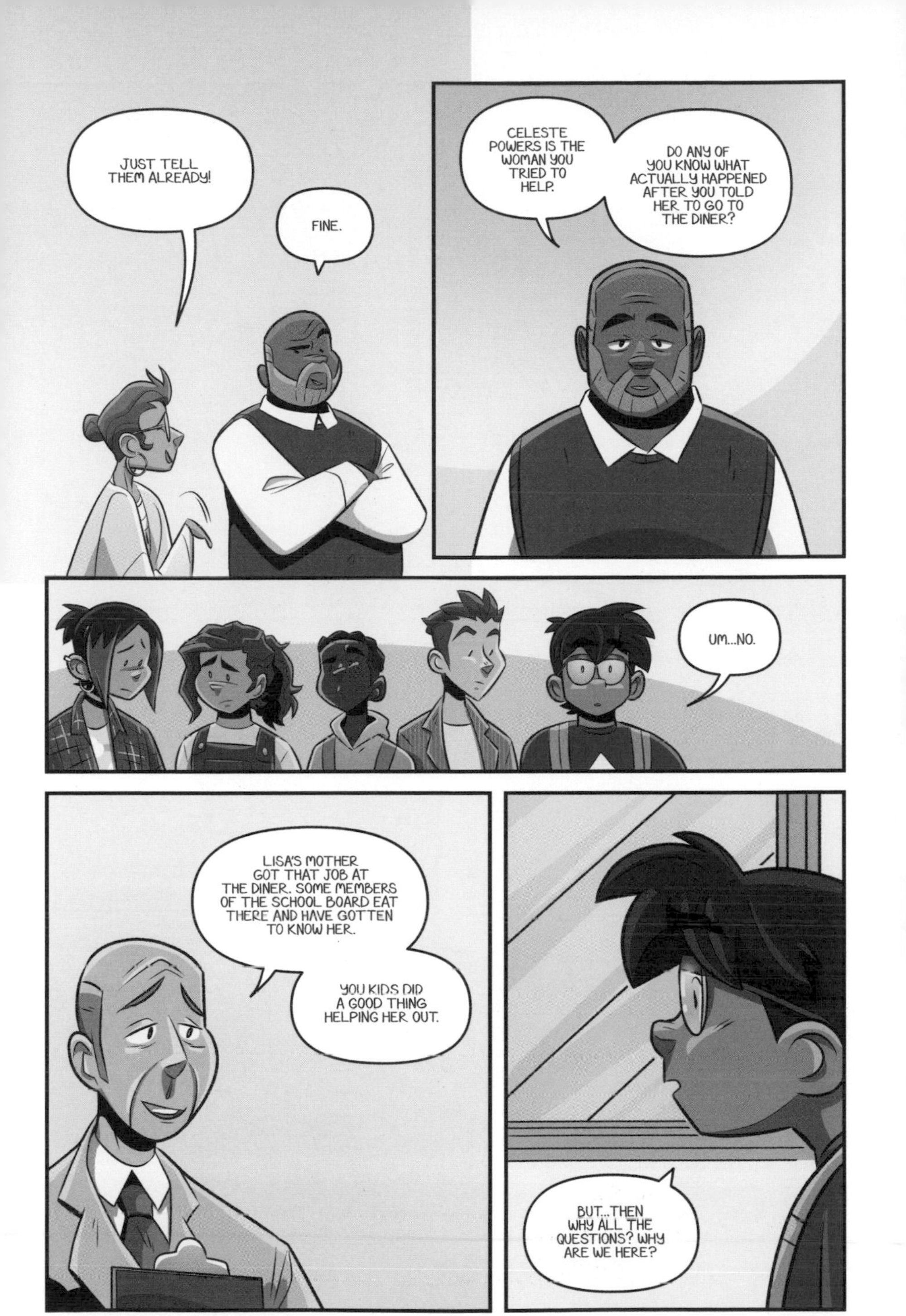
JUST TELL THEM ALREADY!
FINE.
CELESTE POWERS IS THE WOMAN YOU TRIED TO HELP.
DO ANY OF YOU KNOW WHAT ACTUALLY HAPPENED AFTER YOU TOLD HER TO GO TO THE DINER?
UM...NO.
LISA'S MOTHER GOT THAT JOB AT THE DINER. SOME MEMBERS OF THE SCHOOL BOARD EAT THERE AND HAVE GOTTEN TO KNOW HER.
YOU KIDS DID A GOOD THING HELPING HER OUT.
BUT...THEN WHY ALL THE QUESTIONS? WHY ARE WE HERE?

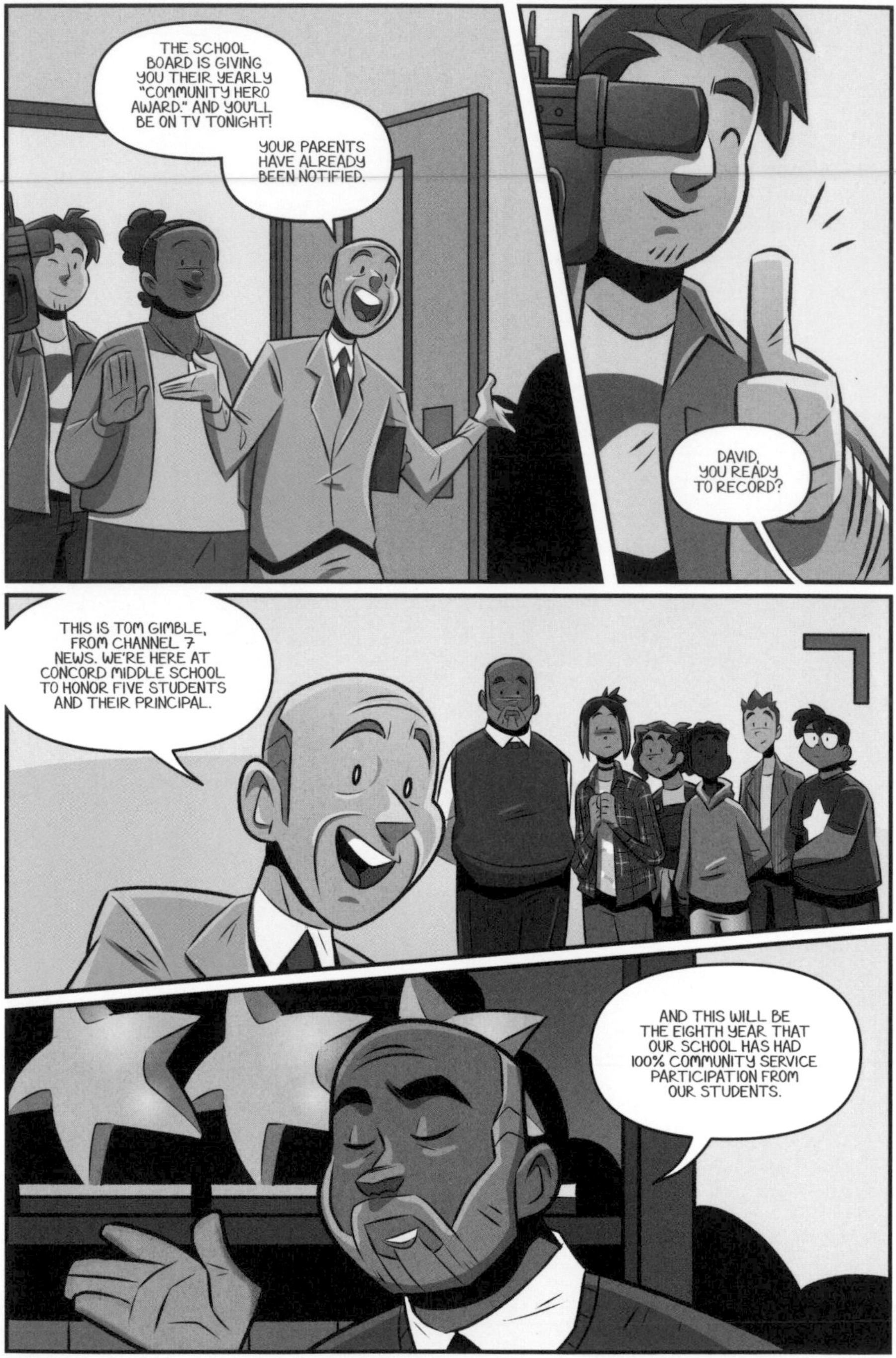
THE SCHOOL BOARD IS GIVING YOU THEIR YEARLY "COMMUNITY HERO AWARD." AND YOU'LL BE ON TV TONIGHT!
YOUR PARENTS HAVE ALREADY BEEN NOTIFIED.
DAVID, YOU READY TO RECORD?
THIS IS TOM GIMBLE, FROM CHANNEL 7 NEWS. WE'RE HERE AT CONCORD MIDDLE SCHOOL TO HONOR FIVE STUDENTS AND THEIR PRINCIPAL.
AND THIS WILL BE THE EIGHTH YEAR THAT OUR SCHOOL HAS HAD 100% COMMUNITY SERVICE PARTICIPATION FROM OUR STUDENTS.

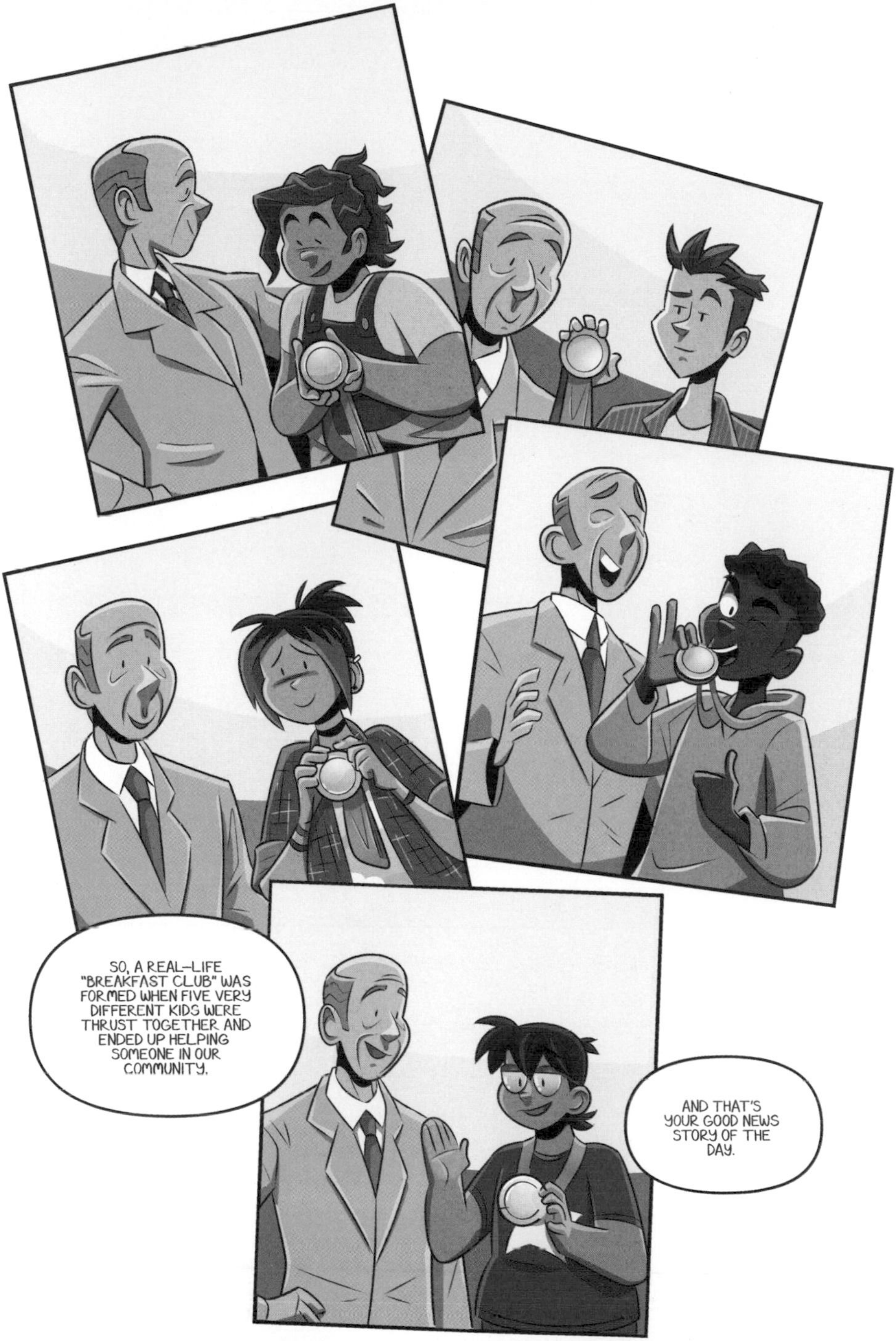
SO, A REAL-LIFE "BREAKFAST CLUB" WAS FORMED WHEN FIVE VERY DIFFERENT KIDS WERE THRUST TOGETHER AND ENDED UP HELPING SOMEONE IN OUR COMMUNITY.
AND THAT'S YOUR GOOD NEWS STORY OF THE DAY.

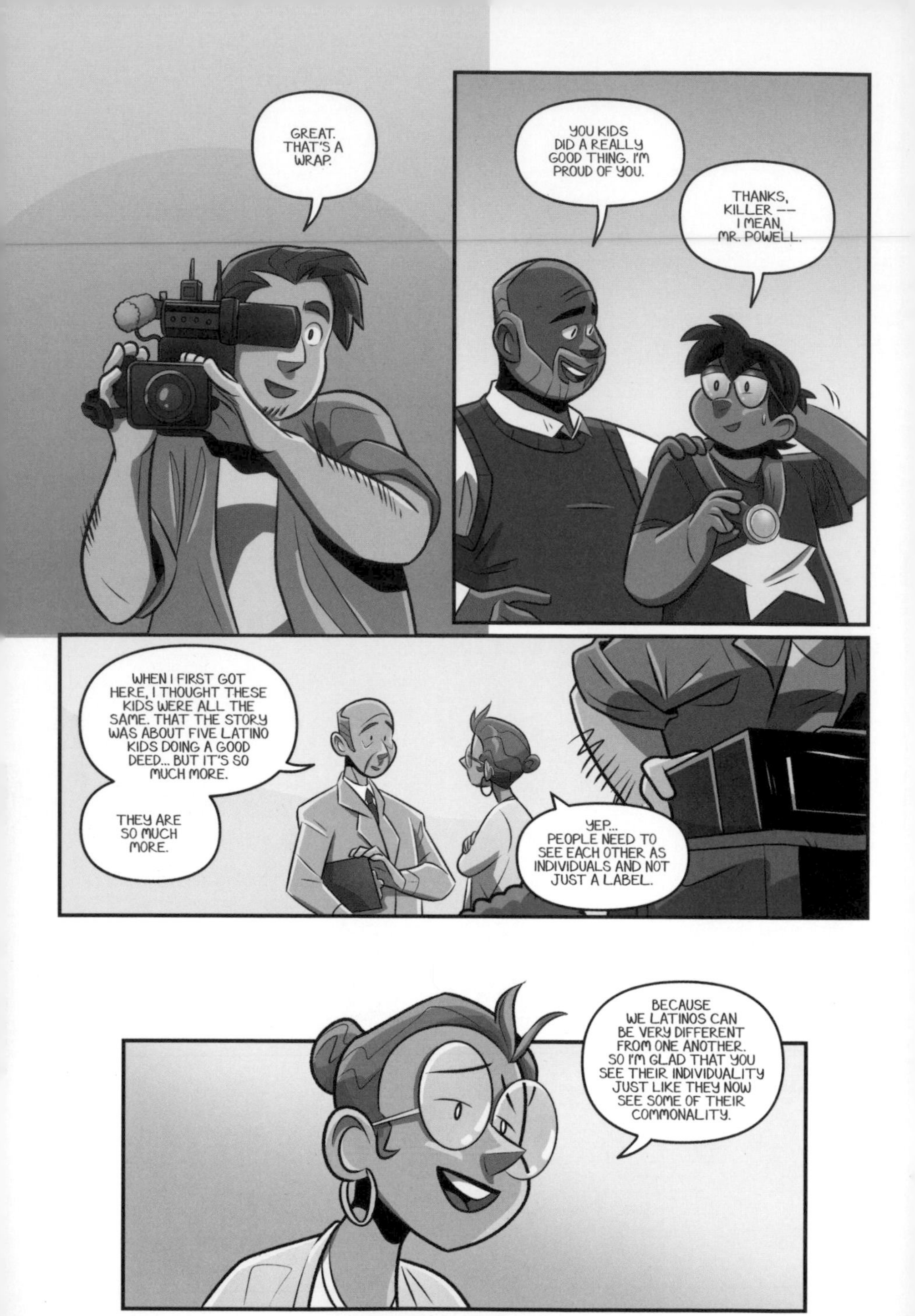
GREAT. THAT'S A WRAP.
YOU KIDS DID A REALLY GOOD THING. I'M PROUD OF YOU.
THANKS, KILLER -- I MEAN, MR. POWELL.
WHEN I FIRST GOT HERE, I THOUGHT THESE KIDS WERE ALL THE SAME. THAT THE STORY WAS ABOUT FIVE LATINO KIDS DOING A GOOD DEED... BUT IT'S SO MUCH MORE.
THEY ARE SO MUCH MORE.
YEP... PEOPLE NEED TO SEE EACH OTHER AS INDIVIDUALS AND NOT JUST A LABEL.
BECAUSE WE LATINOS CAN BE VERY DIFFERENT FROM ONE ANOTHER. SO I'M GLAD THAT YOU SEE THEIR INDIVIDUALITY JUST LIKE THEY NOW SEE SOME OF THEIR COMMONALITY.

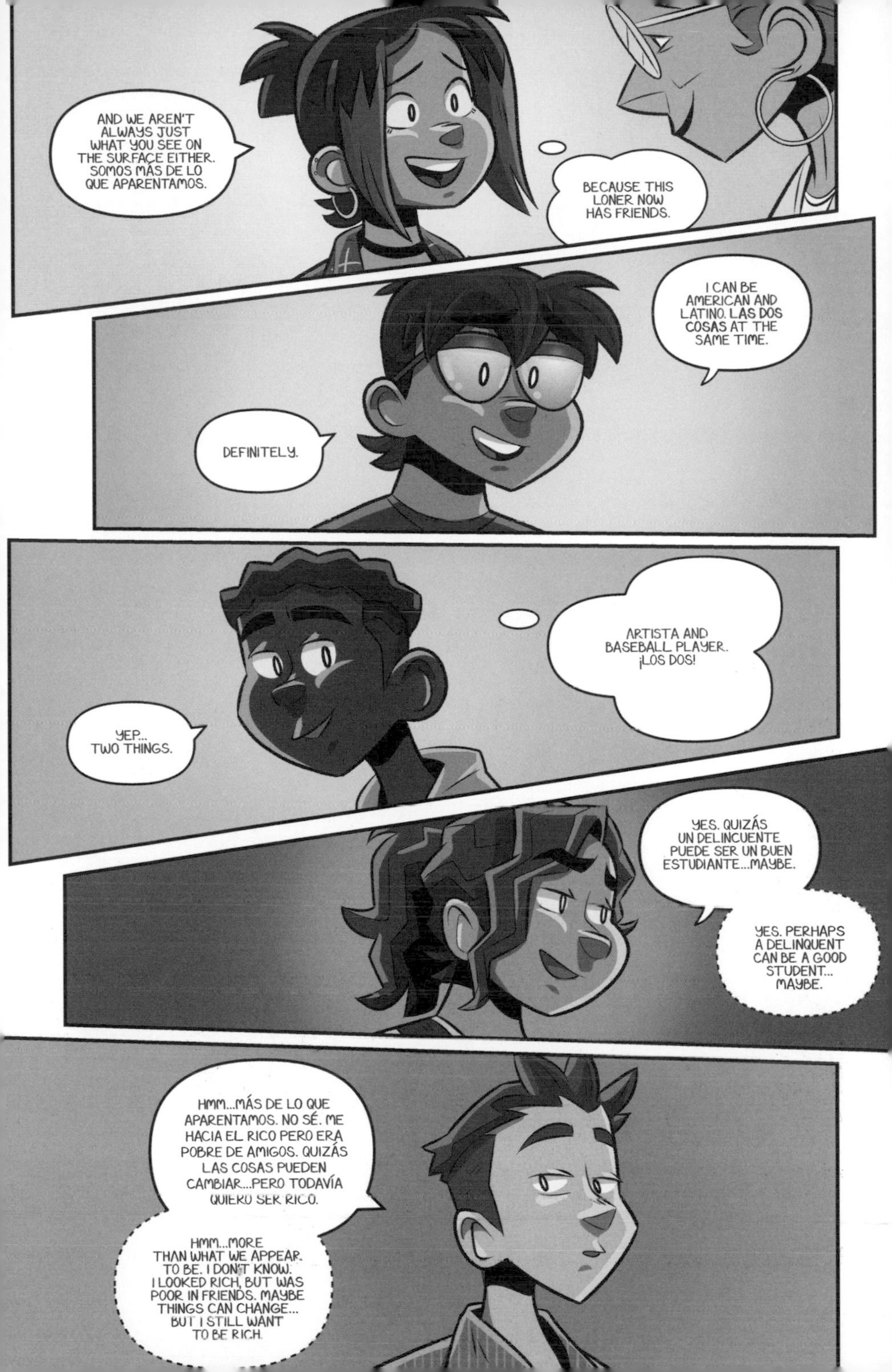
AND WE AREN'T ALWAYS JUST WHAT YOU SEE ON THE SURFACE EITHER. SOMOS MÁS DE LO QUE APARENTAMOS.
BECAUSE THIS LONER NOW HAS FRIENDS.
I CAN BE AMERICAN AND LATINO. LAS DOS COSAS AT THE SAME TIME.
DEFINITELY.
ARTISTA AND BASEBALL PLAYER. ¡LOS DOS!
YEP... TWO THINGS.
YES. QUIZÁS UN DELINCUENTE PUEDE SER UN BUEN ESTUDIANTE...MAYBE.
YES. PERHAPS A DELINQUENT CAN BE A GOOD STUDENT... MAYBE.
HMM...MÁS DE LO QUE APARENTAMOS. NO SÉ. ME HACIA EL RICO PERO ERA POBRE DE AMIGOS. QUIZÁS LAS COSAS PUEDEN CAMBIAR...PERO TODAVÍA QUIERO SER RICO.
HMM...MORE THAN WHAT WE APPEAR TO BE. I DON'T KNOW. I LOOKED RICH, BUT WAS POOR IN FRIENDS. MAYBE THINGS CAN CHANGE... BUT I STILL WANT TO BE RICH.

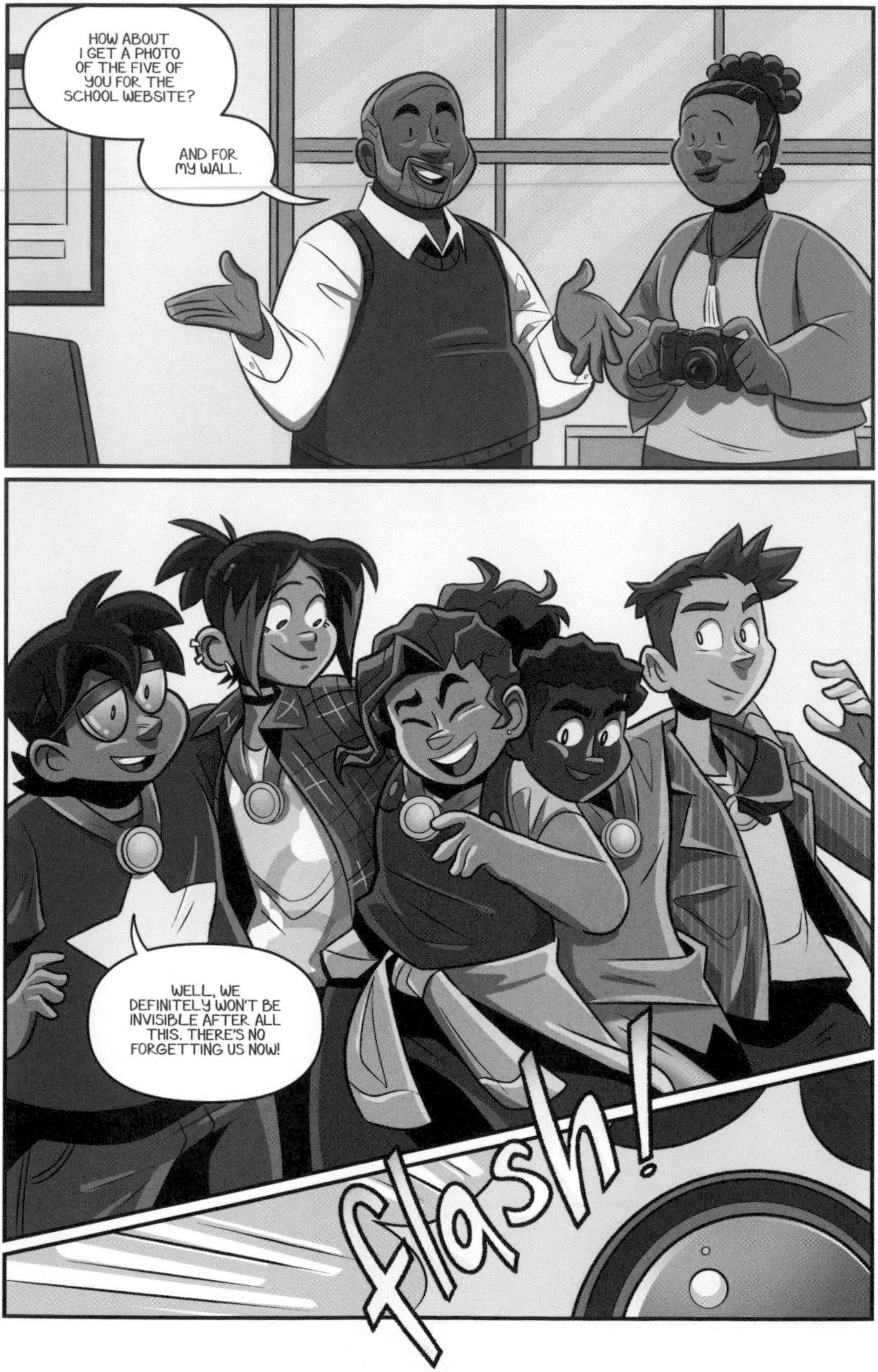
HOW ABOUT I GET A PHOTO OF THE FIVE OF YOU FOR THE SCHOOL WEBSITE?
AND FOR MY WALL.
WELL, WE DEFINITELY WON'T BE INVISIBLE AFTER ALL THIS. THERE'S NO FORGETTING US NOW!
FLASH!

WHAT'S IN MY BAG?

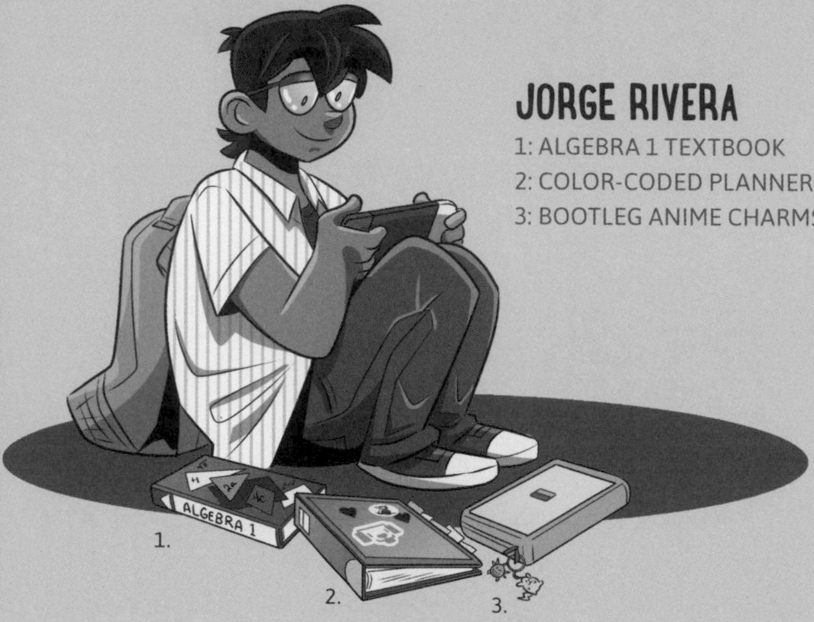
ALGEBRA 1
1.
2.
3.

JORGE RIVERA

1: ALGEBRA 1 TEXTBOOK
2: COLOR-CODED PLANNER
3: BOOTLEG ANIME CHARMS

DAYARA GÓMEZ

1: PAPER PLANES
2: YO-YO
3: SNACKS!

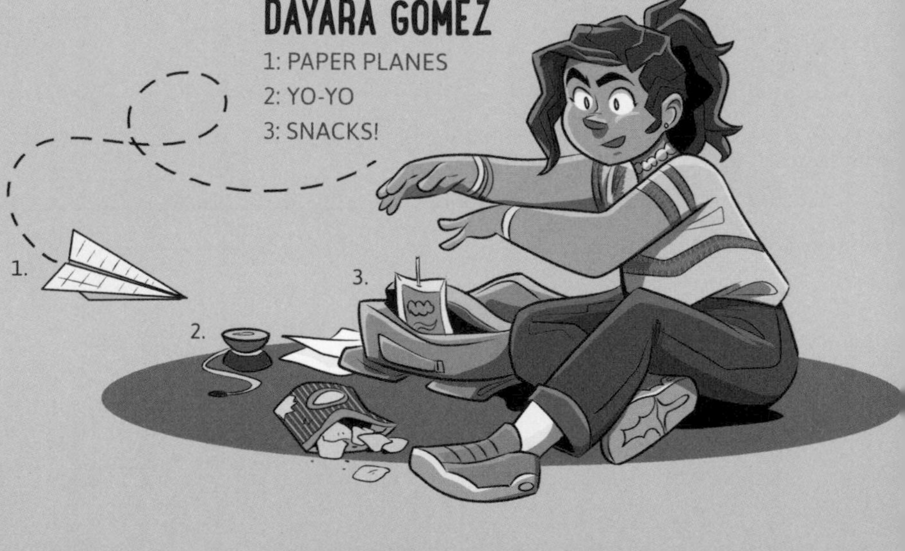
1.
2.
3.

NICO PIÑEDA

1: LO-FI BEATS
2: LATEST LAPTOP
3: EXTREMELY STRONG COLOGNE

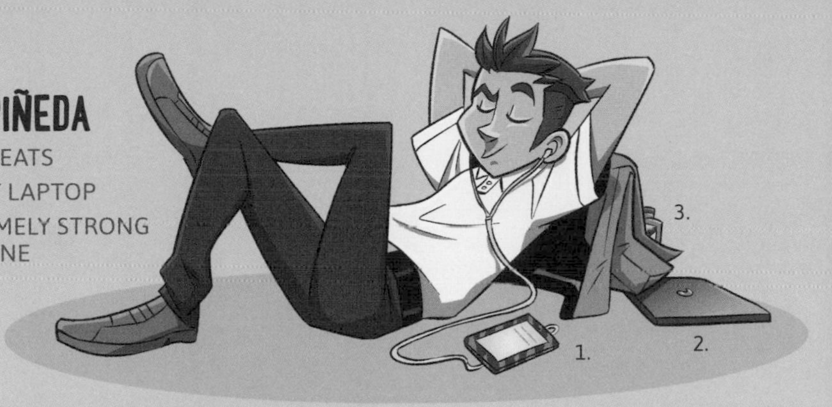
3.
1.
2.

MIGUEL SOTO

1: BASEBALL GLOVE
2: COLORED PENCILS
3: COMIC BOOKS

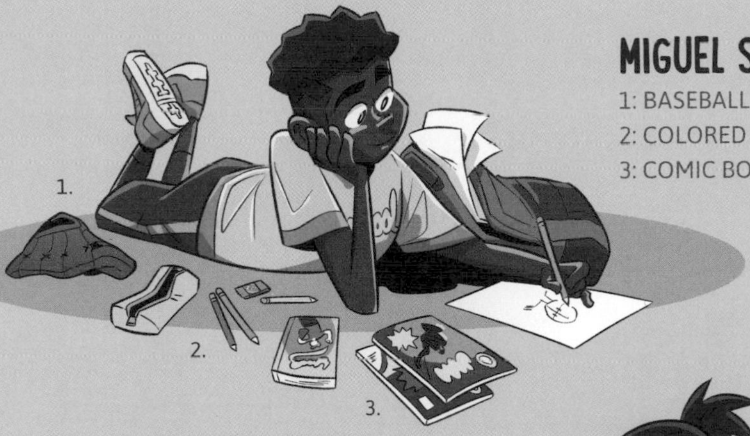
1.
2.
3.

SARA DOMÍNGUEZ

1: FANFIC IDEA JOURNAL
2: NEKO PENCIL CASE
3: FANTASY NOVELS

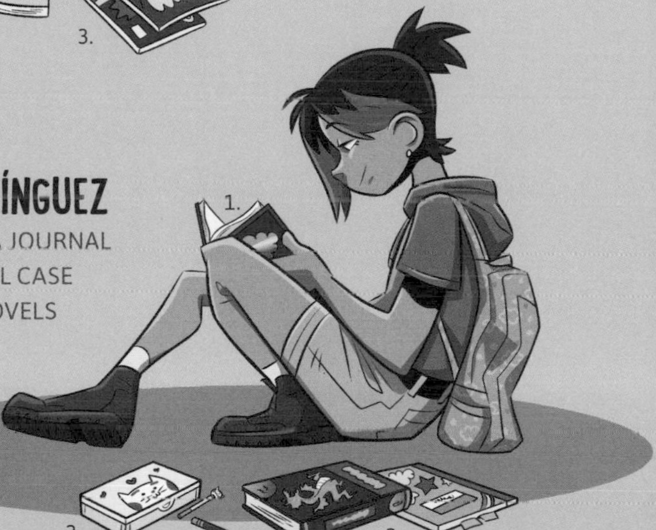
1.
2.
3.

A NOTE FROM CHRISTINA DIAZ GONZALEZ

¿Que dice? It was a question I'd often ask my parents while watching TV, since all the shows were in English. My parents had made the decision to teach me Spanish first, knowing that I would become bilingual once I started school. The only catch was that, in the small southern town where I grew up, none of my fellow students or teachers spoke Spanish. I turned to the skills of deciphering visual and context clues — learned from watching cartoons — to try and understand those around me. After weeks of staying quiet and smiling at anyone who spoke to me, I learned English and soon had the lifelong advantage of knowing two languages.

Today, when I visit schools, I always try to search for those ESL students who may feel a little lost like I did when surrounded by words that they don't yet understand. It was during one of these visits that I realized the tremendous value graphic novels can afford those learning a new language. The pairing of the written word with the visual representation of the story was powerful for these students, but they were not seeing themselves in the stories they were reading. Plus, the books themselves were either all in English or a full translation. It made me wonder if there could be something in between. A single book that could be read and enjoyed no matter which language you spoke or how proficient you were in either language. One that could help with fluency in both languages. An idea took hold and — paired with Gabriela Epstein's wonderful illustrations — a story for kids who speak English AND Spanish was born.

Christine

A NOTE FROM GABRIELA EPSTEIN

Invisible is a story I wish I had growing up. I never knew how to contextualize my identity and, as a result, always felt like an "other." It has taken a long time to divest my self-image from stereotypes and understand that Latine has no one "right" way of looking, speaking, or behaving. We are a beautiful, diverse group of people.

And we have a unique perspective that can change this country for the better, too. No matter the language(s) you speak or the color of your skin, no one can erase your history. No one can tell you that you aren't Latine, or not Latine enough. You are born of something much stronger than the systems used to divide us. Just as Jorge and the crew unite to help their community in their own way, so can you!

Con mucho amor,

Gabriela

AUTHOR'S ACKNOWLEDGMENTS

First, I'd like to thank God for blessing me with an incredible family and a group of friends that fill my life with love and happiness. I am so grateful for each one of them. A thousand thanks to the many people who have helped shape this story from an idea to an actual book. I am especially appreciative of my extraordinary agent, Jen Rofé, and my wonderful editors at Scholastic, Emily Seife and David Levithan, who have believed in this book from the very start. Muchas gracias to friends Jennifer Cervantes, Angela Padron, Angie Torres Moure, Jorge Corona, Jenny Torres Sanchez, and Danielle Joseph, who offered valuable feedback and shared with me their unique perspectives. I am also so thankful to have been able to work with the talented Gabriela Epstein, who interpreted my words into the vivid illustrations that you see on these pages, and Lark Pien, who brought them all to life with her color. My sincere appreciation goes to the entire Scholastic/Graphix team, specifically Phil Falco, Shivana Sookdeo, David Saylor, Lizette Serrano, Emily Heddleson, Jordana Kulak, and Meaghan Finnerty, whose enthusiastic support for this book has been incredible. Finally, to the librarians and educators out there who work so tirelessly to provide a safe, welcoming place for all students, thank you for all that you do to make each student feel *visible*.

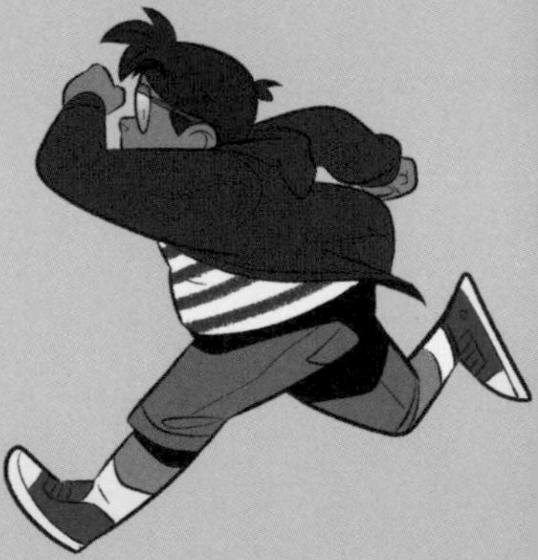

ILLUSTRATOR'S ACKNOWLEDGMENTS

I'd like to thank Christina for writing such a wonderful, inclusive story. These characters have been a blast to draw, and I'm so grateful that they'll live in children's hearts for years to come. Thank you to the incredible editorial and design team at Graphix who came together to make this book possible: Emily Seife, Phil Falco, Shivana Sookdeo, David Saylor, and David Levithan are heroes in their own right. A big shout-out to my agent, Steven Salpeter, for being the best of the best — I could not have done this without you. Lastly, I'd like to thank my parents and family for always being there for me at every stage of my artistic journey — I love you!

CHRISTINA DIAZ GONZALEZ is the award-winning author of several books, including *The Red Umbrella*, *A Thunderous Whisper*, the Moving Target series (*Moving Target* and *Return Fire*), and *Concealed*. Her books have received numerous honors, such as the American Library Association's Best Fiction for Young Adults distinction, the Florida Book Award, the International Latino Book Award, and a Junior Library Guild selection. Christina currently lives in Miami, Florida, with her husband, two sons, and a dog that can open doors. You can read more about her and her books at christinagonzalez.com.

GABRIELA EPSTEIN is the creator of the *New York Times* bestselling graphic novel adaptations of The Baby-sitters Club installments *Claudia and the New Girl* and *Good-bye Stacey, Good-bye* by Ann M. Martin. She graduated from the Rhode Island School of Design with a degree in illustration and has worked as a character designer for TV animation. When she isn't making comics, she enjoys yo-yoing, listening to spooky podcasts, and playing ice hockey. She lives in Austin, Texas. Visit her online at gre-art.com.

LARK PIEN, the colorist of *Invisible* and the Sunny Side Up series, is an indie cartoonist from the Pacific Northwest. She has published many comics and is the colorist for Printz Award winner *American Born Chinese* and *Boxers & Saints*. Her characters Long Tail Kitty and Mr. Elephanter have been adapted into children's books. You can follow her on Instagram @larkpien.